Razarkha's Revolution

Matthew J. Dave

Table of Contents

Special Thanks

Thank you to Jimi Simmonds, for making the map and creating this vast world alongside me, as well as pointing out worldbuilding issues when they come up.

Additional thanks to Milly, Sara and Nino for sticking with the series throughout its creation. An additional thank-you to Nino for illustrating the cover.

Prologue

Tei Fel'thuz, a toddler of three, played alone in her creche with a stuffed toy resembling a spellbinder girl, complete with a tail. She didn't know her own tail was crooked, nor that she was small for her age. All she cared about was the story in her head. She'd named the doll Rina, and she was a mother figure to the other toys in her collection.

"You're mean and you're mean too," Tei said in 'Rina's' voice, making the doll point to one of Rakh's soldier toys and a small skull necklace. "You both get no dessert."

Surrounding her island of imagination was a lounge, where shelves of books and velvet couches covered the chilly ilmenite walls of Castle Selenia. Count Rani Fel'thuz sat in a distant armchair, his flat nose stuck in a book, while his eldest daughter, Razarkha, read over his shoulder.

They were practically copies of each other; while Rani was a man and Razarkha a girl of eleven, they both wore pale foundation, black makeup around their eyes, purple dye amidst their black hair, along with cloaks of black and lilac. Eventually the girl lost interest and approached her little sister's creche. Upon seeing Razarkha, Tei stopped her storytelling and gripped Rina in a tight hug. The older girl said nothing and stepped over the creche's walls, her preteen lankiness towering over the toddler.

"What are you playing with?" Razarkha asked.

"I don't want you," Tei said, backing from her sister.

"You don't want me? What kind of stupid sentence is that? You really ought to grow up," Razarkha said, effortlessly catching up to Tei and grabbing her ear. "What did you mean by 'you don't want me'? It's not nice to say that about your kin."

3

"Go away! I don't want you!" Tei pleaded as Razarkha twisted her ear.

"I don't want you around either. You killed mother, and I won't let you forget that. You're an ugly, stupid brat and I hate you," Razarkha said. "See? That's how a grown-up speaks. You're just an ugly little imp."

Tei lost what little patience a toddler had and wriggled from Razarkha's grip, then bit her finger. Razarkha screamed and slapped Tei as hard as she could.

"You little brat! How dare you—"

She stopped talking when she noticed that, somehow, her father had seamlessly moved in front of her. Without a word, Count Fel'thuz slapped his eldest daughter in the face.

Razarkha looked at Tei, rubbing her face and evading her father's withering glare. She opened her mouth, but Count Rani cut her off.

"It hurts when someone bigger and stronger harms you for no reason, doesn't it?" Rani asked. "Do you think you're powerful for harming a girl of three? Do you? Because I don't feel powerful hurting you."

Razarkha clenched her fists. "Why did you do that? You're a grown-up!"

"And you're almost a woman," Rani said. "Your first blood will be any day now, yet here you are, tormenting a girl barely out of her swaddling clothes. Even for a child, that's pathetic. Do you want to be like the Plague Emperor?"

Razarkha's eyes welled up. "The Plague Emperor destroyed the weak! He killed his enemies! Tei's my enemy, she's a kinslayer!"

"The Plague Emperor humbled the haughty and protected the oppressed. What power is there in abusing the lowly? You ought to strengthen the weak, not abuse them. You can behave like the Plague Emperor, with dignity, power, and honour, or you can behave like a spiteful little girl who thinks a baby is capable of murder."

4

Razarkha trembled, formed a few non-words, then fled from the room.

* * *

Rakh Fel'thuz, heir to the House of Fel'thuz, stood at the top of a shiny, slick staircase. There was a bannister, but he was too short to properly hold onto it. It was dinnertime, and Count Rani insisted that as his heir, he had to join he and Lord Nemeron at the table. He told himself that Lady Torawyn was downstairs, a grown-up woman who made him feel funny in a good way, but even this couldn't make him go down alone.

He looked around for a servant; maybe they would carry him down. He sat and shook his head. He was eight, he couldn't be treated like a baby anymore. Suddenly, Razzie appeared by his side, sitting cross-legged, a red hand-mark ruining her white makeup.

"What's the matter, Rakh? Are you being a coward again?"

"Go away, Razzie."

Razarkha paused. "Father told me that the strong need to help the weak. They need to strengthen them."

Rakh looked to Razarkha. "Why are you telling me this?"

"Are you afraid of stairs?"

"Yeah. They're so slippery and if I fell it'd be a long way down."

"It's not that bad, even if you did fall," Razarkha claimed.

"You don't know that—"

Before he could finish his sentence, Rakh's perception became a tumbling blur. His shoulders, head, legs, and torso smacked against bump after bump of hard ilmenite until he found himself at the foot of the stairs, aching all over. He struggled to get up, and as he did, Razarkha skipped down the stairs.

"See? That wasn't so bad, was it? Now you're stronger for having—"

"I hate you, Razarkha!" Rakh screamed.

The girl's eyes widened. "But I—"

"Father tells me that I shouldn't be sad about marrying you and that you'll be better when you're a woman grown, but I know he's lying!"

"Rakh—"

"You're a horrible bully! You're mean to Tei, you're mean to Waldon, you're mean to *everyone!* I hope you die, Razarkha! I hope you die, so I never have to marry you!"

His older sister couldn't find any more words. Her lips quivered, then she vanished.

Boxed

Count Rakh Fel'thuz twitched as he sat, his chair wobbling with him due to its uneven legs. His foot tapped against the ilmenite floors of the Castle Selenia council chamber, and he drummed his remaining hand against the similarly quasi-metallic table. Surrounding him were the councillors to Overlady Kagura Selenia, their words blurring together in his mind.

At the newly-knighted Minister of Criminal Affairs, Plutyn Khanas's insistence, the chamber had undergone a renovation. The three dark blue Selenia banners to one sky-blue Fel'thuz banner ratio had since shifted to two Selenia banners on opposing walls, while their adjacent walls had a Fel'thuz banner one side and the Plutyn Khanas's personal banner on the other, in honour of his daughter's betrothal to Rakh's heir, Rarakhi.

Aside from the overly influential Minister of Criminal Affairs, the council consisted of an old human woman with sunken eyes, a couple of old high elven men, a gruff, middle-aged orc, and Wisdom Erwyn Yagaska. At the head of the table, Overlady Kag'nemera Selenia leaned over the table like an eager child, her womanly beauty contrasting the childishness in her pale red eyes. Erwyn shuffled his papers, glanced at Rakh, then spoke.

"Now that minor intracity management issues have been discussed, we should move on to provincial issues. As of late, Genna Oswyk and Marissa Gemfire's feud has subsided, but only due to shared anger over something worse. Lady Gemfire's youngest daughter, Amerei Gemcutter, has gone missing following a visit from Wisdom Yugen of Parakos."

Rakh groaned. "The last thing we need is the Gemfire army occupied fighting the most powerful army in the kingdom."

7

"Indeed. I've prepared a few suggestions for Lady Gemfire. Overlady Selenia, would you be willing to put your name to a letter I've written up?"

Kag, blithe as ever, cocked her head. "What does it say?"

"It commands Lady Marissa not to wage war against the Parakosi, and to accept any peace offerings they put forth."

Kagura put her finger on her lips. "But the Parakosi just abducted her daughter! I'd be angry if someone hurt *my* family."

"Amerei has simply gone missing when Yugen happened to visit," Erwyn pointed out. "For now, we need to keep the Parakosi blameless and ensure our allies are unoccupied."

Rakh nodded. "We don't know when Razarkha is returning, and if she does, she'll likely have powerful tools at her disposal. Every able-bodied man needs to be ready."

The orc, Blueprint, Minister of Works, spoke up. "No disrespect, Count Fel'thuz, but didn't you handily beat your sister without trying? Also, weren't it you that spared 'er in the first place? I remember the foremen bitchin' about how she should've been executed."

"People change," Rakh replied. "The Razarkha I exiled was a pitiful bully without a sound thought between her ears. However, she's since caused a stir in Ilazar, and in the worst-case scenario, has acquired a soulstealer."

One of the older high elves, General Kareon Moonspawn, fixed his collar. "You speak a 'soulstealer'. What do we know about such devices?"

"There are seven in the world, and they can absorb souls, then destroy them to provide arcane power," Rakh exposited. "If Razarkha has one and returns to Arkhera, we'll need every man we can get."

"No offence, Count Fel'thuz, but I'm the one with the military experience," Kareon replied. "If there's a woman who can drain souls from a given area, the only chance we have is shooting her down from afar. Even then, if she can use her acquired arcana to protect herself, then our only option is evacuation."

Rakh slumped in his seat. He'd asked himself the same question repeatedly, and the only solutions he'd conceived were generic and sloppy. Regardless, provincial unity was a preferred state to the estrangement that currently characterised the Forest of Winter.

"Ensuring our vassals' cooperation will open more strategic options," Rakh insisted.

General Moonspawn grunted. "We ought to research counter-magical strategies too. Perhaps we can enlist the help of the Order."

Erwyn swallowed. "Moving on, Ashglass has recently banned all imports and exports. I sent a letter asking Wisdom Khalver why this was, but he hasn't responded."

"It doesn't add up," the sunken-eyed woman, Chancellor of Vaults Enva, remarked. "Being candid, Ashglass's economy has outperformed Moonstone's for years. Implementing a trade freeze in the middle of a boom is bizarre."

Lady Kagura stopped stroking her hair to interject. "Perhaps Lady Foenaxas finally realised she was showing me up! I've grown tired of outsiders acting like Ashglass is the true capital of this province. Perhaps Mor'kha *is* respectable if she's holding back for my sake."

"My lady, we rely on Ashglass's copper and tin," Enva explained. "Even if this *was* Lady Foenaxas's reasoning, it would only hurt the province in the long term. Additionally, with no trades to tax in Ashglass, Moonstone will lose months' worth of income."

Lady Kagura slammed her hands on the table. "Then we must investigate the issue!"

"Are you willing to authorise the deployment of scouts?" Erwyn asked.

"Absolutely! Send them, see why Lady Mor'kha sees fit to choke *my* city of metals!"

Minister of Criminal Affairs Plutyn Khanas creased his brow and cut in. "Wisdom Erwyn, if I may, I've got an additional provincial issue to bring to your attention. As a family man, Count Fel'thuz may be interested too."

"You've got information on Razarkha's whereabouts? Perhaps a report from Tei?" Rakh asked in an increasingly desperate tone.

"Something like that," Plutyn answered. "I sent a spy to Winter Harbour to uncover the anonymous Ilazari source for Baron Oswyk's report on Razarkha's antics. I can confirm it's Anya, granddaughter of the infamous Ilazari gangster, Elki Kasparov."

Lady Selenia snorted with laughter, which drew the attention of every councillor in the room. The necromantic knight tented his fingers and sighed deeply. Once the guffawing was over, Plutyn spoke in a low-pitched, deathly grim tone.

"What's so amusing, my lady?"

"Your source must be wrong! Why in the world would my vassals be in cahoots with foreign gangsters?"

"That is the pressing concern," Plutyn said. "My source is trustworthy, but you are correct to question your baron's behaviour. Hence, I'm going to enlist some familial assistance. Count Fel'thuz, you've been biting at the champ to combat Razarkha in some way, correct?"

Rakh's face warmed up and his phantom hand itched. "It's true that I'm worried, but why wouldn't I be?"

"Then I'm sure you'll be willing to help. As a *knight,* I lack the new-system influence to make this request. I have a cousin in the Crystal Palace serving Overlord Verawyn Vcrawor, and I'll need you to negotiate a temporary release of that duty," Plutyn said. "I suspect that Anya Kasparov's connection to Giles Oswyk is through blackmail. I'm going to call in a family favour and have Cousin Rowyn investigate Winter Harbour's many oddities."

"I don't see how this helps us find Razarkha."

"Let me finish," Plutyn snapped. "Once he's extracted as much information as he can from the good baron, I intend to have my cousin find wherever Anya Kasparov and Razarkha Fel'thuz are hiding. Don't worry; he's a reliable man. Content with being a knight."

"Just like you, I hope!" Kagura said with a wide smile.

"Just like me," Plutyn muttered.

The high elven lady prodded her own cheek and made more vacuous noises. "Should I help? I'm much more influential than Count Rakh. See, he's a count, and I'm an overlady, that means he only gets to live here and advise me while I rule over the province. Maybe I should be the one to negotiate with a fellow overlord."

Plutyn's face twisted into the most hideous facsimile of a smile he could muster. "As overlady, you doubtless have more important things to tend to. I wouldn't worry your pretty little head about it."

Though the Minister's face tightened as he noticed the line he'd crossed, Kagura's expression lit up the room.

"I always wondered if you thin, tall, scary types thought elves were pretty!" she gleefully said. "I'm glad you think so, I work ever so hard to stay the most beautiful woman in the world. Speaking of which, Erwyn, I have a project for you, but it's special and secret."

Wisdom Erwyn shifted in his seat. "As you say, my lady."

Plutyn sat back. "What do you think, Count Fel'thuz? Can you secure Cousin Rowyn's services? I believe it's in everybody's interests."

Rakh wanted to tent his fingers as Plutyn was wont to, or play with his hair, or scratch the itch of the phantom hand possessing his wooden one. He'd spent the last two

11

weeks pacing about, ranting about the sister he'd foolishly spared. As opaque as the Minister of Criminal Affairs was, every lead needed to be pursued.

"I may as well," Rakh answered. "If there's anyone suited to spying on someone like Razarkha, it's a man of magic like yourself."

"Indeed. I'll brief you on the details later."

* * *

The *Dikamonstra* cut through the blackened waters of the eastern Accursed Sea. Wind swept through Razarkha Fel'thuz's black-and-lilac hair as thunderclouds roiled above her. Weil, her slightly fat-faced, dun-haired partner in crime, stood beside her at the fore of the oversized skiff. His hand trembled beside hers as they watched the dots on the horizon grow larger.

Razarkha was too busy clutching the Soulstealer of Craving to hold hands. While she spent the artefact's bluffing potential in the process of acquiring it, Nortez and Sula were full of its intended targets. Her biggest conflict was not if she would use it, how discriminate she ought to be.

She lifted the treasure and admired her grin, which was multiplied across every facet. The device was an amalgam of enchanted crystals; the upper half a three-strand 'rope' of rose quartz, carnelian and aquamarine, while deep blue topaz formed a bowl at the bottom. Sometimes it would glow on its own, and rarely, a hateful miasma appeared to surround it.

"Am I useless to you now?" Weil asked in Isleborn Ilazari. *"You have a soulstealer and are about to enter the second-most ascendant-filled nation in the world. I presume you'll visit Sula afterwards. Conquering them will be easy."*

Somehow, Weil's perfectly rational concern hurt Razarkha. In principle, an unpredictable chaos-speaker was a liability, especially in a pair of nations where chaos-speech was still discriminated against. He may have proven useful when Razarkha was at the bottom, but he was disposable now. Contemplating this caused her to wince.

"You're not useless to me."

"How could I possibly help?"

Razarkha shook out a few disjointed syllables, then gave up on her sentence. What was stopping her? A voice came from the soulstealer, perceptible to her alone.

"Are you really playing out this denial? A madwoman you may be, but you're not the monster you fancy yourself as."

Razarkha didn't give the god in the soulstealer the satisfaction of a response and spoke to Weil instead.

"You can open portals and unleash terrifying tentacles—"

"How does that harm an incorporeal enemy?"

"Not every enemy we face will be ascended!" Razarkha snapped. *"You helped me get to this point and lost your house for my sake. I'm not about to leave your loyalty unrewarded."*

Weil shrunk into himself. *"I'm still your Plague Emperor?"*

Razarkha smiled and put her arm around his tentacle-shaped tassels. *"Of course you are. Provided you appreciate your Plague Empress."*

"Why wouldn't I? You freed me from the Kasparovs. I'd be nothing without you."

"I know," Razarkha said with a smirk that died upon checking the horizon.

The specks had become boats. Unlike the wooden hull and cloth sail of the *Dikamonstra,* they were made of metal, and were monstrously large. They lacked sails and flew orange flags with red suns instead. Mounted upon their bows were long, cannon-like contraptions, while the deck was outfitted with other incomprehensible weaponry.

13

"What are those? How are they afloat?" Weil asked.

"The flags are Yukishiman, and they— Weil, we need to turn back!"

"Turn back? If we cannot make it to Quattrus, we'll run out of food!"

"Use your chaos-speech to drag up some fish, I don't care what we eat, just help me turn this ship around!"

Weil rushed to the aft of the ship and turned the rudder-wheel, while Razarkha scrambled to the mast. The ship was experiencing an until-then fortunate tailwind, so her personalised sail, a black flag with a red-eyed purple rabbit staring forwards, billowed proudly.

She folded the sail and pulled it down, then rushed to the fore to check their trajectory, staying focused on the metallic behemoths as the skiff turned. To her horror, two of them had already pointed their unusual cannons the *Dikamonstra*.

"No, not now, not here!" Razarkha ranted in the Common Tongue, then shifted back to Isleborn. *"Weil, hurry the turnaround, open a portal and get a tentacle to push the ship, anything!"*

"The Great Rakh'vash is more likely to push the ship over if I ask that of them!"

"Shut up, it's helped us many times!"

"It's helped us destroy things. It doesn't appreciate constructive efforts, as I'm sure I've said before."

Razarkha tugged at her hair as the metal ships grew unavoidably closer. *"Gods, you're useless! Hand the wheel to me, we're—"*

A crash drowned her speech out, followed by a deafening creak. The starboard side of the *Dikamonstra* had been transformed into scattered mess of driftwood. Razarkha and Weil desperately attempted to stay balanced on what remained of the aft, but the waters quickly swallowed it. Weil grabbed Razarkha's hand, opened a portal beneath them, and from it a tentacle large enough to hold an aurochs emerged. The monstrous limb wrapped around them, keeping them suspended as the *Dikamonstra* sank beneath them.

"*What now?*" Weil asked.

"*You're the one summoned your tentacles, I thought you'd have a plan!*"

"*We could take a chance with a portal jump, but I don't trust the Rakh'vash to—*"

Loud, repetitive bangs filled the air, and the tentacle released its mortal affiliates. With a screech, it slipped into its rapidly closing portal, leaving Razarkha and Weil to fall into the water like any other flotsam. Razarkha flailed and screamed, pushing herself towards a shard of her ship, while Weil removed his heavier clothes and treaded water. Once she was safely gripping some driftwood, she ranted at Weil.

"*What are you waiting for? Open another portal!*"

"*The Rakh'vash has refused me!*" Weil yelled back. "*He says those people wield the knotweed, some vile infection of reality!*"

"*Tell it that I'll do something much worse if it doesn't brave this 'knotweed'.*"

Weil's head briefly slipped underwater, then bobbed back up. "*It doesn't believe your threats.*"

"*Oh, your god is insufferable!*"

One of the boats began lowering a pinnace, and a loud, crackly voice projected itself over the waters in a Yukishiman-accented rendition of Common Tongue.

"*Are you Razarkha Fel'thuz and her accomplice, Weil?*"

"*What is he saying?*" Weil asked.

"*He recognises us, somehow,*" Razarkha replied in Isleborn.

"*Shout back if you're Razarkha,*" the fuzzy voice demanded.

"Why do you want to know?" Razarkha yelled back.

"If you are Razarkha, we were told to spare you by high command. Do you have your soulstealer? You're only relevant if you have that."

Razarkha opened her hand briefly. She had clung to the artefact despite everything.

"Very well. I'm Razarkha Fel'thuz, and I possess the Soulstealer of Craving. I presume we're your prisoners."

"If you want to live, yes."

Her conquest of Galdus would have to wait.

"Very well! We accept your proposal."

Weil was almost sinking. *"Razarkha, what are they saying? Are they sparing us?"*

"They are. Just relax and do what they say. I'll figure something out."

The pinnace reached the water, and a tall, human oarsman rowed over to the scattered remnants of the *Dikamonstra*. Once Razarkha was aboard the rowboat, her hands were forced behind her back and cuffed with something that drained the heat from her head through her wrists. As the oarsman rowed to the barely-afloat Weil, Razarkha let her body slacken, reserving her strength to grip the Soulstealer of Craving.

Wrangled

A dank stench permeated the cell Razarkha Fel'thuz languished in. The tide was sickening without the horizon, and within the *Celestia's* brig, the closest thing to a landmark was a small, golden lantern attached to an opposing wall. Weil had been taken to a different part of the brig, and no pre-existing prisoners were there to keep Razarkha company.

Despite her efforts and protestation, she'd lost the one reason she was headed to Galdus in the first place: The Soulstealer of Craving. If she were against the Nortezians, fleshless, death-fleeing ascendants, she'd be relishing in destruction and power. Thanks to a Yukishiman fleet she couldn't have possibly anticipated, the soulstealer had been rendered useless.

Razarkha pulled against her cuffs; somehow, the Yukishimans had were able to suppress her arcane expression without true magitech. She kicked a nearby wall, then became unbalanced from a stray bob. She landed on her back, and a dearth in her soul prevented her from getting back up.

Once, she was strong enough to tolerate solitude. It was all she knew aside from verbal sparring with her brother-husband. Fate had placed Razarkha amidst antagonists and idiots from birth, so books were her best friends. Weil had weakened her. His eagerness to please, his kindness during her nadir, his connection to the Rakh'vash, all contributed to her addiction. When she was a friendless countess, she didn't know what she was missing, but now that the taste was on her lips, she needed more Weils in her life.

Without the soulstealer or her conquest, what was she? Weil doubtlessly craved her company too, but if he knew the truth, that wouldn't be the case. He'd have killed her before she dragged him away from Ilazar, and his father would likely have an honorary grave to visit.

"I'm sorry, Weil," she said to the air.

An apparition of Count Rani Fel'thuz appeared as she sat up. He was much taller than he was in life, looming twelve feet tall and staring at his eldest daughter with disappointment. No words escaped his mouth, but Razarkha shook her head and averted her eyes.

"I'm not the problem, father. Everybody hates me, why shouldn't I hate them back?"

The figure slipped into the shape of Weil, in the red and black cloak he shed to stay afloat. His doughy face was red and streaked with tears.

"I know *you* don't hate me. I know you're different, and I know I wronged you, but I did it for your own good!"

Weil swept away as though sand in the wind, and in his place stood a human woman with blonde hair whose curls appeared to be fixed in place. She wore a dress that rivalled Ilazari fashion; the cut of the fabric was a simple dark blue, covered in glittering silver sequins that formed stripes from her neckline.

Beside her was a wagon containing a bizarre metallic column. On top of it was a spherical glass chamber with numerous golden-glowing nodes sticking out of it. Staring from within was a cloud with glowing pale green embers in place of true eyes. Despite its expressionless nature, it filled the air with resentment.

"Greetings, Razarkha Fel'thuz," the human said in a lilting Yukishiman-accented rendition of the Common Tongue, keeping her hands behind her back. "I trust you're enjoying your stay on the *Celestia?*"

"Kill me or release me. Don't waste my time with pleasantries," Razarkha spat.

"Ah, good, you're much better at speaking Common than your friend," the human said with a smile. "Young Weil said *'I no speak Common Tongue'*, it was quite adorable.

18

Thankfully, I know Isleborn Ilazari to a functional level. He told me a lot of things about you."

Razarkha rolled her eyes. "If you're trying to break me with claims of betrayal, you're fighting with shadows. Weil would never turn on me."

"You're correct, he hasn't. In fact, he wouldn't stop talking about all the ways he admired you. It's a shame; he's quite handsome."

Now Razarkha knew she was playing a game. Weil, despite the days of sailing, was still too fat to be good-looking. His cheekbones were barely visible, and from what she'd seen, his ribs weren't defined. Perhaps he could fit in as a grotesque human, just like her brawn-obsessed brother, but Razarkha liked Weil for purely non-physical reasons.

"Can you get to the point? If you've heard of me, you'll know I single-handedly brought down the Kasparov Family. You don't want to enrage me."

The woman burst into laughter, and once done, nodded to the glass sphere beside her. "My friend says it was your lackey's doing. You didn't do much aside from pretend to be her."

"Your friend— pretended to— no, that isn't—"

"Hello again," the cloud echoed in Isleborn-accented Common. *"It's me. I'm a lot less beautiful than I was the last time you saw me, but I suppose it's better than sharing my grandfather's fate."*

"Anya Kasparov?" Razarkha asked.

"No, Parthezad of Arkhera. Of course I'm Anya Kasparov!" the cloud mocked.

"My apologies, all ascendants look the same to me. Why bother preserving yourself? Life without a body is like pork without seasoning," Razarkha retorted in Isleborn.

"Meanwhile death is akin to complete starvation of experience. I would rather be here, experiencing things partially, than experiencing nothing at all," Anya's wisp explained.

"Is the inside of that Yukishiman trap an enjoyable experience?"

"I will be released before long," Anya claimed. *"First, I must assist the good engineer. I've always been fair to my associates. Weil's betrayal still breaks my heart, as does your betrayal of him."*

Razarkha's heart jumped into her throat. *"What have you told him?"*

The human answered this question before Anya got the opportunity. "She's not relevant to my interrogations of Weil. I had him all to myself. I don't like to share tall, meek men."

Razarkha's temples burned up. "Shut up. You can't trick me, I know you haven't seduced him—"

"Why would it matter if I had?" the human asked. "Weil remembered something you said vividly. He said that you called him useless."

"That was in the heat of the moment! You can't hope to poison him against me!"

"Tragically, he's still loyal to you," the engineer said, her hands still hidden. "Most people treat you like the vermin you are, but he's different. Poor boy. Perhaps there's still time for him to realise who he's serving."

"I'm not falling for this!" Razarkha spluttered. "Just ask me what you need to ask, tormenting me is pointless!"

"It isn't pointless to me," the human said, her eyes glinting. "Would you like to know what's in my hands?"

"Is it the—"

"Come now, I know you Arkherans are unknowledgeable, but I'm sure you've heard of manners. Ask me nicely."

Razarkha's teeth ground against each other. "Show me what's in your hands."

"Even Weil would know that wasn't polite, and he sounds like a deep-voiced child in Common. Try again. Say 'please Imperial Engineer, if you would be so kind, reveal your hands'. It's not hard."

"I hate you," Razarkha muttered, before shifting her tone. "Please, Imperial Engineer, if you would be so kind, reveal your hands. Are you happy?"

"Overjoyed," the human said with an unexpected tweeness.

She revealed her left hand, in which dangled the Soulstealer of Craving. She held it daintily by the 'rope', swaying its ladle-shaped lower half in front of Razarkha.

"You want this, don't you? It won't get you any closer to escape, if that's what you're hoping. It's closer to a stuffed toy. Empty comfort for a child such as yourself."

Razarkha's chest tightened. "It's rightfully mine and I want it back."

The Imperial Engineer paused, then shrugged. "Very well. When we investigated it, we were dismayed to find that its energies matched those of the Sovereign. Additionally, it's bonded to you, according to the voice within the device. There would be public outrage if we were found to use Sovereign-based artefacts. You know how it is, Mother worshippers infesting Wrenfall. Ah, I suppose you don't."

Razarkha cocked her head. "You're returning it without protest?"

The woman threw the soulstealer into the cell, keeping her right hand behind her. "Go ahead. It's all yours if your cuffs allow you to pick it up."

Anya shifted within her glass prison, and Razarkha conceived a plan of action. She scrambled as best she could with her legs alone, pushed the soulstealer along the floor, and sat down with her back to the artefact, slipping her unburnt hand over it. By the time she properly got a grip on it, the Imperial Engineer's expression had twisted into a barely repressed smirk. Razarkha pushed down her own glee and whispered to her soulstealer's god.

21

"Bold Individualist, have the soulstealer consume that—"

Razarkha writhed as agony shot through her body from her cuffs. The Imperial Engineer revealed her right hand, which held a slab of overly smooth material with several buttons upon it, one of which she was pressing.

"You couldn't help yourself," the Imperial Engineer remarked. "I'll try again later. Keep the soulstealer for all the good it'll do you. Say goodbye, Anya."

"Goodbye, Fel'thuz. It was good to see the woman who broke Zemelnya. I hope you get sent back to your home country," Anya Kasparov said. *"Your family will receive you with open arms. Or is it loaded arms?"*

With that, the Yukishiman and her gaseous friend left Razarkha with her soulstealer, just as alone as before.

* * *

The train to the Crystal Palace was nearing its terminal station. Outside the clattering contraption, lush hills and arable farmland gave way to industrialised stretches filled with refineries and adits to the mines from which House of Verawor derived their riches. Gargantuan knuckle-walking beasts carried geodes from mines to refineries, while diminutive men sat on their shoulders, pointing and calling.

Rarakhi, newly made heir to the Fel'thuz name, beheld the creatures with morbid fascination. After a particularly long stare, he shuddered, and with difficulty, ripped his eyes away. Rakh met his eyes and broke the silence.

"What's wrong, Rarakhi?"

"Just wondering what those things are," the boy replied.

"What things?" Rakh Fel'thuz asked.

"Those beasts that look like huge men on four legs."

Rakh scratched his prosthetic hand and frowned. "I think they're ogres. You don't see them beyond the Harvester's Peaks and Iron Hills."

Rarakhi unknotted a piece of his hair. "Are they men?"

"Well, those people on their shoulders are probably ogretamers, which are a kind of beastmaster. I'd say they're beasts, but the distinction is muddy," Rakh remarked.

"Some necromancers can control people when they're still alive," Rarakhi claimed. "Plutera told me control is all about the spine or something. It's hard to tell what she's saying when she gets excited. Anyway, what I'm tryin' to say is just 'cause they can be controlled with magic doesn't make them any less people."

"I suppose. Humans were in a similar position in the Golden Galdusian Empire, though your mother and aunt know more about that than I."

Rarakhi put his hands behind his head. "Aunt Razarkha's the reason we're down here. Would she enslave humans if she had the power?"

This question gave Rakh pause. The word 'Razarkha' brought many things to mind; his attempted murderer, the mother of his dead trueborn children, his angry, lonely sister. She would ramble about the Plague Emperor and his fight against the Golden Galdusian Empire with a passion usually reserved for bullying Tei.

"I'm not sure. If she were to enslave people, I think she would be indiscriminate. She always idolised the Plague Emperor, and his struggle against Galdus dismantled the old practices of augmenting humans for magical enslavement."

"But she's still bad?"

"Just because she believes in some good things doesn't mean she isn't dangerous," Rakh explained. "Her greatest strength is her unscrupulous determination. Only brute force can stop her from doing something once she puts

23

her mind to it. I was wrong to exile her. Killing her is the only way to stop her for good."

"You really fucked that up, didn't you?" Rarakhi said with a laugh.

"It's not funny," Rakh snapped, his sternness apparently bringing the train to a stop. "Come, let's get our things and make this quick."

Beyond their window was a metropolitan train station with a reinforced glass roof and paved platforms, numerous pillars holding up the ceiling where it dipped. The pair of spellbinders got their suitcases and left the station to meet the city it lay within.

Before them was the Crystal Palace's city centre, a well-paved, pleasantly hot tangle of winding roads and beauteous expressions of the lower class's backbreaking labour. Jewellers dotted almost every street, while a restaurant at the end of the station's road had seerish and elven customers queuing beyond the premises for a seat. While many of these prim money sinks stood tall, none could dwarf the centremost building: The palace for which the city was named.

Preceded by a publicly accessible fountain and twenty acres of gated-off gardens, its size made Castle Selenia look quaint. Its upper levels were sculpted elegance, mimicking the curved and bulbous aesthetic of Ilazari architecture, while its lower level had the edged, compact and pillared style of the Galdusians. As Arkhera had been ruled by both cultures at different points in time, it was unclear which empire oversaw the building's creation, if either.

As Rakh neared the gates, a pair of armoured seers raised their halberds. Perched atop posts were a squad of goblins with small musket rifles pointed at him and his son. All wore the maroon, black and gold of the Verawors, with the seers closest to them having a tentacle-wrapped iron rod with an eyeball on top etched into their breastplates.

One seer's eyes glittered red and green through his visor as he spoke. "Who are you, and why do you want to see Overlord Verawor?"

Rarakhi hid behind his father, his teal gaze fixed upon the goblinese guards' rifles. Rakh put his hand on his son's shoulder and answered in a calm voice.

"We're here to request the services of Sir Rowyn Khanas. He lives in this city, correct?"

"He does. Seems the overlord caught you with his third eye, 'cause Khanas got his shift reassigned to honour guard duty with barely a day's notice," the seer said. "Bloody lucky, are the Verawors. I wish I could have visions that help my career."

"What visions *do* you have?" Rakh asked. "I've made love to a seer before, and believe me, satisfying her was a nightmare when everything was predictable."

The seerish guard gave a gruff laugh. "All I see are different ways I could die. Makes me a great fighter, but a terrible businessman."

"I'm sure the businessman seers lament needing to part with their coin to hire seers like you. Someone has to save their skins from assassins and disgruntled workers."

"That sounds like the rich trying to stop the poor complaining," the guard said with a shrug. "If you're just here to talk, you won't mind a pat down. Leave your suitcases with us."

"As you wish. Rarakhi?" Rakh said, checking on his shaking son.

"Dad, I— I'm sorry, I'm still a little uneasy. The Selenia guys are like ol' Bloodmetal to me now, but I don't know if I can stay calm with all these strange guns on me."

Rakh softened his voice. "They're just going to check you for weapons, it's nothing serious."

"Something the matter, boy?" the previously silent guard asked. After a pause, he dropped his halberd and caught Rarakhi in a wrist lock.

"What the fuck, what did I do?" the lad spluttered.

"You have a knife, don't you?"

Rarakhi's eyes pled with Rakh, but as a visiting nobleman, he took diplomacy's side.

"Please tell me you didn't bring a knife with you."

"It's for self-defence! I'll give it to you, I'll hand it over no problem, I promise!"

"No funny business," the second guard demanded as he released the boy. "You spellbinders are tricky, and illusionists are the worst of all."

"How many illusionists have you met in your time?" the first guard asked.

"Shut up, I know their magic's all about trickery," he said as Rarakhi handed a shiv over.

"The pat down won't reveal anything else, will it?" the first guard asked.

"Hopefully not," Rakh said, shooting a glare at his son.

The guards seized their suitcases, and after they patted their bodies, the pair were sent on their way through the Crystal Palace courtyard. Beastmaster-ran apiaries and seer-controlled vegetable patches lay behind the goblinese watchmen, and further within was an ornamental section consisting of shaped hedges and even more patrolmen.

Rakh hardened his tone. "I know it's hard to let go of the past, but you're not part of the underground anymore. You don't need to bring a knife to a word fight."

"I had that for people on the street, not this lord we're visiting," Rarakhi claimed. "What if we came across a mean son-of-a-bitch at the inn we're staying at?"

"Still, you see how this looks, don't you?"

"Of course I do, I'm not stupid."

"Keep it in the suitcase next time. Put it in your pocket when you think you'll need it. We're not going to get mugged in the most heavily-fortified building in Arkhera."

Rarakhi clenched his fists and his face reddened. When they reached the palace itself, the opulence was more evident than ever. Towards the top of the supporting pillars, massive rubies, jets and topazes were in-laid, and draped above the entrance were rich velvet banners, maroon with a black iron bar upon it, wrapped by the tentacles of a golden octopoid creature with a single red eyeball.

"Their sigil is outright daemonic," Rakh said, his missing hand hurting more than ever.

"Not so nice facing horrible shit from your past, is it?" Rarakhi remarked.

"Rara, you don't need to do this while I—"

As the sound of his right hand's bones being crushed flitted through his mind, the castle doors opened, revealing a young woman about Rarakhi's age. She was seerish, with mousy features, brunette hair, and a lanky body on its transition to adulthood. Her eyes, like most of her race, shifted in colour from red to green depending on the light they were beheld in.

"Oh, you must be Count Fel'thuz. My father's expecting you," the girl said with a clumsy curtsey.

"Ah, are you Veran Verawor?" Rakh asked. "I'll admit I only know you as a name on your family tree. It's good to meet you nonetheless."

"I suppose that's all I'll be," she said with a sigh. "Eldest child, but not eldest son. It's just the way life is. Come with me."

Rakh followed the young woman inside. The foyer was vast and dappled from the marble that formed it, and though myriad halls branched from it, it was sparsely populated. Two servants rushed about, dusting a room whose size would demand twenty servants in Castle Selenia. A wide staircase stood at the back of the lavishly barren expanse, which Veran quietly walked towards. She appeared to be pleasant, but as a passed-over elder girl, she had the potential to become a Razarkha. Unable to contain his curiosity, Rakh spoke.

"What's your brother like?"

"Which one?" the girl asked.

"Your eldest. Verik, is it?"

Veran chuckled. "Oh, the precious heir. Mother loves him, father hates him. He's cruel, to be honest. He bullies poor Anver every day, and sometimes he stares at Woraga in a way boys his age shouldn't."

This wasn't a situation Rakh had insight on after all. There was no point in commenting. He needed to get Rowyn Khanas's services and deal with the current monster. The Verawors would deal with the next generation's Razarkha.

"I'm sorry, who is this Woraga?" Rakh asked. "I thought Verawyn only had three children."

"Woraga's my step-aunt, silly," Veran said with a laugh. "Though she is young enough to be my sister. My mother *hates* her, but you know how it is. Women her age hate any woman that benefits from their spouse."

Rakh tried to play with his hair, only to remind himself of his wooden prosthetic's lack of articulation. "I don't think every woman behaves like that. You wouldn't if you were your mother's age, would you?"

"I suppose not."

Rarakhi chuckled. "Maybe your mum's just an insecure bi—"

"Rarakhi, remember where you are, and don't leap to conclusions."

Veran, a model of inelegant elegance, rose above Rarakhi's blunder and took them up the stairs in silence. Through the palace they walked, navigating labyrinthine, near-abandoned halls and climbing many more staircases, some thin, some twisting, some without bannisters. The eerily quiet quest ended when they reached a room with a heavy mahogany door.

Behind it, voices bickered. One stumbled over his words, while the other spoke clearly and confrontationally. Veran knocked on the door, and the latter voice silenced itself. After a short wait, a tall figure clad in emerald-tinted light armour opened the door. They met Rakh's eyes, stepped back, and allowed the Fel'thuzes to enter.

The council chamber was warm-coloured, with a simple, circular mahogany table in its centre and two windows that allowed light to flood onto a variety of potted plants. Sitting on one side of the table was a blonde-haired seer with a face beset by the ravages of time. His somewhat feminine-featured face was obscured by a yellow-grey beard, while the maroon and gold of his family was expressed through a rich silken jacket and cravat. He was accompanied by what appeared to be a floating, floral-themed cowl that housed a cloudlike figure with jade-green lights for eyes.

Opposite the seer was the spluttering figure, a high elven businessman with a frayed black cape. Even as Veran led the Fel'thuzes in, he continued to babble to himself.

"As I was trying to say, Lord Verawor, my business represents the vast majority of Renewalist prayer bead production in this city."

"And yet you did not save enough to protect yourself from the downturn that's affecting all businesses that export to Ashglass," the old seer said. "Businesses are not tax-funded services, Aryndel. If yours is failing, I will not bail it out."

"What happens when Ashglass starts importing again and I'm not there to sell to them?"

"Somebody else will fill that niche. Get out of my sight before I have Parthezad put you to sleep," the seer commanded.

The high elf shakily stood, gave the floating cowl a nervous glance, then dashed away. The seer groaned, then turned to Veran with a tired smile.

"Thank you for finding them, dear," he said. "Was I right on the timing?"

"I only had to wait ten minutes," she said with a smile, before rushing to hug him.

The two Verawors embraced, and the tall knight shut the door behind the Fel'thuzes. Rakh scanned the lithe metallic figure and noticed that the back of his gauntlets had flaming skulls etched into them, much like the banners Plutyn insisted covering Castle Selenia with.

"Rowyn Khanas, I presume?" Rakh asked, but before the knight could answer, Lord Verawor spoke.

"Do not assume you can poach my men so easily. Fel'thuz, is it?" Verawyn said. "You're shorter than I expected. Aren't spellbinders supposed to be taller than necromancers?"

"We Fel'thuzes aren't known for our height," Rakh stammered. "Please understand, Lord Verawor, we're here because of Plutyn Khanas. He wants to call in a family favour."

The old seer pulled out a chair for his daughter, then sat down. Veran sat beside him, an excitement flickering in her unusual eyes. The lord glanced at his floating cowl, then spoke.

"Parthezad, is he being truthful?"

"Of course," the green-eyed cloud expressed in a simultaneously male, female, young, and old voice. *"Oh, that's quite amusing, but irrelevant."*

"What amuses you?" Verawyn asked.

"Rakh Fel'thuz similarly evaluated you as short, but unlike your assessment he wasn't surprised at all. He considers the spacious palace and gem acquisition compensatory."

"Ah, you're the sort that, while benefiting from the class system, looks down upon those who act according to their station," Verawyn remarked. "Hypocrisy makes me itch. State your reason for borrowing— allow me to stress that, *borrowing*— Rowyn Khanas's services."

"Our Minister of Criminal Affairs, Plutyn Khanas, wants a favour from his cousin to make up for past events. Apparently Rowyn refused to marry his daughter—"

"Oh, he's *still* bitter about that? Bloody Plutyn, he can't let things go like an ordinary person, can he?" the knight broke in, his tone surprisingly unthreatening.

"Quiet, Rowyn," Verawyn commanded, and when he wringed his hands, his daughter mimicked him. "Regardless of familial bickering, temporary release of duty is a decision *I* make, not some Khanas in Moonstone."

"Yes, my lord," Rowyn stammered.

"Continue, Fel'thuz."

Rakh gave the overlord a shallow bow. "Thank you. Plutyn wishes for Rowyn to visit Winter Harbour. He believes Baron Oswyk is hiding criminal activity and wishes to find his associate, Anya Kasparov. She recently revealed to Oswyk that my sister, Razarkha, has risen in power, so theoretically, if we find Anya, we find Razarkha."

"Kasparov is an Ilazari name, and your sister is exiled. How are either relevant to Arkheran affairs?"

The flowery cowl echoed in its androgynous way. *"My lord, he's afraid of his sister returning to Arkhera with a dread weapon that can massacre ascendants like us. Perhaps you could use your third eye with this in mind."*

Verawyn rolled his eyes and began to mutter. "I'll do it just to humour you, Parthezad. How much turmoil could a—"

The seerish lord cut himself off and rubbed his temple.

"What's wrong, father?" Veran asked.

"You need to go with him, Rowyn," Verawyn insisted.

The necromantic knight folded his arms. "Did you see Plutyn's bitterness festering into a monster great enough to destroy Arkhera?"

"This is no time to joke, Khanas," Verawyn said. "I foretell great destruction, but there's one detail that has me confused. When were you expecting Razarkha to return?"

"Honestly, any day now," Rakh answered. "Part of stationing Rowyn at Winter Harbour was in case she returned mid-investigation."

Verawyn pressed his hands together. "The good news is it seems her return is much further in the future than that. Months, perhaps years away. The bad news is she represents great destruction when she does. That is, unless Rowyn can stop her ahead of time."

Rakh swallowed and faced the unfamiliar Khanas. "I'm sorry to put this upon you. Plutyn believes a necromancer like you would appeal to Razarkha's sensibilities, especially if you claim to have left Verawyn due to disdain for 'weak' races."

Rowyn shrugged. "It works out well for me. I've needed a break from this city for a while. Don't tell Plutyn, but me and the beastmaster girl I rejected Plutera for didn't even marry, and she's made my life miserable since we parted ways."

Rarakhi butted in. "Don't think you can claim Plutera now. She's mine, you hear?"

"Oh, I wouldn't dream of it. Marrying cousins half my age? That's an old system thing. Plutyn can keep his old system. What I'm after is an adventure away from Umbria."

"It's settled, then," Rakh said. "Meet us at the train station tomorrow morning on the seventh hour. After your briefing in Moonstone, your adventure will begin."

Deployed

"Last I saw him, Plutyn was headed to Castle Selenia," Bloodmetal said with a shrug. "Plutera's practically the mistress of the house at this point. Guess the boss likes the high life."

The undead orc was guarding Plutyn Khanas's manor with his mute co-worker, Notongue. His crushed breastplate was still encrusted with the same gore it was the first time Rakh met him. He, along with Rarakhi and Rowyn, had assumed Plutyn would have preferred to arrange matters in the privacy of his own home, but it appeared sending a message was more important than comfort.

"Wait, Plutera's here but the boss isn't?" Rarakhi asked. "Can I come in? You know, spend a little time with my betrothed?"

"Yeah, but there's conditions," the guard said with a grin bordering on rictus. "The boss told me that if you return and want to see Plutera, there's got to be a chaperone. It's not that he don't trust you, but three years is a long time, 'n' if you do anything you can't take back, cancellation of the betrothal becomes difficult."

Rakh laughed. "It's a fair concern—"

"Shut up, dad," Rarakhi scoffed. "You fuck peasant girls and ruin 'em for marriage all the time. I'm your bastard, do you think I'd repeat your mistakes? I'm a good guy and Plutera loves me for that."

"Actually, she quite likes the steady stream of bodies you once provided," Bloodmetal claimed. "She said she misses you being a scary underground ghost sometimes."

The boy's face reddened. "Now I'm nervous. Fuck you, Bloodmetal."

"Now, now, don't hate me, hate a world that makes girls crave violent men. It's same with orcish women, not that I've enjoyed any since dying."

Rowyn had been looking over the revenant with silent fascination. It was this remark that finally coaxed words from his mouth.

"Plutyn raised you, yes?"

"That's right, the boss wanted a smart, nigh-unkillable undead guard, so he got me. Then he thought I needed an idiot to keep me in line and raised Notongue."

The mute orc beside him hissed and flicked his compatriot's nose. Bloodmetal took the hit unflinchingly even as blackened ichor dislodged from his nostril.

"If that breastplate's stayed on you since you were raised, I can't imagine it's a pretty sight inside," Rowyn said. "Admittedly I'd *love* to find out. Disasters have a certain beauty to them."

"Har, you're just like Plutera," Bloodmetal said. "Anyway, you adults, go and find the Boss. I'll babysit the two young lovers."

Rarakhi glanced at his father then walked past the guards. With that, Rakh headed back through the Khanas estate. Rowyn walked behind him, admiring the undead workers on his cousin's gardens.

"I'll admit, Plutyn knows how to put his powers to work," Rowyn said. "These zombies are autonomous to a degree I couldn't possibly achieve."

"Why is that?" Rakh asked.

"My powers don't seem to have come through," Rowyn admitted. "My mother assured me I was a late bloomer, but even now, the best I can manage is stabilising dying organs during surgery. I'm a useful part time aide for medics in training, but I'm no true necromancer."

"I hope that's not important to you."

"I wear armour and swing a sword around, which is technically a new skill to replace the one my forefathers passed down," Rowyn said with a shrug. "It's a shame I won't see Plutera before I leave, but given what Plutyn intended for us, perhaps that's for the best."

Together, they left the Khanas estate and stepped into the snow-covered streets of Moonstone. Recent snowstorms had overwhelmed even the richer districts, and efforts to grit the area had only left the streets soggy and partially cleared.

"You escaped an unwanted betrothal simply by saying no. I'm sure the distance between you and Plutyn helped. I was raised to be my sister's husband and patriarch," Rakh said. "I should have said no. I was never dominant enough to control somebody like Razarkha."

"Are you sure dominance was the issue? I confess I know little of your sister, but you both coexisted for at least the forty or so years you've lived—"

"Thirty-five."

"As you say. My point is, if she was an insatiable monster, wouldn't you have reached an untenable point sooner?"

"Perhaps," Rakh said. "I failed Razarkha, but worse, I failed Rarakhi and Tei."

"What's Tei got to do with your situation?"

Rakh's words caught in his throat. "She was regularly bullied by Razarkha, that's all."

The knight adjusted his visor. "I see. My apologies."

Rakh's black overcoat and Rowyn's emerald-green spaulders had become white with accumulated snow by the time they reached Castle Selenia's grounds, and within the building, shelter was the only respite. The merciless chill of the outdoors was perfectly preserved by the ilmenite interior of the castle, and Rowyn was shuddering in his armour.

"Tell me there's a hearth *somewhere* in this castle."

"There's a few lounges with fireplaces," Rakh replied. "They're Plutyn's preferred haunt when he isn't talking with Erwyn. The two get on remarkably well given how they were introduced."

Rowyn folded his arms. "Do I want to know?"

"It involved blows to the crotch. Not the fun kind."

"Ah. Lead the way, Fel'thuz."

After moving from lounge to lounge, Rakh and Rowyn found the self-proclaimed Lord Khanas in the games room, playing *Wraiths and Wyverns* with Lady Selenia. As Rakh expected, the lady was hopelessly losing, yet she advanced a single zombie with the enthusiasm of a grandmaster making a winning gambit.

"See? I blocked your wyvern! You can't take my ghoul!" the lady said with a squeal.

"No, but my other wyvern is free to do this," Plutyn said in his usual dour tone. He moved the appropriate wyvern and threatened Lady Kagura's necromancer. "Check."

"But that's— how am I supposed to— isn't that checkmate?"

"No, there's a—"

"Let me figure it out, I'm smart enough, just give me time," the lady commanded, staring a hole into the board.

Plutyn turned to Rakh and Rowyn, an unimpressed glower consuming his face. Silence lingered until the Khanas family's more metallic half broke it.

"Smiley as ever, Plutyn," Rowyn remarked.

"Thuglike as usual, Rowyn," Plutyn retorted.

"Oh, come off it. I'm a guard, I need protection. Have you ever been hit by a musket ball? It hurts," Rowyn said. "You called, and I answered. Let's save the insults for when these two aren't listening."

Plutyn's hands tensed, and without a word he made Lady Selenia's move for her.

"Oh, that's how save myself," she said with a wide smile. "Thank you, Sir Kha—"

"You're in a fortunate situation, dear cousin," Plutyn said, ignoring his employer. "I took in a boy with three times the pride you've exhibited, someone I'll be happy to call my son. You had that opportunity, and you spat upon it for some beastmistress. That's the past. The present involves restitution."

Kagura put a finger on her cheek. "Cancellation of betrothals could upset somebody? But mistakes happen. Like my father betrothing Yarawyn to a *dark elf*. What was he—"

"My lady, refrain from talking about matters... beneath your station," Plutyn said as he squeezed a game piece. "You answered my call, Rowyn, so presumably you are willing to pay your restitution. That implies you know how you wronged me."

"I'm doing this for a change of pace," Rowyn replied. "I have a troop of Verawor soldiers specifically loyal to me waiting at the *Wendigo's Head*. Just tell me what to do and I'll have fun working on it."

Plutyn hopped a wraith over his own zombie, then over one of Lady Selenia's wyverns, capturing it. Following this, the necromancer stood.

"You're lucky we share the old blood of Galdus," he said, taking out a pipe, a small sachet of bhang-weed, and a matchbox. "Let's discuss business. Fel'thuz, continue my game for me. I trust it will be a more even match."

"Wait," Rakh stammered. "I want to know how you intend to find my sister. That's my right, isn't it—"

"I'm the Minister of Criminal Affairs. When it comes to tracking criminals *you* wrongly reduced the sentence of, I shall handle the specifics. You're an advisor to the lady; feel free to understand the forest while *I* deal with the trees."

With that, Plutyn left the room, pouring his bhang-weed into his pipe as he walked. Rowyn followed, though not before turning to Rakh with an apologetic half-bow. The count sighed and sat opposite his lady.

"The minister is growing haughty," Rakh remarked to Lady Kagura, who was engrossed in her game board, but her gambit appeared to be a mystery even to her.

"I think it's because Erwyn is showing him so much attention," Kagura finally said. "They both like cutting open bodies and other scary wisdom things. I wanted Erwyn to work on my special project but he's always talking with the minister."

"About what?"

"Ashglass. I know Razarkha's scary, but I don't want to make friends with Lady Foenaxas. She worships the wrong god, she looks like a man, and when I last visited her brother didn't even greet me!"

"Probably something to do with the betrothal you denied him," Rakh said. "What's this special project?"

The high elf hurriedly moved a zombie forward. "That's a secret, counts like you can't know about it. It's a tree and you need to see a forest or— you know, what Sir Khanas said."

Rakh moved a ghoul into the open. "Of course, my lady."

* * *

The mockery of Imperial Engineer Hildegard Swan had become unbearable. Every day, the human arrive at the brig and spout a new titbit she'd gleaned from Weil, waggle Anya Kasparov in front of her, then wait for Razarkha to try and kill her. It didn't matter how she attempted to subvert the engineer's test; she always ended up pressing the 'pain button'.

Razarkha didn't bother insulting the pair on sight anymore. She stared, took the abuse, then watched them leave. She adjusted her sleep to match their visits, and as she was currently unable to sleep, a visit was forthcoming.

On time, Hildegard Swan arrived, wearing a practical fusion between a business suit and a skirt, her lipstick so red it could be seen in the brig's dim light. Beside her was Anya Kasparov, no longer within her machine, but instead wearing a flowing Galdusian cloak, black with pale green embroidery. Affixed to her clasp was a malachite gemstone to match her cloak, glimmering with arcane energies.

38

"Hello again, Fel'thuz. Do you like the new look? It represents freedom," the ascendant echoed. *"You're not too familiar with the concept, are you?"*

"Shut up," Razarkha spat.

"I'm with Fel'thuz," the Imperial Engineer remarked. "I granted you freedom, yet you now see fit to speak ahead me. I hope you don't consider our allegiance an equal one."

"Of course not, great engineer, your authority is vast and unstoppable."

"The word 'sorry' is sufficient."

"Sorry."

"Good girl," Hildegard said. "So, Razarkha, Anya Kasparov is here, out of her SAIC— sorry, to brown-neckers like you that means 'special machine that contains ascendants'. While she's freer to move than she's been in weeks, she's more vulnerable to your soulstealer than ever. Before, your attempts would have likely triggered my SAIC's mechanisms, killing her before your soulstealer could complete its job. Now she's all yours."

"What?" Anya spluttered. *"You said that this would be the last time I saw her—"*

"Quiet, Kasparov. I have a transponder with me and can signal the activation of my latest ANF generator with a word. Don't make me regret my mercy."

"Of course, Imperial Engineer."

A week ago, Razarkha would have mocked this shell of Anya Kasparov. She was no longer an elegant gangster who struck fear into those she met. She'd been reduced to a bodyless lackey to the madmen of Yukishima. While Razarkha was the good engineer's prisoner, Anya was a fellow victim. Razarkha clung to the Soulstealer of Craving and stood.

"If I try to steal her soul, you'll hurt me or worse. Don't insult my intelligence," Razarkha said, rising to her feet. "This is your final test, isn't it?"

"Perceptive," Hildegard remarked with a raised eyebrow. "I'm glad you understand the situation. Why don't we negotiate the terms of your release?"

"Terms of— you're going to let me go?"

"Of course," the Imperial Engineer said. "Why throw a perfectly good resource away? The Soltelle Imperial Navy can't be seen using Sovereign-based magitech, but say there was a rogue madwoman who happens to be moving through Nortez removing elements that are problematic to the empire. Convenient for everyone, wouldn't you say? We'll allow your behaviour to go unchallenged but distance ourselves from your divine allies. Our thread prevents us from using the soulstealer to its full potential anyway."

"You want me to be a patsy, is that it?" Razarkha said with a scoff. "Act as though I'm working alone, when in truth you'll be whispering in my ear?"

"I think you'll be more convincing if you behave as you always do, though I do have a preferred initial target for your massacres. Weil told me about your idol. The Plague Emperor was certainly a fascinating character. He would be on our side, to be sure."

"Not so. You Yookies dominated Northern Amerist with typical imperial oppression. The Plague Emperor fought for freedom."

"Then consolidated that freedom by forming his own empire. The clue is in his title," the human said with a titter. "There was the Golden Galdusian Empire, then the Ilazari Plague Empire, then the Jaranese-Na'liman Empire. On and on, round and round. We Yukishimans are strongly opposed to Old Galdusian ideals. We consider eternal, miserable life, and enslaving humans to be abhorrent. If you intend on massacring ascendants who cling to the old ways of Galdus, we have a common enemy. Of course, killing civilians is distasteful—"

"Whereas I don't care what they call themselves. Civilians, soldiers, if they cling to their existence and accept

40

slavery, all they're good for is arcane fuel," Razarkha finished. "I understand. You truly offer freedom. You won't stop me taking what is mine?"

"If you kill our allies, we'll respond as though we weren't the ones to release you. You'll be branded an enemy of the empire and eradicated. But you have the sense not to let it come to that, I hope," Hildegard said.

Of course," Razarkha mumbled.

"Good. Have your little shindig, enjoy consuming the ascendants that trouble our imperial interests, and be free."

With that, the Imperial Engineer unlocked the cell, and opened the door for Razarkha. She walked out, allowed the human to unclasp her cuffs, then stared. She was short and fat-faced like any other human, without magic beyond her technology. She stood, unfazed by the freshly released spellbinder before her, which itself made Razarkha's blood boil.

"What are you thinking about?" Hildegard asked. "Let me guess, you're excited to eat soup with a spoon rather than your face."

"No."

Hildegard chuckled. "Oh, how stereotypical, you're thinking of how you could kill me, aren't you? Don't bother. If I die, you'll never leave this boat. Not in one piece, at least. Sharks need food too."

Razarkha gritted her teeth and looked to her soulstealer. There was no way to betray this woman without dying. Weil was also on this boat; if she angered the great and mighty Imperial Engineer, he'd be killed too.

"Take me to Weil," she demanded.

"Oh, how sweet. You *do* love him. I debated with myself whether it was possible for… things like you to love. Don't worry. I was so confident in your reformation I released him early. He's waiting for you in a cabin. I could lead you to him, if you wish. There's also some fresh clothes to replace your sea-soaked rags."

Razarkha almost smiled, then pushed it down. In an artificially flattened tone, she replied, "Excellent. Let's not waste any time."

Hildegard grinned, then signalled Anya Kasparov to leave. When she was away from the brig, the engineer put her hands behind her back and followed the ascendant, then turned away from her at the first split in the corridor.

"Are you still figuring out how to kill me?" Hildegard asked. "Remember; though I'm an engineer by trade, humans generally beat spellbinders in fistfights. Further stacking the odds, I have a handgun. Even if you're willing to die in the process, remember that the chances of you killing me at all are laughably low."

"I gave up after your first warning," Razarkha said. "I'm not going to betray you. Not now, at least. I know it's madness."

"Good to know you're still open to future betrayal. I'd hate to think that I broke you completely," Hildegard said with a dismissive wave. "Just remember to choose your timing wisely. The Soltelle Empire has a lot of resources."

Razarkha opted against a response. The journey through the *Celestia's* corridors was eerie, each stretch as repetitive as the last. Eventually, they reached a metallic door coated in rust. Hildegard knocked it with a simple three-beat rhythm and spoke in basic Isleborn Ilazari.

"Weil of Zemelnya, your woman."

The door opened, and there stood the boy, too good to be true, in his usual uncertain posture. She may have been in rags that stood to ruin his fresh clothes, but she couldn't stop herself. She charged at Weil and clutched him. A harrowing pain seized her chest, and her eyes began to leak.

"Is that truly you, Weil? You're not an illusion or a trick, are you?" she babbled.

"I'm not."

"Say something I wouldn't know about yourself."

Weil paused. *"I've used to have a strange infatuation with Anya Kasparov even though she terrified me. Until she had my father killed, of course."*

Razarkha let her relief consume her, and she soaked his new clothes with tears as heavy breathing took the place of intelligible dialogue.

"I'll leave you to it. Don't be too loud, remember that sailors leagues away from their wives live here," the Imperial Engineer said, shutting the door once she was done.

After voiding her eyes of liquid weakness, Razarkha released Weil and as though a toppling tree, collapsed onto the cabin's lint-addled bed. Despite her utter defeat, a part of her couldn't stop laughing.

"What was funny? What did the woman say?" Weil asked.

"I'm not laughing at her. She just made another hackneyed implication that you and I have a conjugal relationship."

"To be fair, you did ambush me with your tongue that one time—"

"Shut up," Razarkha snapped, then widened her eyes. *"Wait, don't shut up, tell me what that human bitch said to you. Did Anya Kasparov speak to you?"*

"Anya Kasparov is on this ship? We must kill her immediately—"

"Don't be stupid. We'd both die if you tried that."

"I don't need you to kill her. I'll make the Rakh'vash corrupt her orderly stasis with my portals. You will survive because I'll take my vengeance alone," Weil insisted. *"You don't need me anymore. The Imperial Engineer said she'll deploy you in Pentatum because of some Nortezian still dealing with the Sulari. With your soulstealer and your freedom, I'm worthless to you."*

Razarkha thrust herself out of Weil's bed and stalked towards the young man, then took him by the collar. Tears were forming again, and her words became strained.

"Listen to me, you fool. I'll always *need you. You're not just a set of tentacles and summoned daemons. You're the only person who's believed in me."*

"How can that be possible—"

"It's possible," Razarkha interrupted. *"If you think you can get yourself killed without harming me, you're mistaken. I will not have you throw your life away. You will take your vengeance on that cloud bitch, but not here, not now. I want to see you live to enjoy your revenge. Am I clear?"*

Weil bit his lip. *"Very clear."*

"Then let us savour this freedom. Where are the baths?"

This made the boy smile with uncharacteristic warmth. *"I'll show you the way. It's good to be with you again."*

Purged

Marching towards the walled-off town of Winter Harbour were seerish spearmen and mounted goblinese musketeers led by Sir Rowyn Khanas, armed with steel and paper alike. If they were civilians, they would have been able to take the train but given they were adversarial to the local nobility, they had to approach according to royally sanctioned rules of engagement.

Rowyn's reading of the law was that despite acting on behalf of Baron Oswyk's overlady, they could not use crown-funded public transport as a form of military insertion. Plutyn insisted otherwise, but Rowyn wasn't about to take legal advice from a proud criminal.

Therefore, he and his men did the honourable thing. They'd marched from Moonstone, through the Ashpeaks, reaching Winter Harbour drained of pep and patience. By the time they reached the gates, the Oswyk guard force had closed them. One trembling human in furs and metal stood beyond the town while the rest watched from the safety of the battlements.

"What's the meaning of this?" the lone Oswyk beyond the walls asked. "By what authority are you approaching with your thugs? I see a green banner with a blue-burning skull, that's no house I recognise."

"I'm Sir Rowyn Khanas of the Crystal Palace, and I'm here on the authority of House Selenia's Minister of Criminal Affairs," Rowyn stated, opening a satchel to present a warrant bearing signatures of Plutyn, Lady Kagura, and Wisdom Erwyn.

"Warrant for the criminal investigation of Baron Oswyk?" the guard asked with a hoot. "Your piece of paper means nothing."

"There's an extra copy of it retained in Moonstone," Rowyn said. "We want to keep things as transparent as possible and I hope his sake that your baron shares that desire. Open your gates to us and we won't need to escalate the situation. We approached your town fairly and honourably. If you turn us away, we'll deploy enough men to break these gates down."

"No you won't. The Forests of Winter needs—"

"Garzag, shoot this man," Rowyn snapped, turning to one of his musketeers.

As the goblin lined up his shot, the Oswyk guard panicked. "All right, all right, we'll open the gates!"

Rowyn smiled beneath his helmet as he raised his hand. "Gun down, 'zag, don't waste your ammunition. Consider yourself fortunate that you're dealing with me. My cousin would not be so lenient."

Oswyk men scrambled to open the gates, and Rowyn loomed over the human guard as he walked past, snatching the warrant back as he did. Domination wasn't always necessary, but knowing when it was separated the good knights from the bad. His men followed him into the town, his goblinese scouts swiftly beginning a search for decent vantage points.

They clambered the relatively short terraces and pointed out routes the Oswyk guards were likely to march along. The knowledge proved irrelevant in execution, as most guards cringed away once they saw the troops. Rowyn turned to his seerish second-in-command, Officer Verwile.

"Do you predict any trouble with the remaining Oswyk men?"

"The town guards are incompetent, but I predict resistance at Baron Oswyk's manor."

Rowyn sighed. "Plutyn's suspicions were correct. Typical corrupt priorities. You know what to do."

"Of course," the officer said. "Spearmen, form a perimeter as we approach Baron Oswyk's manor. Musketeers, stay back and pick off resisting guards from a distance."

The men shifted accordingly, albeit limited by the streets they were traversing. Women grabbed their children's hands and fled, while some guards attempted to stop them, then thought better once muskets were aimed their way.

Rowyn adjusted his visor. Honourably speaking, he should have assured the civilians that they were safe, but the guards were hypothetically as afraid for their charges' lives as their own. Throwing away a bargaining chip was never a prudent military tactic. Verwile kept his arms folded, speaking once they reached the edge of Oswyk Manor's estate.

"This is it, Sir Khanas. Be prepared."

Unlike most of Winter Harbour's buildings, Oswyk Manor lay behind steel gates and had numerous watchtowers within its grounds. Behind the gates, elven patrolmen wielded long-barrelled magitech guns surrounded by metal coils and beyond them, mace-wielding orcs stood tall.

"Third eyes open," Rowyn commanded his spearmen, before addressing the guards. "You all work for Baron Giles Oswyk, correct? We have a Selenia-approved warrant to take him in for questioning and investigate accusations of criminal conduct."

"Too bad, he's not coming out," one of the orcs called back. "Why don't you come closer, dog? Stop barkin' and put yourself ahead of those little men with the spears."

"Honour does not require suicidality," Rowyn stated. "If I were you, I'd ask your baron if he wants to escalate this situation. You're illegally speaking on his behalf as it stands."

"The baron doesn't have to answer to people like you."

Rowyn couldn't afford mercy. The armoured behemoths towered over his seerish spearmen, and if they made the first strike, they would kill at least one. If escalation was inevitable, he needed the initiative.

"As you wish," Sir Khanas muttered, then raised his voice. "Musketeers, focus fire on the mace wielders. After that, we break the gates down."

The goblins were swift and efficient, peppering the metal monsters with lead until the bulk of them fell. They weren't completely incapacitated, but the spearmen were smart enough to stab through their armour's gaps while the goblins reloaded. A single orc remained active enough to smash through the spearmen's line entirely, charging Rowyn with their mace raised. He didn't have time to draw his sword, but he'd trained against orcs before. Defeating them was as simple as acknowledging their weight.

He sidestepped the brute's first charge, but the orc didn't overshoot as far as he'd hoped. The orc turned and swung, knocking Rowyn to the floor and dinting his tasset. The beast roared and held his mace high, ready to finish him with a single crushing blow, only to be mercilessly hammered by another set of musket balls. If that didn't kill the orc, his shocked dropping of his own mace onto his helmet did. Rowyn scrambled across the floor before the monster fell on top of him, and when Verwile offered a hand, his breath wavered.

"That was too close. Where are the interior patrolmen?" Rowyn asked, taking his second-in-command's hand and rising to his feet.

"They're retreating, but I don't think that's a good thing," Verwile said. "Scouts, what do you see?"

One goblin, perched atop a horse, pulled out a telescope. "They're taking position at the watchtowers. I think they intend to hold a standoff and make this operation too bloody to carry out."

"Break down the gate regardless," Rowyn commanded. "We need a pyromantic goblin strong enough to melt metal on the locks and scouts ready to call out whenever they see their sharpshooters—"

Something whizzed through the air and hit the telescope-bearing scout in the head, killing him instantly and spooking his horse. Rowyn lowered himself and continued.

"Quickly, melt the locks and end this effort. Any musketeers who're loaded, shoot back at the watchtowers. Make them regret resisting us."

The resultant firefight cost minimal spearmen but more musketeers than Rowyn preferred, leaving only five by the time the gates were opened. Some had organs that could be stabilised by his powers, and though he kept them in operable condition, they would not be worthwhile soldiers for months.

Rowyn turned to his second-in-command. "Verwile, I trust you to kill every patrolman you can. Take all but ten spearmen through the gates, then bring Baron Oswyk to me, alive, along with any healer that serves him. His wife and child are to be left unharmed."

"What are you going to do?"

"Stay here, maintaining the injured and ensuring the regular guards don't get any ideas."

"Of course," the seer said, inclining his head. "I hope to still be alive when the baron reaches you."

"You will be," Rowyn promised, lifting his hand as he forced a goblin's lung tissue to twist over a bullet-hole. "Go, while you can."

Verwile nodded and pushed his allocated men forward, while Rowyn stayed behind with the ten or so men who required maintenance but weren't irreparably damaged. Of these men, only two were conscious, a seer and a goblin.

"Thanks for this," the seer said, wincing at the hole in his plackart.

"It's the least I can do for the men putting their lives in my hands," Rowyn stated. "Tell me if you're in pain and I'll endeavour to reduce it."

Somehow, the bullets used by Oswyk's personal guard had torn straight through the spearman's armour, so

Rowyn forced his stomach to plug its own leak by inducing muscular contraction. It was a hackneyed trick by this point in his career of on-field 'medicine', but it did the job until proper medical help arrived.

"Those elves were holdin' some weird fucking guns," the goblin remarked between gasps. "Seems like the baron has some friends in high places."

"It doesn't matter how many friends he has. He'll talk."

Snow continued to fall as Rowyn held his living troops steady. Eventually, Verwile and his men returned, their armour caked in blood. With them was a human with light olive skin, blue-and-grey velvet clothing, and messy, overgrown brown hair, along with a short, pudgy gnome that wore the same colours and hid his eyes with dark-lensed goggles. The pair were dragged to Rowyn and thrust before him. Verwile nodded to his higher-up.

"Here they are, Sir Khanas. Baron Giles Oswyk, and his wisdom, Mack."

"Thank you," Rowyn said, silently balancing the well-being of his men as he spoke. "Baron Oswyk, I must ask you a question. I have a warrant to investigate you of suspected corruption signed by your overlady, the woman you swore to serve when you accepted your title. Why were your men so eager to resist us?"

"You trespassed on my land without notice!" Baron Oswyk snapped. "You may serve the overlady, but this is *my* town, and you should know that my imports are the only things that keep the Forests of Winter relevant!"

"It does appear this port is helpful. It'd be a shame if Overlady Selenia used her authority to seize control of it," Rowyn said. "You'll cooperate with us, or you'll become a commoner, or worse, fertiliser. Am I clear?"

The baron spat at Rowyn's feet, and with a gesture of the hand, a spear was at his throat. Sir Khanas lowered his pitch, almost resembling his cousin.

"Reconsider your attitude, Baron."

The minor noble swallowed, then huffed. "What do you want?"

"You have an overseas associate; Anya Kasparov, if my information is correct. She's linked with criminal groups in Ilazar, and I believe she had something on you. You've got enough money to spend on advanced magitech for your personal guards but not enough to invest in the rest of your town's infrastructure. What makes you so afraid for yourself that you'd bankrupt your subjects just to save your skin?"

Oswyk's face sprouted a smug grin. "You're working with hunches. I could be regular selfish arsehole like that Lord Verawor in the south."

"One moment," Rowyn said, opening his satchel and foraging through the evidence Plutyn provided. He pulled out a set of papers. "Here we are. Receipts from a Rainbow Fort ascensiologist who enchanted a piece of malachite with soul-binding properties for one Giles Oswyk. The testimony from him is glowing, he was ever so excited to work for a nobleman.

"My cousin's spies recall hearing a malachite-powered ascendant have a conversation with you, answering to Anya Kasparov. Incidentally, they heard this outside the house of your secretary, which I'm sure Baroness Genna would be interested to know—"

"Your cousin had men following me, so what?" Oswyk asked.

"Why would you give away an ascension stone? Anya Kasparov had something on you. What dirt incentivised your fostering of incompetent town guards while saving the competent men for your manor?" Rowyn asked. "I'll make this easy for you. Which crime family do you work with? Lie to me and I'll ensure this spear finds its way into your throat."

"I yield! I've been helping the Malassaian Traffickers for years! The eastern ports to the south cracked down on them, but they cut me a deal where I could enjoy some women if the guards went easy on them!" Oswyk spluttered.

Rowyn narrowed his eyes and adjusted his visor. Plutyn intended to extort Oswyk once unless the criminals he'd enabled were the Traffickers. In that case, Plutyn promised to send in a 'clean-up crew'. He steadied his breath and moved onto his second objective.

"You were the one to inform us about Razarkha Fel'thuz. Your friend Anya told you about her, yes? Did she mention her current location?"

"Anya wittered on about Zemelnya collapsing because of that Fel'thuz woman, but I haven't seen her since. Perhaps she got herself killed or blown away by a stray breeze," Oswyk said. "Am I supposed to know her every move? She's a bloody magic cloud."

"Zemelnya was Razarkha Fel'thuz's last known location?"

"Yes."

"Very well. Have your wisdom treat my injured men, and if he tries to botch the surgery, I'll kill your entire household. You'll also arrange my passage to Zemelnya. Verwile, you're in charge of Winter Harbour's matters until Selenia reinforcements arrive. From now, every Malassaian Trafficker who reaches this town dies."

*　*　*

The skies of Pentatum were blackened from the permanent storm gathered about the Nortezian megalopolis's centrepiece; a grand citadel whose height pierced the clouds and the skies beyond. Its obsidian majesty was veined with glowing redstone visible from throughout the supercity, with orderly portals opening around it with regularity.

Consigliere Vieri hovered through the southern outskirts of Pentatum, yet despite myriad miles between him and the citadel, he beheld his base of operations with a bittersweet fondness. Order defined the Galdusian way; the buildings were square, simple, and functional, the people uncomplicated even in their messy, pre-ascended forms.

The outer city contained far more breeders than Vieri preferred. These selfish citizens opted to indulge in carnal pleasures irrelevant to man's true calling, cursing further souls with fleshly existence. Moderate Ascensionist philosophers argued that breeders were a necessary evil as the only means to create new souls, but when ascendants persisted for eternity, what use did the new serve that the old could not? The truly orderly avoided complications, and thus ascended all that could consent. Unknown factors like new generations would be moot.

The days of the Plague Emperor were over, and ascendants were free to live eternally. Yukishima sought to disrupt this balance, however. Duke Revidus Erasmus of Pentatum was eager to make peace with the humans as Duke Weldum of Quattrus. Much like breeders, the duke retained his fleshly form despite lacking a wife or any intent to breed. Vieri tolerated this madness as he had with Revidus's forebears. His role as consigliere was to steer the decaying young man of sixty towards wisdom, but when he refused to listen, unorthodox methods were necessary to preserve Nortez's greatness.

The consigliere had visited the Sulari capital of Nova Tertia and seen the grandiosity of Darvith, the greatest ascendant conglomerate that was or will be. His towering, roiling form contained multitudes of souls, with enough power that his swarm of arcane lights had fused into a great cyclopean lantern. Grand Ascendant was a citadel unto himself, visible upon all horizons containing Nova Tertia.

Quattrus's allegiance with the Yukishimans was foolish and hasty, yet Hextolis agreed with their decision, and in spite of Vieri's objections, Duke Erasmus agreed too. There was no defeating Sula. Darvith was but one of the monstrosities the elder Galdusian continent wielded, and with the upsurge of easily smote breeders in the most vulnerable parts of Pentatum, Nortez stood to lose numerous souls if Sula declared war. Breeders were selfish and short-sighted; all lives were precious, and they chose to entrust theirs to such brittle vessels.

The ascendant moved through another perfectly sized block of cuboid buildings, marked by Old Galdusian numerals. Five more repetitions and he would be at the rendezvous. He was to meet with a group of breeders that hadn't abandoned Old Galdusian principles: The Sons of Sula.

So many had been corrupted by debauched Ilazari notions such as individualism and borscht. Maintaining order was the only way to serve the nation, and as for cuisine, fungal food parcels were all Vieri required in the faded days of his fleshly form, and they were all any pre-ascendant required. A caterpillar did not philosophise over the leaves it consumed before its transformation into its final, beauteous form, so why should a pre-ascended child do so?

Vieri drifted towards the southern edge of Pentatum, a strict division between civilisation and the consumed. Behind the ascendant was a bastion of order, whose only blemishes were the pre-ascendants that milled about its streets. Before him was degradation given form in a sweeping expanse of trembling, red-leaved trees and pale, luminous grasses.

Nature was redundant, twisted as the Ilazari beast who toppled the old empire. It rose, it expanded, it rotted, forever changing until becoming naught but compost. It was in Nortez's interest to expand Pentatum until Nortez was composed of three supercities and nothing else. On contemplation, Liberium and its upstart human residents deserved to be absorbed. He would have to bring the idea to Duke Erasmus's attention.

Finally, he found the fleshlings he sought, and more importantly, the wand in their possession. They were all youths of sixteen or younger, wearing plain white clothing lined with the gold of the old empire. Their faces were variable, as all fallible pre-ascendants were, and one appeared to be a different sex to the others. In the hands of one youth was a wand the height of a human, a uniform double helix of jadeite and nephrite topped with a redstone-and-norvite conduit whose power lit the entirety of the outer block. Vieri's inner embers burnt a pale blue as he approached them.

"My dear Sons of Sula," he said in Old Galdusian. *"You've done well. As promised, here are the relevant texts."*

From within his billowing, smoky form, Vieri telekinetically produced a set of text-tablets containing transcripts of the dukes of Pentatum and Quattrus discussing the recent Yukishiman alliance, along with ancient paper texts on the major losses of the Ilazari Plague Emperor.

In exchange, he telekinetically snatched the wand from them. Its norvite-redstone conduit would amplify his arcane potential by a factor of hundreds; hopefully enough to overpower Duke Erasmus's hopelessly loyal ascended guards. The brutes didn't understand that embracing foreign ideals meant betraying their very decision to ascend, and if they stood by their delusions, compulsion would be necessary.

"Keep Nortez strong, Consigliere," one of the youngsters said. *"With your help, Galdus will be great again."*

"Your devotion at such a young age brings great joy," Vieri said. *"The Yukishiman menace is a temporary bump on the great journey of the Galdusian Empire. May your feeble forms remain preserved until your ascension."*

The three looked to each other, then quietly moved away from the consigliere. Trailing his new acquisition along with his deep blue cloak, Vieri began his journey back to Pentatum's inner city. Fleshlings wittered in the bastardised language colloquially known as 'Nortezian' as he passed, most decked out in the simplistic clothing of laymen. There needed to be unity in the people, and while their fleshly incongruence couldn't be helped, their clothing could. After another block of the breeders' empty gazes, Vieri noticed an inconsistency.

Two fleshlings arrived, decked in garb fashioned from sections of Ilazari and Yukishiman cloth, sewn together in a bizarre mockery of self-expression. One stank distinctly of the Rakh'vash, while the other bore the dread of a different dark god.

"You two. State your names, ages, and precinct of residence," Vieri demanded in Nortezian.

"My name is Erre, or R if you prefer the Common Tongue, and I hail from Arkhera," the thin one stated in fluent Old Galdusian while presenting a strange magitech device. *"My friend, meanwhile, speaks the Golden Tongue terribly. I couldn't help but overhear the conversation you had with those young men. Very interesting in these changing times."*

Vieri backed off as he noticed soul fragments emanating from the foreigner's device. Still, he was surrounded by numerous loyal breeders. These stains would be easily scrubbed from the city's moral fibre.

"What of it? You aren't a Nortezian citizen. You don't have a right to life."

"You, meanwhile, are a traitor to Nortez's progress. Your life is actively harmful."

Before Vieri could react, the woman raised the magitech device and chanted in a dread tongue that could only be the language of the dark god of Ilazar, the Great Disruption. Vieri's ascension sapphire glowed with an intensity not seen since he first bound his soul to it, and his cloudlike form pulled towards the device against his will.

Vieri split in two, one half within the soulstealer and the other within his ascension stone. His cloak, wand and sapphire fell to the floor, and fragments of memory gripped his fractured soul with a feverishness he hadn't experienced since his fleshly days, when he craved a young woman and sang foolish songs.

"I don't want to be trapped!" he screamed, but nobody could hear. *"I don't want to stay there forever!"*

His final scraps were wrested from his original vessel, and he writhed within the Soulstealer of Craving, its owner peering into it with an expression much unlike the dullness of a typical breeder. The woman took Vieri's wand and raised it, making a declaration in broken, Old-Galdusian-polluted Nortezian.

"Fleshly folk of Pentatum, heed my words! Nortez shalt change, as the Empire of Human Suns, that is, the one of the Snowy Home, comes for us all. Ascended fools such as this one aim to hold thee back, clinging to the past as the future comes to decimate it. They shalt claim it is in thy interest to cling to the past with them, but all thou shalt share in is their demise. The Snowy Home comes for us, and with it progress. Art thou content being part of an outdated system where one cannot enjoy the simple fruits of the flesh? If thy answer is nay, thou shalt cheer with me as I partake of this wretched soul!"

To Vieri's horror, the woman tipped his new vessel towards her mouth in a symbolic gesture, and in doing so, began tearing his very being into pieces. The people cheered for the monster while he sputtered in futility. His generations of advising the Erasmus family, consistently failing to make the patriarch of the decade ascend as an eternal duke, crafting numerous customised wands, working as a librarian of a magical theory archive, commanding a human augmentee to sit and stay, all appeared before his soul, before being ripped away.

Lingering to the bitter end were his eighteen years of fleshly life. His mother's hateful, bloated visage reminded him of breeding's innate misery. A woman who would never return his love sneered with contempt. His father smiled at him before losing his face in the ascension process.

"I don't want oblivion. I don't want this."

An unnerving, divine voice responded. ***"You made your choice when you ran from mortality."***

Vieri ceased to be amidst thunderous applause.

Contaminated

The people of Pentatum's outer city were surprisingly easy to sway. Razarkha stood before a crowd, drinking in the soul of a consigliere while they screamed in adulation. According to both Yukishiman and Nortezian sources, this ascendant deserved his fate, but Razarkha didn't particularly care.

As arcane energies flowed from her soulstealer to her body, all she could think about was the Plague Emperor's vengeful quest through Galdus. He'd massacred thousands of ascendants and was celebrated for it. She'd longed for the same appeal; to be applauded for her strength as Rakh was for his weakness.

She was an idol to the shifting flesh that made the straight edges of Pentatum interesting. Her head buzzed with the anxiety arcana imposed, but there wasn't a destructive enough outlet for her energies. Weil stood beside her, his posture withdrawn as ever.

The people's adoration wasn't as satisfying as Razarkha had hoped. She'd told herself that in a world where strength was celebrated, she would be happy. Yet these people didn't know, love or empathise with her. She was merely a killer who targeted the right person.

"Is this the start of meaningful change?" one young man shouted over the crowd's incessant chatter.

Razarkha cleared her throat and began a speech in her antiquated attempt at Nortezian. *"The people shalt rise as a force of progress and slay the notion that the greatest state is static order. The old must be cast out, and the new welcomed. Those who have embraced their mortality and..."*

Distractions swarmed within Razarkha's head. Fears of incomplete message delivery, Weil's unnerved expression, and an emptiness she swore she was rid of stayed her lips.

"They're waiting. Did you pause for suspense? Have you angered them? What's going on?" Weil asked in worried Isleborn.

"Shut up, Weil, I'm thinking," she snapped in his language, then shifted back to her juggling act between Nortezian and Old Galdusian. *"The fleshly ones, unafraid to die, who take merriment from their… ability to sire new life, art truly the ones with power. For once an ascendant vanishes, they hath no legacy. Thou? Thou hast thy legacy growing within thy bellies, dangling between thy legs. Thee and thy children shalt remain as the old is cast away."*

"What change do you fight for?" the same man asked, causing the crowd to quieten into a milder rumbling of tongues.

"The death of conservative ascendants such as Vieri, who view thee as verminous chattel. These creatures have no value for thee, so thou hast no reason to value them. All that wish to claim their rights and not fall victim to the ascendants' desperation must claim them with their own hands. Who shalt join me?"

At first, the response was lukewarm, but the few voices that agreed soon encouraged more to call out. By the end, all who hadn't walked away were yelling a Nortezian word she had no translation for: 'Inissureon'. From her knowledge of Old Galdusian, the closest word it resembled was 'immiscireum', which translated to insurrection in Common.

"Yes! Insurrection! Insurrection against all who hamper progress! While thou hast nothing to fear from these death-fleeing clouds, I have seen the human Sun-Empire's fleet with mine own eyes. They are kind to their friends and terrible to their enemies, so we shalt do well to avoid friends of the Snowy Home."

"Duke Revidus cannot be a target? You're a false insurrectionist!" a breeder called out. *"He may side with Yukishima and the Isle of the Plague, but he's the reason we*

breeders have simple, worthless food. He's done what every Erasmus has done. He's kept his body, while relegating other fleshlings to the outer city. We want access to the inner city!"

"We also want food people of the proximal outer city eat!" another Nortezian added.

"How do you expect us to start a revolution when there's only one ascendant-killer, and it's in your hands?" yet another asked.

Questions kept coming. Razarkha had some answers thanks to the Yukishimans who'd deployed her, but she couldn't quash them quicker than they came. Some concerns, like access to the inner city, were entirely foreign concepts to her. If the inner city was populated exclusively by ascendants, there'd be no food, no greenery, nothing to allow an unascended being to exist. Perhaps it was akin to the exclusive section of the Zemelnya Central Library, or Antique's ever-locked vault. Something to enter, but not live in.

Razarkha sighed. In the time she'd spent mulling over a single question, tens had piled on top. She wondered if this was how Rakh felt, sitting on the council seat his masculinity afforded him, listening to councillors bring up issue after issue.

Before she could ruminate further, Weil raised a tentacle the size of a small spire behind her, which flinched and screeched as something powerful crashed against it. A feminine voice echoed through the identical streets of the Pentatum's outer city, speaking in Nortezian so formal it bordered on corrupted Old Galdusian.

"Civil unrest detected in Pentatum Distal Outer City, sixth-hour sector, vein fifty-two, tissue forty-eight. Breeders unaffiliated with this unrest shall return to their residential complexes. All compliant breeders are permitted additional dance hall privileges. Squads deployed to expunge non-

compliant breeders. All inner-city citizens visiting are advised to return to their sectors."

"What is this, Weil?" Razarkha stammered in Isleborn.

"I don't know, you're the Galdusian expert, all I know is a fireball flew towards you while you were busy staring at nothing!" the chaos-speaker replied.

"They said something about—"

Another impact struck Weil's tentacle, making it collapse into a pile of flesh and inky black goo. In the distance, a pair of ascendants flew amidst the towers of Pentatum, their green embers shining from metallic bodies fashioned after wyverns. One of them clung to the side of a residential tower, while the other hovered and summoned a fireball large enough to consume most of the crowd Razarkha had attracted. Weil raised his hands and brought up another tentacle, but this one buckled after a single hit. Razarkha's potential revolutionaries scattered, albeit the occasional pyromancer and geomancer readied some retaliatory magic.

"What do we do?" Weil begged. *"I can't make another portal without the Rakh'vash growing angry at using its body as a shield!"*

"Then we don't use it as a shield," Razarkha said, and she turned to her loyal few. *"Those who wish to fight, use whatever means thou must to move quickly. Distract them as my grand chaos-speaker doth, ensure they cannot focus on me."*

"Insurrection!" they called in return.

The pyromancers started to fly, while the geomancers tore up parts of the road and surfed upon them. Once the wyvern-ascendants were occupied with raining fire upon the newly radicalised Nortezians, Razarkha turned to Weil.

"Throw me with one tentacle, catch me with another," she commanded.

"Towards the ascendants?" Weil asked.

"No, into the wilderlands behind us. Of course towards the ascendants!"

"That's high. Are you sure—"

Razarkha gestured to the inferno the ascendants were stirring up in an attempt to massacre their new allies, and Weil nodded.

"Sorry. Throwing you now."

Weil muttered in Chaostongue, and a portal opened beneath Razarkha. A tentacle rose from within, wrapped itself around her, and after stretching itself upwards, flung her with disorientating force. Razarkha clung to her soulstealer with all her strength, vanished with her own natural magic, and through the nauseous exhilaration, found coherent speech.

"Bold Individualist, Sovereign, whatever you want to be called, I need you to make this soulstealer suck up the two ascendants as I pass them!"

"A paltry request for a god. Consider it done."

As she careened through the air, barely cognisant of the square-shaped blurs passing her by, arcane mists drifted towards the soulstealer as her arc reached its plateau. Razarkha revealed herself once more, ready to be caught. If Weil knew the truth, these would be her final moments.

Instead, a tentacle emerged in front of her and cushioned her body with a slimy, sucker-pad-laden landing spot, wrapping around her before she could slide down its length. Her clothes were covered in daemonic sludge, and she was lowered to the ground with only a limp to contend with. Her new fighters, where alive, were cheering and grieving all at once. Weil rushed through the thoroughly desecrated street to hug Razarkha while she shuddered from the soulstealer's latest victims.

"You're safe. Thank the Rakh'vash I caught you."

"You did well, Weil," Razarkha assured him.

"What now?"

"We ask our new friends how to reach Hextolis. That's where the Imperial Engineer wants us—"

"Civil unrest has reached critical status in Pentatum Distal Outer City, sixth-hour sector. Full curative measures authorised," the feminine voice from earlier echoed. *"Breeders are not permitted to evacuate and must comply with all ascended officers. Use of magic by breeders will be presumed hostile and excision will be mandatory. Operation: Clamp, cauterise, expunge."*

Razarkha panicked and rushed to the nearest pyromancer, a tall, white-haired spellbinder woman with the same kimono-cloaks as her fellow Pentatum civilians. *"Dost thou know what yonder voice means?"*

"Clamp means they wish to restrict movement, cauterise that they wish to use fire, and expunge means— well, making us do what we mortals do best," the pyromancer responded.

"Not today," Razarkha promised. *"Spread the word! We shalt gather all that we can and punch a hole in their clamp, then escape to the other sectors."*

"The Watcher will find us there too."

"Then we shalt move until we find a way to Hextolis. What would be the fastest way?"

"The only way a breeder may move between the great cities is through the Gates, but they are controlled by ascendants."

Razarkha grinned. *"Take heart, sister. Our journey to greatness is just beginning."*

* * *

Wisdom Erwyn's laboratory had seen more use as of late, not only as a place for discussion between he and the ever-active Minister of Criminal Affairs, but as a site of experimentation. Lady Selenia's secret project had him importing numerous magical substances: Malassaian unicorn hair, enchanted jadeites, powdered redstone, a bizarre magical deposit found off the cliffs of Syron Isle, and even liquid shade.

His goal was to create an elixir that would grant Lady Selenia eternal youth. Not the immortality an ascendant achieved, stripped of bodily pains and pleasures, nor eternity as angels and daemons knew it, persisting as glorified servitors of a god. Lady Kag'nemera wished to be her beautiful self forever. While Erwyn had initially protested, he realised that despite who requested it, research into bodily immortality was not entirely in vain. If he could receive funds to research an interesting, possibly revolutionary topic, was it not his duty as a wisdom to seize that opportunity?

He finished preparing his first experimental batch, squeezing precisely one red drop of aqueous silicate of arcana from a pipette into a colourless solution within a vial. Upon the drop meeting the body, a cloudy white precipitate formed, and Erwyn smiled.

"As expected. Now for the difficult part. Who in the world would volunteer to take—"

The door to his laboratory opened without warning, and Erwyn hastily put the vial in a rack. He then turned to his intruder; it was Sir Plutyn Khanas, sucking on his pipe as usual.

"I keep telling you to knock, Minister Khanas. You may provide an invaluable service to the House of Selenia, but you aren't allowed to enter any room you please," Erwyn said.

Khanas responded in his usual grim tone. "You were talking to yourself. A lonely man shouldn't begrudge company."

"You're the last man I consider company. It's always business with you, and I'd prefer to keep it that way," Erwyn replied.

"Then we're in agreement. I have more news from Ashglass," Plutyn said, closing the door and sitting at Erwyn's reading desk.

"Stand, Khanas," Erwyn commanded. "Don't pretend that I'm oblivious to your little power plays. You remain king of your underground operations, but in this castle there's a different hierarchy."

"You don't want to hear the news? A shame, it's of great personal significance to you."

Erwyn walked over to his cabinet of poison and antidotes. Addressing the reflection of Plutyn in the glass, he spoke with reservation.

"Remain seated if you wish, but once you're done informing me, you must leave me to my studies."

"Count Fel'thuz grows worried about you," Plutyn said. "Hiding in your laboratory, performing secretive experiments for an imbecile. It's pitiful that he admires you."

Erwyn's tone sharpened. "Tell me the news."

"While some organ runners have fled Ashglass despite their duties, the ones who've returned reported a boom in organ sales. Not only that, it was exclusively coming from an old woman receiving noble patronage. The district she was in was in chaos, guards arresting and killing people who appeared to be rabid. Other districts were burnt to the ground. The woman who bought organs in bulk was, according to my sources, a wisdom of sorts."

"Melancholy," Erwyn said. "The economic disturbance must be due to an epidemic."

"I presumed it was your mentor."

"It's the only conclusion that makes sense," Erwyn stated, turning around. "Melancholy only approaches nobility in cases of city-wide disease. She's a travelling healer who generally evades official notice, but when she has an opportunity to save scores and conduct valuable research in the process, she offers her expertise readily."

Plutyn frowned. "Which disease is afflicting Ashglass? Their lockdown hasn't just affected the above-ground economy, but my personal economy too. If there's a way we can offer aid and lift the lockdown, we should pursue it."

"I agree," Erwyn said. "In addition, a noble display of solidarity between the Selenias and the Foenaxases would strengthen the Forests of Winter before Razarkha's return."

Plutyn stood and left a pregnant pause before he spoke. "You were correct to consider poisoning her."

"I know I was," Erwyn replied. "The symptoms were akin to rabies, you said? Is there any other information regarding the disease?"

The necromancer took a long hit of his pipe. "When my runner saw Melancholy in person, she was cutting open a man's nether regions—"

"Rapeworm. By God, no wonder Melancholy's invested in this outbreak."

"What do you mean?"

Erwyn took a seat by his laboratory equipment. "Melancholy's full title as a commoner would be Melancholy of Thornwrit Heath. Younger generations haven't heard of the town and for good reason. It was utterly ravaged by a rapeworm epidemic of which Melancholy is, as far as she's told me, the only survivor."

"That would explain how she rose from commoner to wisdom. Most commoners can't afford to educate themselves and forge connections with nobility," Plutyn remarked. "But those who have something to fight for, a true urge to climb, will find a way regardless. So many fine young men have rose from the dregs in my old-system fiefdom."

Erwyn ignored Plutyn's verbal screed and continued. "The worm infests the genitals of its host, initially through eggs present in contaminated water, but once it finds a host, it'll spread in a much more destructive way. It forces its hosts

67

into a mad, hypersexual state in which they'll rape any nearby person, spreading their eggs to other hosts. The waterborne form is dormant and usually limited to foetid ponds, but once within a host, rapeworms are capable of destroying entire towns within days. Melancholy herself was attacked by her own father—"

"If that's the case, how did she remain sane?" Plutyn asked. "Wouldn't she be driven to a similar state of nymphomania?"

"She's uncertain why she was granted the trauma but spared the madness," Erwyn admitted. "Nonetheless, if this is a rapeworm epidemic, the woman your man met was almost certainly Melancholy. She claims her greatest enemy is no man, but rapeworm itself. Summon Lady Selenia for me."

Plutyn frowned. "Very well, Wisdom Yagaska. May your personal connection with Melancholy not tarnish your decision-making. Between you, Fel'thuz, and Selenia, at least one should be capable of clear thought."

"You've delivered the information," Erwyn snapped. "You have no further reason to be in this laboratory."

The necromantic knight put out his pipe. "Of course, great and wise Count Yagaska. Or would you prefer I didn't note the inherited title you spat upon?"

"Summon Lady Selenia, Minister."

"Of course."

Erwyn watched the necromancer leave and sat at his reading desk, rubbing his temples. An epidemic, his latest research, and the ever-looming threat of Razarkha, piled alongside the day-to-day running of Moonstone, made him want to smoke Plutyn's weekly bhang-weed supply in one sitting. Rakh's 'good news' of Razarkha being further away than expected according to some overprivileged southern seer wasn't believable evidence on its own. Even if it was, it came with the caveat that her presence stood to change Moonstone forever.

Rowyn Khanas's staging of a hostile takeover in Winter Harbour hardly assisted in provincial unity, though the deployed troops would at least ensure a forced peace. If the King had any issues, Rowyn's letters detailing the extent of Oswyk's crimes would mark House Selenia's actions as reasonable force for managing unruly vassals. Erwyn rested his head on his desk, before being forced into alertness by a peculiar, wood-on-wood knock on his door.

"Rakh? I told Sir Khanas to summon Lady Selenia."

"He did, Rakh just accompanied me," Lady Selenia's voice responded. "He's been teaching me *Wraiths and Wyverns* but also talking about hard things I don't want to talk about."

"Oh, I see. Come in, both of you."

Seeing his count enter slackened Erwyn's shoulders, even as Lady Kag waltzed in behind him, her gaze absent as always. She tottered over to the rack of experimental vials and beamed.

"You've been busy!" Lady Selenia said. "I've been busy too. Count Fel'thuz has really made it hard for me to beat him."

Erwyn glanced at her, then adjusted his monocle and focused on Rakh. "Of course, my lady. I'm sorry I haven't had time to rest lately."

The count shook his head. "It's all right. I've been unable to sleep these last few days. I keep remembering Lord Verawor's face. I can't stop thinking about what he might have seen."

"It's good to see you," Erwyn said with a soft smile. "It's fortunate that you're here. You may be key to helping this situation. Lady Kagura, please take a seat and— *don't touch the vials!"*

The elven woman pulled her hand away from a rack as her face reddened. "I was just curious, I wasn't going to drink it or anything."

"I find it worrying that you had to specify that," Erwyn muttered. "Please close the door, Rakh. We need to discuss the Ashglass situation."

"It's Lady Mor'kha, isn't it?" Kagura said as her count shut the door. "She's finally gone mad from her stupid fire renewing god! This is why dark elves shouldn't be in positions of power—"

"No, it's an epidemic," Erwyn interrupted. "Rapeworm."

Rakh swallowed. "God, you mean the same illness that got your mentor's town? Thornwrangled something-or-other?"

"Thornwrit Heath, yes," Erwyn stated. "Speaking of Melancholy, she's reportedly working with the Foenaxases already. Ethically and personally, I'm obliged to aid her efforts."

Kagura became indignant. "Why? You're responsible for Moonstone's wellbeing, not Ashglass's! If you ask me, Mor'kha Foenaxas was cursed for following the wrong god."

"Funny how divine retribution targets the poor when a rich woman sins," Rakh remarked, his tone the sharpest Erwyn had ever heard. "Diseases don't need to be explained away by a god, and what's more, Mor'kha is your vassal. Your attitude towards the Foenaxases has been disgusting throughout this crisis, but now I'm truly sickened."

The lady's lip quivered, and she backed away from the two men. "This is what I've had to deal with, Wisdom Erwyn. Rakh's been mean to me, just like his sister was before. Whenever I talk about Ashglass or the Foenaxases, he always takes the filthy dark elves' side like it isn't their fault their city's locked down!"

"In light of the new information, locking down is the most responsible thing Lady Foenaxas could have done," Erwyn stated. "What have you been telling Lady Selenia, Rakh?"

Rakh folded his arms. "That her attitude is repulsive. She knows nothing of her own people, yet makes assumptions about Ashglass simply for worshipping the wrong god and being the wrong race."

Erwyn tugged on his cravat. "Lady Selenia, that isn't bullying. Rakh is doing his job and advising you. Now I'll do *my* job and act as your auxiliary decision-maker. I will leave Moonstone and assist my mentor. For diplomacy's sake, you and Count Fel'thuz will accompany me."

Lady Kagura began to witter. "Wait, no, that's not right! I'm the lady of the city! Who will rule in my absence?"

"The man who won't stop reminding us he wasn't made a lord. If you two come with me, Lady Kagura can make peace with the Foenaxases while Rakh corrects her blunders—"

"I never make blunders," Lady Kag claimed.

"Yes you do, my lady," Erwyn stated. "You and Rakh can handle diplomatic exchange with the Foenaxases, while I assist Melancholy. Plutyn Khanas, meanwhile, can enjoy a taste of power, hopefully reducing his passive aggression."

"What passive aggression? I think Sir Khanas is very kind and intelligent, even if he's not a lord," Kagura babbled.

"If you're so fond of him, you won't balk at naming him acting lord," Erwyn said. "Like it or not, my lady, you *will* accompany us to Ashglass. If you're to live forever as Lady Selenia, you're in dire need of real-world experience."

"What's this about living forever?" Rakh asked.

"It doesn't matter. My lady, do you accept, or will you continue to delay your acceptance?" Erwyn asked.

It took moments for the lady to crumble. "Fine, I'll go to Ashglass, but only if you stop being mean."

Erwyn exhaled. "That's good enough for now."

* * *

"This is far as I take you," the *Calamarnica's* captain told Rowyn in Ilazari-accented Common. "No sane man docks at Zemelnya without strong mage now that Plagueborn scum have control. First dropping daemon takes sea, now madness takes land."

Rowyn shielded his eyes with his unarmoured hand and peered to the distant Ilazari port city. "How much do you want to recompense the loss of your pinnace?"

"Two of your Arkheran silver, friend. I trust more than Ilazari credit while Zemelnya burns."

"Very well," Rowyn said, searching his pockets before producing two grey coins with a flattering profile of Landon Shearwater's swollen face. "Thank you for taking me this far."

"I do as Baron Oswyk says, and he fears you. Good luck, friend."

Rowyn picked up his bag of armour pieces and satchel of food, then clambered over the side of the *Calamarnica,* where a pinnace was waiting. He got comfortable, took hold of the oars, then nodded to the crew hands. Slowly, he lowered into Ilazar's murky waters and started rowing.

He was naked without his emerald armour, but it was a necessary vulnerability considering that he'd sink like a brick if he fell into the water. His arms were technically rowing, but Captain Yumanov's words had somewhat robbed them of their purpose. If Razarkha was still in Zemelnya, she was likely already dead.

The *Calamarnica* swiftly grew distant, and even in his cropped, helmet-ready hair, Rowyn could feel the tailwind the ship had suddenly benefitted from. As his vessel bobbed over each wave between him and Zemelnya, dread festered within his heart. The peculiar feeling seized hold of his tongue and forced words out of his mouth.

"I'm Rowyn, rowin'," he said, mirth peaking and falling with a single bob.

With each oar stroke, the *Calamarnica* became increasingly inaccessible, and behind Rowyn lay what the Ilazari-blooded sailors were convinced served as the hell of this realm. He was approaching a shale-covered beach from what backward glances could provide, while off to his left were sheer cliffs. Beneath them lay jags sharp enough to gut man or ship alike.

"It won't be so bad. I'll ask the locals about Razarkha, confirm her death, then go home," he told himself.

The scraping of the pinnace's hull against the rocky shards of Zemelnya's beach seemed to serve as a fitting interruption to quash his strained optimism. A nearby young woman, blonde-haired and decked out in what appeared to be treated, stitched-together seaweed, stared with a disconcerting lack of inhibition. As if to complete her look, she also wore two abalone-shell bracelets and a necklace of shark teeth and mermaid's purses.

Rowyn paused. "Do you speak Common?"

"In small piece," the woman said.

"I speak Isleborn only small piece too," Rowyn admitted with a laugh, then hauled his armour and food out of his boat. *"What language is comfortable?"*

"Speak Old Galdusian well. I Plague-blooded, very poor, but read many book."

"Thankfully I was educated in Old Galdusian," Rowyn said in the appropriate tongue. *"It's a common language for magical textbooks in Arkhera."*

"Oh, you come from brown-neck land. My sister hated brown-neckers, but then again, she hated a lot of things."

"I see," Rowyn said. *"Did you lose her recently? I'm sorry if I made the wrong assumption, but the use of the past tense made me—"*

"No, no, you're correct. She was flaunting her new wealth in father's face one moment, the next, she couldn't be found anywhere. One of her clients' houses fell into ruins,

73

and I think she must have been there when it collapsed. Mother doesn't want to accept she's gone, but what else can I believe?"

"Mothers never accept their children's deaths, even if it happens in front of them," Rowyn claimed, taking his armour out of his bag and putting it on, piece by piece. "I should have had two little brothers, but neither of them made it past the age of two."

The woman looked him over, her tone growing wistful. "We all have loss and misery in our lives, but lately, it's been worse. I should be happy. The Isleborn oppressor, Elki Kasparov, along with his clan, are dead. The Plagueborn are rising, or so War'mal says, but I've not seen a credit of this so-called rise."

"So you're beachcombing for accessories?"

"It's a Plagueborn tradition for the poor. Self-expression above all. If you cannot afford fabrics to show your style, then you create your own."

"It looks good," Rowyn said, completing his armour assemblage. "A beastmaster from where I live uses spiders to form her clothing's silk. What's your name, friend?"

"Vi'kara. Yours?"

"Rowyn Khanas. If I may, could I ask some questions about what happened here?"

"Of course," Vi'kara said. "Come with me, I need to be with my family. Loots begin in the early evening, and if I'm don't help build the nightly ice wall, our family may fall victim."

Rowyn eyed her stretching tail and smiled. "A cryomancer. That's good to know. I'm a necromancer, and not a very good one."

"I could tell that from a distance, fool," she said with a chuckle. "No spellbinder has a tail as short as yours."

"Is that a problem?"

"No. In fact, I think you're rather handsome, especially in that metal garb."

Rowyn let the warmth run through him. If the sailors were to be believed, there was naught but misery ahead. Seizing happiness where possible was crucial to surviving this mission with his sanity intact.

Warped

Rowyn awoke to see his misty breath above him. His head rested atop a worn-down cushion while his body depressed a sofa so scratchy he'd elected to sleep in his clothes. Morning light barely reached him through the ice wall beyond Vi'kara's house, illuminating a dank, frost-covered sitting room with a single armchair and the couch he lay upon.

He grimaced and sat up, certain that Vi'kara's family didn't have means to freshen up. While Rowyn didn't speak their tongue, he could see that her father was dismayed to have a stranger inside, while her mother berated the poor girl for something else. Despite her convincing them to let Rowyn stay, he was barred from their upper floor, and most of their cupboards were locked.

Rowyn started putting his armour on when a door opened above him. Vi'kara descended from upstairs, clad in naught but a scarf and a seaweed girdle. The knight cleared his throat and translated his thoughts to Academic Galdusian.

"I never got to properly thank you—"

"What are you doing, Rowyn Khanas of brown-neck-land? Are your people truly the unwashed savages Yukishimans claim they are?" Vi'kara asked.

"Excuse me?"

"You've only just awoken, yet you hope to put on your armour? I know I wear seaweed, but I treat it first to ensure its cleanliness," Vi'kara explained. *"You must at least freshen your clothing, then after that, use your Arkheran knight money to get something better. I like your metal shell, but you need something that makes you handsome without it. Let me at least beautify your scent."*

Rowyn reddened. *"I didn't know you had soap—"*

76

"Oh heavens, no, we can't afford imports from Ubiyscht Kashalot. We have oils, though; Vi'khash gave us a variety as gifts. I think she did it to insult father after he chastised her for her falseness. I never thought she was lying, even if she was hateful."

"What was she allegedly lying about?" Rowyn asked, unstrapping his greaves.

"The healing power of oils!" she said, putting herself into a closet while her tail stuck out. *"One moment, you shall be amazed."*

Rowyn unlaced his sabatons and frowned. *"What manner of healing are you referring to? Fragrant oils certainly mend the soul a mite, but if you're implying they do much beyond that, I respectfully disagree."*

"You speak from experience?"

"I'm a combat medic whenever I'm deployed."

"Oh," Vi'kara mumbled. *"I won't bother you with them."*

"No, no, I'd appreciate being freshened for the journey, I didn't mean to imply you're wrong to offer," Rowyn babbled. *"What oils did you have in mind?"*

"Peppermint oil, to awaken you and free your clothes of contaminants, oil of bergamot to keep your mind forever alert, perhaps some sea salt to keep you safe on your next sail."

Rowyn smiled. It was mostly nonsense, but she meant well enough. Masking his sweat's stench for a while harmed no-one. She left the closet with a set of bottles balanced atop a platter that looked more expensive than the entire house, and set it out on the floor, folding her legs nearby. She beckoned towards Rowyn and grinned.

"Take off your clothes."

Rowyn jumped; the woman to see him naked was Umbria, and she was hardly satiable. Memories of the beastmistress's sultry dances entrapped him, before Vi'kara butted him back into the present.

"Well? I can hardly infuse that silly tunic with healing power if it's on you, can I?"

"My apologies, I was distracted," he claimed. *"What if your father walks in on us? He could misinterpret my intent—"*

"And if he does? Fathers in Ilazar are not the brown-necker men that fret over their daughter's sexuality. All exist to be free, man and woman alike. Men who seek to possess women are hardly men at all if you ask me."

"If you're sure I won't be treated as monstrous, go ahead," he said, removing all but his undergarments and sitting in the armchair.

She took his clothes and scanned his body shamelessly, laughing to herself as she applied numerous oils. Rowyn rubbed his arms and looked away from her, afraid to break the silence. Vi'kara took the burden instead.

"Your body is interesting. Spellbinders usually desire thinness, and I believed necromancers were the same. How did you get such odd, bulging muscles?"

Rowyn sighed. *"I don't have arcana-intensive powers. The muscles come from moving about in metal, swinging a sword, and eating plenty of poultry. I'm aware I should probably have darker marks beneath my eyes and more visible ribs, but I—"*

"I didn't say I disliked it," Vi'kara said. *"I'm sure you're quite beautiful to the humans in brown-neck-land. They like that sort of body, don't they?"*

"I think so."

"It must be nice being exposed such variety. I want to meet a goblin before I die," Vi'kara remarked.

Rowyn's throat tightened, and without thought, he blurted out a suggestion.

"You could come back to Arkhera with me if you want. You wanted to show me through Zemelnya, but if your nightly routine is anything to judge by, it's dangerous here."

Vi'kara's face brightened into a smile that thawed the room. *"You Arkherans take after your land's natives. Your orcish ape-men may kidnap beautiful young women and marry them, but here we believe in romance."*

"That's not what—" Rowyn spluttered in Common, before correcting his tongue. *"I didn't intend that as a proposition, merely an offer to reside in a safer land to make up for your generosity."*

"True generosity has no expectation of repayment," Vi'kara said, holding up Rowyn's tunic. *"Your clothes are done. You're going to hide your interesting body again, aren't you?"*

The necromantic knight took his tunic back with a playful grin. *"Sadly for you, yes. I really ought to ask you about the condition of Zemelnya. Is it related to—"*

"Yes, yes, you want a tour of the city. You'll need a cryomantic bodyguard for your vulnerable, meaty body, so I'll guide you!"

Before Rowyn could refine his question, Vi'kara rushed upstairs. He shrugged, then began his armouring process all over again. Surprisingly, he was done before Vi'kara returned, as her father's awakening resulted in a lengthy Plagueborn argument. Rowyn opened his mouth but Vi'kara spoke ahead of him.

"Come, let's see what the War'mal Group did this time!"

Rowyn pointed upwards. *"Did your father say anything concerning me?"*

"Oh, just that he wants you out of this house by the evening," she said with the wondrous tone she'd maintained since recovering from his oil scepticism. *"Come, I'm just as curious as you are!"*

The young woman wandered to her creaking front door, which she swung through a rectangular hole in a massive, icy wall. Rowyn picked up his gear and gave her a nod.

79

"Melting sections of ice is harder than forming them to a cryomancer, correct?"

"Of course."

"Consider me impressed; that's one clean melt."

Vi'kara giggled and covered her mouth, then walked ahead of Rowyn, her motion ever so slightly springier than the evening before. Her behaviour was completely at odds with the city centre she led Sir Khanas into. Colourful terraces stretched before being abruptly cut off by splintered ruination, and in the city square, numerous pikes protruded from makeshift stands, bearing various spellbinder heads. Accompanying them were signs marked in Plagueborn or Old Galdusian runes.

The pattern gleaned from the writing Rowyn could read was that Isleborn collaborators with the Kasparov Family were considered worthy of death. Colourfully dressed thugs patrolled the area, forcing nearby citizens to spit on the heads or mock them. In the centremost square, a head stood impaled above numerous others, paired with a sign that read *'The highest of all carrion'*.

"Who was he?" Rowyn asked in Old Galdusian.

"Duke Markiz Mayenev," Vi'kara muttered. *"He was the one who ensured the Yukishimans could deal with our great isle and share in their riches. He was also indebted to the Kasparovs for numerous political favours. War'mal had made loud claims of replacing him with a duke that would represent Plagueborn interests, and it seems he's completed the first half of that plan."*

"This War'mal, who is he?"

"The leader of a group of incredibly powerful Plagueborn mages. They once fought against the Kasparovs for control of the city's debts and contraband, but since Elki Kasparov was proven to be powerless and his kin slaughtered, he's ran without competition. Other families have briefly stepped into the space left by the Kasparovs, but they've died for their audacity."

"Are you glad Duke Mayenev is dead?"

"I don't care. He was a man who lied to Yukishimans and Ilazari alike. Sometimes the world needs a good lie to keep it from collapsing, wouldn't you say?"

Rowyn's chest deflated. It was a shame this woman wanted to stay in Ilazar. Momentarily his true objective buzzed in his face, but personal interest swatted it away.

"Order may be the greatest lie of all. If that's the case, I've been lying since I was old enough to swing a sword."

"You've apprehended savage Arkherans all by yourself, then?" Vi'kara remarked with a raised eyebrow.

"Of course."

"Such a metal brute. Come, I'll show you the Central Library."

She moved on to charred set of foundations, backed by a towering, light-drinking obelisk of pure nasite. A set of construction geomancers were raising a building nearby, and were currently lowering onion dome onto a completed spire with the assistance of a floating telekinete.

"Where's the library?" Rowyn asked.

"There," Vi'kara said, gesturing to the ashes. "The War'mal Group looted the old library and burned it to the ground. It's odd, usually there would be an ascendant protecting the building, but just before Elki Kasparov died, the ascendant vanished. Without him, this was inevitable."

"What was?"

"The reclamation of knowledge as a Plagueborn import. The Plague Emperor gifted the Isleborn with Galdusian insights that helped the Isle of Dreams claim its independence. War'mal no doubt wants to use this precedent to monopolise arcane secrets."

Rowyn swallowed and slung his satchel over his shoulder. "Was the person who overthrew the Kasparovs with the War'mal Group?"

"I hear she was a brown-necker like you," she said. *"War'mal gave credit to some woman, Raz-something Fel-something. He revealed that the soulstealer that kept the Plagueborn in line for years could only kill ascendants. Fleshly folk had nothing to fear. After that, the Raz woman defeated Kasparov in an honour duel and left the Isle. While I hate the chaos and looting left in her wake, I must admire her."*

"How so?" Rowyn asked, measuring himself appropriately.

"She appeared from nowhere, it is said, as though an apparition. Then she granted War'mal the crucial knowledge that Elki Kasparov's soulstealer threat was a lie and paved the way for a Plagueborn uprising. All she asked for was to keep the soulstealer Elki dropped. Oh, and a ship that could cross an ocean."

Rowyn frowned. *"I know who she is. Was her ship headed to Arkhera?"*

Vi'kara let loose a raucous laugh. *"By the dark gods, no, why would she go there with a useless soulstealer? She left from the eastern port, meaning she's either seeking more magical artefacts in Ikinami, or she's headed to Nortez to kill some ascendants."*

"When ascendants are killed by the soulstealer, what happens?"

This gave the young woman pause. *"Perhaps Elki Kasparov's lie had some truth to it. He claimed souls absorbed by his soulstealer could grant arcane power used in spellwork beyond the user's natural spellbinding."*

The pieces fit together. Lord Verawor claimed Razarkha's threat would be delayed, but devastating, and that was easily explained by time spent consuming ascendants in Nortez. He needed to catch up with this woman before she became immune to assassination.

"Please can you take me to the harbour? I need a new ship."

* * *

The common room of Razarkha's residential-block-cum-hideout was bare, with chairs and tables pushed to the edges while she trained. Fortunately, it was windowless, lit only by the veins of cyan-glowing magical stone that spread throughout the walls.

Razarkha stood in the centre of the room, surrounded by the few followers who'd escaped the sixth-hour sector of Pentatum. Weil and the block's overseer, a fleshly librarian named Sorelli, stood closest to her, the latter garbed in a gold-and-white Pentatum kimono adulterated with red.

In her hands was Vieri's wand, a twisting green staff that required both arms to aim. As such, she kept her soulstealer stuffed in the upper half of her newly acquired Pentatum kimono. She shakily pointed her wand's red-and-white conduit towards a mark on the wall furthest from her followers, then glanced at an open book on the floor.

"The words are easy, Praetor Erre," Sorelli said in Nortezian. *"Use them as a guide, not a true incantation. 'Lux recentio' is merely a sound used to apply focus. In truth you are speaking to part of the Great Light, the Creator above Order. You must use your natural aptitude in light manipulation and your plentiful arcane power to convince the Starforger that you are worthy of focusing this light."*

Razarkha frowned. *"I knoweth the concern is not wording."*

"Our brains and souls are intrinsically linked to the Father of Arcana. Find him, and his light will be yours," the librarian promised.

While she'd hoped to conceal her weaknesses from her followers, she needed to learn spellwork if she hoped to use the ascendants she'd consumed. Otherwise, she'd remain an illusionist with excessive arcane energy. Spellwork was the means to grow beyond her watered-down, hybridised abilities.

The hideout lay within the fourth-hour sector of proximal outer Pentatum, which according to local recruits was the closest outer-city area to the Fourth Gate of Pentatum, a transportation device within the inner city. This was their path to Hextolis, the capital of Nortez and a hive for the Sons of Sula.

Between the inner and outer cities was a large, magically protected wall which Sorelli referred to as 'the Membrane'. As its purpose was to prevent breeders from entering the ascendants' den, Razarkha presumed only power comparable to ascendants could force it apart. Therefore, learning spellwork was imperative. Elki Kasparov had demonstrated lumomantic spellwork that shattered rocks, and as a fellow illusionist, she would do the same.

"What's the matter?" the god in the soulstealer whispered within her head.

"You plainly know what I'm thinking," Razarkha muttered in Common. "Why ask?"

"I find forcing mortals to state their thoughts aloud often helps them to process their implications," the god explained.

"If you must know, I'm worried that this device isn't enough," she whispered. "Elki Kasparov had this for years, yet only learned how to shoot lumomantic beams."

"How do you know that was the extent of his power?"

"People don't hold back in a fight to the death."

"I despised Elki Kasparov. His potential was limitless, yet he contented himself with superiority over lesser men. He never strived to be the best man he could be."

"He was lazy even to the grave?"

"He was quite panicked when you challenged him, but he didn't have time to branch into spellwork his body wasn't already equipped to assist with."

Razarkha smirked. "So he stuck to lumomancy. Thank you, Bold Individualist, I think I can make sense of this."

"What were you saying? Communication with your dark god won't help," Sorelli interrupted.

"I doth require time to join with this Father of Magic. My brain shalt assist, moving arcana as mine words guide it."

Weil interjected in Isleborn. *"Look at it this way. Though I am a chaos-speaker, my speech is powered by arcana. Every spellbinder talks to this great, perverse light, but normally you only ask it to cast illusions. Convince it to open the rest of magic to you!"*

Razarkha's forehead burned. *"As you convince your chaos god to obey you? Give me time!"*

"Sorry," he said, slumping his figure.

The boy had been desperate to prove useful throughout their journey to the fourth-hour sector, unintentionally piquing the Watcher's interest on multiple occasions. He was even bold enough to suggest portalling across the Membrane, only to be reminded of his failure at sea.

Razarkha's eyes creased. *"I'm sorry, Weil. I know you're trying to help."*

Weil stepped back and squatted by a wall without reply. Razarkha kept her staff steady, then closed her eyes. It was just an extremely bright illusion that moved infinitely forward. Her body's personal magic just needed a small stretch; surely, the Great Light could provide that in exchange for a scrap of ascendant soul.

"Here you are, Great Light, whatever your true name is. Have a piece of Vieri," she muttered to no-one, channelling energies from her chest, through her burning head, into her arms and up the jadeite-nephrite spirals of her staff. "Help me cast *lux recentio!*"

The redstone in her wand's conduit briefly rivalled the norvite in brightness, then unleashed a pure white beam that consumed not only the mark she aimed at, but the wall it was painted on, leaving a steaming hole the size of a fist.

Sorelli's expression shifted from a grin, to a grimace, to a modest smile. *"Well done, Praetor Erre! It's a shame you were unable to control the strength of the beam, but thankfully you didn't destroy anything crucial—"*

The light-veins of the common room shifted from cyan to red, and sirens began to wail. A familiar projected voice droned its monotonous, feminine Nortezian.

"Unusual magical ability detected in residential block three, Pentatum Proximal Outer City, fourth-hour sector, vein seventy-six, tissue one. While this malady is currently asymptomatic, all breeders within this block must exit the building and report to deployed ascended officers in the standard submission position. Identity checks will be conducted, and unusually powerful breeders will be reported. Powerful breeders who collaborate will be rewarded with imported Ilazari delicacy 'Shashlik' or an ascension ritual of their choice."

The librarian yelled a Nortezian word whose roots were too modern and vulgar for Razarkha to figure out, then paced and repeated the word ad nauseum. Weil stood and faced his mistress.

"We need that gate beyond the wall," Weil insisted.

Razarkha hyperventilated and drew some arcana from her soulstealer. She winced as her agitation spiked, then addressed her people. *"We leave this complex; Sorelli, thou shalt accompany us, no matter how lucrative thou deem thy overseeing job. Thou gave it up the moment thou sheltered me. Insurrectionists, follow me! We're going to cross the Membrane!"*

"Insurrection!" the followers cheered.

With that, they rushed from the common room and into the streets of Pentatum as Weil hurriedly flung Sorelli's books into a chaos portal. Looming over the block-filled street was the Membrane, a deep red crystalline structure so smooth and tall that even Weil couldn't climb it. Obfuscated wisps rose behind the wall, no doubt hoping to unleash a magical barrage from the top. Razarkha turned to her geomancers and pyromancers.

"Pyromancers, fly to the top if thou canst. Thou cannot slay the ascendants, but thou canst stop them attacking downwards. Geomancers, thou must tear up every part of the street thou canst to form a battering ram. I shalt assist with illusory copies of all."

The group split up, and Sorelli turned to her. *"Praetor Erre?"*

"Thou shalt hide until thy path is clear," she said, casting copies of her followers that flew with the pyromancers and swarmed the streets with her geomancers.

As Sorelli rushed into a nearby alley, Weil eyed the Membrane. *"How do we break this wall? Is there anything I can do?"*

"I saw Elki Kasparov shatter boulders using lux recentio," she explained in Isleborn, cloaking her and Weil. *"If I can make a crack in the Membrane, I may need your assistance, though I the geomancers' work should be enough. If they can form a ram, they'll open the crack with ease."*

"As you say. I'm sorry about before—"

"This isn't the time for that."

The ascendants reached their positions atop the Membrane. They all resembled Kasparov's husk; simple clouds surrounding themselves with cloth. They were swift to act; in moments, a lightning bolt fell from the sky and decimated the geomancers' first attempt at a ram, sending shards throughout the residential blocks.

Terrified breeders ran into the streets, and more lightning bolts struck, smiting pyromancers from the sky and cutting further ram-building efforts short. Razarkha's throat tightened as she rushed towards the Membrane beneath her cloak. She inhaled, dragged arcane energies into her head, then held Vieri's wand upright. Arcana danced through the double helix and into the conduit.

"First Light, grant me this power. *Lux recentio!*"

This time, the blast was large enough to consume a full humanoid and left the wand so hot that Razarkha dropped it. The beam scorched the edge of the Membrane, and following a wall-wide luminous wave, pieces shattered off it. Chunks of crystal collapsed atop tens of residential blocks, and Razarkha took a deep breath.

"Now there's scores of weaknesses the geomancers could exploit, but—"

As if to complete her sentence, the storm above the panicked geomancers demolished yet another attempt at a ram, and her followers continued to drop like flies. Weil's expression hardened, and he ran towards the closest crack in the Membrane.

"Weil! Where are you going?" she yelled in Isleborn.

"If your geomancers can't build a ram, I'll pull this wall apart myself!"

Razarkha wasn't about to let him become a target. She left Vieri's wand behind and sprinted after him to ensure her cloaking would cover him too. Before she could issue orders, the chaos-speaker raised his hands and started a Chaostongue chant. Erupting from a pair of grounded portals came two tentacles, who jutted into either side of the Membrane's crack. Then, like an octopus prizing open a clam, they created an opening.

The ascendants must have noticed the problem, as soon, their storm focused on the area closest to the Membrane's crack, but with Razarkha's obfuscation, their electromancy was as accurate as a natural thunderstorm. Weil's face was twisted with concentration, and briefly, Razarkha considered kissing him.

Soon, the crack was widened into a hole large enough for ten men to fit through, and though her followers were scattered, they noticed the gap. The pyromancers descended, the geomancers abandoned their construction, and behind them, Sorelli huffed, puffed, and screamed as he narrowly avoided the increasingly desperate lightning strikes. Razarkha's revolutionaries charged into the inner city, only to be instantly surrounded by ascendants, some cloth-wearing, others armour-clad, in humanoid and non-humanoid forms alike.

Razarkha grinned and took out her soulstealer. Weil had his moment, and this was hers.

"Bold Individualist, you know what to do with these cowards!" she called out.

"Your instructions are vague, try again," the Sovereign teased.

"Kill them all, you stupid god!"

"Blasphemous, but all right."

Without delay, a storm of magical fog swirled into the Soulstealer of Craving, with cloth and metal falling all around them. It was enough that the device singed her already-burnt left hand, before cooling as it vented its excess energies by housing them within its owner. Anya Kasparov's cloudy form, Hildegard Swan's mockery, and Rakh laughter surged through Razarkha's mind as at least fifty souls fed her insatiable appetite for arcana. Distant ascendants noticed the massacre and retreated, leading to a resounding cheer from the revolutionaries.

"Praetor Erre has delivered us to the Inner City!"

"None shall intimidate us again!"

"We shall finally see the truths they have hidden from us!"

Razarkha took a triumphant breath, but her joy was interrupted by a siren blaring through the inner city, along with more of the Watcher's announcements.

"Emergency alert for Pentatum Distal Inner City fourth-hour sector residents; outer city civil unrest has metastasised and is assisted by Plague Imperial Technology. Those untrained in combating sociocidal activity are advised to evacuate. Reiteration: All ascended residents unfamiliar with Plague Imperial Technology must evacuate."

"Even the Watcher fears us!" a pyromancer called.

"All of Galdus will fear us, friends!" Razarkha called. *"Enemies of progress will be afraid to drift through the streets. None will oppress breeders while we exist as a spectre in their minds."*

Sorelli cleared his throat. *"We destroyed many residential blocks—"*

"Sorry, thou art speaking too colloquially for me," Razarkha snapped. *"Librarian, thou shalt lead us to the Fourth Gate, so we may spread our freedom to Hextolis!"*

"Of course," the librarian stammered, and with that, Razarkha reapplied her cloak.

The inner city was largely akin to the outer city, though in place in overly regular residential blocks, singular, wide buildings lined with ascendant-filled capsules overlooked the streets. Occasionally, Old Galdusian architecture could be seen, bearing the hallmarks of marble, pillars and alabaster statues, though unlike Galdusian-Arkheran architects, none depicted humanoids, instead portraying wyverns, wyrms, and in many cases, a six-winged orb.

Atop a set of marble stairs was the Fourth Gate, a shimmering arch of norvite bright enough to illuminate the storm-beset blocks around it. Standing beside it was an ascendant whose armour was fashioned in the shape of a nine-foot-tall crane. Its metallic beak was sharpened to an absurd edge, and pieces of cloudy energy spilled from its armour.

"We must be careful," Sorelli whispered. *"That is Praetor Lissandrum, and his power is directly linked to—"*

Razarkha pushed past the rambler and lifted her soulstealer. "I won't be vague with you this time, Bold Individualist. Murder this bird-man."

"It would be my pleasure. I hope you enjoy the results."

"Wait, what do you mean by—"

Before she could finish her sentence, the soulstealer glowed, and the crane armour keeled over as though an avian rendition of an insect's moult, while its magical essence entered the soulstealer as planned. Sorelli rushed behind her and ranted in rapid Nortezian.

"What in the fuck did you do that for? I told you to be careful! See how this gate is an empty arch? It required Lissandrum's orderspeech to function! What do we do now?"

The Watcher spoke once again. *"Malignant civil unrest located. All trained ascendants, switch locations from site of membrane breach to Fourth Gate. Praetor Lissandrum non-cohesive."*

"Now they're coming for us and we have no way out!" Sorelli screamed. *"You've doomed this revolution before it could begin!"*

Razarkha trembled. Every soul she consumed made her crave another five, and with so many ascendants to savour, she'd forgotten this wasn't a feast; it was a massacre, and people had more uses than food. In the corner of her eye, Razarkha noticed Weil approaching the gate. She turned and called out in Isleborn.

"Weil, what are you doing?"

"Fixing this gate," he claimed, touching the norvite and chanting in Chaostongue.

Sorelli swallowed. *"What he's proposing is madness. Norvite is as much the Grand Order's as nasite is the Living Entropy's. If a chaotic portal appears in this gate, there's no telling where it'll—"*

A blast struck the edge of the gate's stairway, and Razarkha talked over the librarian. *"There's no time. Men, to the gate!"*

The group rushed to catch up to Weil, who stopped his chanting. After a delay and another five or so blasts blocked by the geomancers, a purple and red rift opened within the arch, the Rakh'vash's myriad eyes staring out of it.

"The Rakh'vash promises this gate will take us to Hextolis," Weil said in Isleborn. *"It may be unreliable in its priorities, but it never lies."*

Razarkha hesitated, but she didn't have the will to quash Weil's hopeful expression. She turned to her crew and pointed to the portal.

"Close thy eyes and step forth, insurrectionists! The God of the Plague Emperor has promised us passage to Hextolis!"

"Insurrection!"

The followers charged into the portal, Sorelli being the last through. Weil nodded to Razarkha and hopped in, leaving her to bite her thumb at her assailants before diving into the Chaotic Realm.

Arranged

An unknown portal spat Razarkha out so that she landed on Weil, who was surrounded by the fifteen or so revolutionaries that survived their active transport through Pentatum's Membrane. Sorelli groaned, but Weil seemed quite comfortable with Razarkha on top of him.

"We made it," the boy said with a smile. *"We're safe for now."*

Razarkha had her doubts. Wherever they were, the sky wasn't visible. The floors were smooth and blue-grey, with pipes of glowing, red matter lining the surrounding walls, and though whatever structure they were in presumably had a ceiling, it was too high for Razarkha to see. There were no windows, and the nearby lamps were large, bright, and sweeping, akin to watchtower's spotlight. Echoes rang through the inorganic expanse, and Razarkha turned around to see their way in flicker, then vanish. The norvite device that once contained the portal was mounted on another pipe-ridden wall, and above them, further spotlights swept, some appearing to be disconnected from the walls.

"Where are we, Weil?" Razarkha asked in Isleborn. *"Hextolis may be the capital of Nortez, but I refuse to believe it's this devoid of life."*

Weil's excitement drained from his face. *"The Rakh'vash said it would take us to Hextolis and that we'd be able to kill the one maintaining Nortez's accursed order."*

Razarkha's face burnt with rage. *"Oh, you idiot, that's not what we're here to do! Has your god taken us to Hextolis's citadel? Ask it, ask it now!"*

"All right, all right!" he stammered, before beginning his Chaostongue babble.

As Razarkha climbed off the fool, she found her own answer. Spotlights focused on the group, and the scream of

93

sirens filled the echoing halls. Her insurrectionists shot upright and prepared however they could. Pyromancers conjured flames, geomancers tore molten red rock from the glowing tubes, and Sorelli dove into the centre of the group, trembling on the floor.

"We're in the Citadel," Weil concluded.

"No, really? I despise your chaos god!" Razarkha spat, kicking Weil in the crotch and addressing her Nortezians in shaky Old Galdusian. *"Do not fear, fellows! If they send ascendants, they shalt only empower me. We must hold our own until they're forced to let us flee. If they're foolish enough to send every ascendant in the citadel after us, Hextolis is ours! Insurrection!"*

Her hands trembled as the sirens continued to blare. Weil writhed on the floor, clutching his nether regions, Sorelli babbled in fearful Nortezian, and numerous revolutionaries whispered to each other in doubting tones. Rakh's smug assurance filled Razarkha's head, and Anya Kasparov's fleshly face smiled teasingly at a figment of Weil.

"Bold Individualist?" she asked her soulstealer.

"Yes?"

"I'm going to survive this, aren't I? You've seen the interior of a Galdusian citadel before, you're a god, you see all, don't you?"

"Are you asking me to preserve your life despite knowing my disdain for those who flee from death? If it's your time, it's your time."

"I'm not done yet!"

"Then ensure that you remain a little longer."

"Oh, *that's* helpful, that's brilliant, why didn't I think of that, to *live,* I just have to *live!* Thanks for nothing, you worthless, complacent, sitting-around godly incompetent!" she ranted. "How in the world did the Plague Emperor gain anything from working with you—"

Agony split through Razarkha's head, spreading through her neck and down her spine. Her legs failed her, and between intermittent eye malfunctions, she beheld her fellow revolutionaries falling to their knees. Some clutched their heads, plenty screamed, and all were incapacitated. Eventually, it was too much, and the world became shrouded in darkness.

Shapes danced before Razarkha's subconscious. She was small, and a monstrously tall rendition of her mother eyed her with disdain. She mouthed inaudible words to an equally huge version of her father, likely saying that they needed more nannies, that she couldn't take the little monster any longer.

An adult Rakh passed her by, shifting her parents into colourful dust that painted a warm, inn-like environment. The taste of rich, Arkheran bone gravy washed away the dull aftertaste left from the Galdusian fungal parcels she'd subsisted on. For a moment, she was happy, until she noticed Rakh glancing at a high elven waitress.

The inn and Rakh collapsed, then reformed themselves into a Weil whose eyes had degraded into a saline waterfall. He towered over her, flooding her surroundings until she had no choice but to swim. Whenever her head was underwater, she heard distant echoes of Ivan struggling as she pressed a pillow onto his face.

Razarkha's back shot upright as she gasped for air, and she found herself back in Hextolis's citadel, in a rectangular cell large enough to fit three standing spellbinders and nothing else. Three of the walls were the same smooth, blue-grey substance as the rest of the citadel, while the fourth was a transparent field that didn't appear to be solid.

She reached out to touch it, only to flinch from a sharp, burning sensation. Once again, her soulstealer was confiscated, and once again, she was a failure. Weil's final experience of her was a violent outburst. He doomed them all, but perhaps it was fate's will. Rakh treated her as a laughingstock, why would destiny be different?

Hours went by, and eventually, her cell was approached by a pair of spellbinders. One was bald, with skin that glowed a sickly teal, clad in black and cyan robes adorned with silvery pouldrons and tassels, while the second was a long-haired man with a perfect spellbinder physique and tight, simple, Yukishiman-styled clothes that showed it off.

Accompanying them was a short, almost-humanoid collection of disembodied stones, held together by an extremely localised set of whirlwinds, whose 'head' was a carved, mask-like rock with a pair of redstone eyes. It lacked legs, instead floating within a small tornado. Occasionally, flashes of lightning flickered between its pieces.

Razarkha squinted and came to the realisation that the creature must have been an augmentee. Conditor was depicted as a man of magma and served as a geomantic constructor before he was freed by the Plague Emperor. If Razarkha was correct, this former human was likely aeromantic.

"This is the ringleader," the bald spellbinder said in soft, formal Nortezian, quietly walking towards the cell. *"Praetor Erre, I believe she's known as."*

The young man covered his mouth but said nothing, and the augmentee hovered in silence. The robed fellow stopped in front of Razarkha and stared with his blue-green eyes.

"'Praetor Erre'. On whose authority did a fleshly foreigner become a praetor?"

Razarkha scoffed. *"If a fleshly being may rule Nortez, why shalt they not become a praetor?"*

The old man laughed in a single short burst then turned away. *"Your actions have cost countless lives in Pentatum, according to the city's Watcher. It's likely damages are underreported. Whoever dubbed you a praetor has no grasp on a praetor's true duty."*

"'Twas the librarian Sorelli who dubbed me," Razarkha said. *"All I claim to be is a revolutionary, campaigning against the conservatives of thy nation. Who art thou?"*

"I'm Grand Duke Varus Kiraxas, ruler of Hextolis and Nortez," the old man said. *"Beside me stands Consigliere Lesteris, my trusted advisor."*

Razarkha's eyes darted to the man with the buttoned-up Yukishiman shirt. He was one of the Soltelle Empire's closest friends according to the Imperial Engineer, on par with Emissary Quissera of Quattrus. She had her gripping point.

"Lesteris," Razarkha remarked. *"Thou art quite the contrast to thy duke."*

"Like what you see? It's a shame we must be enemies. I believe in the right clothes you would be quite striking," the consigliere said, earning a sharp glare from his superior.

"You killed Consigliere Vieri of Pentatum, then carved a path through numerous ascended soldiers and civilians by the Pentatum Membrane," Varus Kiraxas said. *"I have no reason to spare you and your friends."*

"Consigliere Vieri was thy enemy," Razarkha claimed. *"I believe thy consigliere brokered peace between Yukishima and Nortez. He would be dismayed to know Vieri attempted to leak information to the Sons of Sula in exchange for a wand."*

This rattled the Nortezians, and Lesteris rubbed his smooth, narrow chin. *"The Sons of Sula? Are you sure? They've been a constant hassle for our reformation efforts, but we didn't believe the Sons had spread to Pentatum."*

"I killed the deliverymen myself," Razarkha explained. *"Then I had breeders take the wand and pretend*

to be them. Vieri accepted it, handed over confidential text-tablets, and then I killed him. He was a traitor."

The old man took what sounded like a breath through three throats, then conjured a gold-and-white portal. Within was a blindingly bright light, with which he had a lengthy, incomprehensible conversation. Lesteris undressed Razarkha with his eyes during the wait.

"It's good to see Arkheran spellbinders aren't too dissimilar to Galdusian ones."

"If thou hope to impress me, thou art woefully ill-equipped," Razarkha replied.

"Of course, you have that overweight consort of yours. You can do better."

Razarkha folded her arms. *"At least he doesn't keep augmentees. They art thine, are they not? Were they male or female before thou augmented them?"*

"Does it matter? It's a human."

"Considering thy allies are humans, I wouldst say so."

"Amusing," the consigliere remarked. *"Very amusing."*

Duke Kiraxas closed his portal and addressed Razarkha. *"The Rakh'norv has confirmed your tale. Still, you massacred civilians. Duke Revidus is demanding your body gated to him, arranged as a map of Pentatum, vein for vein."*

Lesteris broke in. *"Grand Duke, isn't that rash?"*

"Rash? She massacred scores of civilians. Soldiers are made to embrace possible mortality, but those civilians by the Membrane did nothing to deserve their fate!"

Lesteris nodded. *"I understand, but consider this. The Sons of Sula have been killing breeders and Yukishiman emissaries throughout the transition, and this woman is opposed to them. Any ascended allies the Sons will vanish before that dread device of hers. We cannot ethically use such a device, but she evidently has no such qualms. Why not let her have her little counter-counter-revolutionary group destroy our enemies?"*

Kiraxas paused. *"She's too wilful. She must be honed before she can be used. That will be her punishment. Contain her in an antimagical training room and keep her isolated. Return her blasphemous device, but ensure no ascendants enter her containment chamber."*

"You are merciful and wise, Grand Duke," Lesteris said with a bow.

Varus Kiraxas gave a disdainful huff and left the room. Once the exit was sealed, Lesteris lifted his hand, deactivating the light screen and the spotlights.

"You can thank me later, in any way a beautiful woman like you pleases," Lesteris said in a way that made his augmentee shift. *"Don't give me that look, Ariel. You had flesh once."*

"Once," she muttered in a grinding, rocky tone.

Razarkha walked out of her cell, immediately making distance between herself and the consigliere. He maintained his smirk, then clicked his fingers, causing the floor to descend. As the room drifted downwards, it passed several other rows of cells, some containing augmentees, others containing wizened and emaciated breeders. It stopped moving once it reached a level that contained an exit instead of more cells. The opening led to a separate chamber as blue-grey as the rest, and, as he walked towards it, Lesteris started to ramble.

"I was the one who requested covert Yukishiman help dealing with Vieri and the Sons of Sula, but I never realised you were the help I requested. If it wasn't for me, you'd never have started this little festival of yours. I'm also why Duke Kiraxas doesn't know of your explicit connection to Yukishima. Some gratitude would be appreciated."

Razarkha frowned. *"I shalt thank thee, but little else."*

"I'm sure you'll change your mind. Don't tell me I'm not the most beautiful spellbinder you've ever seen. Ariel thinks so, doesn't she?"

"You're beautiful and wise, Master Lesteris," the augmentee replied.

"Isn't she adorable?" Lesteris said with a short squeal.

As they moved into the chamber, Razarkha felt a sharp pain in her throat. The faces of the Malassaian women she'd freed in Winter Harbour flickered before her, and for a moment, Lesteris saw them too.

"Oh yes, you're an illusionist, aren't you? You truly are helpless without a soulstealer. Speaking of which, here you go."

The man dug into his trouser pocket and produced the Soulstealer of Craving. When Razarkha attempted to retrieve it, he pulled it away.

"Give me a kiss first."

"Thou art despicable," Razarkha spat.

"Is that a yes or a no? I know killing you would transfer this device's ownership to me, and unlike Duke Kiraxas I'm quite willing to take it for myself."

"As you wish," Razarkha muttered.

She breathed in, then gave Lesteris a chaste kiss on the cheek. The consigliere handed the soulstealer over with a self-satisfied grin, then gestured to the blank, hexagonal room.

"This will be your training arena. I shall provide you with as many books on spellwork as you require, and additionally, I'll teach you modern Nortezian. Your Old Galdusian hybrid tongue is hilarious, but impractical if you want to sway unpretentious minds. For now, you'll sit and wait, like a good girl. I'll have Ariel craft new clothes to your specifications. No doubt you want to look like a leader, not some bedraggled rat on the run."

"Provide the cloth, I'll make my own outfit."

Lesteris stifled a chuckle. *"Do you doubt Ariel's obedience? I assure you, she's good at taking orders."*

"The strong don't rely on the weak," Razarkha snapped.

"Oh, you actually believe all that talk about ending Galdusian conservatism," Lesteris remarked. *"I thought you just wanted an excuse to kill ascendants. To me, you're just a means to suppress the Sons of Sula. I hope you enjoy your stay, Praetor Erre. I'll return soon."*

With a click of his fingers, the chamber's entrance shut. Before Razarkha could say anything else, the consigliere opened a gold-and-white portal of his own, spiriting he and Ariel away. Once again, Razarkha had nothing but her soulstealer for company.

* * *

For some reason, the Ilazari were even less willing to sail east than they were to stay in Zemelnya, and so buying a ship was simultaneously easy and a pain for Rowyn. He'd failed to amass a crew, so the only boat he could sail without killing himself was a one-man skiff.

As Rowyn carved through Nortez's deep, dark waters, his memory fell hostage to Vi'kara's face. She'd begged him not to go east, figuring that if sailors were avoiding the Nortez route, he should too. It was a fair concern, but what else could he do? Hide out with her until her father inevitably murdered him in cold blood? Return to Arkhera, where Plutyn would use his myriad connections to ruin his life?

Duty had always been his priority, and there was no need for that to change. He'd seen Razarkha's work on the streets of Zemelnya, and if she was wielding a soulstealer in Nortez, her work would only worsen. Rakh Fel'thuz was a nervous wreck, but his fear was justified.

101

A fleet could be seen ahead. Its peculiar, metallic appearance was plausibly Nortezian, from what Rowyn knew. Plutyn's idea of Galdus was long dead, and in place of crafted marble angularity, featureless towers and arcane, crystalline structures stood. If any nations were to master metallic boats, it would be Nortez or Yukishima.

The latter wielded metal in every facet of their military operations, but there was no reason for a Yukishiman fleet to linger in front of their enemies. Rowyn's stomach twisted; perhaps the Nortezians feared all incoming boats as potentially Yukishiman, and that was why Ilazari sailors were unwilling to travel there.

As the fleet grew closer, the truth revealed itself. Cannons on the rear ships' sterns were mounted, long monstrosities Rowyn had seen at Jadeport. Rippling in Galdus's perpetual winds were orange flags with red suns upon them. The Ilazari who sold him the skiff had mockingly provided him with a black-and-white flag of surrender, and now that he was irreconcilably drifting towards the maritime equivalent of an ogre's fighting ground, its time had come. Rowyn took the flag in one hand and shimmied up his mast, calling to the nearest boat in a panicked, hoarse voice.

"Hello! Anyone who can see me, I come in peace! I repeat, any Yukishiman vessels who can see me, I'm friendly! Please hear my words!"

The skiff drifted closer, and a boat's cannon tracked Rowyn's movements. When he got a good look at its crew, he noticed they were preparing a ladder. A projected, crackling voice called out to him in Yukishiman-accented Common.

"Ilazari sailor, your surrender has been acknowledged. Please align your ship with the Celestia *and prepare for retrieval. The crew will fire flares to mark its location."*

As expected, flares shot from the closest ship, and Rowyn brought his boat into position. He didn't know why the Soltelles were playing sitting duck in enemy territory, nor why they were blockading their Ilazari allies, but he supposed they'd have an explanation. What he couldn't guarantee was if the *Celestia's* crew had useful knowledge on Razarkha. A ladder was lowered down the side of the monstrous, barnacle-encrusted vessel, and the fuzzy voice spoke once again.

"Climb aboard, sailor. Prepare for a thorough check before your capture."

Rowyn put his satchel and bag of armour around his shoulder and started his ascent. Yookies weren't an unreasonable lot; Lord Verawor appreciated their business above any Arkheran's. Still, being a prisoner of the world's strongest empire was hardly a joyful prospect. A set of rifle-wielding soldiers in heavy clothing met him at the top, backed by white-suited skippers with pistols Rowyn hadn't seen before. The knight put his hands up and spoke.

"Check anything you like. I don't want to be your enemy."

A soldier smirked as he approached, then patted Rowyn over, cuffed him, unsheathed his sword, and took off his satchel so he could look through it.

"Such primitive weaponry and gear. Not even Ilazari would be happy with— oh, I see. Someone get the Imperial Engineer over here, I think we've got another brown-necker," the soldier commanded, and a sailor was quick to follow.

"You can just ask me. I speak the Common Tongue," Rowyn said. "If by brown-necker, you mean Arkheran, then yes, I'm one of those. There's no need for—"

"We make the decisions here, armour boy," the soldier snapped, giving his fellow riflemen a nod. "Consider yourself lucky we didn't blow your ship clean out the water. That's what happened to the last brown-necker who came this way."

Rowyn grunted. Yukishima prided itself on being a beacon of civility and progress, but its armies were as infested with sadists as any Arkheran guard force. The guns aimed at him were accepted and expected, but soldiers that mocked their quarry were walking worms. Suddenly, his resentful thoughts faded as the Yookie's words echoed through his mind.

"Wait, who was the last Arkheran who passed?"

"That's classified, brown-necked snake," the soldier said as he finished his inspection. "We leave that shit to the Imperial Engineer. Oh, there she is. You're gonna *love* her. She likes talking to prisoners."

The soldiers parted to let a short human woman with unmoving blonde curls saunter towards Rowyn. She grinned, then gestured to the soldiers around her.

"Good work, men. Take him to the brig, we need to have a talk."

Rowyn stammered. "Wait, I beg you! You're the Imperial Engineer, yes? You'd have access to classified information, wouldn't you? Do you know anything about Razarkha Fel'thuz? I have a strong suspicion she sailed this way!"

The Yookie men prepared to drag Rowyn away, but the Imperial Engineer lifted her hand. "Stop. I have a better idea. Uncuff this gentleman."

The soldier who conducted the check began to splutter. "But he's a brown-necker, he admitted it himself. Don't you need to break him an' all that?"

"He's not my type," she claimed. "Uncuff him, or I'll let Admiral Lunscar know you're refusing the commands of a member of Imperial Intelligence."

"Of course, Imperial Engineer."

The man uncuffed Rowyn, allowing him to bow to his supposed saviour. "Thank you. What's your name, if I might ask?"

104

"Hildegard Swan, but please, call me Imperial Engineer. Or Lady Hilda, I hear you brown-neckers are sticklers for antiquated noble titles. Follow me."

The woman waltzed off, her posture assured. Her dress-suit could have hidden all manner of weaponry, and she exuded an air of smug competence. Rowyn followed her into the ship's hull, through a set of salty-smelling metallic corridors, then finally into a personal cabin the size of Verawyn Verawor's bedroom.

Within, a rifle-wielding woman stood by a double bed, nude save for a collar and a utility belt. Rowyn averted his eyes, focusing instead on Hilda, who sat by a desk covered in files. A couch and shelf resided nearby, the latter chock-full of books.

"Please, get comfortable," the Imperial Engineer commanded. "And by all means, look at Ana. She got uppity again, so she's an exhibit for all visitors."

Rowyn shuddered. "I'd rather not be an accessory to a stranger's fetish."

"Suit yourself," Hilda said with a shrug.

"Why did you opt against keeping me in the brig? Razarkha sailed by here, didn't she?"

Hilda began writing a note. "Of course. She intended to visit all manner of destruction upon Quattrus, but now she's something of a controlled agent. I'm somewhat impressed."

Rowyn chuckled. "Your tone doesn't imply that."

"Oh, I'm not impressed by *Yukishiman* standards. But given brown-neckers are known for— well, their necks being brown, you tracked Razarkha down relatively quickly. Who are you, and what do you intend to do to her?"

"I'm Rowyn Khanas, and I intend to kill her," he stated. "Razarkha possesses a soulstealer if my information isn't outdated. Did you seize it from her?"

"Heavens, no, if we were caught retaining Sovereign-based technology it'd be a PR *nightmare* back in Wrenfall. No, we let her loose in Pentatum with it."

"You did what?" Rowyn spluttered.

Hilda's voice became wry. "Now, now, don't get upset. Ana's more than just an exhibit, she also knows fifty ways to kill you. Given you're unwilling to look at her, they're considerably easy for her to execute."

"Why in the world did you release her?"

"Nortez has officially surrendered, but that doesn't mean there aren't niggling little political problems. Conservatives unwilling to accept change, counter-revolutionary groups, et cetera. Of course, we Yukishimans hold ourselves to a higher standard, and we'd never assassinate political enemies."

Rowyn narrowed his eyes. "So you released Razarkha knowing she'd erase your enemies while being officially unrelated to you."

"Wow, you're sharp for a brown-necker!" the Imperial Engineer said in a sing-song tone. "I wonder if you'll process the next statement of the obvious with such proficiency."

"I presume you won't let me kill her, then," Rowyn said. "At least, not while she's useful to you."

Hilda nodded as she finished a jot and tittle. "Very perceptive. Still, I imagine you intended to infiltrate her group."

"Yes. I hoped to bond with her over shared Arkheran culture and claim concern over the greatness of our equally minor houses. I'd say I wanted a powerful friend and sought her out to find glory with her."

Hilda scoffed. "I'll help you change the story based on her current situation. I've just received word from a friend in Hextolis that she's currently training in their citadel."

Rowyn creased his brow. To a woman like this, the previous statement's implication was likely obvious, but this time he didn't have a 'sharp' interpretation on hand.

"I'm sorry, I don't understand. You don't want me to assassinate her, yet you're willing to assist with my infiltration?"

Hildegard rolled her eyes. "Must I explain everything? You're going to be a mole. Someone who will report Razarkha's movements to the nearest Yukishiman radio tower whenever possible. We just got done with a military campaign in Nortez, so believe me, there's a lot of them. As a bonus, if Razarkha misbehaves and kills our allies, you have full permission to assassinate her. Oh, I'm feeling generous. One more bonus, just for you."

Rowyn's throat tightened. "Please, for the love of every god there is, don't offer your guardswoman's body."

"Don't flatter yourself," Hilda said. "What I mean to offer is a telegram relay. If you keep me informed, I'll send messages to Arkhera using a miraculous Yukishiman technology you wouldn't begin to understand. Is the Sandport Radio Tower still up and running?"

"The Sandport What Tower?"

"That's a yes," Hildegard said. "Just tell me which city and recipient you want your message to reach, and I'll endeavour to transmit it. Don't say I'm not spoiling you."

While it was tempting to tell her exactly that, something told Rowyn that exaggerated deference was the only feasible option he had.

"Thank you, Imperial Engineer," he said. "Let me know when I'm to be deployed."

Educated

Ironically, Razarkha's isolation chamber contained more than one person. While she sat and sewed her own dress, Ariel floated in one of the room's six corners. She was silent save for the whistle of her body's natural cyclones with the occasional buzz of electricity when her storms churned too strongly. Despite Razarkha's protestation, Lesteris had lent the augmentee's services to her, but she refused to stoop to his level by having the former human work for her. Yet as she finished frilling her outfit's collars, Ariel's stillness became infuriating.

Razarkha lifted her eyes from her textile work, glanced at the piles of Galdusian text-tablets she'd used to train in spellwork, then over to Ariel. She sighed, picked one of the tablets up, and lent the smooth red-and-black device a piece of her power. Its polished obsidian screen lit up, and displayed Nortezian text; with a swipe of her finger, the words changed, as though flicking the pages of a book.

The wondrousness of the devices had become mundane, and as Razarkha read, she grew anxious at the quiet winds Ariel brought to the room. A creature as violated as her didn't deserve to be a breeze; her rage should have been an unstoppable tempest. If she was a sinchild of the Bold Individualist, Razarkha would have easily convinced the augmentee to rebel. As she was, Ariel was trapped within her weakness. As word after word on multi-purpose geomancy met Razarkha's eyes and escaped through her slack jaw, an unrelated idea sprang to mind. She put down the text-tablet and turned to Ariel, Nortezian edging from her mouth.

"You don't talk often, do you?"

"No. If there isn't a reason to talk, I shouldn't," Ariel replied.

"And why is that?"

"Because Master Lesteris said so."

Razarkha frowned. *"Who gave Lesteris the authority to rule your life?"*

"The Demidium Breeding Facility," she stated. *"They raised me, let me breed, then when I had my allotted children, I was augmented and sold to Lesteris."*

The thought made Razarkha itch. *"People shouldn't be bought and sold."*

"Why not?"

"Because we're people. Humans may be weak, but they ought to live as wild animals. You can speak, you can solve problems, you're— you're a person, and that..."

Razarkha trailed into silence. The way Ariel floated in unending patience, not once cutting her off or expressing rage was all Razarkha required to conclude that the woman was lost. If she couldn't be an ally, then perhaps she could be used.

"You serve Consigliere Lesteris closely, yes?"

The augmentee's body shifted its two rocky hands together. *"Yes, I serve him well. He always lets me know when he's happy with me. I live to hear his words, 'good girl'."*

"What happens when you displease him?"

The cyclone beneath Ariel briefly intensified, and sheet lightning formed between her segments. *"Why do you want me to think about those times?"*

"I want to know what the true Lesteris is," Razarkha admitted. *"It's funny, I'm reminding myself of my worthless brother. He told me that a man's true self is exposed by how they treat their inferiors, not their superiors. He used this philosophy to chide me for disciplining foolish, complacent servants, but the core reasoning isn't wrong. Besides, Lesteris lent you to me. You need to answer my question."*

The augmentee's winds howled, and eventually, a rumbling answer was produced. *"He temporarily disincorporates my body."*

"Does that mean what I think it does?" Razarkha asked.

"It means the magic in my body is temporarily seized. I become a pile of rocks, unable to move. My redstone eyes remain active, so I can watch Master Lesteris move about freely while I stay still. I need to be taught a lesson; how else will I become obedient?"

"Those lessons are stupid," Razarkha snapped. *"Even if he wasn't pathetic for relying on a weaker species, disincorporating you just leaves him a woman down. You're not learning anything but blind fear."*

"Fear helps you survive. I was fortunate. I got to breed with a strong man before I was augmented. His name was Ferrus, and he had big arms that held me wonderfully."

"If that was when you enjoyed life, why continue to live without your flesh? Why not go out in a blaze of glory, striking against your master?"

A wave of sheet lightning spread through Ariel. *"That's not what I'm supposed to do."*

Razarkha pinched her nose-bridge and rested her back against the closest wall of the chamber. *"You're irretrievable. I thought I could be a hero. Nobody I meet wants to be saved, and when somebody does, I ruin them."*

"I'm sure that's not true," Ariel said in a bland, polite tone.

"You like to make Lesteris happy, correct?" Razarkha asked, hoping the change of subject would make the whipped dog forget her moment of sincerity.

"Oh, of course!"

"You've probably noticed that he's taken a liking to me, much as your human man took a liking to—"

"Oh, no, humans don't do things like spellbinders do," Ariel claimed. *"We're simply selected, then the overseers help us copulate. We don't get to do anything on our own, but it felt good when it was happening."*

Razarkha's expression darkened. Humans may have been different to spellbinders, but this was wrong. She'd heard Rakh with his human women before, grunting, tousling and defiling their marriage bed. Humans, when wild, chose their mates, even if that choice was objectively incorrect.

"Anyway, you've noticed Lesteris likes me, yes?" Razarkha continued.

"Yes, I have. He's fond of visiting the outer city and inviting breeders into the citadel, where he'll mate with them. He'll probably mate with you, too."

Razarkha smirked. Finally, this broken creature was betraying her master.

"Does he do anything strange when he mates? Does he require anything unnecessary for breeding?"

Ariel's arm-pieces separated and orbited her before rearranging themselves into a neutral position. *"Sometimes he seeks out breeders who have already chosen partners. If they become angry, he'll even bring them along to watch as he mates with their partner. Most spellbinders seem to want privacy to mate, but Lesteris doesn't."*

"That oddity is known as cuckoldry. He does it because he wants his fellow spellbinders to suffer," Razarkha explained. *"Do you suffer, Ariel? Is disincorporation painful to you?"*

"I no longer feel outer pain, but whenever Lesteris is hurt, I feel an inner pain."

"Because you care for Lesteris, or because you fear disincorporation?" Razarkha said, her tone growing insistent.

"Why are you asking me that? The thoughts of a human are worthless."

Razarkha shook her head. *"Not so. Did you know Lesteris is allies with a human? Her name is Hildegard Swan, and she works for an extremely powerful nation. This*

111

human frightens me, but I had no choice but to value her thoughts."

"She must be an exception to the rule."

"No, Ariel. Beyond Galdus, there's a world full of humans. I don't like most of them. They're short, they're fat, they have hair in the ugliest of places, but they're all willing to make their thoughts heard," Razarkha said. "Forgive the requests of a peculiar Arkheran. I want to know the thoughts of a mere human."

Ariel's cyclone quietened to a hollow whistle. "Whenever Lesteris asks for honesty, it's a test. Honesty leads to punishment."

Razarkha smiled at the aeromantic construct. "Think of it this way; if Lesteris lent you to me, I can treat you as I wish. I have no intention of punishing honesty. Do you want to tell me something?"

Ariel's body became overcast, and a harsh rocky scrape replaced her usual rumbling voice. "He mocks me for my obedience but torments me for disobedience. He hides me from foreign diplomatic meetings, telling me I'm a disgrace to his reputation. He's had me hold down male spellbinders as he killed them in front of their partners. Lesteris is— I don't think he's an ordinary spellbinder. The farmers told me spellbinders were a civilised race."

"You're right to hate him," Razarkha assured her. "Thank you for talking to me. That is more valuable to me than any service. If you want to talk again, don't hesitate. I might say your thoughts are stupid or wrong, but at least you've said them."

"I understand. Thank you, Mistress Erre."

"Don't call me mistress. Erre is enough," Razarkha said. "I'm going to work on my lumomancy. Would you like to mock my failures?"

"No, that would be rude," she said. "But if you want, I can finish off your outfit."

Razarkha folded her arms. *"Have you learnt nothing? I don't want you to serve me against your will."*

"You misapprehend me, Erre. I want to work for you."

Razarkha swelled with an unfamiliar exhilaration. This was the missing piece of the Plague Emperor's success. It wasn't the Sovereign's magic, or an illusory, Rakh-like lie. Weil was her first, and this augmentee was her second. The key to loyal servants was the truth.

"Very well, Ariel. I'll let you know how I want it, then you're free to make it happen."

* * *

A chill ran through Melancholy's spine as a gust of wind billowed into her paraffin-lit operating tent. Tied down to a slab with his penis constricted at the base was a dark elven fellow who'd received twice the standard dose of poppy milk. It was only appropriate for Ashglass's grim circumstances, and as she cleaned her scalpel, a pain gnawed at her abdomen.

She'd eaten the appropriate foods, drank hippocras, stretched and straightened her spine throughout her middle years, yet time's unavoidable regress came for all. It was less than five years before she'd be seventy; she should have had a permanent home and some children to look after her in her advanced age.

Instead, she was in yet another tent, taking on her oldest enemy. The wretched beasts that stole Thornwrit Heath from her wouldn't claim every settlement in Arkhera; her experiments would make sure of that. Once satisfied with her scalpel, she removed a vial from a rack and gave it a tentative flick, jarring the precipitate within.

She smiled as the suspended white flakes shifted, then moved over to her anaesthetised patient-cum-experiment. He was already nude when captured and slicing through his penis was a simple enough procedure once blood supply was cut off. With one lengthways glide, the fleshy tube opened to reveal numerous writhing, white strands.

Melancholy picked one of the rapeworms out with a sharp tug. "You don't know what horror you've wrought. You just want to live, like any other creature. But your existence is a problem to people like me."

She moved the flatworm into a dish filled with a jellified bone soup, then moved the sample into a small, ice-lined box beside her desk. It was a portable cryomancer the gnomish inventor family known as the Gatleys had gifted her, and it had proven useful for preserving food throughout her journeys. This time it'd serve a much greater purpose.

After a short ponder, Melancholy returned to her operating table with her precipitate. She poured it with one hand and separated the man's tissues with another, ensuring every wriggling mass within the white clump received their dose. Once the creatures relaxed their mouth-grippers, they would be easy to remove. The only issue was if penile function would return following the operation.

Penectomies and hysterectomies were an admission of defeat. Rapeworms had claimed the humanoid reproductive system as their territory and removing them was man forfeiting their right to reclaim what was theirs, torching the land and fleeing. True pioneers fought back, and if Melancholy was more than ready to be the only pioneer against rapeworm.

The rapeworms steadily became easier to scoop out in bunches, and the dark elf's stretched penile skin relaxing to an appropriate flaccidity. She dumped the white mass into a bucket, and once she was sure he was free of exogens, she took the bucket to her desk. There, she opened a small jar of paraffin and scooped a chunk into the bucket, then used a handheld pyromancer from within her pocket to light the accursed beasts on fire.

She lingered to watch another population of her sub-sapient nemesis flare up and reduce to ashes, then moved back to her patient. His penile tissues were just as damaged by the precipitate as the worms were, with mucous and spongy tissue ravaged by acid burns. Melancholy shook, then left the slab to kick the blackened bucket over.

"Curse you wretched creatures!"

Nothing could make the pile of charred worms hear or care. She took her scalpel, washed it all over again, and prepared for a penectomy. As she moved to declare her figurative surrender, the sound of her tent's guards speaking killed her focus.

"I 'unno if you should distract 'er, milord," one of the guards said.

"Yeah, she'll probably just send you back out, you know how she is," another added.

"I don't care," an Elarondian-accented voice replied. "I'm lord consort of this city, and I'm well within my rights to ask this so-called healer questions."

"Yeah, but she's— well, y'know how she is," the first guard said.

"I command you to let me through," the accented voice demanded. "Well? Are you going to disobey commands during a crisis?"

"No, milord."

The clatter of armour preceded a dark elf entering the tent, garbed in a traditionally feminine Elarondian tricorn. His rich outfit consisted of colours combining the yellow and orange of his blood house, the Solerros, with the black, red, and gold of House Foenaxas, his family by marriage. He swaggered in, then wretched at the sight of a cut-apart penis.

"Don't trouble your delicate stomach, Lord Consort Solyx. That thing is coming off the moment you leave me to my work," Melancholy muttered, approaching the unconscious dark elf and evaluating the best point to cut.

115

The young man faltered before finding his words. "As you say, Melancholy. Not to cast doubt upon you, but you've insisted on days of humanoid experimentation and judging by your remarks, you still haven't produced a method of rapeworm control that doesn't kill or sterilise the victim."

"Not to cast doubt?" Melancholy said with a raised eyebrow. "You speak louder than you ought to, Lord Consort. You call me a so-called healer, as though a penectomised dark elf is somehow less preferable than a rabid monster stalking the streets raping everything from old ladies to little boys. Why are you here? Speak quickly, then get out."

"You've asked a lot of us. Our children are asking why the city's burning. Mor'kha's weeping in the Temple of Renewal every day before attempting to revive the city's morale. Even she can't believe her own speeches anymore. You offered us help, but your work is too slow."

"I am *one woman,* Solerro," Melancholy stated. "If your wisdom was helpful, I would drag him into this, but the only thing he's good for is pessimism, as is typical of his kind."

"What do we do, then? We can't burn more districts, and if a cure isn't forthcoming, the next generation of Ashglass will be the smallest yet. We need an answer, now!"

Melancholy groaned. "What do you want? An incorrect answer now or a correct answer later? You mistake impotently demanding untenable results with leadership. Next time you want to raise a concern, send your wife. She's infinitely more respectable."

The dark elf's nostrils flared. "I— Ashglass has lost *thousands* from your advice!"

"And retained hundreds of thousands more. I won't tell you again, Lord Consort. Leave me, so that this potential worker may live, childless as he may be."

"You're not taking this seriously. This is just a laboratory for you to experiment in, isn't it? King Landon was right to throw you out of his court," the lord consort spat.

Melancholy closed her eyes and muffled her laughter with her hand. Once she stopped, she approached the youngster with the determination of a woman half her age.

"Believe me, you jumped-up second son, nobody cares about eradicating rapeworm more than I. If I die before this curse upon Arkhera is gone, my ghost will personally haunt the land until a cure is found. You stand before me, hold up my work with your complaints, and deliberately bring up my past with no intent other than to insult.

"Despite this, I stay while you highborn brats spit on me, just to cure your city of rapeworm. I have no special love for your glorified Renewalist cult, no more than I love Deathsport, Godswater, or the Divine Halls. Ask yourself, do you want me to stay, or should I leave you and your ungrateful city to their fate?"

Solyx Solerro tugged at his cravat, then turned his back on Melancholy. "So long as you're taking this matter seriously. If I find you've been artificially prolonging this process, there shall be consequences."

"As would rightly be the case. Now leave, preferably without another word."

Thankfully for Melancholy, the lord consort left in silence.

Confounded

"I'm going to die," Lady Kagura repeated for the fifth time. "I'm going to die, I'm going to die, I'm going to die, please don't let me die, Rakh, I'm too beautiful to die!"

Rakh rubbed his face while his lady continued to rant. The carriage had been like this since Moonstone, and though the drivers ignored their lady's panic, he was still glad that Kag hadn't thought to give them a direct order to turn around.

Horse-drawn carriage was their only travel option while the train lines to Ashglass were blocked, and that meant there was no escape from Lady Selenia. Rakh was to her right, Erwyn was to her left, while Rarakhi was squashed against the carriage's door, and flanking their vehicle was a set of cavalrymen.

"When I die they're going to eat my face, my beautiful, beautiful face. Rakh, you're not even listening, are you? I'm very concerned about everything and you were wrong to call me evil or apathetic or whatever you called me when you forced me to do this!"

"Don't fret, my lady," Erwyn told her. "The Minister of Criminal Affairs told us which districts are unsafe, and the drivers will approach the south-eastern side of Ashglass, as he advised us to. Remember when you told us how much you trust the minister?"

Lady Kagura began to hyperventilate, then grabbed Rakh by shoulders. "Why did Erwyn answer before you? Are you angry at me because of the *Wraiths and Wyverns* games? Is that what this is all about? Answer me, Rakh!"

Rakh faced her as much as the carriage allowed him. "I'm not sure what to tell you, my lady. This isn't about spite, it's about expecting you to be a good overlady to Ashglass."

"I *am* a good overlady! I could have started a war with them to get their horrible Madaki faith out of my province, but I never did, just like Erwyn told me! I've never failed them before, even if I don't like them! I'm a good lady, I am, I am!"

"Will you *shut the fuck up?"* Rarakhi suddenly broke in. "Dad and Erwyn may give a shit about all this 'my lady' nonsense, but I don't. Stop being a fucking child. I'm scared too, ain't we all, but you're crying like you're six."

"You're a child, you don't know what being a lady is all about," Kagura spluttered. "Why did you bring your bastard along, Rakh? His lowborn insights aren't helpful!"

"He's here to dig up information the Foenaxases may not be willing to tell us. They know I'm an illusionist and will keep an eye on me, but I won't be introducing Rarakhi to Lady Mor'kha. He'll instead be covertly investigating the districts," Rakh explained.

"That idea's stupid, he just insulted me," Lady Selenia said with an upturned nose.

Rarakhi scoffed. "Get used to it, pointy-ears."

The argument erupted further, so Rakh cast his illusionism on himself, muting the pair and staring out the carriage's window. The snow here was closer to sleet, though once they crossed the Peatwater River's bridge, it became adulterated with grey.

As they neared the city, Rakh's face whitened. The ground was dry, yet the pale flakes kept falling. Within Ashglass's slick, dark obsidian walls, a glow reached above the battlements, and an endless pillar of smoke rose behind the black, phoenix-bearing banners of the Foenaxases.

"By God, what's happening in there?" he mumbled, returning his own hearing only to realise he was drowned out by Lady Selenia's whimpering.

"I don't want to see the Foenaxases," she whined. "Lady Mor'kha's going to burn me at the stake for being an Eternalist, I just know she is. Then her people will throw tomatoes on my corpse and—"

"Calm down, my lady. Lady Mor'kha's will appreciate any help she gets," Rakh claimed. "If you appear helpful, nothing bad will happen. Can you do that?"

Kagura sniffled, wiped away a tear, then nodded. "I can do that."

"Good."

Erwyn folded his arms. "Where were you before, Rakh? You shouldn't have let her get to this state. I was trying to get your attention, but you were staring out the window."

"Sorry. The ashes caught my eye."

The wisdom's voice lowered. "It's a necessary evil. Melancholy's made many decisions like this."

"I can't imagine how Lady Foenaxas is coping."

"I imagine she's dipped further into her religion," Erwyn speculated. "Whatever you do, my lady, do not insult the God of Renewal. Are we clear?"

Selenia's lips trembled. "Am I a burden to you two?"

Erwyn paused. "Of course not. But you won't insult Lady Foenaxas's faith, am I understood?"

"You're understood," she muttered, flitting her red eyes away.

Rakh scratched his false hand and wondered if Lady Selenia was like him, with some matters of the mind as out of reach to her as shooting a bow and arrow was to him. The carriage stopped outside Ashglass's south-eastern entrance and was quickly surrounded by dark elven guards bearing the Foenaxas colours of black, red, and gold while another stayed by the gates.

"Out the carriage, *now!*" one guard yelled.

"This city is off limits, haven't you read the signs?" another said.

"Get out, explain yourselves, and turn back!" a third added.

Kagura put her head in her hands and began to weep, while Rakh turned to his son. "Rarakhi, open your door and get out. You know how it is."

"Yeah, yeah, cooperate when caught. I do this shit better than you," he replied, leaving the carriage without question.

Rakh stepped out after Rarakhi, and Erwyn followed, while Lady Kagura rocked in the carriage. Behind them, Selenia cavalrymen were pointing spears at the Foenaxas guards.

"Threaten our lady further and we'll have your heads," a high elven cavalier said.

A Foenaxas gunner pointing at Erwyn paused. "Your lady? Who the fuck is—"

"Zaxar, look," another gunner said to the onlooker. "Their flag. Blue an' a moon."

"Shit, it's the overlady!" he replied. "Right, you brutes back off and leave this to me."

Rakh raised an eyebrow as the men lowered their weapons while the guard approached. "Forgive my scepticism, but your men raised weapons at a carriage bearing the colours of your overlady. I think leaving this to you isn't in anyone's interest—"

Erwyn elbowed him then took over the conversation. "My apologies for the misunderstanding. I'm aware that Ashglass is going through an ordeal. Lapses of memory are to be expected when circumstances are dire. I sent Wisdom Khalver a request to visit so we could discuss measures to solve the issue."

The guard adjusted his visor and looked to his men, who shrugged in response. Following that, he addressed the group.

"I'll get confirmation, but I don't think I've been briefed on it. Wait here, I'll be as quick as I can."

With that, the guard sprinted through Ashglass's gates as fast as his armour would allow, while the rest fiddled with their weapons from a safe distance. Erwyn muttered under his breath and Rarakhi trembled in the cold, likely recovering from the firearms pointed his way. Lady Kagura was still in the carriage, swaying and hugging herself.

Rakh took a deep breath, then opened the carriage door. "Lady Selenia?"

"Go away, you can't kill me, it's treason!" she yelled, then slackened her body. "Oh, it's you, Rakh. Why are they all attacking? I thought Erwyn sent a letter!"

"I thought so too," Rakh replied. "Come out, we can ask him together."

"Why would Erwyn lie?"

"I don't think he did," Rakh assured her. "Please calm down. Remember, you're Mor'kha Foenaxas's overlady. If you're this afraid, imagine how afraid she must be of you."

This seemed to perk her up, as she soon left the carriage with a puffed-up chest and put on a deep voice as she walked up to Erwyn.

"Wisdom Yagaska, how could you fail to inform the Foenaxases of our arrival?"

"I didn't," Erwyn muttered through gritted teeth. "I don't know what happened. I know Wisdom Khalver must be as busy as Melancholy, but surely he found the time to open his letters. By the Ghosts, it's half a wisdom's job!"

Lady Kag'nemera tapped her lip. "Perhaps he struggled to read your handwriting?"

Erwyn groaned. "I don't think that's it, my lady."

Rakh sidled over to Rarakhi. "Good job being brave, Rara."

"Don't patronise me," he snapped.

"As you wish. Are you still willing to stay at a commoner establishment?"

Rarakhi smirked. "Of course I am. You babysit that idiot elf while I find out what's *really* going on."

Razarkha and Tei's words came from the boy's mouth without either's influence. Rakh put his arm around his son's shoulders and patted him with his prosthetic hand.

"I know I failed you, but I'm glad you've grown to be so self-sufficient. Many in your position would have fallen into despair. You remind me of your mother in that respect."

"Let go of me," Rarakhi said with a squirm.

Rakh pulled away and averted his eyes. The boy probably wished death upon him, and he was right to do so. Count Fel'thuz let Ashglass's false snow fall upon him in silence, waiting for a Foenaxas representative to arrive.

After minutes masquerading as hours passed, a short man in maroon and gold robes rushed out of city gates. He puffed as he reached the Moonstone four, made to address them, then burst into a coughing fit. Even Lady Selenia knew not to speak until he was done, and once the hacking stopped, he spoke.

"By the Ghosts and every other god there is, I'm sorry," the diminutive man said, revealing his peculiar red-green, seerish eyes. "I received your letter, Wisdom Erwyn, but after consulting my third eye, I saw your lady crying and regretting her journey."

"So you sat on the letter and did nothing?" Erwyn yelled. "Your guards almost killed us!"

The seer held up his hands and backed away. "Now, now, Yagaska, let's not get heated, I thought your lady was likely to have her carriage turned around, that's all. It really is in your best interest to—"

"I shall assist Melancholy in combating the rapeworm epidemic," Erwyn stated. "Lady Selenia and Count Fel'thuz are here to share solidarity with the Foenaxas family."

"How did you know about Melan— oh, that doesn't matter," the Ashglass wisdom said. "I'll lead you to Lady

123

Mor'kha. She's currently giving a speech at the evening mass."

"Can I split off?" Rarakhi asked. "I'm Count Fel'thuz's bastard son, and your high lady probably doesn't want to see my sort. I'll just find a place in a safe district."

Khalver paused. "Actually, Mor'kha adores her two bastard cousins-once-removed. If you want to avoid the dull Renewalist mass, though, feel free to find lodging. Just be sure to obey the city guard. They're an invaluable resource in these trying times."

Despite the carnage behind Ashglass's walls, Rakh couldn't help but smirk. The so-called intellectual had just provided Rarakhi with an excuse, and of course, the boy seized upon it.

"Yeah, you're right," Rarakhi said with a shrug. "Guess you seer sorts really can look into the future."

Khalver chuckled. "Well, you don't need to be prescient to know children hate dull religious ceremonies. Come with me. You wouldn't mind pretending that this visit was a surprise, would you?"

Rakh opened his mouth, but Erwyn spoke first. "I would rather die."

"But if I—"

"You made a potentially deadly mistake, Veritas," Erwyn continued. "I will not feign incompetence to cover up yours."

The seer faltered, then evaded the critique altogether. Once through the gates, Rarakhi edged away from the group, and as Rakh watched him leave, the boy didn't look back once.

* * *

Razarkha was finally reinvented as Praetor Erre, and though she had no mirror, she knew that a black cape with purple inner lining suited her. Her chances of blending in

124

with Nortezians were non-existent, but with Lesteris backing her up, that was hardly a concern. Ariel floated in the corner, watching Razarkha lift a floor panel with the spellwork incantation *elevatio manuum.*

She kept her hand elevated, praying that her will was still being transmitted to the First Light. The panel held steady, so she made a sweeping gesture, flinging the panel in the exact opposite direction to her intent. It flew towards Ariel, who calmly caught it in a localised whirlwind.

"Almost, Erre," she said. *"Would you like to catch it as I did?"*

"I haven't started on aeromancy yet," Razarkha said. *"I could attempt a telekinetic grab. Go ahead, throw it back."*

The augmentee threw the panel, and Razarkha held out her hand.

"Nolite en aere!"

Though the incantation was declared, and magic flowed from her soulstealer to her body, the energies failed to reach the First Light in time. The panel smacked her in the chest and fell to the floor, shattering.

Razarkha stumbled, and Ariel floated over, her rocky hands covering her non-existent mouth. *"Erre, are you all right? Please don't tell Lesteris, he'll disincorporate me!"*

"It was my failure," Razarkha muttered. *"You did as I asked. My telekinesis still needs work."*

So far, her varieties of spellwork were limited to basic lumomancy, low-range geomancy, and poorly executed telekinesis. Mixing them with her natural illusionism was the only way they were remotely practical in battle.

"I'm glad you're uninjured," Ariel remarked.

Razarkha paused. *"You're much more talkative now."*

"My apologies."

"Don't apologise!" Razarkha said with a roll of her eyes. *"It's a good thing. You may never grow strong enough to strike against the weaklings who forced you into this predicament, but the fact you're speaking for its own sake means you're stronger than you were before."*

"But to be as strong as you, I need to fight my keepers, correct?"

"Yes," Razarkha said. *"Whenever I don't like a situation, I get angry. I scheme to take my vengeance no matter what. I reason I'm here is because I fought my tyrannical brother. We were forced to marry each other."*

"You had keepers too?"

"Yes, he was called 'Count Rani Fel'thuz'," Razarkha scoffed.

"I thought you said humanoids weren't domesticated in your homeland."

Razarkha stumbled over her Nortezian and clarified herself. *"It was a joke. Count Rani was my father, and he wanted to have a pure-blooded grandson."*

"Oh. Ha ha ha ha ha ha ha," Ariel stiffly blurted.

"What did I tell you about pretending to like things I say?"

"To not do it," Ariel said in a shameful tone.

"Lesteris will pay for what he's done to you," Razarkha promised.

As though summoned by name, a gold-and-white portal opened in the centre of the room, revealing Lesteris's lithe frame. He stepped out of his portal, wringing his hands and whipping his tail about.

"Hello again, Praetor Erre," the consigliere said. *"How is your training going?"*

"It's going—"

"Don't answer," Lesteris interrupted. *"Regardless of your progress, it's time to put it to use. Being partially trained will add to the illusion."*

Razarkha groaned. *"And this illusion is?"*

126

"That we're unaffiliated. I've checked what I can regarding the Sons of Sula, and as expected, they're restricted to the outer city. The inner city is too well-monitored for their tastes. In addition, I've traced magical transmissions from both Demidium and Nova Tertia. The Sons of Sula have a leader named Axas, and he's likely not in this city. Like most cowards, he's hiding far from the conflict."

"What do you propose I do about that?"

Lesteris smirked. *"Right to the point. I've located numerous Sons of Sula cells within Hextolis. I want you to exterminate them, and never fret; if you and your rabble fail, I have a personal elite squad who will clean up whatever mess you leave behind."*

Razarkha's eyes lit up. *"You want to deploy me? Does that mean you'll release Weil and the rest of my insurrectionists?"*

"Of course," Lesteris said. *"Once you're done, stand by the Membrane in the fourth-hour sector.* Without *destroying it. An associate will meet you and take you to your new residence within the citadel. I think you'll like it."*

"I'll only like it if my insurrectionists share it with me."

"I designed it with that in mind. Your little area is easily the size of your paltry Arkheran mansions. I even gave you a double bed, in case you become overwhelmed by my beauty. Don't blame yourself, it happens to a lot of women," Lesteris said, punctuating himself with a flick of his hair.

Razarkha grinned. *"Would you have a problem if Weil shared the bed with me?"*

The young man huffed. *"There's no accounting for taste."*

"Oh, come now, surely that will give you an idea or two," Razarkha replied, bringing her tail upwards so that she could stroke along its tip. *"Enough preamble. Tell me where*

these Sons of Sula cells are, then bring Weil to me. If you've harmed him, you'll have to watch me kiss him better."

Lesteris's smooth face creased. *"Of course, he's— yes, he's completely unharmed. Let's get you briefed."*

Exalted

Walls blurred as an elevating cell ascended through the Hextolis Citadel. Razarkha was flanked by Ariel and Lesteris, the latter of which regularly stared at her tail while his own whipped about. He'd failed to start conversations throughout the ascent, and was apparently insane enough to try again.

"Your Nortezian appears to have improved," he said. *"I'm glad you took my criticism to heart. The breeders have their eyes blotted out, but eventually they will come to see Old Galdusian as the antiquated, worthless relic it is."*

Razarkha didn't respond. She'd told him that until she saw Weil she was unwilling to entertain his soliloquys, yet his irritating voice was like a harmless fly beckoning to be swatted.

"I'm amazed at your resolve, Praetor. I believe we have a true connection. You were from that dirt-ridden, uneducated nothing that is Arkhera, while I was born in the Distal Outer City. Seventh-hour sector, if you're curious. It's a good thing a local librarian noticed my orderspeech or I would never have been elevated. I was granted concubines so my seed would spread to more breeders then granted a position as consigliere. Quite like your story, I imagine. What were you, some unwilling wife? Your former husband was no doubt half the man I am."

These words buzzed close to her ear. The young man's neck was so exquisitely exposed. Her hands could easily wrap around such a slender throat, and his face would be prettier stained blue. If there was any man Rakh exceeded, it was Lesteris.

"I see a fire in your eyes! What sparked it? Was it mentioning your husband? Ah, you're probably wondering how I knew you were married. It's quite simple. Your outfit

occasionally exposes your hips. They bear the stretches of pregnancy. How many children do you have—"

"If you don't stop talking, I'm going to strangle you to death," Razarkha snapped.

The consigliere ceased his prattling and Razarkha adjusted her cape. *"You're much more beautiful when your mouth is shut."*

Silence accompanied the trio for the rest of the ascent, and eventually, the floor stopped moving. An opening formed within the nearest wall, and Lesteris headed through it, gesturing for the others to follow. Before them were a set of cells, each with a transparent field, and she soon found her main concern. Weil was slumped against a wall, overgrown hair covering his eyes. Razarkha rushed towards him and spoke Isleborn.

"Weil, it's me! Can you hear me? If you can't I swear Lesteris will die in front of—"

"Razarkha!" the young man shouted, flinging himself onto his feet. *"It's been terrible in here, all they do is provide food and take away our— wait, did you get new clothes?"*

Razarkha couldn't help but smile. *"It's good to see you."*

Weil found the strength to return her warmth. *"I never stopped believing you'd find a way out. You overcame Elki Kasparov with nothing. This must have been trivial."*

"That's not quite the case," Razarkha said, gesturing behind her. *"I've made a deal with Consigliere Lesteris, but we'll still be fighting ascendants. For now, we serve him."*

Weil's admiration fled from his face, and Razarkha turned to Lesteris, shifting her tongue to Nortezian. *"What are you waiting for? Release my men."*

Lesteris chuckled and put his hands behind his back. *"Ask politely."*

"Please release my men, High Consigliere," Razarkha said in a flat tone.

"Better. You're much more beautiful when you're polite," Lesteris sneered, sauntering to a nearby wall.

While it started as the usual grey-blue, when he touched it, a glowing set of runes appeared. He touched the runes in a few places, swiped his hands, then, following a chime, raised his hand, deactivating the screens holding her men in. Sorelli staggered out first, her pyromancers and geomancers stirred awake, but Weil stayed within his cell. Razarkha decided to approach him instead.

"What's wrong, Weil?" she asked in Isleborn as she took his hands.

"I failed you," he said. *"I thought you'd fix my mistakes, but instead, you've surrendered the freedom of this movement, all because you trusted me."*

Razarkha suppressed a scowl. While he was correct to blame himself, the last thing she needed was a demotivated Weil. She may have augmented her repertoire with lumomancy, poor geomancy, and terrible telekinesis, but it wasn't enough to storm cells of organised Sulari supremacists. Weil's chaotic energy was a vital component of her revolution.

She glanced at Lesteris, whipped her tail a little, then whispered to her Isleborn devotee. *"I don't care about your mistakes, Weil. I've missed you too much to dwell on them."*

Before Weil could formulate a response, Razarkha ambushed his mouth, infiltrating it like a poorly controlled circus python. The messy experience came to an end after excessive fumbling, and while she needed a mint leaf to chew afterwards, it appeared to have the desired outcome.

"I'm glad I have you," Weil said, holding Razarkha tightly. *"If you weren't around, I think my father's death would have broken me."*

"I know," Razarkha falteringly replied. *"Thank you for believing in me."*

Lesteris harshly cleared his throat. *"When you two are done lovemaking, I have a briefing to assign. Once deployed, I don't want to see you until you're done."*

* * *

Rakh, Erwyn and Lady Kag walked through the empty streets of Ashglass, escorted by black-cloaked, dark elven guardsmen and the long-haired, short-statured Wisdom Khalver. The obsidian city walls had slipped from view, replaced by stone-and-wood terraces with the occasional Elarondian spire reserved for high-class establishments. Rarely, a peasant drifted through the streets, cloaks wrapped around them, but those who weren't guardsman had guilt written upon their faces. As they neared their destination, it became clear why.

Stretching from beyond the Renewalist Temple of Ashglass was a crowd of commoners, eagerly leaning towards the entrance. The building contrasted its Elarondian-Arkheran surroundings; it stood as a towering, tapering Madaki building of dun and black rocks with rangoli engraved into the walls. Two Foenaxas banners were draped around its entrance, which was barely larger than a double door.

"Quite the turnout given the epidemic," Erwyn remarked.

"Those who are infested are easy to spot and neutralise," Khalver said. "Mor'kha's speeches are more popular than ever. The people need hope in these dire times."

Erwyn frowned. "They need a cure."

Rakh intervened before Erwyn killed the seer. "Until a cure's found, I think giving the people hope is reasonable."

Erwyn tutted. "I suppose. Veritas, have your men separate the crowd."

"Allow me time," Khalver said, then clicked his fingers. "Soldiers, you know what to do."

The armoured men shrugged and grumbled amongst themselves before yelling at peasants while pointing their weapons. The mood shifted from pleasant to fearful in moments as the previously adulating commoners complied. Rakh briefly considered vanishing as the common folk rightly pointed their blameful eyes at him.

They walked through the steadily parting crowd until they were basked in the warm, crackling light of three hearths, positioned at the left, right, and back of the packed Renewalist Temple. There were Arkheran-styled pews, but no pulpit for the speaker, only the trust that the people would give her the space she needed. Mor'kha's speech was technically audible, but was nestled behind a layer of murmuring from her alleged listeners.

The guards settled for the back of the room, and Khalver shrugged. "I can't get you any further unless one of you has magic that could shrink every man in this room."

Lady Selenia folded her arms. "I'm the overlady of this province. I think you should put in extra effort."

"He's already terrified a group of peasants just to get us inside. Be quiet and wait for her speech to end," Rakh whispered back.

"What good does she even have to say?" Kagura muttered.

"Open your ears and you may find out."

Rakh used his height to his advantage and peered over the crowd. Gesticulating and orating was Lady Mor'kha Foenaxas, a doughy-faced, golden-eyed woman whose ashen grey hair stretched down to her ankles. Her features and body were distinctly masculine, especially within a black leather jerkin and cloak. Despite this, her tone was gentle and motherly.

"Know that all who have burned in this calamity will have a gentler life upon their reincarnation. The God of Renewal knew that karmic balance was not enough, and generously provided a recourse. For if every man's karma was fully accounted for, no men would remain; only innocent plants and animals. Death by fire was the recourse offered.

"While many of your loved ones have fallen to this wicked curse, know that saving their souls has always been my concern. We cannot save every vessel, but when that option is exhausted, when there is nothing that can be done to bring your loved ones back, know that their souls have drifted to a better life.

"Ashglass will recover from this. We are a resilient people. We've braved the cold, hostilities from north and south alike, sanctions against our God-given duties, and so much more, yet every time, we come out stronger for our struggle. Grieve for your loved ones; that is the beauty of a life well lived expressing itself. But against every impulse you have, hold onto your hope. For only in despair shall this pestilence have its victory. Otherwise, our triumph is assured. Fight against acedia, and you will surely win!"

The applause was initially sparse, but soon, the adulation gained momentum, growing into a true celebration as Mor'kha turned her back to them. She quivered as the roaring continued, and eventually faced them again.

"Thank you for braving the city streets to hear my words of encouragement," Mor'kha said, her yellow eyes shiny with tears. "Though God is my guide, you are my inspiration. I never cease to be amazed by your resilience. Cry, scream your grief, but never give up. My love goes to you all. Leave in peace, knowing that I share in your pain."

The people left the temple, some in tears, others with defiant hope, though all appeared to have a sincere love for their lady that Kagura simply didn't inspire. Eventually, the temple was empty enough that Mor'kha could be easily walked to.

Naturally, others had reached her long before her extra-city visitors. A set of five children, four boys and one girl, surrounded her, while a tricorn-wearing man with golden hair held his lady. To the side was a dark elf in light armour, with golden eyes and similar facial features to Mor'kha, his ashen hair tied in a top knot. When he spotted Khalver approaching with the Moonstone trio, he pointed to them half-heartedly.

"Mor'kha, I think the overlady's here."

Lady Foenaxas glanced over her husband's broad shoulder, and abruptly broke from his embrace. "Overlady Selenia, what a pleasant surprise! I didn't expect to see you here. My apologies, Ashglass is not in an ideal state, but it's nothing we can't push through."

Kagura turned her nose up. "You stopped exporting goods, so we investigated the cause, didn't we, Erwyn?"

Khalver stammered as his lady's eyes drifted towards him. "Lady Foenaxas, I know what you're going to say. I foresaw them learning about our issues, but I didn't expect them to visit! After all, if they knew of the rapeworm, why would they?"

"I sent you a letter," Erwyn stated.

Mor'kha maintained her glare. "Is this true?"

"Yes, but I foresaw Lady Kag'nemera panicking on the approach. I assumed she would turn back," the seerish wisdom said, crumbling from the eyes pinned on him. "Not that I think she was wrong to keep going, her visit is no doubt well-intentioned, I just didn't think you—"

"Enough, Khalver," Mor'kha commanded. "I'll review your salary in the coming weeks. Considering the situation, a pay cut is the best you can hope for."

The seer hung his head. "Of course, my lady."

Mor'kha looked to her family, then to Lady Selenia. "Why have you visited, despite knowing the danger?"

Rakh cleared his throat before Lady Selenia had a chance to answer incorrectly. "May I speak in my lady's stead?"

"Is there any reason why?" the armoured dark elf asked sharply.

"I simply believe I can explain it well," Rakh claimed. "We're here to offer our unwavering support during these hard times. We know of Melancholy's presence, and Wisdom Erwyn wishes to reunite with his mentor so he can work with her. With two brilliant minds working in tandem, a cure is sure to be forthcoming."

"And what about you two? No offence, but there's nothing an invisible snake and a home-breaker can provide us," the dark elf replied, stopping when Mor'kha raised her hand.

"Enough, Irikhos," Lady Foenaxas said. "I apologise for my brother's harsh words."

Kagura scratched her ear. "It's all right. I'm not sure what he means anyway. I'm not an invisible snake *or* a home-breaker."

"She knows what I mean," Irikhos snapped.

"Irikhos, *stop,*" Mor'kha commanded.

"I'm so confused. What did I do to you? If anything I helped you," Lady Kag said. "Don't you remember when my father made that silly betrothal? I put a stop to that and allowed you to remain a fun, free bachelor! Why would a dark elf want to marry a high elf?"

Irikhos clenched his gauntlet. "I'm leaving. If you let that halfwit into our castle, keep it as far from my room as possible."

With that, he stormed off, and Kagura put a finger on her lip. "You know, I'm afraid of spellbinders, but they aren't stupid. Why did he call you a halfwit, Count Fel'thuz?"

Rakh covered his face with his hand. Lady Mor'kha, meanwhile, bowed to her liege.

"My deepest apologies, Lady Kag'nemera. The guards will show you and Count Fel'thuz to the castle. Wisdom Erwyn, would you like to be escorted to Melancholy's tent?"

"By you, my lady?" Erwyn asked.

Mor'kha gave him a small smile. "I can hardly let you and Khalver be alone with each other. You've been ready to kill him this whole time!"

Erwyn nodded. "You're insightful, Lady Foenaxas. Please, lead the way."

* * *

A young man named Asmodius entered a dance hall, filled with blaring noise played by magitech speakers. He was in the coastal side of Hextolis, the Distal Outer City of the third-hour sector, the very eastern edge of the megalopolis. He arrived by ship two hours earlier, received his bland, Nortezian rations, then travelled to the designated spot.

The boy was Sulari, so Nortezian dance halls were something of a novelty. Breeders that would have ascended in Sula instead revelled around him, flailing their arms about in a mockery of artistry. Ballroom dancing was dead, murdered by the flashing lights and synthesised music of the Nortezian government-approved distraction.

His flowing Sulari clothes no doubt drew attention from the largely monotonous, kimono-clad Nortezians, but it didn't matter. Consigliere Vieri still held sway in the fifth city, so he couldn't be arrested simply for being Sulari. The Yukishiman hegemony wouldn't fully encroach on Sula's little sister while brave ascendants like Vieri stood for decency.

He pushed through the thrashing Nortezians until he reached the rightmost bar in the dance hall. Serving at it, as expected, was a black-haired necromancer with a blatantly extended tail and an eyepatch. He prepared a glass, then leaned over the counter.

"Please show your alcoholic beverage privilege pass before you are served," he stated in Nortezian.

"Axas has given me verbal permission to partake in all this dance hall has to offer," Asmodius responded in Sulari.

The necromancer opened the counter, speaking Sulari in turn. *"This way, friend."*

Asmodius's heart raced. This was it; he'd made it to the cells where the most difference could be made. Varus Kiraxas may have forgotten what serving Nortez meant, but the Sons of Sula hadn't. The necromancer took Asmodius into a back room, where numerous spellbinders, ascended and unascended, sat before a magitech projector on rows of marble benches. Asmodius sat next to the nearest pair of spellbinders, a dun-haired man in a gold-and-white Pentatum kimono, and the strangest woman he'd seen in his life.

Much like a Sulari spellbinder, her clothing was individualised, with a tall-collared cape covering her back while her front was barely covered by the silken dress upon her body. She struck him as neither Sulari nor Nortezian yet possessed an aura that distinctly reminded Asmodius of Nova Tertia. Specifically, she evoked the presence of Darvith, the great ascended conglomerate whose persistence kept Sula great even as Nortez languished.

"I haven't seen you at the Nova Tertia rallies, but you'd fit in there," Asmodius said falteringly. *"Your cape is magnificent."*

"Isn't it?" the woman replied in a dialect of Nortezian that resembled the old tongue. *"I worked hard on it, though admittedly I had an augmentee finish off bits and pieces."*

"Brave of you to own an augmentee in this Yukishiman-infested nightmare land," Asmodius replied. *"If you were to imply that spellbinders are superior to those short, tailless animals in public, I'm sure you would be slain on the spot."*

"It's terrible how the current regime endorses silly things like treating humans like they're individuals, isn't it?" she said.

"Absolutely. I'm glad to meet a Nortezian so passionate about the cause."

"I'm the most passionate woman you'll meet in your life," she claimed.

Before Asmodius could continue his discussion with the charming, if odd, woman, the magitech projector displayed an image, projecting a masked, hooded face and little else. The figure moved a little, then his speech echoed throughout the room.

"Welcome to the third-hour sector Hextolis cell of the Sons of Sula, friends. I am your leader, Axas, the man who could be any of the silent majority yearning for a time when Galdus was free to conduct its higher pursuits in peace. Interesting times have come upon us since our last meeting, so let us begin.

"Firstly, congratulations on a job well done regarding Hextolis. There are cells in almost every sector of the Outer City thanks to your hard work, but moving our ideology inwards will be difficult given the Nortezian administration's paranoid surveillance. The cowards fear the Yukishiman gun at their back, not noticing their former greatness prowling before them.

"Soon, Hextolis's breeders will agree with us or fear us, and from there, a new foothold can be acquired. Unfortunately, this comes with some harrowing news. Our former foothold, Pentatum, may be lost. It is reported that the agents who were to retrieve text-tablets from Consigliere Vieri never returned to their post, and my attempts to contact Vieri himself have yielded naught but silence. If he has been assassinated, then the worst has befallen Pentatum."

Asmodius's heart sank. Their protector had martyred himself for the cause, angering the Yukishimans enough that they resorted to assassination. The human brutes had betrayed their own claims of civilisation.

"What I mean by this is that the Yukishiman delegation has either enforced the installation of numerous Arcane Nullification Fields, or, the more terrifying yet likely option, is that a soulstealer wielder has found their way to Nortez."

The woman next to Asmodius covered her mouth, while a spellbinder near the front spoke to their leader.

"What do you mean, Great Axas? Why do you suspect a soulstealer has been used? There are only seven in the world, while the Yukishimans make ANF generators daily."

The projected man adjusted his mask, revealing a gloved hand. *"It is simple. If an ANF generator was in use, and that killed Vieri in Outer Pentatum or within his chamber at the Citadel, I wouldn't be able to transmit to either location. All magitech in the area would be disabled. However, I can transmit and receive information from both areas. The only ascendant-killers that don't disrupt magitech are the soulstealers."*

The group murmured, and Asmodius decided to add to the auditory undercurrent. He turned to his Nortezian neighbour and offered a platitude.

"It's frightening, isn't it? A soulstealer being used in this age."

The woman scoffed. *"It's a worthless relic on its own. Elki Kasparov of Ilazar had one, and he was murdered by some upstart. A soulstealer is only as good as its wielder."*

"Is that so? How can you be sure?"

"Galdusian culture persisted even after the Plague Emperor crushed it. If the soulstealers were a guaranteed path to annihilation, Sula wouldn't exist."

Asmodius laughed nervously. *"I suppose you're right. What's your name?"*

140

"*Erre,*" she whispered. "*Though don't tell the others that, they may get terrified.*"

"*Why is that? Why are you named after a rune?*"

"*Shush, Axas is about to speak again,*" the woman pointed out. "*Don't worry, you'll have some time to solve the enigma.*"

True to her words, Axas continued his address. "*Now that you're aware of a likely soulstealer wielder carrying out assassinations, we must be prepared for a third faction, beyond us and Yukishima's pets. We shall name this hypothetical enemy 'Erre', after the neo-folkloric figure some Pentatum breeders have taken as a symbol of resisting us.*"

Asmodius's heart thumped against his ribs, and he rushed to grab the woman beside him, only to fall right through her flickering image. From thin air, the woman's voice rasped.

"*Now!*"

The Pentatum man beside her opened a red-and-purple portal unlike any Asmodius had seen and slipped within it. Soon after, the rift ejected fleshy, octopoid tentacles that indiscriminately stabbed the Sons of Sula whose bodies were still flesh and bone. A tendril wrapped around Asmodius and constricted his ribcage, shortening his breath with every moment. The ascended members were thankfully unharmed, so he called to the room.

"*That caped woman! She's vanished, but she's Erre! She's the one you need to kill! Save yourselves, make this room inhospitable to fleshlings! Do it now!*"

The ascendants forms began to ripple before they could respond, and soon they were spiralling towards the middle of the room, their ascension stones clattering against the floor. As hope drained from Asmodius's breathless body, fleeting projections of the woman appeared, along with shadows of tall spellbinder men wielding planks of wood.

"No. Axas, are you still watching?" Asmodius croaked.

"I am, friend," the masked projection said solemnly. *"Your sacrifice is not in vain. You have proven that Erre is real."*

"For the glory of Galdus," Asmodius whimpered, before his chest gave way and his body crumpled.

Ravaged

Ashglass's peasants scrambled to head indoors, while Lady Mor'kha treaded through her city's grey snows with Erwyn and her guards in tow. While the terraces around them were intact, the glow Erwyn dreaded was closer than ever, its smoke plume dominating the evening sky. A clearly constructed-in-haste metallic blockade lay ahead them, choking the street's path.

Erwyn inhaled through his teeth as he processed the sheer number of guards manning the structure. "I presume all streets headed to this part of the city are similarly blocked?"

"A necessary precaution. Beyond lies the Realm of Hungry Ghosts made flesh," Mor'kha muttered. "So many have burnt within it. I know I appear disingenuous, voicing my regret despite giving my men orders and watching from afar."

"Anyone in your situation would be consumed by guilt, despite knowing what was necessary."

"Some of the soldiers who set the entertainment district aflame haven't returned to work. I sent others to conduct welfare checks, and some have— I cannot blame them for wanting to die," Mor'kha said. "Those who crumble under impossible pressure aren't weak."

"If it's any comfort, Lady Foenaxas, I believe you made the right decision. No matter how many you kill, it's always better than the alternative. Nobody wants Ashglass to be consumed by this vile parasite. Not even my fool of a lady."

Lady Foenaxas shook her head. "You shouldn't undermine her. Though she may frustrate you, she's who you swore to serve. I cannot claim to know Lady Selenia, but she doesn't seem malicious, simply pure. Untouched by the world's horrors and blind to life's struggles."

"That's an accurate conclusion, but her indifference to Ashglass's plight and the impending return of Razarkha—"

"This is about the warning Baron Oswyk sent? Now I understand why Lady Selenia is here," Mor'kha said. "It's to be expected that you'd act selfishly. It's the way of those yet to be enlightened by the truths of Renewalism. Razarkha has no reason to target us, yet you want my armies to assist in deflecting her. Am I mistaken?"

"You are our vassal."

Mor'kha bunched up in her cloak. "Let us hope your work with Melancholy produces a cure to rapeworm."

They reached the blockade, and the guards momentarily pointed their flintlocks before raising them to offer their lady a salute. Mor'kha returned the gesture, and they opened the way into the wasteland that was once the Ashglass entertainment district. The buildings were blackened husks. Several roofs were completely blasted apart, while some retained splayed pieces of stone and ashen planks. Far beyond the already-destroyed streets were flames still ongoing, and the soldiers occupying the mortal hell occasionally stopped marching to watch.

Soot-covered signs pointed to inns, taverns, music halls and shooting ranges, when legible at all. Cleaner signs painted in red marked the way to Melancholy's base of operations. Mor'kha and Erwyn moved through the revenant district until they reached a set of tents sitting within a notably intact street. Numerous spear-toting guards patrolled the area, with pairs occasionally rushing into a tent with cuffed people on a stretchers.

Mor'kha approached a guardsman. "Which tent is Melancholy in today?"

"I think she's in that one over there, milady," the guard responded, pointing to a nearby tent taking in stretcher after stretcher. "I know you don't need telling, but she'll probably get short with you. You know how she is, very particular about being interrupted."

"I think she'll make an exception for this one," Mor'kha said. "Introduce yourself, wisdom."

Erwyn offered a stiff bow. "I'm her former student, Erwyn Yagaska. If she's been complaining about lack of assistance, I'll be a welcome surprise."

The guard played with his visor. "If you're the one guest she'll be happy to see, I s'pose I can let you through. Just that tent over there."

"Thank you, Private... Arakhal, yes?" Mor'kha asked.

"Oh, you remembered me," the guard said with a small laugh.

"Of course. All volunteers for the curing effort are dear to me, even if I'm terrible with names," Mor'kha said. "Your speech about what duty meant to you touched my heart."

"Well, I— that's kind of you, my lady. Go on ahead."

Mor'kha moved on, her expression shifting from warm to miserable the moment her face was out of the guard's view. Erwyn considered asking her why, but it was redundant; the woman had myriad reasons to be pensive. They entered the relevant tent, and for the first time in three years, he beheld his mentor.

She'd barely changed despite her years of wandering, wearing a red and black smock that covered everything but her wrinkled face and bloodied arms. She covered her bunched-up blonde hair with a net, likely because she was operating on one of the many tied-down, nude patients in the tent.

"Ah, Lady Foenaxas, I see you're here to waste my time again," she said, her brown eyes trained on the phallus she was slicing.

"Not quite, Melancholy," Mor'kha said. "Look up, when you're ready."

145

She finished the cut, then applied a solution with a pipette. Following that, she tore her attention from her patient and noticed Erwyn. Her crow's feet creased, and she groaned.

"Trust you to go snooping through Ashglass's business," Melancholy said, then fanned her hand at Mor'kha. "Leave us, my lady. I'm glad you've brought Erwyn to me, but you must minimise your time amongst these patients. We wouldn't want you to get hurt."

"Of course," Mor'kha said, lowering her head before exiting the tent.

Melancholy waited for her to leave, then turned to Erwyn. "It's funny how nobles love to lord over commoners until the moment they're reliant on one. Then they're as deferential as they expect us to be. Well? Did you lose your tongue since I last saw you?"

"No, I didn't," Erwyn said, and walked over to her patient. "What is it you're doing? Isn't your normal procedure to penectomise and get it over with?"

"Not this time. There are so many infectees here. Realistically, Ashglass will need to incorporate members of the Ashpeaks' villages by force or save at least *some* of these people's reproductive capacity to have a functional population over the next few generations."

"So you're working on a cure. Has any progress been made?"

"I've managed to find a way to consistently relax their grippers for efficient extraction, but the solution produces too much collateral damage and the resulting genitalia are likely non-functional. Every time I fail, I revert to penectomies," she explained with a sigh. "At least I have an abundance of test subjects."

"Perhaps you're approaching this the wrong way," Erwyn said. "Removing the rapeworms may be the instinctive first option, but carriers exist, correct?"

146

Melancholy winced, squeezed her abdomen, then began pulling the stringy white worms from her patient. "Of course. I was lucky, however. I've met multiple carriers, but they're extremely rare. I've never met more than one case per epidemic. If I could compare my rapeworm infestation with a fellow carrier, that would be wonderful, but alas, I can hardly cut *myself* open—"

"You needn't," Erwyn said with a smile.

"As you wish. If we find a carrier, we can run comparative tests," she said, dumping worms into a nearby bucket. "For now, be a good novice and burn these wretched creatures."

* * *

Hildegard Swan's armoured car barely bumped as it drove through the overly smooth streets of Hextolis. Rowyn was in the back with a black-and-green-clad ascendant claiming to be the late Anya Kasparov, watching the city go by. Whatever Plutyn's idea of Old Galdus was, it wasn't killed by Arkheran culture. If anything, the Arkheran Isles had preserved the aesthetic, while hard-edged Galdusian progress murdered its father in its sleep.

Their car was part of a fleet, nestled within the centre, but that didn't stop Rowyn from noticing the fleshly citizens of Hextolis's third-hour sector gathering in distinct groups. Some held up the gold, white, and black of Sula, while others held dark banners with a smattering of red paint in the shape of a Common Tongue 'R'. Rowyn leaned towards the front passenger seat, where Hildegard sat.

"Can you see that, Imperial Engineer? A flag bearing a letter from the Common alphabet, not Galdusian runes. What in the world is that?"

Hildegard grinned. "Come now, Rowyn. Literacy may be a problem for the Arkheran underclass, but surely you know how to spell your own name."

Rowyn groaned. "I know it's a letter 'R', that's not what I'm asking. Why are Galdusian demonstrators holding up letters from the Common Tongue?"

"Think for more than five seconds and you'll figure it out."

After pausing for more than his allotted time, Rowyn pieced the clues together. "Your plant embedded itself."

"So it would appear," Hildegard said. "Apparently Razarkha has acquired a semi-legendary status in Pentatum, and in Hextolis she's known as 'Praetor Erre'."

"A fitting mockery of the Galdusian system," the wisp claiming to be Anya Kasparov remarked. *"I cannot think of a person less worthy of the honour praetors are associated with."*

"Be that as it may, she's become quite the weapon," Hilda said. "Anya and I have had a bet going that she would disobey me the moment it was convenient. However, I remain confident in my ability to break people."

"You haven't experienced the Razarkha I have."

"Relax, Anya. You barely interacted with her before she exterminated your family. She caught you by surprise, but that's her only boon without the soulstealer. Unlike you, I needn't fear that relic."

Anya turned to Rowyn, her eye-embers glittering. *"You will follow Razarkha more closely than either of us. Don't underestimate her as my grandfather did."*

"Of course," Rowyn said. "After hearing her brother rave about the threat she poses, I have a hefty serving of apprehension for this job."

"Apprehension? That's not a good sign. You won't leave the job half-done, I hope," Hildegard said. "You don't want to know what happens to people who disappoint me."

"Unless fleeing is necessary, I'll keep my eyes on her," Rowyn half-lied. "Diligence is a trait you can trust any Arkheran knight to possess."

Hilda chuckled. "Of course, in precious little brown-necker-land, everyone's honourable, and corruption is just a spectre of cynicism. You've been to Winter Harbour. You told me yourself that military force was required to end Baron Oswyk's corruption."

Rowyn wasn't about to let Hilda get the last word in, but a tremor so powerful it shook the car cut him off. He peered out of the window to see a tall building crumbling, with numerous pyromancers flying out of its upper levels. Meanwhile, geomancers surfed down the tumbling edifice on its shrapnel. As the building collapsed under its own weight, a massive daemonic tentacle punched out of its upper floors, wrapping around a pair of spellbinders. It proceeded to fling the pair while ascended troopers floated after them at a suspiciously leisurely pace.

"Ah, reliant on dearest Weil as always," Anya remarked. *"This is the threat Razarkha Fel'thuz represents. Not only does she have her soulstealer, but she has a stupid, immensely strong chaos-speaking brute on a leash."*

"Nothing threadtech can't solve, should she go rogue. Besides, if Weil is so stupid, why don't *you* have control over him?" Hilda asked with a smirk.

"I did. If only I leveraged it while I had the opportunity. Perhaps I could have staged an accident for my dear departed grandfather and led the Kasparov Family with something resembling ambition."

"There's no point ruminating over paths not taken," Rowyn said, then glanced at the glowing pile of rubble as they passed it. "So, that was the result of Razarkha's work? She doesn't appear to be *stabilising* Nortez."

Hilda shrugged. "Disinfecting Nortez of its clingy supremacist ideology can't be done peacefully. It was only one empress ago that we Soltelles outlawed slavery, and there were wars in the streets over such a reform. If that could happen to Yukishima, what choice does a backwards country like Nortez have?"

"If you insist," Rowyn said flatly.

Following the jolt of excitement the collapsing building represented, the remaining ride to Hextolis's Membrane was more of the same: Demonstrators for both Sula and 'Erre', numerous ruined buildings with an 'R' insignia painted upon them, and a monotonous feminine voice echoing in Nortezian.

They stopped at the towering redstone wall known as the Membrane, where a set of ascendants checked their cars for heavy-duty anti-arcane devices. While they found personal ANPs in one of the supply cars, they were quick to drop their aggression once Hildegard spoke to them. Eventually, they agreed to open the Membrane.

The process was a bizarre affair; an ascendant floated towards the barrier and cast what appeared to be advanced geomancy upon it. The wall sagged and flowed while glowing in every colour of the rainbow, then pushed itself up, forming a bizarre liquid-edged arch seemingly held up by sheer force of will on the geomantic ascendant's part. Once a wide enough opening was made, Hilda's fleet drove into the Inner City.

As the armoured car continued its journey, Rowyn's doubts about modern Galdus multiplied. What little personality the outer city expressed through minor architectural variance was erased by its inner-city equivalents. The streets were uniform in width and surrounded by evenly tall rows of towers so seamlessly neighbouring each other that they shared power veins.

Towering over the skyline was the citadel, a huge, blue-grey monstrosity with walls higher than the Plague Obelisk of the Arkhera's Great Lake. The central tower beyond was so high that it superseded the roiling clouds around it, as though stabbing the eye of a massive, unending storm. Rowyn took a deep breath as he let the sight set in.

"Grand Duke Kiraxas and Consigliere Lesteris live there, don't they?"

"How adorable, the Arkheran figured something out for himself," Hildegard cooed.

Rowyn rolled his eyes. "I don't know why I said anything."

"I'm similarly stumped. A mystery we'll carry to our graves."

"Think of it this way," Anya said. *"Though you'll have to stay in that grotesque citadel, at least you don't have to spend further time with the Imperial Engineer."*

"Always a positive," Rowyn remarked.

Hildegard put her hands behind her head. "If you're liked by everyone, you've never said anything meaningful."

The journey carried on, and though Rowyn hoped something would change between the Membrane and the citadel walls, the street was nothing but a dull straight line that went on for five excruciating hours of driving.

There was always a junction every five buildings, always a strange, magical core above the third building of each block, always capsules along the upper levels that contained ascendants. It was a shame 'Praetor Erre' hadn't hit this part of the city, because the scant landmarks were driving Rowyn mad.

Finally, they reached the citadel, dwarfed by its casing alone. Though nothing was different about the street save the huge wall at its end, when Rowyn left the armoured car, the winds were immediately palpable. Above them, clouds grumbled as a great black whorl, spitting rain at the ground. Hilda stayed in the car, while Anya floated out of the window.

"Why aren't you leaving? Isn't this where we meet Consigliere Lesteris?"

"Yes, but I can't enter his portals," she said. "It's a Yukishiman thing."

Rowyn raised an eyebrow. "And you're not going to meet him outside?"

"Why would I? Have you seen the sky?"

151

"Of course," Rowyn said with a frown. "Wait, why are *you* leaving, Anya? I thought you feared Razarkha."

"Oh, I do, but the Imperial Engineer has generously granted me an opportunity to play a little prank on her and Weil. Nothing deadly, just a minor jab between old associates. I'll return to Hilda soon enough."

"How do we meet this Lesteris fellow?" Rowyn asked.

"We wait," Hilda claimed from her dry, hard-roofed car.

After what felt like another hour of waiting in the rain, a gold-and-white portal opened in the wall, and from it stepped a long-haired, skinny spellbinder in what Arkherans would call Yookietown garb. He swaggered past the cars outside his citadel's walls and stopped in front of Rowyn and Anya.

"Let us see," he began in strongly accented Common. "This one is metallic despite being a necromancer, and this one is an ascendant with— oh my, what utterly primitive energies. Your soul-bonding to that stone is about a thousand years out of date, my dear!"

"It worked, did it not?" Anya replied in sharp Common, before saying an Isleborn curse that resembled the words 'sucker bill-rat'.

"Consigliere Lesteris, I presume?" Rowyn asked.

"Much politer than your ascended compatriot, I see. I am glad you're the one staying with me. One moment."

Lesteris moved past Rowyn and spoke to Hilda in whispers. He took hold of a strange device, muttered a few words of thanks, before heading back to the pair.

"Come with me. As for you, Rowyn Khanas of Arkhera, I shall teach you Nortezian. If you know Old Galdusian, it's an easy transition," he claimed. "I have a room set up for you within Praetor Erre's penthouse suite."

Rowyn followed the sauntering, long-tailed man to the portal. The consigliere entered, as did Anya, and Sir

Khanas glanced at the Imperial Engineer one last time. She blew Rowyn a sardonic kiss, and he returned a bite of the thumb before diving through the portal.

On the other side was a surprisingly homely complex, set out like an Arkheran manor, albeit one with grey walls that occasionally moved beneath the building's excessive black banners. There was a living room cluttered with unwashed plates and recently sat-upon cushions, and numerous bedrooms lay atop a flight of stairs. Lesteris led them up to a single room with blank walls and a window overlooking the entirety of Hextolis. He put his hands behind his back and beheld the megalopolis, grinning to himself.

"It's beautiful, is it not?"

"Hextolis? Well, it's certainly... uniform," Rowyn replied.

Lesteris laughed. "You mistake my meaning. It is beautiful for me, not you. I enjoy knowing that this is under my control, save any— how you say— quibbles from the duke."

"This is my room, then?"

"Of course. Feel free to customise it as you wish. Praetor Erre wasted no time customising her room!"

"May I see it?" Anya asked. *"I'm curious to know how the Praetor sleeps at night."*

Lesteris's face twisted into an odd expression Rowyn had spotted seerish investors wearing when they entered high-class cabaret clubs. "Yes, let's look at the Praetor's room while she's out. She shall never know of our intrusion."

"Actually, she will, because I have a gift for her."

"Oh? Please present it, so I may check its safety," Lesteris said.

Anya's cloak opened, and a book floated out of her cloudy form. Lesteris took it and blushed at the cover image. Rowyn looked over his shoulder and immediately understood why. It was a picture of a tall spellbinder woman with a crop whip riding upon the back of a spellbinder man on his hands and knees, blindfolded and gagged. Rowyn remembered Umbria's enjoyment of similar material, as well as the time she recommended some to Lord Verawyn's teenaged stepsister. He didn't know whether to laugh or shudder.

"*A gift in jest,*" Anya explained.

"It must be an Ilazari tradition," Lesteris dismissed. "Place it wherever you wish."

He walked them into a room with an unmade double bed with pillows on opposing ends. Stacks of smooth, rocky slabs were piled in one corner, and they had a similar window to Rowyn's own, covered with black curtains.

Upon a glowing wall panel lay crude drawings depicting a black-haired man watching a brown-haired man kissing a black-haired woman, then beneath it the same woman shooting a beam through the black-haired man. Below this was another picture, this time of the black-haired man's charred legs falling over due to lacking a torso, while the other people squat danced. Anya's wisp made an unusual noise before speaking.

"*I see her art style is as juvenile as her thought process. I don't envy whoever that man is. At least she plans on kissing dearest Weil. It's the least she could do given everything she's done to him.*"

Anya pulled the book from Lesteris's hands and placed it on the double bed, which forced a question from Rowyn's lips.

"If it's not a secret, what's the book about?"

"*The beautiful story of a young man who, following the assassination of his family, is looking for his place in the world. Then he gets taken in by a beautiful dominatrix. A dominatrix is—*"

"I know what a dominatrix is."

"*Very well. This dominatrix, unbeknownst to him, was the one who killed the boy's family, and she in turn*

154

doesn't know this meek boy is the last survivor of the family she murdered. When both learn the truth, the boy goes mad and— well, I needn't spoil the ending. You should learn Isleborn and borrow it once Weil is done with it."

Rowyn chuckled. "I'd rather not."

"Suit yourself," Anya said. *"I'm done here. Best of luck, Khanas. Enjoy living with your seventieth cousin twice removed!"*

"What is that supposed to mean—"

Without answering, Anya slipped out of the bedroom, and Lesteris put his hands on his hips.

"I should leave you to get comfortable. Praetor Erre will return once her mission is completed, then we can have you two properly introduced. For now, we mustn't be seen in her private abode; she is very precious about her time alone with that fat oaf of hers."

Uninformed

Time was unwilling to pass for Rowyn. He didn't have enough personal effects to decorate his new room, he couldn't read Anya's little gift due to linguistic ignorance, and even customising his armour was futile given the suite's drawing tools were exclusively panel-based.

He laid out his armour and started to clean each piece with his sleeves. The faintest aroma of Vi'kara's oils rubbed off from the fabric onto the green-tinted metal. Part of Rowyn wondered what Plutyn would do if he'd have stayed in Ilazar with such a lovely young woman.

Umbria would be targeted, most likely. Perhaps he would spend another decade simmering in resentment. It was never clear just how ruthless Plutyn truly was. Knowing him, it was a deliberately cultivated uncertainty. Still, it was in his best interest to continue his mission. If Razarkha's work in the outer city was any indication, she stood to threaten not only Moonstone, but Arkhera as a whole.

His thoughts were interrupted by a gold-and-white portal opening behind him. Rowyn half expected an entire crew to step out, but instead, it was Lesteris and a peculiar set of levitating stones, connected by the smallest storms he'd ever seen. In the former's hands was the device Hilda handed him, a cuboid with a switch, a button, and a dial, along with some sort of metallic horn.

"I hope I wasn't interrupting anything important," Lesteris said in a wry tone. "I almost forgot to provide you with this. I cannot claim to know the— how do you say— ins and outs of this device. It is abominable Yukishiman technology, after all."

Rowyn took it from him. "Who's that with you? They're certainly an odd-looking ascendant."

Lesteris burst into raucous laughter and wiped away the fit's resultant tears. "Forgive my levity, Rowyn Khanas, but that thing is not comparable to an ascendant. She is Ariel, an aeromantic human augmentee. I bought her from the Demidium Breeding Facility not long before the Yukishimans started their little campaign. Those humans wouldn't understand my keeping her, but— what is it you Arkherans say? What they do not know will not hurt them."

Rowyn frowned. "Was she was modified against her will?"

"Humans from the Demidium Breeding Facility are hardly capable of informed consent, but Ariel doesn't appear to suffer," Lesteris said, switching his tongue to Nortezian. *"You're happy as my servant, aren't you, Ariel?"*

"Every day serving you brings me joy."

"See? She's a treasure. Worth every norvite ingot transferred."

Rowyn shuddered and recalled his briefing. Hildegard claimed that Razarkha appeared to hate ascendants, and claimed that to get on her good side he'd have to feign a similar prejudice, but what was her opinion on slavery? Rakh spoke of her like a mad dog, but even dogs refused to eat their master's corpses.

"And you don't have any directions for this device?"

"I have some, but only paraphrasing that confusing Imperial Engineer," Lesteris said. "This switch activates it, the dial finds 'stations', as though I'm supposed to know what such things mean, and the button allows you to speak to one of these 'stations'."

Rowyn frowned. "It's as good an explanation as I'll get."

"Oh, while I'm here, there is good news! Praetor Erre and her friends are closing in on the desired meeting point. I shall bring her to you shortly. In the meantime…" Lesteris paused, then shifted to a much more confident Nortezian. *"Ariel, keep this Arkheran company. If I find out you've been tedious, I'll be most disappointed."*

"Of course, Consigliere."

157

Lesteris clicked his fingers and a portal opened beneath him, causing him to slip out of the room. Rowyn gazed at Ariel, then closed his eyes.

"My sincerest apologies," he said in Old Galdusian.

"What for?"

"I may not know the nuances of Nortezian, but he treats thee unacceptably."

"How do you know that? I didn't tell you how he disincorporates me," Ariel remarked.

"Disincorporating? If I assume correctly about such a practice, then he's a monster."

Ariel's echoes thawed in tone. *"It's good to know all Arkherans are as kind as Erre."*

Rowyn smiled, then switched his transponder on. Immediately, he was greeted by a crackling akin to the announcement systems on the *Celestia*. As per his vague instructions, he turned the dial. Aside from the occasional warble, the same crackling continued until, for reasons unknown to him, it suddenly spoke Yukishiman-accented Common.

"That's strange, we're picking up one extra transponder. It just appeared; one moment, triangulating... it's coming from within the Hextolis Citadel!"

Rowyn decided to test the button that supposedly allowed him to speak. When he pressed it, the fuzzy voices fell silent.

"This is Rowyn Khanas, I'm with the Imperial Engineer. I'm keeping an eye on the Erre movement?"

He released the button to hear the response, and true enough, it was appropriate.

"Well I'll be damned, that was fast! Ol' Hilda don't mess around, eh? You ain't playing with your transponder in front of that Erre girl, I hope."

"No, I'm not, though there's a human augmentee owned by Consigliere Lesteris with me. It seems he wanted to hide her from the Soltelle Empire," he said, eyeing the oblivious Ariel, who'd drifted towards his desk.

"You're joking. Lesteris, the one who's trying his hardest to be our pal? Wait 'til Empress Marya hears this, there are gonna be sanctions. *Thanks for the help, brown-necker, and remember to keep your transponder switched off and hidden when that R gal's watchin'!"*

"Thank you. What's your name, if I might ask?"

"Kenji, but call me Ken. You may speak to other operators depending on the time of day, so don't hook up next time and say 'hello, Ken'. Misuki would be quite upset to be called a man's name!"

"I didn't understand half of what you said, but thank you, Kenji. I'm going to deactivate this device now. Goodbye."

With trembling uncertainty, Rowyn flicked the device's switch then put it in his pocket, restoring the room's silence. He turned to his desk to see Ariel aeromantically juggling his armour pieces.

"What art thou doing?" he blurted in a terrible attempt at Nortezian.

"I'm picking up your appearance modifiers! It's impressive that despite being well over the usual age of ascension, you're already prepared to undergo the process now that you've reached Galdus. Would you like me to ask Lesteris for a high-quality ascension stone?"

"Nay, those aren't for my ascended form, 'tis light armour made to protect my body."

"What good is this armour at protecting flesh?" Ariel asked. *"Most magical attacks will kill regardless of the apparel a fleshly target wears."*

Rowyn folds his arms. *"In Arkhera, powerful mages art rare. We build armour that defendeth against blades and musket-balls, though with the advent of r— one moment, Old Galdusian fails me— with the advent of 'rifles', armour is becoming irrelevant even there."*

159

"If it is irrelevant here, why are you keeping it?" Ariel asked.

"Thou raiseth a fair point," Rowyn said. *"Wouldst thou like to modify thy appearance with it?"*

Ariel's redstone eyes glimmered. *"I'm allowed? Thank you, kind Arkheran man!"*

The augmentee levitated Rowyn's plates around herself, and she assembled them symmetrically, the only part in the right place was the helmet. Rowyn chuckled and sat back on his chair.

"I am glad thou art able to enjoy this time."

"You mustn't tell Lesteris. Praetor Erre is kind to me too, but Lesteris says I shouldn't let it go to my head."

"The more I learn of this Lesteris, the less I like him."

"A lot of people say that."

Rowyn swallowed. *"I suppose thou must return these pieces to my desk, lest the consigliere arrive and behold thee in such a state."*

"I suppose."

The former human detached the pieces from her body, sparks still dancing between them, and placed them on Rowyn's desk. Despite having no face to read, Rowyn still detected a distinctly miserable breeze coming from the woman.

"Worry not, thou shalt play with my armour again," he assured her.

"Thank you, kind Arkheran."

"My name is Rowyn."

"Then I shall refer to you as Rowyn."

Just after sparks stopped jolting between Rowyn's armour pieces, the stress-inducing golden portals of Lesteris opened, this time as an ensemble. They dumped six spellbinders into the room, one of which was the good consigliere.

160

It didn't take long to spot Razarkha amongst the remaining five; there were only two women, and only one had Rakh Fel'thuz's black hair. Despite their enmity, the sibling-spouses shared similar fashion choices, as while she wore a high-collared cape that flew in the face of Rakh's practical coat, her preferred colours were, just like her brother's, black and purple.

Her four compatriots comprised of a chubby-faced, brown-haired spellbinder with sad amber eyes, an overweight man in a long cloak whose hair appeared to be mostly receded, a white-haired pyromancer whose flames danced around her hands even in this peaceful situation, and a male spellbinder with shoulders broad enough to rival Rowyn's.

"Praetor Erre, I presume?" Rowyn asked.

"Oh, what's an alias between fellow Arkherans? Call me Razarkha," she said in northern-accented Common, playing with a strange contraption made of numerous gemstones. "Lesteris told me a fellow countryman would be joining me. What's your name?"

Lesteris flamboyantly gestured to Rowyn before he could get a word in. *"Praetor Erre, this gentleman is Rowy—"*

"I asked my fellow Arkheran, not you," she snapped in surprisingly confident Nortezian, then switched seamlessly to Common. "My apologies. The consigliere does a disservice to Nortez's reputation, but you'll be glad to know my cause has genuine sympathisers amidst the snakes. Your name?"

"Sir Rowyn Khanas."

Razarkha chuckled. "Oh, *Khanas,* is it? I discovered something interesting about our lineages during my stay in Ilazar, but you don't need to know about that."

"I have the Imperial Engineer's assurance that this fellow's intentions are genuine," Lesteris began, only for Razarkha to cut in once again.

"I'll be the judge of that," she said, and once again changed her tongue. "What inspired you come all the way to Nortez? It can't have been an easy journey, especially if the Yukishimans around Quattrus welcomed you as they welcomed me."

"They were quite understanding, though the brig was the initial option before the Imperial Engineer stepped in," Rowyn admitted.

Razarkha's eye twitched. "Isn't that fortunate? Still, quite the journey. What inspired you to go the distance?"

"Yukishiman traders in Jadeport talked of a woman fighting 'the good fight' in Galdus from the inside. They said she hoped to end ascendant hegemony, and I was inspired. Recently I quashed a trafficking ring in Winter Harbour, so believe me, I'm quite concerned with mankind's shared dignity."

This remark made Razarkha start talking in Isleborn to the brown-haired spellbinder boy, who spoke a more naturally accented Isleborn in return. After an extensive conversation that curiously left Lesteris irritated, she finally turned back to Rowyn.

"While you were that far north, did you speak to my dear brother, Rakh Fel'thuz?"

Rowyn forced a chuckle. "He believes you're a madwoman, but anyone fighting for the freedom of all should be commended."

"It's odd that you're so passionate about ending ascendant rule in Galdus," she remarked. "If I'm not mistaken, you work with an ascendant. Parthus, something like that?"

"Parthezad," Rowyn corrected. "I'm not here to see ascendants die. I simply prefer a Galdus, no, a *world,* where people like Ariel aren't subjected to slavery."

Lesteris's face reddened and he began to blabber in his mother tongue. *"Rowyn Khanas, you're under my* protection, so I would advise you keep such slander to yourself."

"Thou doth keep a slave. Mine words were not slander."

"Oh, using Old Galdusian as an approximation for Nortezian, I'm getting nostalgic!" Razarkha said, putting her arm around Rowyn. "Very well, Sir Khanas, you understand my goals. Provided you can serve the cause, you may follow me."

"I can assist in stabilising otherwise mortally wounded soldiers in battle," Rowyn explained. "If your mages can provide cover, I should increase your retention tenfold."

"It is a bloody affair, revolution. I accept your offer," Razarkha said, releasing him and dancing over to her friends, gesturing to each as she shifted to Nortezian. "Let me introduce you to our leadership. This Isleborn sweetheart is my best friend, Weil, our resident chaos-speaker who strikes fear into the hearts of our enemies. This is Librarian Sorelli, whose insights into Nortezian culture allow us to connect with the common breeder in ways Lesteris fails miserably at, this gentleman is Igneus, our geomantic coordinator, and finally, here is Adolita, perhaps not our most measured pyromancer, but certainly our most powerful!"

Rowyn bowed. "I am honoured to meet thee. May I meet some of the lower-ranked members? I make it a point to know who I'm healing."

"An interesting philosophy for a necromancer," Razarkha said, and took the hand of the boy apparently named Weil. "Stop staring at us, Consigliere. We can take it from here."

Lesteris folded his arms. "Apparently so. Ariel, with me."

"Yes, master," she said before being dragged with her owner through a portal.

Razarkha waited for it to disappear, then nodded to Rowyn. "He's a wretched creature, but don't worry. I've been contemplating... alternative solutions for acquiring establishment support from Nortez."

"I'm not surprised. Shall we?"

"Yes," Razarkha said. "It's good to see a fellow Arkheran who doesn't despise me."

"And it's good to see an Arkheran willing to change the world beyond our little kingdom," Rowyn returned with surprising sincerity.

*   *   *

Rakh stood beside Irikhos Foenaxas in Castle Foenaxas's games room, watching over Lady Mor'kha's five children and the adult child known as Kagura Selenia. The eldest, an ashen-and-gold-haired child named Morganix, was playing *Reversi* with Lady Selenia, and judging from her expression, he was winning.

The second and third oldest, Moryx and Lexana, were closely spectating, while the two youngest boys, Darkhal and Irigax, were busy playing *Chasms and Staircases,* a game determined by dice, not wits. Morganix placed a black counter at the edge the *Reversi* board, then flipped over numerous white counters to reveal their black undersides.

"A conversion of five. You're really fun to play against for a grown-up," Morganix said. "When me and my dad play, he always trounces me."

"Your father may be really good at this game but that's because he isn't a lord in his own right, so he has time to practise silly things like this!" she spluttered.

Morganix immediately raised his voice. "Now you take that back!"

"No! I'm your overlady, I'll say what I like!"

"Mum is my lady, I don't care about overladies or any of that stupid stuff!"

"Well I don't care about your stupid game!" Kag yelled, stamping towards Rakh in a huff. "Count Fel'thuz, put this child in his place!"

Rakh paused in the hopes that Lady Selenia would think for a moment. "By that, do you mean defeat a child at a board game?"

"Yes!"

Irikhos rolled his eyes. "God, you're pathetic."

Kagura's face reddened. "What did you just call me?"

"Pathetic," Irikhos reiterated. "My sister told me to watch over the children, I didn't expect you to be the one throwing the tantrums. Then again, what standards could I realistically hold you to?"

Rakh broke in. "Irikhos, remember what your sister said—"

"I remember. No needless antagonism of Lady Selenia. But if she starts shit with my nephew, she's going to hear some harsh words," Irikhos said, approaching Kagura with a glower. "You can handle that, can't you, *overlady?* A politician as prominent as you must constantly face criticism. Unless you're some figurehead blinkered like a Godforsaken mare."

"I'm not a mare!" Kagura sputtered. "I'm the most beautiful woman in the world!"

"Then become some artist's model and let someone *competent* rule the Forests of Winter," Irikhos said, backing her into a wall. "Imagine what this province would be like if Tor or Yar were around."

Morganix cheered. "Yeah! You tell that mean lady!"

Rakh strode to Irikhos and took him by the shoulder. "With all due respect, Sir Irikhos, you'll give my lady some space or—"

"Or what? You'll cast some illusions? Spare me your—"

Irikhos stopped his temptation of fate as Rakh tapped into one of the harder aspects of illusionism; drawing specifics from a target's mind that weren't merely giving solidity to preconceived images. He found images of fire, lizards, and shadowcats, which he quickly projected to shut the dark elven knight up.

"No! *No!* I know these aren't real, you're tricking me, but— *get away from them you fucking monsters!"*

Kag ran from the room, as did the children save Morganix. Rakh cast the final illusion; a shadowcat descending into the umbra of a nearby lantern, then leaping at Irikhos. The knight screamed, then fainted. After that, the count faced the eldest Foenaxas child and lowered his guard.

"I'm sorry, little Morganix."

The young elf punched Rakh in the stomach. "What did you do to Uncle Iri, you slit-nosed monster?"

Rakh took the hit, but when the boy tried again, he caught his fist in his hand. "Your uncle will wake up. I was afraid he'd hurt my lady. If somebody scared your mother so much she had her back against the wall, wouldn't you do everything you could to protect her?"

"My mum isn't a mean idiot!"

Rakh swallowed. "No matter how mean and idiotic someone is, they don't deserve to be physically threatened."

Flashes of Johansen's final anguished moments flickered through Rakh's mind. The monstrous Yukishiman's pleading eyes as Plutyn's goons kicked his sides and stamped on his head wavered before him. The crack of a wooden panel lingered in his ears, and momentarily, he saw Razarkha lying face-down on the floor.

Another punch from young Morganix brought Rakh back into the room, along with the boy's screaming. "Just wait until my mother hears about this! You'll be out of this city and away from us decent people!"

Rakh accepted each pathetic left-handed blow while maintaining his grip on Morganix's right fist. "Tell whoever you like. Your mother is reasonable, I'm sure her decision will be fair."

Morganix trembled. "That's not the— you're not supposed to be happy about that!"

"Who says I am? One lesson you learn as you get older is that accepting a situation and enjoying it are rarely the same thing."

"I'm not your son, snake, all you have is a bastard! Save your stupid lessons for him!" the boy said, breaking out of Rakh's grip, kicking him in the shin, and sprinting away.

Rakh sat on the floor besides the knight he'd rendered unconscious, covering his eyes and shaking his head. What was this farce? What would unity do against a monster able to kill anyone who came close to her? Ashglass had enough corpses on the pyre, and if they faced Razarkha with Moonstone's men, they'd have survived one horror only to fall to the next.

He looked to the furthest wall in the room and imagined Razarkha standing in front of him. He tried to cast an illusion of her, but the form couldn't stay consistent. She was his wife. His sister. Even when trying to kill him, she wasn't one of the world's Johansens. She was a confused, rampaging bulldog whose nature was to snarl and bite.

"There's no talking my way out of this, is there, Razzie?"

"You still call me Razzie, as though to provoke me. Are you even trying to make peace with me?" the amorphous Razarkha replied.

"I called you Razzie because it reminded me you were my sister. The girl I knew from the day I was born. I wanted things to be different, Raz, we both did."

"You were too weak to do what needed to be done. You can't stand around and promote peace when pacifism allowed me to rise," Razarkha said.

167

"I could have saved you from yourself. I could have comforted you when Razander died. I could have tried to understand you."

"But you didn't. Why advocate for unity when you don't know the first thing about it? Leave the matters of the mind to Tei and Erwyn. All you're good for is impotent righteous fury and alienating your son. You're not bad at losing hands too, now that I look."

Rakh's body became limp. "You're right. All my talk of setting differences aside is hypocritical when I never gave you a chance. I've never made peace with an enemy in a way that didn't involve unconditional surrender."

"Who the fuck are you talking to?" a masculine voice broke in, shattering Rakh's illusions and making him scramble to the side.

"By God, you're awake!" he exclaimed, facing a groggy-eyed Irikhos.

"Why'd you stay? Looks like everyone else is gone," the dark elf remarked. "Obviously not for my welfare given the shit you made me see."

Rakh bitterly laughed. "No, I was too busy giving myself terrible visions. I'm sorry I escalated the situation. I should have responded to your challenge with an argument, not... what I did."

"I wouldn't have listened anyway. Forgive my vulgarity, Count Fel'thuz, but I fucking despise your lady," Irikhos said, his voice fracturing from emotion.

"I know. It wasn't fair of me to expect you to share a room with her and not become aggressive," Rakh said. "If not for her, your son would likely be the heir to the Forests of Winter. I know as a second born it must be difficult. Lord Consort Solyx copes with his fancy hats, you cope by hating the person who stole your opportunity for relevance."

Irikhos scoffed. "You know nothing, snake."

"Then correct me," Rakh said.

This gave the dark elf pause, and his tone softened a few measures. "It's not about political power. Yeah, I was one of the first nobles in Arkhera to be passed over for his older sister. I don't care. Mor'kha deserves it. This isn't about politics. As far as I'm concerned, the House of Selenia can burn to the fucking ground. All I wanted was to marry Yar."

"You were genuinely fond of your betrothed? Unusual for our class," Rakh remarked.

"Yarawyn was everything my previously suggested betrothal, Cousin Elrax, wasn't. It's nothing against Elrax; she's a good woman, but she fears her own shadow. During discussions she was so quiet, too afraid to turn me down even though she clearly didn't want the marriage. I worry about Ellie, but that's 'sides the point. Yar was different. She looked ready to punch her father for treating her like a bargaining chip."

Rakh folded his arms. "She was certainly the most wilful of the Selenia sisters."

"Yarawyn the feisty, Torawyn the motherly, Kagura the stupid."

"If it's any comfort, Yarawyn appeared to like you too," Rakh said. "She resented Lord Nemeron for treating her as a possession but came to look forward to visiting Ashglass."

Tears slipped from Irikhos's eyes. "That doesn't make me feel better. Even now, I remember her challenging me to a duel. She lost, but I didn't expect the fight she put up. Then she gave me a kiss for defeating her honourably."

You'd have been a better couple than Razarkha and I."

Irikhos laughed. "That's like saying we'd be better for each other than matches and everflame. Sorry I provoked you. My quarrel isn't with you. Thanks to her own stupidity, Kag will probably be the last Selenia your family has to serve. She's still waiting on a brother so she can have some pure-blooded offspring, isn't she?"

"She is," Rakh wistfully replied.

"Once she's gone, the Fel'thuzes are probably going to take control. Then that legitimised bastard of yours, Rakhirara or whatever his name is, will be Overlord of the Forests of Winter. He and Morganix should be the ones making friends if you want a united province in the future."

"Perhaps," Rakh said. "Who knows what the future holds?"

"You wouldn't be such a bad overlord yourself," Irikhos remarked. "That's what would happen if Lady Kagura died, isn't it?"

Rakh paused. "I suppose so, but my ascension wouldn't go unchallenged. Baron Oswyk and Lady Gemfire would understandably suspect me of orchestrating my lady's demise."

"You're a tall snake with ridiculous hair, it's hardly the most trustworthy look," Irikhos said with a smirk. "I'd best find Mor'kha and explain the situation. Wouldn't want you to get wrongly charged with attempted murder given I know what Mor'kha does to killers."

"What do you mean by that?"

Irikhos walked out of the room, turning back briefly. "I wouldn't worry about that. You're not the one burning."

Compromised

Acrid smoke filled Rarakhi's nose as he slunk through Ashglass's ruined entertainment district. He'd spent days pondering how to sneak past the guards, and despite his ability to stay cloaked for extended periods, he'd only just found a way to clamber past its northern wall.

If Plutyn and Rakh had anything in common, it was a willingness to send him into dangerous situations. Eventually, Rakh would do the decent thing and die, allowing Rarakhi to live an easy life as a count. Until then, it was naught but hard work.

Soldiers gathered around various buildings, spraying oil through a flame and slinging an inferno at former businesses without hesitation. Occasionally, babbling, grunting people skulked through the shadows, only to reveal themselves too quickly and find a spear lodged within their skull. Some armoured dark elves sat amidst ashes of their making, clutching their helmets as they wept. Rarakhi moved deeper into the entertainment district, where fires had already ravaged the area. Though he hoped to find naught but ash and ghosts, scanning of the area revealed more silhouettes amidst the alleys.

He spotted the ruins of a restaurant, the crumbled walls containing a scorched set of worktops, some blackened, warped pans, and several charred tables. He ventured inside to find a frantically scratching high elven man searching up and down for something, frothing at the mouth while making ragged grunts. Rarakhi backed into a chair, only for it to collapse and trip him up.

"Oh *shit.*"

The high elf's head twisted towards the noise, and he screeched while stumbling towards Rarakhi. He struggled to get up as the rabid elf drew closer, allowing fear to play havoc with his illusionism. Numerous doubles were projected around the room, which only made the elf more frantic, diving into each false Rarakhi with all its might.

By the time Rara found his footing, the sound of blunt metal hitting the elf rang out. A yelp followed, then a thud. Rarakhi checked the site of the attack and found a young high elven woman breathing heavily as she stood over the man, a cast iron skillet in her hands.

Rarakhi smiled, even as he drew his knife. "Holy shit, there's people who ain't—"

"Stay away!"

"What are you talking about—"

"You're going to kill him, aren't you?" the woman asked, holding her pan in a surprisingly martial poise.

"Well, yeah. He's fallen to that rapeworm thing, there's no hope for him."

"You don't know that!" she spluttered. "I— I'm here, aren't I? I can keep him under control. If he ever gets too noisy, I can just hit him. I can leave food for him, I can keep him safe, I just need to make sure he's looking for me."

Rarakhi put his knife away. "Is he someone important to you?"

"My betrothed," she said with a wavering voice. "We were saving ourselves for marriage, but he just came for me. He pushed me down, grunting like a monster, and…"

Rarakhi realised she wasn't going to finish her sentence. "I dunno what to say. Sorry. I can't imagine what it's— wait, how long ago was this?"

"Days. He wasn't smiling like usual, his clothes were torn, there was blood on his face. He attacked my mother too; she went mad not long after. I wanted to keep track of them both, but now I've lost mother. Get away, before he wakes up. I've got to distract him again."

"He's not getting cured if he's chasing you, why don't you—"

"Let the soldiers take him? They'll kill anyone they can't hold down," the woman said, her eyes twitching. "I've seen them torch entire terraces. There's no mercy left in Ashglass. I'll do things my way, and you can steer clear!"

"You can't do this forever, you know that, right?" Rarakhi said moments before getting slapped.

"Yes I can! I'll do it for as long as Farawan stays like this! I can take his strange behaviour, I can keep others safe, just stay out of my affairs!"

Rarakhi made to say something else, only to cut himself off with a realisation. This woman got attacked the same time as her mother, yet she was here, talking and fighting while the mother was off being rabid somewhere else. She may have been mad for her betrothed, but this wasn't the same as rapeworm.

"Look, I think you might be onto something," Rarakhi said. "You didn't go mad while your betrothed and mother did, right? Maybe you're special. That's why you should leave your betrothed behind and come with me to—"

"I'm not leaving Farawan!"

The man began to stir, and the woman hit him on the head again.

Rarakhi shook his head. "Sorry, I'm not leaving you here. If you survived this, Erwyn and his mentor, Sadness or something, need to see you."

"What are you talking about?"

Rarakhi stammered. "I'm not from Ashglass, y'see, I came with this healer guy. He came 'cause his mentor's here. They're trying to cure this place of rapeworm, and—"

"No! I've seen the soldiers cut people down left and right. I've heard the screams of tavern drinkers as the guards burnt them without a second thought! Lady Foenaxas has revealed her true monstrousness!"

"How about we find them together? I have special powers that let me turn invisible, I can help you move unseen. We'll find the healers and you don't need to speak to any soldiers."

The woman stood and pointed her pan at Rarakhi. "And you won't kill Farawan?"

Rarakhi nodded. "I promise. I have a betrothed myself, and you're doing what I'd want Plutera to do if I fell to this."

She hoisted her betrothed over her back. "Very well, spellbinder. Hide us, and we'll search the district together."

He held his end of the bargain, and together, they left the ruined restaurant. Throughout their walk, they remained silent, taking in the shifting shadows and distant grunts from people yet to meet their demise. Soldiers hid in burnt-out corners, talking to each other or alone, staring at their flintlocks or daggers. Tattered Foenaxas banners flew from blackened poles and charred corpses lay by equally destroyed buildings.

At some point, the floor stopped being covered by ash and red, legible signs were seen amidst the wreckages, pointing towards a medical base of operations. Rarakhi's heart lifted, and he gestured to the remarkably persistent woman hauling her betrothed behind him.

"Look! Signs leading us to people who can help!"

The woman frowned. "This isn't a trick, is it? There's more soldiers here than ever."

Rarakhi's voice faltered. "Well, of course the medics are gonna be protected by soldiers, that can't be helped—"

"But they could shoot me and Farawan!"

Rarakhi took a deep breath. "We've come so far. We can't turn back now."

"We can!" the woman insisted. "We could slip back invisibly and stay hidden together forever! I'm good at finding food, we'll survive, I promise!"

"No," Rarakhi said in a stern voice. "I'll admit something to you, all right? I uscd to be a criminal. I know, I'm young, but I did some horrible stuff. Killed people, torched buildings, you name it. I have more reason than most to fear guards. But sometimes, to get further in life,, you've gotta face those scary guards. Erwyn's my friend, well, something like that. He won't have us killed. You've got to trust me."

The woman trembled. "What will they do to me?"

"If you've been attacked but aren't one of 'em, they'll want you alive for as long as possible," Rarakhi guessed. "My boss liked to experiment on folks too, and even with evil experimenters, they don't kill if it loses 'em a subject."

"That doesn't comfort me!" she snapped.

"Look, if you don't take this risk, you're just gonna wander around aimlessly until your betrothed kills you or he dies of exhaustion and you do something stupid. I'm not going to take you this close then let you go. I'm a wrong 'un, but I'm no monster."

The woman readjusted Farawan, then nodded. "I'm sorry. I was hiding from the truth. You're right, I'd be wandering forever."

"Save this for after Farawan's with a healer," Rarakhi said. "I'll be with you, I promise."

Together, the pair followed the signs, and eventually found a set of well-patrolled tents. Rarakhi spoke to the woman one last time before their reveal.

"What's your name?"

"Narina," she said.

"Prepare yourself, Narina. They won't be hostile once they know what's happening, just be ready for weapons pointing at you. I never get used to it."

"Thank you," she replied. "What's your name?"

"I'm Rarakhi," he said. "I s'pose I should put Fel'thuz at the end, but just call me Rara."

"If the guards attack us, I'm going to die blaming you, Rara," she said with sharpness.

"Can't be surprised. All right, I'm removing the cloak. You ready?"

"No, but don't wait for me."

Rarakhi dropped his illusionism, which inevitably made the guards jump into action. In moments, spears were pointed their way, backed up by muskets.

"How the fuck did you appear from nowhere? Who are you lot, and why are you this side of the entertainment district blockade?" one called.

"I'm Rarakhi Fel'thuz, and you'd best not harm me. My dad's a visiting nobleman," Rarakhi said in an unexpectedly assured tone.

"Shit, you're joking," the same soldier said, lowering his spear. "Who's that with you?"

"Narina, and her betrothed, Farawan. Farawan's got the rapeworm madness, but she— well, she got attacked by him, but she ain't mad," he hastily explained. "I think Erwyn'd like to see her, along with Misery or whoever his mentor is."

The rest of the soldiers followed the talkative one's lead, and a tall, broad-shouldered dark elf walked out from the back line. "You two, with me. Fair warning, though, the stuff going on in there's gruesome as all fuck. I'll carry the one with rapeworm."

Narina's eyes widened. *"No!* You're not going to kill him!"

"We ain't gonna, but I'll be honest, he won't be much good as a betrothed once Melancholy's done with him," the soldier admitted. "Please work with us, who knows when he could wake up."

Narina shook her head. "Not until you explain what you meant by him being no good!"

"From what I know Melancholy cuts off people's cocks to stop the madness. I'm sorry."

Narina teared up. "But he'll still be alive? He'll be his old self?"

"As close as he can be without a cock."

Narina laid her betrothed on the floor. "Thank you. I'm sorry for being hysterical."

176

"You're afraid, lass. We all are. I've had friends I've known for years driven to death over this. You're not alone."

Rarakhi watched them pick up Farawan, then walked with them towards a tent marked with a sign reading *'Surgery in Progress'*. Within was a set of unconscious bodies, along with Erwyn and an old human woman in red and black, each operating on their own patient.

"Oi, Melancholy, another patient for you," the guard said.

"When you get the chance, Erwyn, dose him with poppy milk and lay him down somewhere where there's space," the old woman said.

Erwyn finished a cut, then said, "At once, Melancholy—"

The wisdom interrupted himself when he noticed Rarakhi, and he dashed to the boy, almost embraced him, then stopped, likely because of his bloody gloves.

"Easy there, Erwyn, you ain't my dad, and even if you were, hugs ain't allowed," Rara said. "There's something important about this girl. Explain the situation, Narina."

Erwyn prepared a dosage of poppy milk while Narina spoke.

"I was attacked by my betrothed when he fell to this spreading madness, as was my mother. She went mad not long after, but I'm still here. It's been days, and I'm not like him."

Erwyn paused just shy of administering the poppy milk, and Melancholy spoke in his place. "A carrier, just like me."

"Exactly my thoughts," Erwyn replied, injecting Farawan. "Rarakhi, you've just stumbled upon a light in this darkness. Narina, would you be willing to undergo a few tests? If you are, then you could help us find a cure for everyone suffering from this horrific ailment."

Narina looked to her betrothed and shakily answered. "Anything to make this nightmare end."

Melancholy continued her operation. "I'm glad to hear it. Commoner women who survived rapeworm outbreaks are becoming quite involved in this kingdom's progress. I'd like to see the nobility keep up. All right, Erwyn, it's time to test your hypotheses."

Rarakhi raised his hand. "I was hoping I could stay and keep Narina company. She's a little afraid of guards after seeing 'em do scary shit."

Erwyn sighed. "Rarakhi, you've put yourself at more risk than I ever anticipated as part of this mission. I can't refuse your request. Putting himself at risk for others is one of your father's most admirable traits, and it's good to see you inheriting his better aspects."

"This ain't about being like my dad," Rarakhi said. "It's about what's right."

"I didn't mean to imply you were mimicking him," Erwyn said. "Stay here and keep Narina company. I'm sure with Plutera as your betrothed you're quite used to operations."

"Sadly, yeah."

*　*　*

The penthouse suite's guest room was abuzz with the chattering of Razarkha's followers. There had been losses along the way but seeing the fire in each new member's eyes made it all worth it. It was better to die fighting than as a subjugated, unquestioning slave.

While the lower revolutionaries took turns playing the bizarre chime-keyboard hybrid common to Nortez's dance halls and others flailed their arms semi-rhythmically, Razarkha rested against a wall with the Soulstealer of Craving for company. Rowyn Khanas was mingling with her men, and Weil was in their bedroom, resting after his intense bouts of chaos-speech.

The Plague Emperor would have been proud of her. There was no way he would have accepted Nortez's slip back into fetishizing immortality at the expense of those lucky enough to breed without complications. She was continuing his work, and for once, she wasn't infested with doubts.

"Are you satisfied, then?" the voice in the soulstealer asked.

"Satisfied is the wrong word," Razarkha replied. "I have purpose here, but I won't be satisfied until— until I— you're trying to trick me."

"I'm not. If you ask me, satisfaction is overrated."

"You, the Bold Individualist, consider satisfaction to be overrated?"

"Finding joy in the work one does is to be commended, but satisfaction is when that work stops. Contentedness is the end of strife, and existence without strife is meaningless."

Razarkha laughed to herself. "So, a content old man is as contemptible to you as an ascendant? I agree with you on many things, Bold Individualist, but not this. Satisfaction can arrive in small doses without killing drive."

"You misunderstand me. A content old man is satisfied, but their life is already over. By that point, it'll be years, if not months before their physical life ends. Satisfaction should be the work of a lifetime. If one ascends, what happens in those millennia of contentedness? Complacency, emptiness, death of ambition. A loaf of bread left unconsumed grows mouldy and is thus wasted, and a life drawn out excessively is similarly wasted."

"I suppose. If I catch myself feeling satisfied, should I expect a dagger at my back?"

"I wouldn't assume the opposite," the voice said with an odd, echoing chuckle. *"Then again, paranoia would prevent you from being satisfied regardless."*

"If I'm to make a difference, I should never be satisfied," she muttered. "I don't think I'll find a way to stop now that I've started."

"Get as much world-changing in as you can. Remember, your soul is going somewhere quite special when your body expires," the voice reminded.

"Will the souls I've captured inhabit the soulstealer with me if unconsumed?"

"Most of the souls within are already torn to shreds. Whatever scraps of soul that remain wouldn't be meaningful company, if that's what you're hoping for."

Razarkha closed her eyes. "No, this is the answer I wanted. I would like to be alone once I'm dead. Would perfectly intact souls remain active?"

"Until the next wielder dies, yes. Previous wielders are used to power the basic soul capturing process, and any spare energy is hardly going to be turned down."

Razarkha chuckled. "Thank goodness I'm such an eager consumer of souls."

"Your thirst for them is shocking even to me."

"Oh, you're too kind. Now, be quiet, I'm going to sleep."

"Of course, great and mighty mortal cribbing my technology."

Razarkha slipped out of the guest room and headed upstairs to her room. Weil, to her surprise, was still awake, reading a book with Isleborn writing upon the cover.

"What is that book?" Razarkha asked in Isleborn.

Weil lifted his eyes from it. *"Oh, I thought you ordered it as a gift. After all, I've always been curious about this kind of book."*

Razarkha took a better look at the cover, spotting a man on all fours being ridden like a horse by a dominatrix.

A familiar feeling washed over her, and she could almost hear the Bold Individualist's mocking laughter from the soulstealer.

"Why would I encourage your degenerate interests?" Razarkha finally responded.

"If you didn't request it, it must have been Lesteris, what with his odd concern about what we do in this bed."

Razarkha simmered in her cheeks' warmth. There was another possible culprit, but the notion was far-fetched. Kasparov was the Imperial Engineer's pet ghost. For her to have access to this penthouse would be a violation by the only protective force she had. At any rate, it would be one more mark against Lesteris.

"Of course it was," Razarkha stammered. *"One moment, I'm going to ask my fellow Arkheran if he can confirm as much."*

Weil laughed. *"If it's Lesteris, his efforts have backfired, because this book is really enjoyable."*

"Perhaps to you," Razarkha remarked, before slinking back to the guest room.

Rowyn Khanas was drinking Ilazari imported vodka with Adolita, notably staying away from the male revolutionaries. If he was anything like her brother, then she would need to exclude the knight before he impregnated half her mission-critical mages.

"It is as I say; if thy words cannot penetrate the monster's skull, then penetrate their vault secondly," Rowyn said in his clumsy Old Galdusian-Nortezian fusion.

"It's strange. In Nortez, there's such little emphasis breeders' possessions. With Praetor Erre's help, however, I've grown fond of keeping souvenirs of our battles. You should come to my room, I can show you the pieces of rubble I've saved," Adolita replied, then backed off once she saw Razarkha approaching. *"Your soldier is ready to serve, Praetor Erre."*

181

"Rest easy, Adolita. I wish to talk to my fellow Arkheran," Razarkha explained.

"I shall leave him to you," the white-haired pyromancer said, bowing and heading to some of her other friends.

Rowyn Khanas was surprisingly akin to Rakh in his looks, except he did further disservice to his hair and body; he'd cropped the former and sculpted the latter into a bulging abomination. Despite this, his smile met his eyes and he didn't look ready to hit her at the first possible convenience, so he was still better than her usual Arkheran company.

"What appears to be the problem, Razarkha?" Rowyn asked.

Razarkha raised an eyebrow. "Nothing gets past you, eh, Khanas? A form of necromantic telepathy?"

"No, you just looked worried," he replied with a shrug. "I saw you heading out. What brought you back?"

"Weil was reading a book," Razarkha began, then gestured when Khanas appeared to be lost. "No, no, this is significant, I assure you."

Rowyn's expression grew snide, then suddenly softened into concern. "Oh, it wouldn't happen to be an erotica, would it?"

"It is. Its title, translated, is *'The Blinkered Stallion'*. I've never understood that filth's appeal, yet it's appeared in our bed nonetheless. When you arrived at the citadel, did anybody accompany you?"

Rowyn's eyes shifted. "The Imperial Engineer allowed Anya Kasparov to play what I thought was a harmless—"

"Of course it was that Kasparov bitch!" Razarkha ranted, then realised her followers were staring, so shifted to Nortezian. *"Worry not, friends, a minor irritation. Khanas and I are still friends."*

"I'm sorry, is there something harmful about this book? It's just an erotica, Anya said she gave the gift in jest. Lesteris even checked it for traps."

Razarkha scoffed. "This isn't about the content of the book, erotica is simply her favourite genre. The point she's making is the book's mere presence. She's telling me that my operation isn't secure, that she can slip through the cracks when I'm not looking."

She stared at her soulstealer. The Bold Individualist was right. Paranoia robbed her of satisfaction, yet it was necessary to survive. Somehow, Anya knew that such a small act would ruin Razarkha's first happy night in forever. One day, when that Yukishiman wasn't around to protect her, Kasparov would be captured, then preserved so she could watch Razarkha kill the last dregs of her family.

"Are you all right?" Rowyn asked.

"Yes," Razarkha muttered. "Whatever you do, don't let Weil know that Anya Kasparov gave it to us. She killed his father, so he would go mad with rage. Currently, the success of our missions rely on Weil's state of mind, so he must be allowed to remain happy."

Rowyn shrugged. "If Weil enjoys the book, why ruin his fun?"

"Exactly," Razarkha stammered. "Thank you for your honesty, Khanas. I have a feeling you'll be indispensable to this revolution."

"Please, call me Rowyn."

Razarkha fanned with her hand. "You'll be addressed how I wish to address you."

"Of course."

"For now, enjoy the music, such as it is. I'm going to join Weil in bed."

Rowyn rubbed his chin. "Out of curiosity, are you two—"

"That's private," Razarkha said with a grin, before slipping into invisibility and running upstairs.

She snuck into her and Weil's room, changed into her bedclothes, then revealed herself to the still-reading chaos-speaker.

"What did the Arkheran knight say?"

Razarkha found the Isleborn words a mite slower than usual. *"It was a poorly-conceived gift from Lesteris after all. The fool is as incompetent as he is loathsome."*

"Indeed. I'm getting all kinds of ideas from this!" Weil said with a joy Razarkha couldn't help but protect. *"When we're ready, perhaps we could try some of the things these characters do. I think you'd like it."*

"Perhaps. For now, the mission is what matters," she said, getting into the bed so her feet were beside Weil's head. *"Are you prepared to subtract Lesteris from the equation? I'm losing faith in our Soltelle backers."*

Weil's tail writhed beneath the sheets. *"I've been ready for days. Tell me when, and I'll make it happen."*

"I knew I could count on you. Good night, Weil."

"Good night, Razarkha. I love you."

"I love you too," Razarkha replied in a manner as truthful as it was deceitful.

Maladapted

The sky of Hextolis's first-hour sector was alight with the attacks of hundreds of spellbinders. Razarkha Fel'thuz was clinging to Igneus as he rode a shard of skyscraper, sucking up every ascendant in the area while the Sons' fleshly soldiers scattered. Rowyn, meanwhile, scrambled to stabilise every spellbinder that fell from the arcane aerial shootout. Occasionally a piece of tower would crash onto people before he could even try, and even if he made it to them in time, the best he could do was guess probable failing organs at a glance before performing the much more pressing task of lugging them away from the fray.

Each revolutionary Rowyn hoisted was someone he'd drank with days ago. They each had their own idea of what 'new Nortez' meant, their own bugbears with what the Sons of Sula wished to restore, and somehow, they all believed Razarkha Fel'thuz, some Arkheran who wouldn't even tell them her true name, was the saviour they needed. He lifted a pyromancer whose leg was twisted by a short fall, then headed for his hideout for the injured.

"You're the Arkheran necromancer, aren't you? Thank you," she said softly.

Rowyn grunted and maintained his bridal carry. *"The thought is appreciated. My apologies, I am trying to—"*

A slab of red-veined rock landed in front of him, leaving an impact crater on the street floor. Rowyn froze, then rushed around it.

"I am sorry, Kazama, it is difficult to talk when destruction surrounds us."

The pyromancer breathed steadily. *"Are you stabilising any of my organs?"*

"I don't need to. Thou hath a broken leg, so don't attempt to walk."

185

"I couldn't even try, seeing the way it bends."

Rowyn swallowed. *"At least thou art taking it in good spirits."*

He made it to his nook, a spot between two long-since evacuated buildings, close enough to carry injured parties to but far enough that it was out of danger. Revolutionaries sat about, their energies resonating with Rowyn while he held control over their malfunctioning organs. Operating by the dim light of the surrounding walls was Sorelli, who fixed each injured soldier in the order Rowyn commanded.

"A grave fracture, Librarian Sorelli," Rowyn told him. *"No organs need to be stabilised, so if there are worse injuries brought in later, tend to them ahead of hers."*

Sorelli nodded. *"I won't keep you."*

Rowyn returned the gesture, then placed Kazama next to a fellow with a collapsed chest and a pronounced wheeze. From there, he ran back into the warzone, which was finally starting to calm down. Weil of Zemelnya was suspended by a tentacle, summoning portals from the sides of buildings and flinging Sons of Sula into others, mashing them into unrecognisable organic paste.

A Sulari pyromancer zipped between Weil's tentacles, then upon seeing Rowyn, darted away from the chaos-speaker. Instead, he soared above the medic, peppering the ground with fireballs that Rowyn barely dove away from. The knight was grounded, and when the pyromancer veered around to finish the job, he rushed to get up.

The effort was wasted. Before Rowyn got to his knees, the pyromancer was downed by a hastily formed portal and its tentacle, which acted as a trip hazard that knocked him off balance. He crashed into the ground next to Rowyn, and to the knight's horror, was still moving.

The pyromancer struggled to push himself up and gasped amidst the pooling blood beneath his chest. He attempted to conjure a fireball, then whimpered as it fizzled out. Rowyn collected his wits and stood over him, stabilising the man's lungs. Weil's transportation tentacle stretched over to the scene, unravelling next to the pair and allowing the chaos-speaker to stand on solid ground.

The young man folded his arms and emitted a hearty, laughter-filled Isleborn ramble, but Rowyn hadn't the faintest clue what it meant. Still, he tried to communicate with the Ilazari.

"Thank you."

"Oh. You do not understand my words?" Weil guessed.

"No, my apologies."

"I say only 'trus' kill medic," Weil explained. "'Trus' is word for chicken, but also means lesser man who flees."

"Ah, that's 'coward' in the Common Tongue," Rowyn said, scanning the area for more fallen soldiers in the relative quiet. "It appears the battle is over."

"Great victory for Razarkha! She is so beautiful when full of oblichenya."

Rowyn chuckled. "I'll take your word for it."

Adolita was next to join Weil and Rowyn, descending with controlled pyromantic bursts. She looked down on the grunting Son of Sula, kicked him in the side, then cheered.

"Behold! Igneus and Praetor Erre are on their way!" she declared in Nortezian, pointing to the one piece of building still in transit.

Upon it were Igneus and Razarkha, who collectively tore up the street on their approach before coming to an abrupt stop. The revolutionary's cape was ripped, but otherwise, she was disconcertingly untouched. She hopped off her ride then approached Rowyn.

"Well done, everyone," Razarkha said, raising her soulstealer in a mock toast. *"Another batch of Sulari idiots*

187

who think they can halt Nortezian progress eliminated. Why is this one still moving, Khanas?"

Rowyn hesitated. *"I am a field medic above all other duties, Praetor Erre. If an injured party can be saved, their affiliation doth not matter."*

Razarkha scoffed. *"Warfare is hardly known for breeding compassion. Let it die."*

"With respect, thou mistaketh pragmatism with compassion. How often hath Arkhera spiralled into civil war?"

"It feels as though it's one a century. What's your point?" Razarkha asked.

"My point is that almost every conflict was partially won by prisoners of war whose mouths were looser than their enemies'."

Razarkha smirked. *"Good point. All right, Khanas, take care of the wretch. I'll ask Lesteris for some suppression cuffs. Once he's fixed, we'll cuff him and ask questions."*

"Should I be present for the questioning?" Rowyn asked, though as Razarkha's face paint shifted, the answer became clear.

"You're proving yourself quickly, but don't consider yourself a trusted ally just yet. Weil and I are all the manpower needed to question an uncooperative witness."

Weil replied with incomprehensible foreign enthusiasm, and Rowyn exhaled. There was much to report to the Imperial Engineer but knowing there was more information he wasn't able to relay made the back of his neck itch.

* * *

"Ideally, we'd accept liquid assets and men to replace the miners we've lost so we can bolster efforts in the Ashpeaks. Of course, if you're willing to donate ilmenite, we won't need as many people mining obsidian, so it's up to you, Lady Selenia," Mor'kha Foenaxas said.

Overlady Kag'nemera stared through her vassal, having lost concentration ages ago. Instinctively, she detected a silence, and snapped out of her trance to fill the void.

"Yes, yes, of course, good idea!"

"Which course of action would you prefer?" Foenaxas asked.

"They're both good," Kagura bluffed, then turned to Count Fel'thuz.

The three politicians sat around a table, eating a bland rice gruel that Foenaxas no doubt considered herself holier for consuming. For some reason, Rakh forced himself to enjoy the breakfast, but Kagura had no such willpower. The count knocked his own forehead with his wooden hand, then spoke.

"It'd be best if we donate some ilmenite, given we're still recovering from the Church of Eternity's last attempt to extort us," Rakh suggested. "The less time spent mining, the quicker Ashglass can recover."

Kagura seized her opportunity. "It's such a good thing Sir Plutyn joined us when he did, he's made the Church compliant by exposing hard truths."

Lady Foenaxas's face curled upwards. "If it *can* be destroyed by the truth, it deserves to be destroyed by the truth. You shouldn't allow that false church to hold *any* sway if you know it to be corrupt."

"It's not so simple," Count Fel'thuz explained. "Many peasants are Eternalists despite the corruption of the Church itself. They deserve a place of worship, do they not?"

"Perhaps. In that case, waste no time negotiating. Rip the corruption out by the root, as though plucking a troublesome hair, then reform the organisation yourself," Mor'kha claimed. "There will always be pain in such matters, but it is necessary."

189

Count Fel'thuz made to babble some other platitude, but Kagura was the overlady, and she would not have her faith be slandered.

"You know nothing, you just believe that everyone was a slug and that we're all going to become slugs. Your temple is nothing like my church and so you wouldn't know the first thing about negotiating with its priests!" Kagura ranted.

"On that we can agree," Mor'kha said. "Your church and my temple couldn't be more different. So, you'll send us some ilmenite?"

Kagura's blood coursed into her cheeks. "Why should I when—"

"Of course we will," Count Fel'thuz interrupted, causing a sting to lance through Kagura's chest. "My apologies for Lady Selenia's hastiness. Her passion for Eternalism is as strong as your passion for Renewalism."

"Each faith's priorities are accurately reflected in us," Mor'kha stated.

"I'm an overlady, I ought to be listened to," Kagura mumbled. "Why do you keep talking over me?"

"Can we talk about this in private, my lady?" Fel'thuz asked.

"No! I want answers now! Why do you pretend to trust me when you obviously don't? Sir Irikhos called me pathetic, and you— you believe him, don't you?" she began, standing over her untouched bowl of gruel.

"I stood up for you then, my lady, but I won't allow you to jeopardise this alliance when Razarkha could return at any moment!" Rakh replied, looming taller than any elf.

"Razarkha, Razarkha, it's all about her to you! I don't like it here, and I don't like pretending to be friends with Lady Focnaxas!" Kagura shouted. "You all hate me, so I'm not talking to any of you. I'm going to my room."

With that, Kag'nemera strode out of the dining area, clinging her Wrenfall kimono while ignoring her hunger pains. If they didn't want her to starve, they'd feed her something good. Beyond Castle Foenaxas's simplistic dining room were winding halls with rangoli-engraved walls, a fusion of Elarondian civilisation and the sand culture Renewalists came from.

The castle had many lounges, but whenever Kag passed them, they were occupied by playing children, massive musical instruments, or rusted fishing equipment. This only served to remind Kagura that this wasn't her home, and that she was despised. When she made it to the first floor, a mixture of Ashglass commoner and northern nobleman made itself heard.

"You look like you're having a hard time," the man said. "Sorry about my role in that."

The word 'sorry' took Kagura by surprise, so she turned to confirm that yes, the voice belonged to Irikhos Foenaxas. She backed away from him, then remembered her status.

"Well, it's good you know you're in the wrong!" she said. "What do you want?"

Irikhos rested against a spiral pattern on the wall. "I think we started off rougher than we needed to. I shouldn't have brought up matters from all those years ago. I was just thinking that if Yarawyn managed to love you, perhaps I should show you that same love."

Kagura's entire body became warm as she stared at the dark elf's unsettling black skin. "What are you saying? Are you trying to earn my hand in marriage? Because that won't work! I'm better than our fathers, I know dark elves and high elves shouldn't get married!"

The dark elf groaned. "That's not what I meant, you— you misapprehend me, my lady."

"Then what do you mean? You can't blame the most beautiful woman in the world for assuming you want to marry her!"

"Of course," Irikhos said flatly. "What I meant is that if Yarawyn could have sisterly affection for you, I should be able to show you brotherly affection. That's why I've decided we should have dinner together, just the two of us. How does that sound?"

Kagura paused. "And this isn't going to be interpreted as us two courting?"

Irikhos laughed so forcefully that it resembled crying. "Come now, overlady. It's as you said, why in the world would *anyone* think that a high elf as beautiful as you would give a *lowly dark elf* like myself a chance? They'll recognise an inferior apologising to a superior when they see it."

The display eased the pain in Kagura's throat. "See, you understand! You and Yarawyn might have liked each other, and all races should be friends, but dark elves and high elves are different for a reason. Dark elves are only good for dark elves and high elves are only good for high elves. That's the way it should be. Otherwise, you end up with half-witted hybrids like Salekh Moonchild or that Sanguinas Isle bastard, the one who sings and sells her body."

"Ever so insightful," Irikhos said. "How about three days from now? I promise you won't have that terrible gruel Strakha insists we all eat. I appreciate what she's going for, but it's just misery atop misery if you ask me."

"I think we really did start wrong," Kagura replied. "I could like you a lot, Sir Irikhos. I accept your offer of platonic dinner without courting."

"I look forward to our time together," the dark elf said, a small smile on his face. "I'll give you your space, overlady. Thank you for hearing me out."

"It's what a gracious lady does," Kag'nemera said.

With that, she retreated to her room, giddy with a feeling she'd never experienced before.

* * *

Razarkha headed towards her penthouse's back room once her underlings were asleep, content in the knowledge that all injured parties were recovering thanks to the efforts of Rowyn Khanas. Accompanying her was Weil, who'd become overly peppy since starting the accursed book Kasparov left behind.

Perhaps it was unfamiliarity with what a happy Weil looked like, but Razarkha didn't trust his smile. His gait was too assured, his step too springy. The boy was supposed to be a creature of uncertainty, but Razarkha dreaded that she was replacing him in the role. Her soulstealer remained grafted to her hand, a permanent reminder that she would be Praetor Erre if she kept pretending to be her.

"It was a good battle today, wasn't it?" Weil said. *"Remember all those months ago when I thought I was killing pirates when shipwrecking those people? I had to deceive myself just to hide from my own strength. I don't feel that anymore. These Sons of Sula are truly deserving of their fates."*

"They're patriots to a nation that doesn't deserve patriots," Razarkha replied. *"Your sailors didn't fight back, but these people want you dead as much as you want them dead. Their morality has nothing to do with your satisfaction. It's knowing you're overpowering an opponent, not a victim. It's how all war should be."*

"What we're about to do isn't overpowering an opponent," Weil stated.

"No. This is a necessary evil, an old Arkheran tradition. Once upon a time, every noble house in Arkhera had a master torturer in their employ. The most recent attempt to revive the role was by Wisdom Yugen of Parakos, and if I'm correct that ended in misery. The key isn't to hire a torturer that enjoys their work, but one that takes it seriously."

"No smiles, then?"

"No smiles," Razarkha confirmed.

They made it to the back room, where a magical cell had been set up, courtesy of Lesteris. Within was the Son of Sula, his sewn-up chest exposed and his crooked tail as limp as his equally bent leg. His arms were cuffed by arcane suppressors that were functionally similar to Yukishiman ones, albeit with different inner workings.

"Dear Son of Sula," Razarkha said as she touched a wall panel, deactivating the cell's protective field. *"Do you have a name?"*

"None that you should know."

Razarkha shook her head. *"A discouraging answer."*

"Do his lips need loosening?" Weil asked in Isleborn.

"Not yet," she replied, then continued her Nortezian interrogation. *"I'm willing to negotiate with you but know that you shall be grateful for everything I give you. Your very life is in my hands. So, when I ask you for your name, your answer is…"*

"Lindros," he mumbled.

"That's correct," Razarkha said. *"I need to know how you got from Demidium to Hextolis. The first few cells I busted were from Nova Tertia, and that makes sense to me. Both Nova Tertia and Hextolis are on eastern coasts, there's no sailing around entire continents to take account of. But Demidium, west, oh-so-close to Jaranar, it doesn't make sense."*

"Why does that matter?" the Sulari man asked with a scoff.

"Because Lesteris, the consigliere, never informed us. Either he's ignorant or allowing it to happen and hiding information," Razarkha explained. *"According to him, he can track every time a gate is used in Hextolis, and no unusual activity has been detected. The old Demidium gates are deactivated according to Lesteris, and I had my men confirm as much. I want to know how you travelled from*

194

Demidium to Hextolis without using gates. I've got my own reasons for wanting to travel beneath the notice of Nortezian authorities."

"That's a shame, because I'm not betraying my city. Nova Tertia may fall, but Demidium can deactivate their gates and be shielded by miles upon miles of inhospitable wasteland," Lindros bragged. "Nothing you can do will make me—"

"Weil, loosen him," Razarkha commanded in Isleborn.

The boy opened a chaotic portal that unleashed a relatively small, hard tentacle that stabbed through Lindros's remaining functional leg, severing his calf from his thigh.

"Wrong answer, Lindros."

"My fucking leg!" the young man screamed.

"It's all right, when those clouds you worship think you're worthy, these injuries will be moot. Until then, you're going to come closer and closer to a death we will not grant you," Razarkha said. "Of course, we—"

"Razarkha, he's unconscious," Weil pointed out.

"You imbecile, you started with too much force," Razarkha snapped. "It's fine. I'll stay up all night if I have to. Once we have his route from Demidium worked out, we'll leave this accursed city and find ones in greater need of assistance."

Weil assumed a more comforting, withdrawn posture. "And we're still going to say our goodbyes to Lesteris?"

Razarkha lifted her hand and muttered to the piece of the First Light that could hear her. Lindros's cuffs momentarily unlatched, then with a similar muttering, closed again.

"Yes, Lesteris will receive his goodbye gift. Go to bed, Weil. Leave the rest of this interrogation to somebody who understands subtlety."

Weil swallowed, then backed out of the room.
"Goodnight, Razarkha."

"Don't stay up reading that stupid book."

"I won't," the boy lied.

Liberated

Razarkha drained another Son of Sula's soul to telekinetically shift a ball gag from a partially clothed Weil's mouth, allowing him to speak from his corner of the room.

"It'll be over soon. Are you ready?" she asked.

"If you're sure it will work," the boy responded.

Razarkha 'sipped' some more arcane energy. *"Of course it will. The man is more driven by his base desires than you. I'll put the gag back in once you're done with questions."*

Weil tugged at the arcane handcuffs holding his hands back. *"You've explained most of the plan, but I'm surprised Lesteris hasn't become suspicious with the amount of 'love equipment' you've requested."*

"He thinks we use it together. The thought enrages him despite its ludicrousness," Razarkha said.

Weil lowered his head. *"If you believe he won't figure it out, then I'm with you."*

Razarkha approached the subdued chaos-speaker and kissed his forehead. *"Thank you for doing this. We'll be free to move on soon enough."*

"I'm always with you."

Nothing else needed to be said. Razarkha gently put the gag in with her own hands, then checked their room's desk. She found a fruit knife, pressed its blade against her palm, then put it down. Thanks to Lindros's cooperation, their way to Demidium was finally clear. She left Weil behind and moved through the penthouse's halls towards a wall panel. She made the relevant sweeps and within moments, a portal the size of an extremely smug consigliere's head opened with a perfectly fitting object within.

"What do you need this time, Praetor Erre? You haven't killed another enforcer as collateral damage, have you?" Lesteris asked.

"I want to talk to you in private. I've prepared my room, and I'd like Ariel to accompany you," Razarkha replied.

Lesteris's eyes lit up, before he flattened his mouth. *"Are you propositioning the High Consigliere of Nortez?"*

"There's only one way to find out. Open that portal of yours, bring Ariel, and join me here. The underlings are busy downstairs, preparing a feast. I'm sure you'd enjoy it if you weren't such a Nortezian purist," Razarkha said with an uneven grin. *"If you're not interested, I understand. An Arkheran like me could prove more than troublesome."*

The portal quickly shut, and Razarkha didn't even get a chance to breathe before a larger one opened in its place. Lesteris exited with Ariel in tow, his buttoned shirt already open at the top. His breathing was ragged, and it didn't take long for him to lift Razarkha's cape and run his hand along her tail.

"Finally, you've seen reason," Lesteris said. *"Forgive my standoffishness, I couldn't let Duke Kiraxas see me as too eager to accept a proposition."*

Razarkha shrugged. *"Thanks to my recent conquests, I see myself as a hero. Surely a hero deserves a high-class lover like yourself."*

"Most certainly," Lesteris said with a grin.

Razarkha paused, then stamped on the floor twice, receiving a knock on the lower floor's ceiling in return.

"What was that?" Lesteris asked.

"What was what?"

"You clearly signalled to the people on the lower floor."

"I was letting my underlings know not to disturb us," Razarkha claimed. *"Come, every moment we waste is a moment not making love."*

Ariel stared at Razarkha, her winds howling in their own subdued way. *"I didn't think you'd make me watch this like Lesteris would. I don't understand."*

"She betrayed you, Ariel, it's as simple as that," Lesteris said with a laugh. *"Did you think that because she was foreign, she'd care about some rocks that* used *to be human?"*

Razarkha cast a minor illusion to keep her face straight to the consigliere, while mouthing the Nortezian for 'trust me' to Ariel. The augmentee responded with discretion.

"Of course, consigliere. I'm a stupid girl."

"You are. Let's not waste any time," Lesteris said, and with that, he rushed towards the man-sized web prepared for him.

Razarkha stalked after him along with Ariel, and as the trio entered her room, Weil struggled from his corner. Lesteris squealed with porcine joy, then sauntered to the gagged man, putting his hand beneath Weil's chin and forcing them to meet eyes.

"I've never heard you speak Nortezian. You won't express your despair in a language worthy of my time, but I'll feel it in your agonised tone," he gloated, flicking Weil's nose.

"Be careful not to finish before you start. Even my husband fulfilled that *part of his duty,"* Razarkha said as she shut the door.

Weil laughed as much as his gag allowed for, prompting Lesteris to slap him, then turn to Razarkha. *"I'm not some fat Ilazari boy. I've experienced numerous women, I know my way around them."*

"Prove it," Razarkha said, sipping some souls before putting her soulstealer down.

Lesteris's tone became commanding. *"Get on the bed, and Ariel, watch closely. Know that this is the saviour you admired willingly submitting to the* true *ruler of Nortez."*

Razarkha removed her cape and dress, then lay on the bed as commanded. Her mother oft told her that marital duties were about lying back and thinking of the future children she'd raise, but Rakh managed to at least make their miserable marriage bed somewhat variable. Sometimes he'd let her go on top, other times he'd have her lying down, but from the moment she saw Lesteris, she knew he'd be threatened by anything but a woman on her back.

"A beautiful foreign gem," Lesteris remarked as he undressed. *"I want you to look your Ilazari dog in the eyes and tell him how much more you enjoy me."*

"Earn it and perhaps I will," Razarkha said.

"I like you. Resistant," Lesteris replied, looming over her without a shred of clothing.

Razarkha murmured an incantation, slipping Weil's suppression cuffs open from afar. Before Lesteris could slip into her, she was already speaking Isleborn to her 'Ilazari dog'.

"Weil, now!"

A much more welcome fleshy tendril stretched over Razarkha, surging from a purple-red portal and wrapping itself around Lesteris. The consigliere sputtered and Razarkha sat up while the tentacle pushed him against a wall. She took his wrists and held them together, then telekinetically retrieved the cuffs and slipped them onto the nude orderspeaker.

"What is the meaning of this?" Lesteris screamed. *"Take those off immediately!"*

"Why in the world would I do that?" Razarkha said, removing Weil's gag to kiss him.

"Stop! Whatever your intent, it won't work! You'll have all of Nortez after you! Every enforcer, every officer, every ascendant under my command!"

Razarkha raised an eyebrow. *"I've proven quite good at killing those. It's the fleshly Sons of Sula that give me the most trouble. You said it yourself, I have a hard enough time not killing the enforcers as collateral damage. What would happen if I started in earnest? You wouldn't want to make an enemy of the most powerful fleshly woman in existence. I'd suggest not giving me the fuel."*

"Yukishima will hear of this!"

Razarkha moved to her desk, then nodded to Weil. *"Make sure his crotch is exposed."*

"Of course," Weil said, and his tentacle slipped upwards to reveal Razarkha's target.

The Soulstealer of Craving returned to Razarkha's left hand, while the fruit knife was in her right. Lesteris squirmed, causing Weil to shove him into the wall. Razarkha drew closer, then pressed the knife against his scrotum.

"I'd be careful if I were you," Razarkha said with a chuckle. *"One wrong move and you won't experience another breeder girl. What do you think, Ariel? Do you like it when Lesteris indulges himself with outer city women? Be honest. He can't hurt you anymore."*

Ariel paused. *"He's horrible. To the girls, to their men, to everyone. He's a mad stud who needs to be sterilised, like the unruly human men at the Demidium Breeding Facility."*

Lesteris's face reddened. *"Ariel! You traitor! You liar! When we're alone, I'm going to disincorporate you for an entire year! I'll—"*

Razarkha slid her blade against Lesteris's inner thigh, causing a small cut in his flesh. *"You're never going to be alone with Ariel again. If you want to preserve those puny things you call genitals, you're going to let me leave Hextolis, you're going to release Ariel, and you're going to spare your ascendants by not sending them after us. Am I clear?"*

"When Yukishima hears of this—"

Razarkha prodded one of Lesteris's testicles with the knife's point. *"Choose your next words carefully."*

"Yukishima won't hear a word, I promise! Take Ariel, she's a worthless, disloyal creature anyway! Leave this city and never bother me again! Just don't violate my body!"

Razarkha smirked and turned to Weil. *"You heard the serial rapist. He doesn't want his body to be violated."*

"Shall I release him?"

"Not yet. Keep him held up," she commanded, then switched her tongue to Nortezian. *"Good news, Lesteris! Your tools for violating others' bodies will not themselves be violated. Why would we stoop to your level?"*

Lesteris laughed desperately. *"Oh, you're— you're most certainly wise and merciful, very clever indeed, Praetor Erre. You outwitted me as a worthy opponent, then granted me clemency! Truly you have much to teach Galdus!"*

"Indeed. That's why I've saved an old Arkheran tradition for you. Come in, men!"

The bedroom door opened, revealing Rowyn Khanas and a group of cheering revolutionaries with rotten fruit in their hands. Weil shifted his tentacle to present the writhing consigliere to them, whose eyes were filling with tears.

"Khanas! You're not going to allow for this, are you?" Lesteris begged.

"My apologies, but I vowed to join Praetor Erre," Rowyn said with a shrug. *"I enjoy preparing fitting fates for people like thee."*

"No!"

Razarkha took Weil's hand, then left the room with he and Ariel. They stood aside as her followers pelted the naked consigliere with fruit after fruit, laughing at his nudity the entire time. He was free to tell the Yukishimans; where they were going, there were no Soltelle navies.

* * *

The *White Wendigo* was a hearth-heated bistro whose clientele were largely dark elves and humans, though the staff were generally high elven, with similar facial features. If Irikhos Foenaxas hoped to impress Lady Kagura, then he'd sorely misjudged her; the tables were wood, the people smelled of sweat, and none of them recognised her authority. The overlady's eyes danced over a particularly short-skirted waitress serving a rough, bearded human, then back to the Foenaxas sitting opposite her.

"Why are high elves serving other races?" Kagura asked.

Irikhos shrugged. "In Ashglass, there's more dark elves than high elves. The folks who own this place are high elven, though. That girl over there's the owner's eldest daughter."

"She's too beautiful to be serving fat, hairy humans," Kagura remarked.

"Provided they leave her a tip, she's happy enough," Irikhos said. "If somebody's happy with a situation, I say it's best not to meddle, wouldn't you?"

"It depends. What if they're in a situation like your betrothal?" Kagura asked. "You admitted that your match with Yar was silly, so even if you were happy, somebody had to stop it before you got stuck with horrible, useless hybrid children!"

Irikhos drummed his fingers on the table and said nothing. Lady Kagura cocked her head, then lost interest, shifting to a topic she hoped would loosen the dark elf's lips.

"Do you like art? My father loved art. He said that I was the prettiest model to ever pose for him."

Irikhos glanced at an armoured dark elf sitting at the bar before he answered. "I'm quite fond of impressionistic art. Portraits are good for the walls of a vain lord, but impressionism allows you to look through an *artist's* eyes, not what some commissioner wanted to look like."

"My father always said impressionism was pretentious and a waste of good oils," Kagura replied. "But my father was wrong about a lot of things. He wrote a lie before he died, which upset me because he promised me my brother would come."

Irikhos raised a hand and got the attention of a waitress. "Sorry, what in the world are you talking about?"

Kagura's throat stung. "He told me that my mother was on the moon after having Yarawyn. Because of that, I'd need to wait for him to join her to get a younger brother to marry me and become Lord Selenia."

"And what was this lie he wrote?"

"That I would only rule until Yarawyn came of age, then she would marry you and rule as overlady!" Kagura said with sharpness. "He promised *me* that I'd be married one day, that all I needed to do was remember him and one day I'd find love."

Irikhos silently gazed through Kag. She shifted under his golden gaze, checked her clothes for stains, then pondered over her next word. For a person who wanted to make peace, Irikhos wasn't welcoming in the slightest. She decided that Elarond would be a pleasant topic, given House Foenaxas's relations to Elarondian royalty, but a waitress spoke before she could.

"Oh, hello again, Sir Irikhos!" she said with a smile. "Is this one of your girls? She's very pretty. Hopefully you keep this one!"

Irikhos chuckled. "Oh no, this is my superior. Today you have the honour of serving Overlady Kag'nemera Selenia."

"You promised we wouldn't be mistaken as lovers," Kagura muttered.

"It's nothing, don't worry   "

"No! You commoners don't understand that sometimes politicians need to participate in *platonic* dinners with allies to forge diplomatic connections!" Kagura lectured to the waitress. "All you little people think about is carnal relations and sharing beds with strangers and spreading the common itch like thousands of Marissa Gemfires!"

"My sincerest apologies, Overlady Selenia!" the waitress stammered. "If I knew the situation I wouldn't have—"

Kagura wasn't about to let this waitress get away. "How could you possibly know the situation? Go, get me some capon with broccoli before I leave."

"Milady, we have no capon, but there is some pheasant stew with chestnut dumplings if you're after poultry—"

"You don't serve capon? Then why does Sir Foenaxas call this a restaurant? I could get better from my castle staff!" Kagura pointed out.

"You're not in your castle," Irikhos said through gritted teeth.

"Perhaps I should be! Since coming here, everything's been bad. I have to give you ilmenite, everyone's suffering, everybody worships the God of Renewal—"

"Enough," Irikhos said, standing up. "Perawyn, that's your name, isn't it?"

The waitress nodded.

"Get me an *Earthfyre* to drink outside and I'll pay extra to keep the glass. I'm not subjecting you to this anymore," Irikhos said. "Sorry for the trouble."

Perawyn rushed away, and Kagura stood. "What are you doing? Why talk over me? I'm your overlady!"

Irikhos lowered his voice and covered his mouth. "Because these commoners don't understand a refined lady such as yourself. Once she gets my drink, I'll take you to a shrine so we can talk in peace. We won't get to eat, but at least we won't be surrounded by commoners."

Kagura beamed. "You *do* understand! Now I see why Yarawyn loved you so much that she ignored what made sense for her children!"

Irikhos's face twisted in a way Kagura couldn't decipher, and Perawyn returned with a short glass of golden liquid. He dug in his pocket and handed her a single gold coin with King Landon's profile, making the waitress cock her head.

"Lady Selenia was never seen here," Irikhos stated, and the girl nodded.

With that, Irikhos nodded to the armoured man at the bar and led Lady Kagura into the smoky streets of Ashglass, leading her through an area with numerous abandoned stalls and shop fronts. As Irikhos took a sip from his *Earthfyre,* Kagura looked back to see the armoured man was following them. Irikhos's strides crunched against the snow, but no words filled the air, so Kagura dutifully provided some.

"Who is the man behind us?"

"Sir Almarax, a friend of mine. He's going to protect us on the way to the old Eternalist shrine; it's quite abandoned, after all. I wouldn't want you to get hurt," Irikhos explained.

"Oh. There are Eternalist churches here?" Kagura asked. "That's good, because I've been meaning to make a donation."

"There were never churches to Moonstone's degree, but there are shrines. Mor'kha strongly believes that Renewalism is the correct faith, but she's willing to make concessions for her husband," Irikhos said with a sad laugh. "He's handsome enough to get through to her in a way most can't."

"You're handsome too, and as her brother, surely you'd be more convincing to her," Kagura remarked. "Why didn't you marry her? Aren't you concerned about the purity of your family line?"

"I tried to marry a high elf."

Kagura chuckled. "You're so silly. Of course you don't care about purity. But you should. Perhaps as the world's most beautiful woman, I'll convince you I'm right one day."

"Perhaps."

The pair wandered into an even emptier street, close enough to the exclusion zone that peasants no longer clogged Kagura's vision with imperfection. Within it was a small building with the closed circle of the Eternalists atop its entrance. Kagura rushed towards the building, paltry as it was, then checked the interior.

There were no pews, no windows, simply an altar with a statue of Morunius, the trickster who swindled the angels out of their secrets, and a staircase leading downwards. Beside the alter was a pedestal with a dusty copy of the Eternal Word on it, which Kagura opened for old time's sake.

"For immortality is in the grasp of all who diligently prove themselves with good deeds, duty to their fellow faithful, and respect for the most hallowed light of the sky, the moon," she quoted at Irikhos as he entered with his quiet protector. "The Eternal Word's wisdom shines bright even in these dark times."

"You sure you want to do this?" the armoured man said in a gruff, lower class dialect.

"I tried, Al, you heard it all," Irikhos replied. "I hoped that we could have a conversation that didn't involve her horridness, but I was naïve. It's my fault for believing in people."

The commoner shrugged. "I dunno, Iri, prepping for if she didn't show a good side don't seem like believin' in people to me."

Irikhos folded his arms. "Perhaps you're right, Al. For now, stick with the plan."

"I hope you know what you're doin', Iri."

Lady Kagura scratched her head. "What are you two talking about? I think it's important to believe in people that matter, but there's a lot of people who don't matter."

Almarax wordlessly moved towards Kagura, who backed against the altar. "What's your knight doing? Irikhos, he's scaring me."

Sir Foenaxas rolled his eyes. "Lady Selenia, all you need to do is shut the fuck up. Go on, Al, knock her out."

Kag held her hands up. "Wait! Sir knight, Almarax, you don't have to do this—"

Almarax backhanded Kagura with a gauntlet-clad hand, and her vision blurred as she collapsed. As the room darkened, she heard the two knights talking.

"When I made my vows, I thought I'd be protectin' women, not smackin' them," Almarax said.

"You saw how she was behaving," Irikhos said. "Besides, she revealed she isn't the legitimate overlady of the Forests of Winter. Not every woman is an innocent victim. This one deserves everything that's coming to her."

"If that helps you sleep, mate. To me, she's an idiot tryin' to make sense of each day."

"Shut up and take her into the basement," Irikhos snapped.

Kag felt her limp body be lifted by metallic arms, and her consciousness waned.

*　*　*

After the effort of escaping his arcane cuffs and informing Duke Kiraxas of Razarkha's betrayal, Lesteris expected that his meeting with the Imperial Engineer would have at least been expedited. Instead, while Kiraxas was quick to tell him that Hildegard Swan was in Quattrus, once Lesteris gated to the appropriate citadel, he'd faced nothing but bureaucratic blockades. First, a standard Nortezian citadel security check, then an inspection by the disgusting, thread-infested humans that crawled throughout Quattrus, and finally, the highborn of the citadel had the nerve to send Lesteris to a waiting room.

It was at least well-situated, set upon Quattrus's fifth-highest floor, just beneath the clouds. From the wall-wide windows, all Quattrus and much of Galdus could be seen, but the most informative angle was west, over the Accursed Sea. Sprawling magical skyscrapers in perfectly aligned veins and tissues spread into a coastline that refused to adhere to Galdusian values, and beyond that lay the largest fleet Lesteris had seen in his life.

Each ship was a small, grey dot from his vantage point, but Lesteris was aboard the *Celestia* when the surrender of Nortez was negotiated; each ship was no trifle, yet hundreds if not thousands claimed Quattrus's waters. These monstrous fusions of metal and steam were the true threat to Galdus; it didn't matter which dog wielded them, only that they could render Galdus's glorious progress moot if provoked.

The Sulari failed to respect the Soltelle Empire as the juggernaut it was. The Sons of Sula labelled him a coward, Duke Weldum and Kiraxas collaborators, as though there were alternatives beyond annihilation. Ariel demonstrated humanity's true worth; if a human bred to be loyal and humble could betray a spellbinder, what would these Yukishimans do, emboldened by their vile golden parasite? Genocide would only be the start.

As dangerous as provoking the Soltelles was, confronting the Imperial Engineer was necessary. It was her decision to foist the Arkheran upon Nortez, and now said Arkheran was a rogue agent, with nothing stopping her from returning to Nortez once she drained Sula of every ascendant she deemed an acceptable target.

Red-hot anger coursed through his cheeks as the memory of Praetor Erre's ploy filled his mind. He should have seen the Arkheran tease for what she was. It was impossible for savages to understand attraction to a worthy man. She was incapable, deviant, drawn to slobs and chaos-speakers. Khanas's cooperation compounded the incompetence; the Yukishimans had proven to be fierce enemies yet worthless allies. Hildegard Swan would answer for it all.

An orderly portal opened in the waiting room, revealing an ascendant clad in crystalline armour that shaped sapphires, jades and opals into twists and horns about his gaseous form. Within his mists was a single jade that emitted fingers of light through his smoky form. Lesteris knelt appropriately, then addressed him.

"Eternal Duke Weldum, I am honoured to be in your presence," Lesteris said. *"Where is the Imperial Engineer of the Soltelles? I was told she was in this citadel."*

"She's several floors lower, admiring the view. She's ready to meet you and assures me that your misgivings will soon be non-existent."

Lesteris scoffed as he stood. *"Somehow I doubt that. She sent me a mad Arkheran dog."*

"I believe she will render your concerns moot," the ascended duke stated with a steady, echoing tone. *"Perhaps you should take my millennia of experience as confirmation."*

"It's unlikely my concerns could be assuaged by anything, but please, take me to see her."

The Eternal Duke opened a portal whose other side was a balcony with two human women looking over the Quattrus skyline. Lesteris crossed over, which prompted an unnervingly fast shutting of the portal.

Hildegard Swan was drinking wine with a red-haired, freckled woman who seemed grateful for her very presence. Both wore ballgowns, though the ginger woman added to her dress with a holster containing a Yukishiman pistol. Lesteris approached the balcony railings and rested his arms on top of them, looking over Quattrus next to the engineer.

"Well, Lesteris? I know your fragile ego has been wounded. Out with it, let me hear all your little grievances," Hildegard said.

"You're calm for someone whose 'secret weapon' has just gone rogue!" Lesteris ranted in the best Common he could muster. "She's no longer under my control, and has left for, as far as I know, Demidium! She was supposed to stay in Hextolis, deal with the Sons of Sula, stabilise the transition, yet now she's an unknown quantity! Your experiment *failed,* Imperial Engineer, and your so-called check and balance, this Rowyn fellow, failed as well!"

Hildegard tutted and shook her head. "Incorrect, consigliere. Rowyn behaved exactly as I'd hoped. He informed me of Erre's plans to humiliate you, leverage the situation, and escape from your control."

"And you didn't warn me? We are allies, are we not? We signed the terms of surrender just as your Admiral Lunscar demanded. What, exactly, does my suffering achieve?"

Hildegard glanced to her redheaded friend, then swilled her wine. "It's interesting that you bring up the terms of surrender, because I've been reviewing the stenographer's transcripts for that meeting. There was a clause regarding the release of augmentees, was there not?"

Lesteris's voice shook, yet he found the Common Tongue words. "Yes. All augmentees under Nortezian custody must be released to the free settlement of Liberium or given the option to join any Soltelle territory beyond the continent of Yukishima as a naturalised citizen."

"How does Ariel fit into that agreement?"

There wasn't enough time to come up with something convincing. Lesteris prepared an orderly portal, but the Imperial Engineer seized him by the arm, frightening the Rakh'norv into closing his way out.

"It's rude to abandon someone mid-conversation. Rowyn Khanas reported that an aeromantic augmentee

211

named Ariel was still under your employ. Erre plotted to free her, and it would appear she succeeded. Even as a rogue, she's much more loyal to the Yukishiman vision for Galdus than you ever were."

Lesteris tried to escape Hildegard's grip, only to notice her friend unholstering her pistol. Once the bizarre device's deadly muzzle rested against his head, words spilled from his mouth in his mother tongue.

"Think about what you're doing! I'm an advisor for the ruler of all Nortez! If you kill me, this alliance is ruined!"

"You truly are an idiot," Hildegard concluded. "Dukes Kiraxas and Weldum knew of my intentions. They're happy to lose the dead weight. Speaking of dead weight; Ana, make the metaphor literal."

The freckled woman squeezed the trigger, spraying Lesteris's brains beyond the edge of the balcony before slinging the rest of him into the glowing urban abyss below.

Trapped

The *Maresancti,* a commandeered Sons of Sula vessel, had sailed from the southernmost port of Hextolis's fourth-hour sector into the Sunrise Sea, then west to the narrow land between the continents of Nortez and Sula. True to Lindros's word, there was an ancient, disused canal in central Galdus, whose surrounding lush, luminous vegetation served as a reminder of what Galdusian megalopolises destroyed as they expanded.

They crossed it on their fifteenth day at sea and continued along the western coast of Sula. Urban remnants dotted the cliffsides, but for the most part, Galdus's southern continent was an overgrown, windswept forest of shifting trees and the occasional mushroom head the size of Castle Selenia. As the days continued to pass, the greenery vanished, and the straight, invariable skyline of a modern Galdusian city took its place.

Atop the *Maresancti*'s deck, Razarkha beheld the monstrous, glowing towers of what she hoped was Demidium. Within the ship's cabin were the rest of her revolutionaries. Shadows the size of flies drifted from the distant city's towers, and Razarkha turned to Lindros, who lay cuffed beside her, Weil, and Ariel.

"Look ahead, boy. Can you confirm that's Demidium?"

The Son of Sula peered, and for the first time in Razarkha's presence, smiled. *"That's the one. My home."*

"You're joyful for a man who's about to see his home razed," Razarkha remarked. *"If you've withheld any information, don't think I won't take your other leg."*

Lindros scoffed. *"What could you possibly threaten me with? We're all dead."*

Razarkha's eyes widened, and she turned to find that the shadows had grown. Weil pulled at her cape and muttered in Isleborn.

"I think we have ascendants."

"But how? We're using a Sons of Sula ship; they shouldn't recognise us!" Razarkha stammered, then yelled in Nortezian. *"All hands on deck, we have ascendants!"*

Lindros laughed caustically. *"You idiots. Did you honestly think the Sons of Sula would trust ships returning from the north after witnessing the madness in Hextolis? It doesn't matter how many ascendants you kill with your blasphemous device. With your feeble flesh, all we need is for this ship to sink."*

"Weil, throw this fool overboard! Ariel, ensure everyone is on deck!" Razarkha called in the appropriate recipients' languages, then rushed to stern to take to the ship's wheel.

Weil was quick to summon a tentacle that flung Lindros through one of the approaching clouds, utterly failing to slow it down. From there, he raised a set of daemonic tendrils just in time to shield the ship from a barrage of icicles. The insurrectionists rushed onto the deck, and Ariel floated to Razarkha with Rowyn by her side.

"What happens now, Erre?" the augmentee asked. *"If they know we're enemies, they'll send as many as they need. How close do you need to be to use your device?"*

Razarkha gripped the ship's rudder wheel. *"I'll ask the god in the soulstealer. Hopefully he replies with something more useful than riddles."*

Rowyn's eyes shifted. "Best of luck, Praetor Erre. I'm don't plan to die out here."

"Nobody does," Razarkha replied, then checked the Soulstealer of Craving as another volley of icicles impaled Weil's tentacles. "Is there any way you can extend the range of the soulstealer, Bold Individualist?"

"The creation of the seven soulstealers involved negotiation between multiple godly forces, all with conditions regarding their limitations. There are certain forces even I dare not tamper with. Do you think that leaves the soulstealers in an extensible state?"

"Kill yourself," Razarkha spat.

"Doing so would cause all manner of cosmic imbalance. You'd miss me if I vanished."

Razarkha's breathing grew ragged as resilience bled from her soul. Her hands were too shaky to hold the boat steady, and there was no way to harm the incorporeal warriors above them. There was no land for Igneus to surf upon, and Weil's defences grew weaker by the moment. It appeared that every time Razarkha boarded a boat, it was destined for destruction.

An idea rushed into her mind; there *was* a difference between this marine encounter and the last. As Weil's tentacles gave way and the ascendants drifted into an advantageous position, Razarkha charged across the *Maresancti*'s deck, screaming in Isleborn.

"Weil! Open a portal that will take us anywhere within the city before us!"

The boy staggered as Razarkha blundered into him. *"But last time I warped us—"*

"I don't care!" Razarkha said, gesturing to the cryomantic ascendants surrounding the boat. *"Anywhere is better than here."*

"Duly noted," Weil acknowledged, and began frantically speaking in Chaostongue while her underlings scattered.

A large portal opened, and Razarkha called to her men. *"Into the portal,* now! *We don't have time for— by the Gods, it's already coming!"*

An icicle barrage sliced through the air, accompanied by intermittent fireballs, and all Razarkha could do was dive into the portal, hoping others would join her. Black, shadowy tendrils undulated within the purple-red void as myriad eyes beheld Razarkha, producing noises that disgusted her on a primal level.

One by one, her men leapt into the Chaotic Realm, though Weil was notably absent. Razarkha watched the regular world erupt into splinters and flames beyond the portal, but when she attempted to swim back to the mortal plane, a tentacle slipped around her and prevented her escape. Rowyn Khanas and Ariel were flung through the entrance by a tentacle on the other side of the portal, before finally, Weil slipped into the portal, his top shredded and his chest pierced by a piece of ship. His voice was croaky, but comprehensible.

"I'm hurt, Razarkha."

Razarkha stammered. *"Just show us where we need to go, Rowyn will keep you steady."*

"At once, Praetor," Rowyn confirmed.

Weil's wheeze partially cleared up, the portal behind them closed, and he pointed to a floating piece of nasite, sucking the light out of the void like an inverse lighthouse. *"See that? That was once an heirloom in my house, I must have sucked it in here when I— anyway, past that, a portal shall open."*

The many-armed being took hold of the revolutionaries, one tentacle per person, and one by one flung them towards the nasite 'landmark', treating Razarkha with the random priority expected of a chaotic being. As the first revolutionary to be flung neared the nasite, a portal opened, revealing a redstone-lit room on the other side.

Razarkha's momentum was too much to cancel. Whether she liked it or not, her revolutionaries were once again at the mercy of Weil's blind idiot god. She slipped through the portal, and was swiftly reminded that unlike the Chaotic Realm, she was subject to falling in her own world, landing atop a soft object. She soon realised it was Sorelli, who shifted beneath her and opened his mouth, before Razarkha shushed him.

"Be quiet. We don't know where we are, so just—"

Razarkha was cut off by several other revolutionaries being ejected by the portal above her, forcing her to endure the weight of several supposed allies. Once the portal closed, the group spread themselves out, leaving Razarkha to check for each member's presence.

A warmth she didn't know existed flowed through her body; by some miracle, every revolutionary was accounted for, despite every previous operation claiming at least one. She found Weil amidst the crowd and attempted to embrace him before he put an arm out.

"I have a splinter in my chest, remember?"

"Of course," Razarkha said, then shifted her tongue to Nortezian. *"Sorelli, Rowyn, get to fixing Weil. As for the rest of you, remain quiet. I'll obscure our forms as much as my powers will allow, then we can figure out where we—"*

"I already know where we are," Ariel said, floating to one of the red-veined walls and tapping it, lighting the room up and revealing box after box of fungal rations, much like the ones given to breeders in Nortez. *"This is the food storage room for my birthplace!"*

Razarkha's chest tightened. *"Dim the room again so I can obscure us. You may be familiar with this place, but if any overseers spot us, we'll have to kill our way out. Stealth is our priority."*

Ariel did as commanded, and Rowyn glanced away from his patient. *"We're in the human farm Ariel's from, that's what she said, isn't it?"*

"I'm glad to know you're not deaf, Khanas," Razarkha snapped. *"Focus on Weil and don't make him scream. There are humans to rescue, and we can't do that if we're spotted early."*

* * *

217

Morning broke in Ashglass's medical camp, and Erwyn, despite the ugly operations he'd conducted, woke up with a full night's rest. Somehow, his mind suppressed each bloody gouge, each white, stringy soup of maddening worms, each wince from Narina as he took his samples. While he didn't remember his dreams, he knew they were more pleasant than reality.

Melancholy was snoring beside him, while Rarakhi slept sitting upright with Narina resting on his lap, and all four barely had bedding between them. Erwyn approached a table with racks containing vials labelled with the name of a bodily fluid, along with a suffix of '*M*', '*N*', or '*C*'. The former two indicated which carrier the sample came from, while '*C*' stood for 'control', indicating the sample came from a typical patient, mad and frothing.

Erwyn had already fruitlessly analysed their blood, bile, saliva, and lymph. The goal was to find something innate that Melancholy and Narina shared, but the control did not, but so far, nothing was forthcoming. Few options remained; the next course of action was a three-way simultaneous operation.

He walked away from the desk and approached his snoozing mentor, tapping her on the shoulder. The old lady grumbled from her slumber, opened her eyes, and seamlessly began her usual ranting.

"For pity's sake, Erwyn, you act as though I'm half my age," she snapped. "I need more sleep with each passing day, yet you see fit to deny me? There'd best be a breakthrough, or I'm stealing another couple of hours."

"I wouldn't worry about sleep," Erwyn remarked. "The sheer *lack* of a breakthrough is why we're out of options."

Melancholy sighed. "You're going to operate on us both. Render that poor girl infertile despite our promises."

Erwyn put his monocle on. "Not yet. We need to compare at least *one* rapeworm from each colony; yours, Narina's, and her betrothed— Farawan, I believe?"

"Until he's cured, names won't particularly matter to him," Melancholy remarked. "If you think you can non-destructively take a specimen from our bodies, very well. There's one concern I've had throughout this."

Erwyn sat on the floor, next to his mentor. "What is it?"

"Your arrival has been convenient. *Too* convenient. Have you been in contact with anyone from Deathsport?" Melancholy asked.

"Yes, but I don't fully understand," Erwyn admitted. "Tei briefly visited Moonstone, then vanished from our lives again."

Melancholy chuckled. "You're terrible at feigning ignorance, so thankfully this is true dim-wittedness on your part. King Landon stripped me of my title for more than my experiments, and I think that while he couldn't *officially* execute me, he wouldn't be blamed for having me quietly assassinated."

"You're referring to Dana Shearwater, aren't you?"

"She was miserable. Landon wasn't there for her, and she knew I had access to poisons. All I did was acquiesce her requests. I may have known her intentions, but I'm a healer of the body. I'm uniquely unqualified to heal souls."

Erwyn frowned. "I don't think I'd have done what you did. Respecting somebody's desire for death is one matter, but I believe people like that should have a chance to soberly evaluate their decision."

"Perhaps," she said. "My fear was that you'd use this operation as an excuse to off me. Collect a little royal payment."

"You think I'd kill someone entrusting me to heal them?"

"A shrewd wisdom needs to, once or twice in their career."

Erwyn shook his head. "I don't believe that. Life as a vagabond has changed you, Melancholy."

"I prefer to see it as having brought my truest self out," she said as she stood. "We have no time to waste. Let's gather the necessary bodies and compare some worms."

The next couple of hours were spent sedating Farawan in the surgical tent, applying the same poppy milk to Narina and Melancholy, and cleaning the necessary scalpels. Once the preparations were made, three nude people lay before Erwyn, two carriers and one haggard symptomatic case whose genitalia, even in his sleep, remained engorged.

Rarakhi stood by Erwyn and folded his arms. "You need your space?"

"Watch if you wish. If you can, find your father and let him know that under no circumstances must I be disturbed—"

As though summoned by his words, Rakh Fel'thuz charged into the tent, accompanied by a plethora of Ashglass guards and Lady Foenaxas herself. Both were distraught, and all Erwyn could do was hold his scalpel steady as he turned to them.

"What is the meaning of this?" Erwyn asked. "I'm about to start operating."

Rakh found his words quicker than Mor'kha. "It's Lady Selenia. She and Irikhos went out for a dinner and the night's gone by. They haven't returned to Castle Foenaxas."

Spikes of anxiety spread through Erwyn's chest. "This is— why in the world did you trust Lady Selenia to go out on her own? You know she's practically a child!"

Rakh's tone grew defensive. "Irikhos was with her, and we've been getting on well recently. He was talking about reaching out to Kag!"

220

Mor'kha burst into tears. "Irikhos was so admirable. He saw the good in me even when father betrayed his place in the succession, and he's gone missing seeing the good in someone like Lady Selenia. He could be *anywhere* in this accursed city. Why, God? Why did you see fit to curse Ashglass? To curse *me?* Did I not sufficiently grieve with the city? Did I need a personal loss to grant the perspective I lacked? You should have taken me. Irikhos is—"

"This helps nothing," Erwyn snapped. "I'm worried beyond belief, but I don't have time to help you find them. I'm working on a cure that could save hundreds, perhaps thousands. The needs of the many outweigh the needs of the privileged few."

Rakh's face filled with horror. "Lady Selenia sees you as a father. You're not suggesting we leave her to—"

"His place is here, you dumb fucking adult," Rarakhi said. "D'you think Plutera contributes to the family effort by going out and squashing fools? No, she does what she's good at an' fixes the guys who got hurt squashing fools. Erwyn's a fixer, not a finder. I found Narina, though, an' if I recall correctly, you're not so bad in the field either, dad."

Rakh breathed in as Mor'kha wept on her knees. He rubbed his remaining fingers together, then spoke quietly. "You're right, Rara. Would you like to help me find them?"

"Sorry, dad. I promised Narina I'd be there for her when she woke up," the boy replied. "You have any idea where they'd be?"

Mor'kha spoke between sniffles. "Iri said he was taking Lady Selenia to the *White Wendigo,* but when I sent men to ask the proprietors, they said they never saw them."

"They never made it," Rakh remarked. "If they were outside of the exclusion zone, it's not likely they're afflicted with rapeworm. Perhaps it's an opportunistic crime, or—"

Rakh stopped himself, leaving Erwyn to prompt him. "What is it, Rakh?"

"When Irikhos and I made up after our fight, he mentioned how I wouldn't make a bad overlord if Lady Selenia was out of the picture. I don't want to accuse your brother, Lady Foenaxas, but is it in his character to—"

"No!" Mor'kha blurted, standing up and fiercely locking eyes with Rakh. "Irikhos is a dear brother and a wonderful uncle to the children!"

Rakh faltered. "We all treat our kin differently—"

"Don't talk about loving kin when you exiled your own sister!" Lady Foenaxas ranted. "Irikhos would never— he's just as lost as Lady Selenia, he's not— he couldn't—"

"You saw how much he hated Lady Selenia. This isn't about how justified his hatred is, I just want to know where he and Lady Kagura are," Rakh said, his tone remaining level.

Erwyn nodded. "As horrible as it is, Lady Foenaxas, we must entertain every possibility. If Irikhos were to take his vengeance on Lady Selenia, what would he do?"

Mor'kha's breathing slowed. "I'm sorry. I should seek the truth above all, even if it's grim. My brother despises Lady Selenia. He has a motive, but I'm unsure what he'd do if left alone with her. I don't think he'd kill her, he'd want answers. His young love with Yarawyn Selenia was heartening to behold. I don't think Lady Selenia's death would fill that void."

Rakh took Mor'kha's hands. "I'll take your word for it, Lady Foenaxas. If he's kidnapped her, he can't be far. There's only so much lugging around one man can do."

* * *

Kagura opened her eyes, but the only difference from when they were closed was a small mote of light in the distance. She could hear someone breathing and pacing, but their form was impossible to make out.

222

"Where am I? Are you the big man who followed us? You'll let me go soon, won't you? I know Irikhos is angry, but you seem like a nice person even if you're a dark elf."

"I'm Irikhos, you imbecile," the voice responded. "How in the world have you survived as long as you have?"

"Well, I don't like to leave my castle because of all the mean commoners outside. I didn't want to come here either, but Erwyn insisted. Now I see it's not just peasants that are mean," Kagura responded.

Irikhos bitterly laughed. "I'm mean? What in the world do you think counts as mean? Isn't sending your siblings overseas and stealing your sister's inheritance mean? Or is it different when you do these things?"

"I never hit Yar in the back of her head and tied her up in a dark room! Believe me, I'd remember if I—"

Kagura felt a sharp pain and her chair almost tipped over, then Irikhos spoke again.

"I don't understand. How can someone as stupid as you ruin so much? Malice is usually devious, intelligent, conniving, but you just stumble through life poisoning everything around you," Irikhos ranted. "God, I want to punch some sense into you, but it just wouldn't work. You're unteachable, impossible to befriend, a complete waste of air."

"I *do* have friends! Erwyn likes me, Rakh likes me, and even Plutyn Khanas likes me, and most of them are scary snake people," Kagura corrected. "You have people who like you too. You can't hide here forever, your nephews and niece and sister—"

"Don't you *dare* mention my family!" Irikhos shouted, his voice bouncing within the apparently hollow room. "What would *you* know about familial love? You defied your father's dying wish and betrayed your sisters, exiling them for no good reason!"

"Why is that a problem?" Kagura asked. "Father promised Moonstone to me, so I corrected his written lies,

223

then I sent Tor and Yar on an adventure! They're probably resting on some nice white sanded beach and eating Elarondian pizza or something!"

"Or rotting in the nest of some nursing wyvern in the Alaterran Mountains," Irikhos spat. "You could have sent them to die in a foreign country, all for some imaginary brother who's never coming. Don't you feel guilt? Don't you feel *shame?*"

"They're not dead, nobody would get hurt because of what I did," Kagura stammered.

"They can, and they do. So many people have been hurt by my sister's well-meaning attempts to fix this outbreak, and she has something inside her skull. An empty-headed idiot like you? You've probably hurt more peasants than you could count. You're better off dead."

Kagura's eyes filled with tears, and she looked towards what she presumed was her feet. "If you think that, why haven't you killed me?"

"I want you to tell me where your father's will is," he answered. "The one that names Yarawyn as his successor. Once I have that, I'll let you go. You can go off and be some artist's model, I don't care what you do. But you're not going to be a lady. You'd best hope for your sake Yar's still alive in Elarond."

Kagura closed her eyes and struggled to envision the wisdom's chamber of Moonstone. Memories of Erwyn smacking her hand away from vials, books thicker than her arms lying unread on the shelves, and the human wisdom who once occupied the room danced before her, but the will's location was unclear.

"I don't know where it is. Erwyn knows, probably. Maybe it's been destroyed?"

Another sharp pain came to Kagura, followed by Irikhos yelling. "Why the fuck are you asking me? You're the one who hid it! Why don't you know where it is?"

"It was out of the way for so long that I forgot about it, that's all—"

"How in the world am I being outsmarted by *you?*" Irikhos raved. "Either you're expertly playing the fool or I'm so stupid that even *you* can outwit me."

"I really don't know! Keeping me tied up isn't going to help us. Why don't you let me go? You like high elves with Yar's features, don't you? You could marry me! You'd like the most beautiful woman in the world as your bride, wouldn't you? I'll forget you did this mean thing, I won't tell Erwyn or Rakh, we could just be married and have grey elven children and I'll tell my brother to go away when he finally arrives, just *please* let me go. I'm starving and I really need to make water—"

Irikhos slapped Kag so hard that her chair toppled over, crashing her head against the hard, stony floor. His pacing rumbled against her cheek, and his voice echoed even more.

"How could you think offering yourself up would do *anything* other than enrage me? Why would I marry the person who doomed me and Yar to unhappiness? Fuck this, you're too stupid to interrogate. I'll let Al help you make your water and after that, you think *very* carefully about where you hid your father's will."

"And if it's destroyed?"

Irikhos's voice lowered. "Then I have no problem making Fel'thuz an overlord."

Kagura squirmed, and Irikhos's footsteps grew distant, while metallic clattering came closer. Sir Almarax spoke in his rough, common tone as her chair was brought upright.

"All right, milady, I'm gonna untie you while you piss, but you can't try to escape."

Kagura began to whimper. "Please disobey Irikhos. I'll give you a kiss, I'll marry you, I'll be a good wife, I promise!"

225

"Sorry, milady. Got a wife of my own. I don't like what Irikhos is doing, but I gotta do what puts food on my family's table."

"I'm sorry! Tell Irikhos I'm sorry, please!"

"I'll tell 'im, but I don't think it'll change his heart. He's already let it grow hard as obsidian," the knight claimed.

"Even obsidian can shatter."

Almarax sighed. "Here's hopin' you're right, milady. For now, best not make this harder 'an it needs to be."

Subverted

Cutting open people's crotches had become so disturbingly routine to Erwyn that for a moment, even his own mentor felt like another extraction job. As was the case with most female infectees, Melancholy's vaginal canal was lined with white, stringy creatures, though she and the recently sewn-up patient beside her, Narina, had a shared oddity: Their worms were covered with red, blotchy cysts.

Erwyn had already taken a sample from Narina, and took another from Melancholy, opting against the destructive relaxant his mentor used. He instead removed a single worm, accepting the loss of the flesh it took with it. He placed it in a jar next to Narina's sample, then prepared a third for Farawan's.

The young man made him most uncomfortable; it was for his wellbeing that Narina volunteered herself. If there wasn't a cure, then he'd have let a woman who'd faced every hell within this realm down. Despite his jittering hands rendering the process inefficient, he successfully sewed Melancholy up, then moved on to his sample desk. He removed his gloves and accessed a quite different set of medical supplies; a small sachet of bhang-weed and some rolling papers. He left the tent with Melancholy's handheld pyromancer, rolled a smoke, lit up, and inhaled deeply.

His mentor would have told him to get a grip. Rakh most likely considered him heartless. Despite overwhelming presence of the disease he was fighting, Kagura's face dominated his mind's dark expanse. It didn't matter how grown she was on the outside; inside she was a spoilt child. Erwyn wondered if she would have respected her father's wishes if she'd seen Lord Nemeron's body herself. Madness, obliviousness, spinelessness, and impulsiveness defined the late Lord Selenia and his three daughters respectively. Even if the erasure of the House of Selenia was an objectively good thing, Erwyn knew the girls.

Melancholy didn't, yet Erwyn took her advice when Kagura used noble precedent to consolidate power as acting lady. Her advice made sense as an uninvolved observer; if Lady Kagura was an unprepared idiot, her advisors would enjoy the glut of the power. She wasn't wrong; between them, Erwyn and Rakh were the overlords of the Forests of Winter, yet he'd convinced himself that his acts of consolidation were harmless.

Irikhos Foenaxas, if truly taking vengeance for Yarawyn's sake, was simply righting Erwyn's wrong. But if he murdered Kag, what could they do aside from execute him? The bhang-weed calmed his shaking hands yet did nothing to his racing mind.

"Hey, wiz," a familiar voice said. "You going back in there or what? I've seen how that elven guy gets when he's awake, an' you don't want him waking up on the table."

Erwyn flicked what remained of his smoke away. "My apologies, Rarakhi. I was taking a break."

"You don't look very relaxed," Rarakhi remarked. "Honestly, you look a little like the boss. It's uncanny."

"I wonder how Plutyn's doing as acting lord. I hope he's running Moonstone like a city, not a crime syndicate."

"The Boss has honour," Rarakhi claimed. "He wouldn't throw us to the wolves. If he's got a problem, he says it without hesitation."

"You haven't seen the way he behaves with Lady Selenia," Erwyn said, heading back into the tent. "You're his friend. The people of Moonstone don't share that fortune."

"I guess," Rarakhi said. "Anything I can do while you're cutting that guy's cock?"

Erwyn put his gloves back on. "Can you, *with gloves,* pop one of the worms' cysts and collect the resultant liquid? Use a sewing needle if you must."

"You having a laugh?" Rarakhi spluttered. "That's disgusting!"

"You asked for something to do."

Rarakhi shuddered. "Fine."

"Thank you," Erwyn said. "I don't know how often Rakh tells you, but even if you're rough around the edges, you've grown to be a fine young man."

"Ah, shut up," the boy said as he put on some gloves at the sample desk.

Erwyn was once again alone with his patient, and the poppy milk's effectiveness wouldn't persist forever. Farawan's penis, when dorsally cut, erupted with worms. He extracted two separate strands, then moved to his sample jars. One was placed in the jar he prepared, and he readied another for the second.

"Rarakhi, do you have the cyst's discharge?"

The boy lifted a vial with around three drops' worth of yellow-red slime. "Here you go, wiz, don't slurp it all at once."

Erwyn swallowed as he took hold of the vial. "I shouldn't get my hopes up, but if this works, Ashglass may have a cure."

"Do you need more of it?"

"Not yet," Erwyn answered. "We do need those cyst-covered worms to survive, however. Watch carefully."

He took some of the discharge with an eye dropper, then used a needle to prick a hole in one of Farawan's worms. After that, he applied the discharge to the wound and closed the jar then moved to the operating table with the remaining gunk.

"What are you doing? Sorry, I'm not a wisdom," Rarakhi said.

"I think these cysts are indicative of a disease Melancholy and Narina's bodies have given their rapeworms. Just as cholera makes it impossible to properly retain liquids, I believe this disease makes it impossible for the rapeworms to exert control over their host."

Rarakhi squinted. "So diseases can get diseases?"

"In this case, it would appear so," Erwyn stated, pricking open multiple worms within Farawan's penis and adding half-drops to their wounds. "Now for the test: I've just attempted to spread the disease to Farawan's worms. If his madness subsides, we know it's worked."

"What happens after that?" Rarakhi asked.

"If this trial is successful, the rapeworms are about to experience an epidemic of their own," Erwyn said. "It won't matter if infected couples have children with each other. The bloodshed and sterilisation can finally stop. Ashglass will be able to rebuild."

Rarakhi glanced at two high unconscious high elves. "So Narina and Farawan will be together again?"

"Don't use the word 'will' yet," Erwyn advised. "Everything I'm suggesting is contingent on my hypothesis being correct. For now, we await the results."

Rarakhi bundled up in his coat. "I'm sorry for all the times I was ungrateful to you back in the orphanage. You're a good guy."

"You were a child. You're *still* a child. Thank you for helping me."

Rarakhi scoffed. "All I did was pop some horrible red boils."

"You brought me back into the tent too," Erwyn reminded him. "Nobody else could have done that."

"Shit, you're really worried about the lady, aren't you?"

Erwyn nodded. "Regardless of my worries, my current duties are to the people of Ashglass. Even if those duties involve idly waiting for three sedated people to awaken."

* * *

230

Razarkha was unsure if her illusionism worked on ascendants, seeing as it only partially worked on Ariel. As such, Razarkha's revolutionaries stayed hidden behind towers of food parcels whenever ascended overseers entered the room. While they theoretically could have stayed in the warehouse forever due to its abundance of food, each visiting overseer made it more likely that they'd be spotted. Between visits, Weil whispered to Razarkha.

"We must move soon. I could open another portal if you wish," he said. *"My chest hurts, but I can still—"*

"No," Razarkha replied. *"I trust Ariel; this much food can only be for the Demidium Breeding Facility. Even if we have no retreat, we must seize this opportunity to free the humans they've enslaved."*

"But if more allies die, their blood will be on our—"

"I have thousands dead by my hand already, enemies and allies alike. This quest was built on death," Razarkha said. *"At least as Erre, I can free as many as I kill."*

"I remember when you admonished me for telling myself I was attacking pirate ships," Weil remarked. *"It sounds like you're doing the same."*

"I'm a revolutionary. That's leagues apart from a man sinking ships because he allowed himself to be extorted. Our deeds will go down in history, while your deeds on the Sudovykly cliffs will be noted in a lighthouse keeper's diary at most," Razarkha spat.

"Then why are you justifying it to yourself? Isn't such behaviour foolish?"

"This isn't the time to doubt me, we're in the middle of—"

The storage room's door slid open and the walls' redstone veins lit up, causing Razarkha's revolutionaries to freeze. A pair of ascendants entered the warehouse, clad in golden cloaks and little else. Their distorted, Sulari-speaking voices echoed through the room while boxes of fungal rations telekinetically shifted from the top of a stack.

"There's something off about this room's arcane atmosphere," one remarked. *"It's as though a couple of ascendants' worth of raw arcana appeared overnight."*

"A shipment arrived yesterday evening, perhaps it's contaminated?" another suggested. *"Perhaps it's best to open the boxes before we feed the humans this stuff."*

"Breeders and humans all look the same when overdosed on arcane supplements," the first said. *"Let's stay safe. You open the one in front of you, I'll check these three."*

Razarkha's hands gripped her soulstealer. Their search would inevitably be fruitless; she was the 'arcane contamination', and hiding was a rapidly waning option. She slipped around the boxes and approached the cloak-bound clouds. Just as she got into killing range, the second ascendant began to prattle again.

"It's odd, there's nothing strange about these rations, but I definitely felt the ascended presence come closer. Did you, Montaris?"

"I'm not sure if it's an ascendant, it's too—"

Razarkha activated the soulstealer and soon enough, the ascendants were sucked into the artefact, their cloaks and stones falling to the floor. Weil, in a panic, rushed into the open, along with most of her group.

"Why did you do that?"

"Didn't you hear what they were saying?"

"No, I don't understand Sulari," Weil pointed out.

"Oh, you idiot, I'll tell you later," Razarkha said, then shifted her tongue to Nortezian. *"All right, men, we have no choice. We're going to kill our way out, but we'll need to be careful if we're to rescue the humans too. I'll use telekinesis to—"*

"Why should we rescue the humans?" Adolita asked. *"We're here to bring Old Galdus to its knees, to remind them*

that nobody sends instigators to Nortez and gets away with it! We should deny them their human slaves altogether!"

"No. We'll exceed that," Razarkha promised. *"We're going to turn their humans against them! Stay by the storage room's entrance while I perform the first step. Using the cloaks and stones, along with some telekinesis, I can pretend these ascendants are alive. After I've lured as many overseers as I can to their deaths, we'll move on."*

Ariel spoke up. *"Why are we killing the overseers? They raised me, and I'm sure if you asked nicely, they would let the humans go. They didn't know how mean Lesteris was—"*

"They won't let them go without a fight," Razarkha snapped. *"You're not a person to them, do you understand? They sold you to Lesteris not caring how abusive he would be. It doesn't matter if an augmentee goes to a 'good' owner or a 'bad' one, any owner of another person is a wretch whose only good deed is their death. These overseers only facilitate—"*

"Montaris?" an echoing voice from beyond the room said. *"What's taking you so long, the humans are getting impatient."*

Razarkha clumsily floated one of the cloaks out with its appropriate ascension stone, then put on an unconvincing impression in broken Sulari.

"There's something strange in the supply room, cometh here, Lesteris."

"I told you, my name's Lestrio," the voice replied. *"Let's see what's going on—"*

The moment the ascendant became visible, Razarkha claimed her third victim of the day. Ariel's winds began to whip, and once again, she started complaining.

"Lestrio would always give my hair telekinetic pats."

"This isn't the time, Ariel."

Rowyn Khanas spoke next. *"If I may, perhaps we should escape from this facility, then storm it later without Ariel, so she may be spared of such trauma. It is akin to one's hometown being razed, is it not?"*

"I fully intend on razing my hometown when the time comes," Razarkha snapped. *"If Ariel is upset, she'll understand the cost of freedom. For slaves to be liberated, would-be owners like Lesteris need to be exterminated."*

Rowyn stood tall. *"I will not approve of this. Ariel has been through enough."*

"I'm heartbroken. I'll do what I want, and you can grovel at my knees when I save your ungrateful life," Razarkha said. *"Insubordinate, the lot of you."*

"Thou art the face of a revolution," Khanas pointed out. *"Thou wouldst hardly attract obedient folk—"*

Razarkha pointed her soulstealer at the necromancer and spoke in plain Common. "I'm grateful for your work saving Weil, but if you speak out of turn again, you won't have a mouth. Am I clear?"

"Yes, Praetor Erre," he said without hesitation.

"You lot will stay quiet until I say so. Every ascendant that passes fuels my telekinesis."

The resultant process took hours; small groups of ascendants were lured and added to the collection of telekinetic puppets, which in turn lured more ascendants. Ariel continued to whine over the deaths of her oppressors, as though they hadn't robbed her of her body.

Eventually Razarkha moved into the hallway, maintaining her illusionism as her group moved along the smooth, windowless passageways. Occasionally, sweeping lights akin to those in the Hextolis Citadel hovered over them, and while it appeared they hadn't detected them, Razarkha couldn't be sure.

Each hall was near-identical, with an occasional sliding door to the side breaking the monotony. Checking the rooms behind them generally led to moments-long confrontations with doomed ascendants. Each soul added to Razarkha's repertoire made her chest tingle. The fear that she'd alerted the facility grew as a pulling, sinking sensation while magical energies prodded her brain's underside. She turned to Ariel and sighed.

"We're not getting anywhere. Ariel, can you show me where they keep the humans?"

Ariel paused. *"You're going to kill every overseer you come across, aren't you?"*

"There's no other way. These are people who saw your human body and thought it was right to convert it into the rocky form you're inhabiting," Razarkha said. *"They never asked you, they just needed to sell an aeromantic augmentee and then stole your body without a second thought. Aren't you angry about that? Don't you want to spare your fellow humans from the same fate?"*

"The overseers are mostly kind. They told me augmentation would hurt and apologised when it happened," she said. *"They're good people, and I won't help you kill them."*

Razarkha itched to demonstrate her magical power, but she relented. Ariel wasn't her slave; disobeying orders was the beauty of the new life Razarkha had given her. Despite this, the girl didn't realise that with each wasted moment, death closed in.

"Ariel, you're an escaped augmentee, are you not?"

"I am," she said. *"Why do you ask?"*

"I'm sure humans in this facility have attempted to escape before," Razarkha said. *"What happened to them?"*

"Some were caught and given the shock stick," Ariel explained. *"But I was a good girl, I never needed the shock stick—"*

"You will now, unless I get rid of the overseers."

"But I'm augmented, they'll never— oh no. No, no, no, they'll disincorporate me, I can't ask them nicely but I can't kill them, what do I do what do I do what do I do—"

"You help me get to the humans. Then they'll be free, like you, without fear of the shock stick or disincorporation," Razarkha interrupted. "I'm not commanding you, Ariel, I'm asking you as a free woman. I need somebody who knows this facility so I can free these humans as quickly as possible. You're the only one who can help. Make the right decision."

Ariel's winds became a tempest, and her redstone eyes traced towards the closest fork in the way. "I think heading right from here should bring you to the human enclosures. But I warn you, there's a door that requires clearance in the way."

"Then how do you know this is the way at all?"

Ariel's voice briefly distorted. "I was taken down this hall when they augmented me."

"I'll believe you. Insurrectionists, let's get there as quickly as possible," Razarkha commanded, then turned to her Ilazari associate. "Weil, can you punch down a locked door in your current state?"

"The Great Rakh'vash is always willing to destroy," Weil responded.

Razarkha's revolutionaries charged through the halls as per Ariel's directions, and as expected were confronted with a locked door. Weil shrugged, made some guttural Chaostongue murmurings, and a portal opened, producing a tentacle that slammed through the obstacle. With that, all doubt they'd been spotted was removed. Alarms blared and redstone veins within the walls pulsed while the insurrectionists flooded into a room full of pens containing flustered, nude humans. Razarkha's forehead began to ache, and a plume of ascendants flowed towards them, moving through an unfathomably long trail of pens resembling those around them.

"Igneus and geomancers, lift the ground and make protective walls that still allow airflow," Razarkha directed. "Adolita, find a weak enough wall for your pyromancers to

236

melt. If there aren't any, ask me for help, but only after I've killed these overseers."

Ariel checked the magically assisted pens and noticed a young male human with black hair, brown skin, and folded brown eyes. While Igneus and Adolita did as they commanded, the aeromantic augmentee floated towards the frightened human and spoke in Sulari.

"Do not worry, Ferrus! It's me, Ariel! I came back!"

Razarkha briefly broke concentration. *"What are you doing, Ariel?"*

"This is Ferrus! He was the stud who impregnated me during my brief stint as a breeding human! We're body friends, aren't we?"

"Ariel, what happened to you? You sound the same, but we were told you'd become a greater, more beautiful being," Ferrus remarked. *"You look frightening."*

"Oh, this is just augmentation. It's not so bad, except for when an ascendant—"

Igneus's barriers shattered, causing rocks to fly and hit numerous revolutionaries. Rowyn was already scrambling to take account of the injured, while Adolita had her pyromancers blast a wall, which was slowly melting under the heat. Ascendants floated past the former barriers, and Razarkha did what she did best; called upon the Sovereign to consume them all.

At first, she kept count, but as more poured into the dread weapon, it became the equivalent of the slices of bread one has eaten in their lifetime. Arcane sparks flitted from Razarkha's body and soulstealer, and every part of her craved an outlet. She strode towards Adolita and her pyromancers, then gave a dismissive gesture.

"Step aside."

Her underlings were quick to comply, allowing Razarkha to aim the soulstealer at the wall they were melting and unleash an devastatingly powerful ray of light that carved a circle through the wall before her, along with a set of layered walls beyond it. The redstone lighting and alarms cut out, and the only light that remained was white and natural. The soundscape filled with Rowyn's panicked babbling and humans discussing matters amongst themselves. Razarkha stood in front the hole she created, forming what she hoped was a heroic silhouette.

"Humans of the Demidium Breeding Facility! Thou art my—"

Before she could finish, the sapient livestock charged from their deactivated pens, shoving Razarkha aside. She sputtered and faltered, but the human tide was irrepressible.

"No— thou canst— there is— they shalt kill thee if thou— no, no, no!"

She watched the humans rush from the facility before the situation could be explained, leaving only one left: Ferrus. Ariel turned to Razarkha and took on a decidedly twee tone.

"Well done, Praetor Erre! There will be no more shock sticks for my brethren, and I can finally speak with Ferrus again. It's a shame we can't breed together anymore because that felt good at the time."

"Nobody cares about that right now, if those humans run into the streets of Demidium, they're as good as dead!" Razarkha ranted in Nortezian. *"Move out, move out,* move out! *If we lose these humans, we're—"*

"Praetor Erre, half our geomancers hath perished," Rowyn reported.

"You're a necromancer, resurrect them or something, *we can't lose these humans, or I'll be a monster, not a heroine."*

Rowyn stared at Razarkha, and Weil lingered in place, then attempted to speak Nortezian.

"Those who walk, follow me. Raz— er, Erre will join us."

Razarkha gave him a weak smile, then watched her revolutionaries leave the facility. Rowyn stayed by the body of a pyromancer, a blonde breeder named Kazama. Sorelli, the coward brave enough to house a budding revolutionary group, lay bloodied against the floor. In the corpse-filled darkness, a child-sized Rakh appeared above her, sat atop an illusory set of stairs. Then, a faceless child pushed him down, and once he reached the ground, he screamed at Razarkha how she was nothing but a monster.

"I'm not. *I'm not!*"

Rowyn's gaze flitted upwards. "Excuse me? I didn't say anything—"

"Leave here, Khanas," Razarkha said. "I'll follow soon enough, I promise."

"Razarkha, I'm sorry—"

"Don't argue with me or you know what awaits you!"

Rowyn gave her a solemn nod. "Of course."

* * *

Eyes were no longer a relevant term to Darvith. Every soul that joined him was an extra perspective, another creator of portals peering through godly realms into all manner of locations within the mortal realm. His original eyes were vaporised like the rest of his being millennia ago, in the days of the laughable failure known as the Golden Galdusian Empire.

Playing along with the Rakh'norv's mortal experiment despite its inevitable failure had always amused him. It was his handicap; in staying where he could exploit the most pride, he was destined to lose the imperial war against his fellow sinchild, Andros. Loser or not, he'd proven himself by outliving the so-called Plague Emperor. He was greater than any ascendant; few arcane spikes were comparable, visible to him as luminous tendrils jutting from the ground, stretching into the cosmos as he did. Oceans of

239

lights beyond the tiny world he inhabited flickered to greet him, their energies mingling with his own.

Beneath him was the grid-like city of Nova Tertia, perpetually overshadowed by his magnificent being. His gaseous form consumed the citadel, and all had no choice but to behold him. Was it any wonder that every Nova Tertian's desire was to look down on the city when all they ever did was look up? Perhaps Darvith was once capable of humility, but now that he was godlike, what was the point in false modesty?

Within one portal, the adorable exploits of a mortal with one of father's trinkets could be seen. A great spark blasted through the Demidium Breeding Facility's walls, and out flowed the humans. Souls roiled within Darvith's collective, complaining of the beasts running loose like in uncivilised nations such as Jaranar and Arkhera.

He suppressed the groans of the overly sensitive fools who'd traded their very individuality for a taste of superiority. Their lot in life was to suffer while being revered by his next victims; mere conduits that continued his career as the Sinchild of Pride. The followers of the trinket wielder raised rocky walls while trying to control the humans, and ascendants from throughout Demidium descended upon the skirmish before being consumed by the woman in the tattered cloak. Silencing his normally storm-like voice, he breezed words to his soul's divine progenitor.

"Dear father, why do you insist on empowering my enemies?"

The Sovereign spoke in a clear tone to the Darvith that once inhabited Luxifros's body.

"I try to keep my eldest son on his figurative toes."

"Jokes about my non-corporeal nature still appear to amuse you," Darvith responded.

"They'll only stop being funny once the pathetic fate of an ascendant stops being funny. Objectively, that will never happen."

240

"Does that elevated animal intend to kill me? The closer she gets, the more likely it is we'll meet. It would be a shame to kill something so interesting."

"Are you afraid?"

"Of course not. Andros was the closest thing to a test I had, and ultimately, pride prevailed over wrath. By nature, pride is the greatest vice; remorse is impossible for the prideful, so the vice persists no matter what. My contemporary siblings have all ensnared people who have since broken free. Every being who joins me is trapped for eternity."

"Not eternity. Remember our deal, Darvith."

"As far as they're concerned, it's eternity. When I finally die, the Underworld will receive a mass immigration of fools."

"Your death could come sooner than you anticipate."

"Not at all. It would pain me, but if that interesting speck approaches Nova Tertia intending to cut my harvest short, I'll force the same fate upon her. As every voice within me knows, pride always precedes a fall."

Severed

There was barely enough time to take account of what Demidium was like before the battle began to rage, let alone what it was like now that it was engulfed in violence. The sea beckoned to Rowyn Khanas from a squared-off coastline, while the Demidium Breeding Facility's blasted-apart walls lay behind him. Boats with red-and-yellow sails depicting six icons were setting sail with urgency, and given the chaos on the land, he couldn't blame them.

Humans ran amidst the fleshly spellbinders they were supposed to serve, flooding the streets with irregularity. Some of Razarkha's geomancers raised blockades to contain them, only for Sulari mages to demolish their efforts. Weil's tentacles did their part in defending the group, but without an ascendant killer, R's Revolution was woefully underprepared.

On the ground, there was no way to discern allegiance, and Rowyn feared that the Sulari shared the sentiment as ascendants began a campaign of indiscriminate pyromantic bombing. By Rowyn's side was Ariel and her friend, Ferrus, the former levitating the latter with her aeromancy in oblivious joy. He patted for his transponder then called to the augmentee.

"Ariel, come with me."

"But why? Everyone is putting an end to the mean people, just like Praetor Erre said!"

Rowyn gestured to a wyvern-shaped metal ascendant unleashing a torrent of flames against humans and breeders alike. *"No, we art doomed. We must leave with haste."*

"But how?"

"Use thy aeromancy and take Ferrus and I to the coast. We need to board a boat, any boat!" Rowyn commanded.

"What about Praetor Erre?"

"Praetor Erre killed Lestrio and many others without thinking, and even if she was reasonable, I can't find her. We must save ourselves."

Ariel paused, then spoke Sulari to Ferrus. *"We're going to the boats. There might be humans on them!"*

"That's good, because while I'm happy to see you, without overseers it's scary—"

A piece of the revolutionaries' most recent geomantic wall flew towards Rowyn, crashing onto a nearby Sulari breeder. Allowing this former slave her fun was usually worth the time, but Rowyn Khanas had to be a knight in this moment.

"Ariel, hover forth above the crowds and carry us with thee, now!"

"I'm sorry, Rowyn, right away!" the augmentee said in Nortezian.

A gust swept Rowyn up from below, and soon, he was floating within a small cyclone that carried not only him, but numerous breeders and humans Ariel passed as she drifted over the crowds. Rowyn opened his mouth to protest, then shook his head. It may have been less stealthy, but if it was possible to save more lives, they needed to.

The growing collection of people flowed to the edge of Demidium, where cuboid 'piers' jutted into the sea. Most of the red-yellow boats had departed, and Ariel didn't wait for commands. She floated over the sea towards a particularly fast ship as Rowyn beheld the carnage behind them. His cautious relief vanished the moment he saw a caped woman floating above the city, sucking up ascendants like Plutyn would a bhang-weed cloud.

"Oh, there's *Praetor Erre!"* Ariel said, sweeping Rowyn up to her while keeping the rest in her eddy. *"Should we return?"*

"No, no, keep going, reach that ship no matter what!"

"But Erre will—"

243

"She will continue without us. Dost thou wish to be safe with thy love Ferrus?"

Ariel paused, then continued drifting towards the ship. *"Yes. I do."*

When they reached the ship, its sailors were quick to notice the Galdusians dumped upon their deck along with the augmentee responsible. They were human, with the brown skin and folded eyes Ferrus possessed, wearing loose, breathable clothing that exposed the midriffs of women and men alike. Rowyn got to his feet, rushed to the front of the group, and put his hands up. The sailors were almost certainly Jaranese; while holier Arkheran Pantheists read their texts in Jaranese, Rowyn was a man of battle and medicine, not divinity. All he could pray for was that they understood the Common Tongue.

"We come in peace. We just want to leave the city. We're not after trouble."

A bulky, topless Jaranese fellow stomped over to Rowyn, his belly wobbling with each step. His crew cleared the way while he cleared his throat, then spoke in accented Common.

"You think you just fly onto our boat with no thought? What if we were full of cargo and your men's heaviness sank us?"

Rowyn eyed the man's sagging nipples and resisted every grim joke in his head, then put his hands together in a Jaranese-style bow. "My deepest apologies. You saw what it was like on the land. Please, for these people's sake—"

"What is that thing?" the captain asked, pointing to Ariel.

"She's an augmentee. I'm sure, given Ferrus's looks, that your people have been trafficked to Demidium. This is what becomes of them."

The captain's eyes grew large. "Great commiserations to your friend. You Galdusians are safe with us, but you help the crew. Add to our... men power, is it?"

244

"Manpower," Rowyn corrected.

"Ah, you not afraid to correct your leader. You stay by my side. I am Khun-Rax, captain of spice boat *Im si Helang*. Speak your Galdusian and make your people understanding."

"Of course," Rowyn said, and turned back to the scattered, confused Galdusians while the captain yelled in Jaranese, causing the sailors to get back to work.

Before he addressed them, he took his transponder out and found a 'station' with the wheel. Crackling chatter preceded his press of the talk button.

"This is Rowyn Khanas, Imperial Engineer Hildegard Swan's spy on Razarkha Fel'thuz," he quavered. "Is anybody there?"

A fuzzy voice replied. *"Shit, we never pick up signals out here. I take it Razarkha's moved to Demidium?"*

"Yes, but she's not just rogue by Nortezian standards as I previously thought. She's yelling at shadows, and her efforts to liberate the humans of Demidium have gone disastrously. There's so many dead, and there's no way I can assassinate her."

"Hey, hey, just slow down, one thing at a time," the Yookie on the other side said. *"She's delusional, you say?"*

Rowyn stared beyond the *Im si Helang*'s stern to see the clouds above Demidium spiralling into single airborne spot. "I fear she's growing too powerful to think clearly. I know you probably don't understand, but we mages have a term called 'arcane incontinence'. Essentially, fear or an abundance of arcana can lead to psychosis, delusions or…"

He trailed off as the clouds cleared, and beside the former eye of the storm was a tentacle the height of a Galdusian tower. A light steadily built up by the tentacle's tip.

"By the gods! I think she's going to—"

Rowyn dropped his transponder and dived towards Ariel despite the augmentee's lack of physical vulnerability.

245

The two hit the deck as a massive ray of destructive light swept across the waters of Demidium, cutting irreparable holes in every boat it touched. The *Im si Helang* rumbled, then slowly began descending into the waters.

As he scrambled for his transponder, Rowyn shakily spoke. "Ariel, this is it. I'm sorry."

"You... are... sorry?" the augmentee asked in slow, confused Common.

"It means I apologise. To thee and Ferrus. My advice has killed thee."

Ariel brought her rocky pieces upright and conjured an eddy for Ferrus. *"I have only just been freed. I refuse to die so early."*

As the augmentee built her winds up, the transponder kept speaking. *"Hey, Khanas, speak to me! Khanas, confirm your status!"*

Rowyn realised his opportunity and threw his transponder into the ocean, then called to the frantic, weeping Jaranese crew.

"I know it's contrary to everything you know as sailors, but you need to trust this storm! This augmentee is going to save us!"

While most of them didn't understand the Common Tongue, Khun-Rax was quick to acknowledge it, raising his hands and speaking in quasi-religious tones to his people. As Ariel's storm grew, the crew and Galdusian refugees rushed towards her, becoming swept in her winds.

The ship's deck was mere feet from the waters it was meant to glide above, and Rowyn beheld the aeromantic human with awe. In his best Old Galdusian, he called up to her.

"Many thanks, Ariel. Thou hath my eternal gratitude. Keep heading west until thou reacheth land!"

Without further ado, he rushed into the storm, allowing himself to be buffeted into the air once more. In the whipping winds, he looked back to see Weil's tentacle had vanished.

* * *

Razarkha watched the Jaranese ships sink from atop one of the few towers remaining to the sector, grinning at her handiwork. Beside her were Weil, Igneus and Adolita, while the streets below contained her revolution's remnants, along with what little humans they'd preserved. As she beheld a distant artificial storm, she sighed, then turned to Weil.

"See? I told you. Ariel and Rowyn were cowards. Ariel deserves a new life, but Khanas swore to serve me. He was growing insubordinate. He let Sorelli die."

Weil folded his arms. *"You only needed to sink one."*

"They were probably trafficking ships. You saw the farmed humans' features. Those who sell their own people into slavery are the worst kind of scum."

Weil paused, then turned away. *"If you say so."*

Igneus tapped Razarkha's shoulder before she could respond to Weil.

"What happens now? We've lost so many."

"The insurrectionists beneath us will serve as a distraction. If I'm correct, the largest ascendant conglomerate in the world exists in Nova Tertia. We need to punch through the Demidium Membrane, find a gate to Nova Tertia, then take this conglomerate by surprise. Once I've consumed them, fear will be obsolete. I'm already becoming one with my magic. The First Light echoes through my mind, its speech growing louder with each soul I take."

Adolita turned her nose up. *"If that's the case, can you tell us what you're going to do with your power? While I'm happy to see Sulari dogs die, you claimed you were going to save the humans, and they don't look very 'saved' to me."*

Razarkha telekinetically levitated and pointed her soulstealer at Adolita. *"My body is begging me to vent my excess arcana. I don't even need words to perform familiar spellwork anymore. The arcana of the world simply responds to my will. You saw what I did to those ships. You won't live to know what it does to your pretty face."*

Weil, despite not knowing Nortezian, stood between her and Adolita.

"Stop this. We've seen what you do to those who betray you. We aren't traitors. Whatever she said, it's not worth killing another ally. Please. Let us move to our next goal."

Razarkha lowered the soulstealer. *"You're lucky I've grown fond of your fat cheeks."*

Weil moved out of the way, and Razarkha hovered towards Adolita. *"Once I've consumed the conglomerate, I'll be a mortal goddess. Provided you've been loyal, I'll grant you whatever your heart desires. Does that answer your question?"*

Adolita nervously smiled. *"Your authority remains unquestioned, Praetor Erre."*

"I'm glad to hear it. Come, we have a Membrane to cross."

* * *

Though Mor'kha claimed she had men investigate the *White Wendigo,* Rakh believed that Irikhos arrived at the pub after all. If Sir Foenaxas was in control of the encounter, then he could have taken Kagura to dinner in earnest, then changed his mind and done something rash. It was just as likely that he never arrived at all and set out rid himself of Lady Selenia, but Rakh refused to believe this line of reasoning.

He'd drawn from Irikhos's fears. The knight was more of a family man than Rakh could ever claim to be, and

248

even allowed him to explain himself after being illusorily tortured, resentfulness aside. Surely, he'd give Lady Selenia a chance before doing something so drastic. As Count Fel'thuz invisibly approached the *White Wendigo,* Irikhos's voice echoed.

"You wouldn't be such a bad overlord yourself. That's what would happen if Lady Kagura died, isn't it?"

Rakh shook his head. Investigating as though Lady Selenia was dead wasn't productive. The door of the *White Wendigo* opened, and a drunk dark elf staggered out, bringing a waft of hearth-warmed air with him. Rakh took the opportunity to slip in while remaining invisible, then weaved through the serving staff in a manner he regrettably considered serpentine.

He claimed a corner by the toilets' entrance and used it as a vantage point. Numerous high elves served as staff, but most customers, as expected in Ashglass, were dark elven, with a human minority sprinkled through the establishment. There was precisely one waiter who seemed to specialise in charming older, female clientele, while the rest of the serving staff were waitresses dressed in, by Ashglass standards, provocative clothing. Given Irikhos's obvious preference for lighter-skinned women, it was unsurprising that he was a regular.

Rakh had his strategy mostly figured out, but it required him to put advanced sound alteration to use. He slipped through the tavern, ducking under platters and slipping behind rows of bar-bound dark elves, before scanning behind the counter. As expected, there were shelves of beverages, including a bottle of malt whisky labelled *'Earthfyre'*, advertised as an Ashpeaks speciality endorsed by Irikhos Foenaxas himself. More importantly, there was a door where staff occasionally retreated to; judging by how long it took for them to emerge, it must have been a break room.

When the bartender was sufficiently distracted by one of his punters bursting into inebriated tears, Rakh snuck behind the counter, crouched, then applied an illusory 'disguise' mimicking one of the high elven waitresses. From there, he stood, cleared his throat to check his voice was sufficiently altered, then entered the presumed break room before the woman he'd based his form on noticed she had a twin.

Within were numerous high elves with similar noses, along with the odd apron-wearing dark elven man. They were mostly chatting between each other, though one waitress addressed Rakh with annoyance.

"Are you joking, Alawyn?" the silver-haired high elf remarked. "You just took a break, why are you always so lazy?"

This was it, his all-or-nothing bluff. Rakh prayed that his feminine voice would hold.

"Sorry," he said. "I'm just shaken up about the overlady we served the other day. Sir Irikhos disappeared the night after, I heard."

"Oh, shut up about that," the waitress responded. "Perawyn split the gold she got nice and fair. I don't recall you complaining when you received your share."

Rakh's breathing slowed. This was an easily squandered opportunity. He stroked his hair, mimicking the actions in his illusion, then continued.

"The guards don't know, so whatever happened is probably bad, don't you think? Has anyone seen the overlady since then?"

"Who cares? It annoys the fuck out of me," the waitress ranted. "How do those morons expect us to care about spoilt idiots who issue commands from their faraway castles we'll never see in our lifetime? Especially the King, we've got his face on every coin, but we're never going to greet Landon Shearwater in our lifetime—"

"Actually, he stopped by Ashglass about a decade ago an' I cooked for him," one of the apron-wearing dark elves claimed. "Obviously this was before he became king—"

"I'll believe it when I see it!" the waitress interrupted. "Anyway, what happened to the overlady isn't my business or yours, just leave noble idiocy to the noble idiots."

Rakh frowned. He'd always tried to make commoners treat him like any other friend, but if they knew he was a noble, he'd always be an exception in their eyes. He hoped that Moonstone's working class didn't regard him as this waitress did, but he couldn't be sure.

"I guess you're right. The snob probably treated Perawyn like shit, anyway," Rakh said.

"What's worse, 'sides from him giving her that gold which is probably worth less than a copper to his spoilt arse, he sided with the bitch! Said something about going to a shrine, as though holy people would hate an Eternalist any less."

"There are more shrines than Renewalist ones, surely," Rakh said.

"Yeah, but like fuck Lady Ascetic would let them be. Surprised any Eternalists stick around, if I'm honest," the waitress remarked. "I suppose with rapeworm going around, they have even more reason to abandon us."

Rakh rubbed his chin, then put on an exaggerated sigh. "I should probably get going. It doesn't matter how shaken up I am, the boss won't pay me for sitting here talking."

"The boss? Since when did you start calling dad 'boss'?"

Rakh hid his blush and backed off. "Sorry, sis, I've just been finding it hard to see him as a father lately, what with all the shifts. Anyway, I'll see you around, goodbye for now!"

With that, he bolted out of the break room, projected a copy of his disguise moving behind the counter while his true self became invisible, sneaking back over the bar and through the *White Wendigo*. If Irikhos was foolish enough to broadcast his next move, then Rakh's goal was clear: He needed to find an Eternalist shrine.

As his break room 'sister' said, Lady Foenaxas wouldn't let Eternalist establishments stand without considerable challenges. If anyone knew where the shrine was, it would be an Eternalist close enough to Mor'kha to be tolerated despite her faith. Only one man fit such a description, and Rakh could only hope that Lady Foenaxas hadn't badgered the Elarondian Eternalism out of him.

Ambushed

Rakh Fel'thuz pounded Solyx Solerro's office door with a force only a wooden hand could take. He stopped to check the prosthetic for scuffs after realising his excess, only for the door to open and force him to focus on the dark elf before him.

"How in the world are you knocking so loudly? Are you using your illusionism to amplify the noise?" Solerro said with an upward flick of his hat.

"Sorry, I got overexcited," Rakh said, hastily applying bloody grazes to his illusory hand. "I've found a lead for where Irikhos and Lady Selenia might be, but I need your help."

The dark elf gestured over his shoulder. "Come in. I'll get a woodworker on the door later."

"Thank you for understanding, Lord Solyx."

"There are missing people at stake. Save your flattery. I'm a consort, little more."

Solerro's office was full of hunting and fishing paraphernalia. Mounted upon the wall was the stuffed head of a terror bird and impressionistic paintings of Elarondian wyvern riders. A path towards his desk was carved from the clutter, though as Solyx sat, it became clear that the only other chair was hidden behind a pile of dusty, mould-eaten books.

"The terror bird's nice," Rakh remarked. "Killed on Sanguinas Isle, I presume?"

"Did you not hear me the first time, snake? Your flattery is unimportant," Solyx chided. "What's the situation?"

Rakh paused. "I disguised as a worker in the *White Wendigo,* and they saw Irikhos with Lady Selenia, but were bribed to ensure they wouldn't report their sighting to the guards."

Solerro scoffed. "Commoners. Their persistent hunger makes them simple to control. Who bribed them?"

"Unfortunately for your lady wife, Irikhos," Rakh answered. "That's why I think it's best to consult you. That and you're more likely to have the information I require."

"Enough preamble. What do you need?"

"Irikhos reportedly offered to take Lady Selenia to a shrine, which would have to be Eternalist to successfully lure her. You were born to Eternalist parents, correct?"

"Yes," Solerro answered. "You want to know which Eternalist shrine Irikhos would be familiar with, don't you? There's only one, and thankfully it's not in the rapeworm-affected areas. Would you like me to lead you there?"

Rakh nodded. "If it's not too much trouble."

Lord Consort Solyx stood. "Too much trouble? Whether Irikhos is missing as a victim or stupid enough to have harmed his overlady, we must find him, for Mor'kha's sake. Incidentally, if he *did* wish to harm her, he wouldn't need to move from the shrine."

As he backed towards the exit, Rakh almost tripped over a stray catgut fishing line, catching himself before he spoke. "Why is that?"

"Because my beloved wife did what she does to all Eternalist shrines. She doesn't want me to complain, but at the same time doesn't want non-Renewalist religion in Ashglass. So, she strangled the life out of the Eternalist churches and shrines with taxes. The priests at the Potter Street Shrine had to give up and become tradesmen about a year ago. There's nothing left the pews, the altar, and a copy of the Eternal Word."

"It's a squatter's haven, then," Rakh remarked.

"Exactly," Solerro said. "Knowing Irikhos, he'd want to keep street rats out, so he probably brought muscle."

"Should we do the same?" Rakh said, successfully leaving the office.

"No, we should jump into the shrine unprepared," the lord consort snapped.

"It was a foolish question," Rakh admitted. "Let's muster who we can at the barracks and then you can lead the way."

* * *

The Sons of Sula's bleating may have been filtered through one of Darvith's many portals, yet it still drove him to distraction. Each of the Nortezian coordinators had proven incompetent, and Siendros, Demidium's coordinator, had the gall to complain about the city's condition, safe in the second-hour sector while the ninth-hour sector fell apart. Darvith had given the tiny wisp of an ascendant a portal's view of the situation, along with a direct connection to his fleshly puppet, the ever-pliable Axas.

"What do we do?" Siendros asked, gesturing at the riots consuming the ninth-hour sector's outer slice with gilded gauntlets. *"Even as the soulstealer-wielding madwoman demonstrates her destructive intent, the fleshly join her as often as they resist. Incorporating fleshly soldiers into the Sons of Sula was a mistake. The only way to unite Galdus is to eliminate the new and work with the previously ascended. We cannot trust mortal troops."*

Axas, hooded and masked, grew adorably irate. *"You wish to slander fleshly allies? Remember it is I, a fleshly Galdusian, who appointed you as the Demidium coordinator!"*

"You are an exception, not a rule, surely you see that! With every wasted moment, the madness spreads closer to Demidium's inner city. Prestalis failed to understand that intimidation alone doesn't secure the loyalty of the breeders, and that's how Pentatum's membrane fell!" Siendros ranted, his ruby-red embers glowing with every syllable. *"We should raze the ninth-hour sector, remove human, breeder,*

255

and insurrectionist alike, then remake it. The Breeding Facility was the only use the fleshly had, and now it's destroyed!"

"I refuse to let the brave fleshly recruits who fight for Galdus's unity be squandered by your extremism!" Axas replied. *"If we fight Praetor Erre, who I remind you wields a soulstealer, with ascendants alone, failure is guaranteed. All we'll do is fuel her increasing magical power. I'm starting to think you're a Nortezian saboteur!"*

Darvith pondered the exchange as he eyed Demidium with his many sky-portals. The insurrectionists were uncoordinated; the only significant threats were the soulstealer wielder and the chaos-speaker. The latter was consistent only in his inconsistency, the farce to Andros's tragedy.

He could encourage Siendros's genocidal, incompetent nature and rob the Sons of Sula of their few soldiers immune to Erre's crutch. Then again, if he were to openly sabotage the Sons of Sula, the group would vanish from his little game. He needed a response that weakened his Galdusian experiment, masqueraded as a wise compromise, and fattened Praetor Erre's pride before her slaughter.

"Enough," Darvith echoed through both the Sons' portals. *"You shall cease these futile attempts to stop Praetor Erre and her jesters."*

Axas scoffed. *"You expect us to let her run roughshod through Demidium?"*

"Precisely," Darvith said, watching another purity inspection bureau collapse from Erre's blinding rays. *"Ascended enforcers are worthless against her soulstealer, and fleshly soldiers break too easily when faced with her spellwork."*

"We can't let her get away!" Axas spluttered.

"Indeed. Though Axas and I disagree on the method, surely her death is the most important goal for the Sons of Sula," Siendros added.

256

Darvith slipped his attention away from the pair and looked through his primary eyes, beholding the majestic urban square of his own creation. Nova Tertia stretched towards the horizon even from his massive height, and the billions within the supercity worshipped him. He was too perfect for these fools to comprehend.

"Siendros, have your local Sons evacuate those unwilling to join the madness," Darvith commanded. *"When other sectors hear of the Sons' heroism, sympathies will shift towards you. You shall be hailed as a hero despite your prejudice against the fleshly."*

Siendros appeared to suffer from a mental stammer. *"You think my attitude is wrong?"*

"You forget you were once fleshly yourself. Ascendant or fleshling, each soul is just that: A soul. Corruptible, imperfect, ambitious and flawed. You and the fleshly are equally capable of failure. Mobilise your ninth-sector men and arrange evacuations."

"Should I tell Malderis and Mythria to prepare for inner-city insertion?" Axas asked.

"No. I shall personally clean up the insurrection once they gate to Nova Tertia," Darvith assured them. *"I allowed your little social movement the time it needed to grow, Axas. You and your coordinators shall not disappoint me."*

Before they could answer, Darvith closed the portals connecting him to them and basked in his beauty once more. In truth, the evacuation efforts were irrelevant. The Sons would enjoy their contemporary reverence, while Darvith maintained the Sula that would go down in history; delusional failure held together by one sinchild's efforts.

"Are you really going to kill her so soon?" his godly father asked.

Darvith opened a portal above Demidium, spotting a swarm of rioters crushing themselves with their own successful demolition. He answered with his original body's soul, muffled amidst the millions he'd harvested.

"Of course."

"I thought this disunited parody of the Golden Galdusian Empire was an intentional failure," the Sovereign remarked. **"Don't tell me you've grown too attached to watch it fall apart? Or perhaps you're akin to the terrible Ilazari artist that claims their works are parodic in an ill-conceived defence of their ego?"**

"I'm not attached to Sula," Darvith snapped. *"Praetor Erre is too insignificant to give me a worthy end. Andros was my first rival, and if I must die, I shall die to a fellow sinchild, not some pretender."*

"That chaos-speaker is almost Andros. Perhaps you could accept your end here and bring me your souls ahead of time, then let this society fall as it will? It would certainly prove your point about you being the sole factor tying Sula together, would it not?"

Darvith's emotions surged through his massive, cloudy body, rumbling like a thunderstorm. He almost responded with his public voice, barely quietening down in time.

"Why are you asking me this now? Why do you instil doubt at such crucial junctures? Is this about my ascension?"

"Our deal was contingent upon you eventually ending. You cling to life as though you fear me," the Sovereign stated. **"I want my souls, Darvith, every soul that forms that abomination you call a body. If Razarkha Fel'thuz consumes them all, I must accept that as a side-effect of the soulstealers' production, but you will have backed out of your side of the deal. Sinchildren become wardens in my Underworld, but for a sinchild that's failed me? I'll admit, you'll be the first outright failure I've had. I'll have to tailor an afterlife just for you."**

258

Darvith remembered his original body, small and weak, alone in the food repositories of Old Tertia, abandoned by his pride-consumed parents. He screamed for hours, yet nobody in the sector heard him.

"I am not swindling you, father," Darvith assured the god. *"Praetor Erre will be squashed like the historical footnote she is, I will harvest a million more souls, then finally, I'll die a worthy death to an opponent of my station."*

"There is no-one of your station," the Sovereign pointed out. ***"Enjoy 'squashing' this supposed footnote, Lucy."***

Though Darvith's godly father fell silent, the damage was already done. He needed something to pick himself up. Perhaps the collapse of the Demidium Membrane was imminent; he didn't know if days or weeks had passed since his conversation with Axas and Siendros.

He checked to see that the Demidium Membrane already had a hole punched in it. There were a surprising number of living insurrectionists, which meant Siendros evacuated the ninth-hour sector as commanded. He could see, as a tangle of spectral strings stretched taut through the wilderlands, the connections between Demidium and Nova Tertia's gates.

The insects spread into the inner city, sucking up every ascendant they passed, yet the closest gatekeeper was spared Erre's rampage. Darvith opened a portal nearby to sate his curiosity regarding this impromptu mercy. Upon closer inspection, the lauded Praetor Erre was far from impressive. Her cape was a torn-apart mockery, her Ilazari-style makeup was smudged, and dim, discoloured strands of hair lingered where dye once persisted.

She was pointing her borrowed weapon at the gatekeeper, an ascendant who'd formed herself into a metallic tortoise, ranting in broken Sulari about how she would consume the gatekeeper unless she opened the gate to Nova Tertia. Amusingly, the ascendant pointed out that if she killed her, there would be nobody around to operate the gate.

A similar event transpired in Pentatum, according to Prestalis, and it would appear Erre didn't want to repeat her mistakes. The self-proclaimed praetor argued with the true praetor until Darvith's patience waned. He opened an orderly portal even closer to the situation, sucked the ascendant to safety, then forcibly opened the pathway between Demidium and Nova Tertia, eagerly yet silently observing both sides' gates.

Razarkha Fel'thuz questioned the situation, but the beaten and bloodied remnants of her insurrection couldn't provide an answer. Minutes passed like days as the fools debated fruitlessly. They wished to travel to Nova Tertia before Darvith's intervention, so why they hesitated to dance to their doom was anybody's guess.

Eventually, they travelled through, arriving in the third-hour sector of Nova Tertia's inner city. Ascendants rose to fight them, but Darvith, finally able to directly toy with the false praetor, invoked a storm above the sector, winds whipping so violently that ascendant and insurrectionist alike were swept up. He was sure to be gentle; he wanted to speak to his would-be assassin first. His massive body drifted from the citadel, casting a shadow the size of the southern Jaranese Isles over his parodic city. It had been a while since he'd personally overseen the expansion of the Golden Galdusian Empire; it was good to agitate his ancient wisps.

Once he was close enough to the storm, he raised a great column of arcane gas that resembled an arm, ending the storm, then cast a telekinetic net that caught the four leaders of Erre's Insurrection, while the rest of the riotous fleshlings plummeted to the unblemished towers below. The local ascendants cleared while Darvith stretched his other 'hand' to give the impression of levitating the four spellbinders above his palm.

"And so, the insurrection that crippled Duke Weldum's 'perfect state in the making' is foiled in moments," Darvith said, keeping his glimmering eyes focused on Fel'thuz's miserable face. *"Did you think that gate opened at random? Your revolution was always at my mercy. The traitorous citizens you recruited through your rampages are dead, scattered upon the floor like the insects they are. It will be troublesome to scour their remains from the streets, but your despair makes it worth the effort."*

"You killed them!" Razarkha screamed, her tone fittingly impotent.

"How many ascendants have you killed? If we count the years we've each cut short, we're close to equals," Darvith said. *"Even so, this insignificant rabble was everything to you, while the ascendants you've consumed are nothing compared to the body you behold."*

Though all four insurrectionists were limp, the most broken was a tall man with long hair wearing a Hextolis kimono. His arcane signature implied he was the geomancer who attempted to wall in the humans they inadvertently killed.

"What's your name, child? The geomancer."

"Igneus," he responded flatly.

"You look crushed, Igneus," Darvith responded, his laughter akin to a thunderclap. *"What's on your mind?"*

"Everything's gone," Igneus muttered. *"I didn't want the Sons of Sula ruining the future Nortez had. I didn't think I'd be responsible for all this death."*

"Your suffering will soon end," Darvith promised, and with that, he telekinetically flicked him into the distance.

The pyromantic woman screamed, Andros's laughable copy squirmed, but Razarkha Fel'thuz was queerly still. Darvith clumped his myriad shining eyes together into one multicoloured sphere, aimed directly at her.

261

"Nothing to say, Praetor Erre? No condemnation of the society you attempted to destroy? I've watched you from afar and know you're more bombastic than this."

"Why are you toying with your prey?" the Sovereign asked, and in the moments it took for Darvith to quieten himself, he felt a tugging sensation at his extremities.

It was the ascendants his hand consisted of being sucked into the Soulstealer of Craving. Darvith retracted his 'arm' and released his telekinesis, allowing them to fall.

"You did that deliberately, didn't you, father?" Darvith said as the three fleshlings fell.

"You're already sabotaging yourself. Why shouldn't I add to the sources of your downfall? Oh, watch out, they're not done yet."

"What?"

Darvith looked down to see a portal beneath the trio, and though he reached out with his telekinesis, the three made it into the Chaotic Realm before he could swipe them. He made one last effort, directly plunging his 'arm' into the rift, only for its gaseous matter to corrupt into black sludge, the result of orderly matter touching its antithesis. Darvith severed his 'limb' before the inky plague consumed his entire body and shifted his form to a negligibly smaller rendition of the one he had before the 'battle'.

"At least some of your souls are now in my hands," the Sovereign remarked. **"I'll consider this a repayment instalment."**

"You cannot slip your mockery beneath my notice, father," Darvith replied.

"Why wouldn't I want you to notice my mockery?" the god jeered. **"If you didn't spend so much time merged with your victims, you wouldn't be so cripplingly prideful. Velzha's a virgin, Mayza's thin and healthy, and Ma works tirelessly to maintain his pleasure house. You're the only sinchild who's fallen so thoroughly to his own sin."**

262

"Silence!" Darvith exploded, unleashing a magical blast that demolished half the sector's buildings. *"It doesn't matter. I've already tracked their rift's destination. They're headed to Ante Tertia, a worthless set of ruins."*

"That's a fine way to refer to your birthplace."

"It doesn't matter what you say. If they return, they're dead, and if they leave Galdus, they've proven their irrelevance."

* * *

Kagura had hoped Irikhos was as tired as her, but the younger Foenaxas sibling was still ranting with ragged determination. The shrine basement was still naught but darkness, though time had transformed the dank stench of mould into a sewer-like aroma.

"If you don't know where the will is, I have no choice but to kill you," he rambled. "I don't care what you think about dark and high elves, I don't care what you intended when you undermined your own father's will. None of that matters anymore. I can't sleep knowing that if I let you go, you'll just go back to ruling our province without a hint of remorse."

"But I really don't know where it is!" Kagura insisted. "It's not my fault, Erwyn was the one who hid it, he said he knew a really good place and—"

"That fucking wisdom knows?" Irikhos screamed as his pacing grew frantic. He reached Kagura's chair, took her by the shoulders, and shook her. "You're telling me Wisdom Erwyn conspired to put you in power? What in the world would— oh, it's obvious, isn't it? Minor count syndrome, if you don't have worthwhile lands, become an advisor to a weak person with a powerful birthright."

"I don't understand, he said he did it because I was the rightful ruler—"

263

"Have you learned nothing?" Irikhos fulminated. "Nobody, and I mean *nobody* likes you. The fact your father disinherited you with his dying wish should prove that. Even Erwyn's using you. You're a pathetic idiot who doesn't even realise how evil she is for sending her own sisters to their possible deaths."

"My father loved me. He said that mother was on the moon, that he'd be joining her soon to give me a brother. He promised me I'd marry him, he loved me, he did, he must have," Kagura mumbled, her words growing increasingly hollow even to herself.

Irikhos put his mouth next to Kagura's ear. "He never trusted you with the truth. You were a disappointment."

"No!"

Sir Almarax's voice called from a distance. "There's no need, Irikhos! The fuck you doing kicking her while she's down? You got what you wanted, you know who can show you the will, just think of what we're gonna do now that we're stuck with a fucking *overlady.*"

Irikhos moved from Kagura. "There's no need for you to start asking questions!"

"Maybe I'm having second thoughts agreeing to this stupid scheme."

"Do you want to move out of this city or not? You and your family in the Sunfort, away from all this disease and horror, that's what you agreed to," Irikhos reminded him.

Almarax paused. "I'll shut up, but only if you give what you promised right now."

"Fine."

The sound of hands fumbling was heard, and misery overcame Kagura. It didn't matter if she was an overlady; she was as weak as any commoner down here. Torawyn would have spoken her way out, and Yarawyn would have beaten Irikhos half to death before letting him kidnap her. Kagura was the worst sibling, and even her father knew that.

"Irikhos, before you kill me, I'm sorry," Kagura mumbled.

The dark elf's voice faltered. "What?"

"I'm sorry. You're right. My father's will wasn't a lie. I didn't want to think my father hated me, but he did. Razarkha said so too, and Rakh probably thought the same. Maybe Erwyn and Plutyn believe it too. Everybody hates me. I didn't want to be some forgotten person, so I became the overlady. I'm sorry I ruined your marriage even if I don't know why you won't just marry a nice dark elven woman. I don't hate dark elven women, I really don't! Your sister's ugly but I've seen dark elven servants who are really pretty—"

"Be quiet," Irikhos snapped. "Your apology is enough. If you keep talking, you'll just make me hate you again."

"I know. I'm sorry."

Irikhos rested against something solid. "Did Yarawyn love me back? She always seemed to, but maybe she was just putting on a show for her betrothed."

"You just told 'er to be quiet," Almarax pointed out.

"Of course," Irikhos said, allowing the despondency to ferment. "What now?"

Suddenly, light flooded into the room with a crash. A group of Foenaxas soldiers rushed down the freshly revealed stairs, and Irikhos raised his hands in surrender. Almarax pressed his back against the wall and slumped in defeat. Behind the squad was the first familiar face Kag had seen in days.

He may have been snakelike, with ridiculous purple dye in his hair, but he was a friend. Rakh rushed to Kagura's chair and untied her, then stepped back to let her stand. Amidst the Foenaxas soldiers was Solyx Solerro, who was the first to speak.

"I'm glad you had the sense to yield," the lord consort called to Irikhos. "What in the world were you thinking? Ah, it matters not. Men, arrest them both, but ensure they're in as comfortable a cell as can be provided. Is your lady faring well, Fel'thuz?"

Kagura could only stare at her saviours, and without thinking, she collapsed into Count Fel'thuz's arms, weeping uncontrollably.

"I know you hate me, Rakh. I know you hate me and I'm sorry."

"What for?"

"Everything. Being me."

Rakh's embrace was as comforting as her father's, but knowing both were lies only made Kagura's legs weaker. Despite this, she held him as though her life depended on it.

Defeated

Rakh, Solyx and Lady Selenia approached Castle Foenaxas with Irikhos and his armoured friend in tow while the rumbling of an organ played far too loud travelled through Count Fel'thuz's very body. The tune mostly made sense, having an Arkheran sense of harmonics and the occasional Elarondian-style glissando, but odd dissonant slip-ups revealed that whoever was playing the organ, they were either unskilled or extremely distracted.

"Strakha's really taking this hard," Irikhos remarked, his voice delicate as snow.

Rakh turned to the dark elf. "I don't know why you took such a drastic action. She's been inconsolable ever since I *suggested* you kidnapped Lady Selenia. What in the world were you thinking?"

"If I told you, you wouldn't believe me. You're probably in on it," Irikhos muttered. "Why don't you ask Lady Selenia?"

Rakh paused, then addressed Kag. "What is he talking about?"

"I had Erwyn hide father's will," Kagura mumbled. "I was only supposed to be lady until Yar came of age. Once she got married to Irikhos, she'd be the overlady."

Rakh stopped walking just shy of the castle gates, an action Kag mimicked while Solyx pressed on with his men.

"I thought you were just paranoid about your sisters. In truth, you were going to lose everything, at least in your eyes," Rakh said, hoping that Kagura would correct him.

"I was selfish and evil. You hate me too, don't you? I know I'm stupid, but I can see your eyes," Kagura said. "I like you, Rakh, and I'm sorry you and Erwyn always have to stop me doing stupid things. If you want me to die, I understand."

Rakh gazed at his lady, her skin barely more colourful than the snow around her. She shivered in her Wrenfall kimono while her matted, unclean hair billowed in the winter winds. Even when confessing to wilful subversion of her father's dying wishes, she was a pitiful soul. Count Fel'thuz removed his coat and put it around her.

"You wronged Irikhos and more importantly, your own sisters. That said, I'm in no position to lecture you about fairness to one's kin," Rakh stated. "Irikhos wronged you too. He gained your trust and then violated it. Ask yourself what can be done to make things right."

"Irikhos committed treason against his overlady," Kagura said. "King Landon would have us kill him."

"Not if the injured party objects," Rakh suggested.

"If I let him live, do you think he'd hurt me again?"

Rakh hesitated. "He's a decent man— decent as any kidnapper can be, at least. At any rate, he's not stupid enough to try the same trick again."

Kagura bunched herself up in Rakh's coat. "Thank you for the advice, Count Fel'thuz."

With that, the lady moved forward, as did Rakh, entering the obsidian maw of Castle Foenaxas together. He followed the footprint of Solyx's men, which led them towards the increasingly deafening organ music. At some point, the music abruptly stopped, and Rakh only had the raised voices of the Foenaxas family to guide him to the castle's music room.

It was a spacious area with numerous seats and a wall-consuming pipe organ, populated by Solyx, his muscle, the Foenaxas siblings, and the children. Young Morganix was with his parents and uncle, listening to the adults' argument, while Moryx and Lexana played lutes together and the youngest two, Darkhal and Irigax, bickered over some stuffed toy. Rakh glanced at his lady, and she took her borrowed coat off her shoulders. Lady Mor'kha was

268

screaming at her husband, and as Rakh approached, he barely gleaned words from them.

"This can't be! There must be a mistake, Sol, a misunderstanding! Iri, you're not the monster he says you are, tell me you're not, please!"

Irikhos lowered his head, prompting the wild-eyed lady to dart towards her overlady. She took the latter's hands forcefully, and as Lady Selenia squirmed in her grasp, she continued her tirade.

"Overlady Selenia, my dear liege, you're able to clear all this up, aren't you? Solyx got a little overzealous maintaining his neutrality, and now he thinks Irikhos is a kidnapper!"

Rakh swallowed. "Lady Foenaxas, you allowed me to investigate the possibility—"

"But my hope was that the truth would be found, clearing Iri's name!" Mor'kha said, shaking Kagura's hands. "My overlady, surely you know what *truly* transpired! It was the common oaf, Almarax, wasn't it? *Wasn't it?*"

Kagura couldn't find her words, but Irikhos spoke for her. "Strakha, stop. Almarax just followed my orders. He deserves to be released."

Mor'kha released Kag, then turned to her family. "I'm becoming erratic in front of Morganix. I'm sorry, Morgan, I'm just concerned Uncle Iri will be falsely accused of—"

"It's not a false accusation," Irikhos interrupted. "I'm sorry, Strakha, but I did kidnap Lady Selenia. I committed treason, and I can't let you threaten them until I go free. Moonstone would rightly march upon Ashglass in retribution, and you know we can't afford that."

Mor'kha's expression reminded Rakh of his father whenever he spotted Razarkha bullying Tei. She turned to her husband, who shook his head, then to Lady Selenia. Morganix stared at his uncle, then spoke in a cracking, shaky tone.

"Why? That stupid high elf is going to have you executed, and there's nothing I can do! Mum can't help, mum can't help, Uncle Iri, why?"

The boy burst into tears and hugged his uncle, who returned the gesture with a grip tight enough to lift him. Mor'kha fell to her knees and Solyx approached her, crouching and bringing her into an embrace.

"It'll be all right, Feeny, it'll be all right," he assured her, but she pushed him away.

"It *won't* be! Moonstone needs Irikhos's head! I tried my hardest to rule, to honour my father's generosity, and just as I thought I could be comfortable, rapeworm blights this city, and now Irikhos is going to *die!* Mother would accuse me of setting this up, you know she would, just like the commoners who think I somehow had the rapeworm target the entertainment district. What did I do to anger God, Sol?"

Kagura unsurely approached Mor'kha, and though every instinct told Rakh to stop her, she was the victim. Regardless of her childishness, she needed to be heard.

"Lady Foenaxas?"

Mor'kha hung her head. "I know, my liege. Irikhos deserves to die."

"Does he?" Kagura said. "I was the one who was kidnapped and I'm the overlady, so I decide what happens to people who commit treason against me."

Rakh swallowed. Whenever Lady Selenia began swinging her birthright around, the best he could hope for was meaningless posturing. Still, his tongue had to hold; as impractical as it was, it was the only correct course of action.

"Your vassal is ready to accept your verdict," Mor'kha said, her voice devoid of inflection.

"I don't want the King to think he's gone unpunished, but recently, my count set a— a— a pattern, a pa— a *precedent,* that's the word!" Kagura rambled, causing Irikhos, Mor'kha, Solyx, and Rakh to stare at her as she continued. "Anyway, Razarkha, Rakh's wife, she tried to kill him, and Rakh exiled her instead. While that turned out to be a bad thing, I think Irikhos is a good man. He doesn't want Almarax to be punished, which is good, because he was so nice to me while I was in the shrine basement, so—"

"Overlady, are you saying you're willing to preserve Iri's life?" Mor'kha asked, soul returning to her voice.

"Yes, but I think after he educated me—"

"No, no, Lady Selenia, I'm sorry," Irikhos began, releasing his nephew. "All the horrible stuff I said was just kicking someone while they were down, like Almarax said."

"I am your overlady and I won't be interrupted!" Kagura shouted. "I don't want you to be exiled forever. I want you to find my sisters in Elarond, then take them home. After that, I'll have Erwyn help you. Am I clear?"

Irikhos stared at Kag. "Are you serious?"

"Why would I joke about this?"

Mor'kha stood, and without hesitation, hugged her overlady. "I don't fully understand, but you're showing a mercy I never thought Eternalists capable of. I must offer my apologies. I oft found myself considering you foolish, arrogant, even evil, but you've proven yourself to be as noble as your station demands."

Lady Kag silently accepted the embrace. Rakh turned away and watched the Foenaxas children, ignorant of the drama surrounding them, then smiled knowing that Lady Kag had distinguished herself from them.

* * *

Weil's portal dropped the three remnants of Erre's Insurrection onto a stony plaza, surrounded by deadened, pale husks that resembled modern Galdusian towers. They were occasionally broken up by angular, pillar-supported marble and alabaster structures which Arkherans would call 'traditionally Galdusian'. In the sky, swarms of cloaks drifted aimlessly.

Razarkha rubbed her eyes, then checked her sides, spotting a dazed Adolita and a long-since-recovered Weil, who was staring at the clusters of ascendants above them. Strangely, they lacked magical smoke, and had no variants beyond the typical animated cloak.

Wherever they were, the city's citadel was non-functional, as while it dominated the horizon, it lacked the usual urban glow, and there were no signs of the permanent storms that Pentatum, Hextolis, and Demidium possessed. Twisted lianas and mushroom heads fought for dominance with the rocky remnants of whatever settlement this used to be, their battle illuminated by a friend Razarkha didn't know she'd miss: The sun.

"Those ascendants haven't noticed us," Weil remarked in Isleborn. *"I wonder why?"*

"They don't appear to be ascendants at all," Razarkha added. "Bold Individualist, your thoughts?"

"There are no souls here beside— oh, that's a fond memory."

Razarkha scowled. "I've just lost everything, Bold Individualist. Elaboration would be appreciated."

"This is Ante Tertia, and aside from you three, there are only two souls. One of them is eternally immune to soulstealers, and the other I haven't met before. Perhaps it was born beyond my reach? How fascinating."

"What did the Bold Individualist say?" Weil asked flatly.

"A load of nonsense, but between the blether he claimed there are two souls here," Razarkha relayed. *"These ascendants must be telekinetic puppets akin to the ones I used in Demidium, but why bother animating them? Who are they attempting to fool?"*

A false ascendant trimmed a tangle of lianas from a nearby tower, while another brushed past a fungal fruiting body, causing it to pop into multicoloured spores that stained its cloak. Razarkha glanced at the seemingly catatonic

Adolita, then jumped at a shadow of her father, great and slender, like a massive upright snake. Weil's voice made the apparition fade.

"It's over, isn't it?"

"It's not. We'll find a way to overcome this Sulari monster."

"Everyone's dead, Razarkha."

Praetor Erre wouldn't give up. Even Razarkha Fel'thuz died hard. This couldn't be the end of her crusade. The Sons of Sula weren't the problem anymore, nor was Galdusian enslavement of humans. Razarkha always killed those in her way; Vi'khash, Ivan, Elki Kasparov, Rowyn Khanas had all learnt that. This great conglomerate ascendant saw fit to oppose her, and just like Rakh, his day of reckoning would come.

"We will overcome him!"

Weil groaned. *"Why fight at all? We should return to Ilazar. We tried to change Galdus and got everybody killed, time to give up and go home."*

"I can't go home until I'm powerful!" Razarkha shouted. *"I'll prove this creature wrong, then I'll prove Rakh wrong too! Do you think I'm weak, Weil?"*

"Against an ascendant like—"

"I'll prove you wrong too," Razarkha snapped. *"Fortunately for you, you're my friend, and you saved my life."*

Weil turned away from Razarkha, his brow furrowed. Adolita rose from her daze and, predictably, began complaining too.

"It wasn't a nightmare," she said in Nortezian. *"All the triumphs we celebrated were for nothing. That ascendant killed us like we were vermin. He singled out Igneus for sport."*

"This is no time to give up," Razarkha spluttered.

"Really?" the pyromancer asked, approaching Razarkha with flames around her hands. *"Our revolution*

utterly failed to save humans I didn't even want to save, that augmentee abandoned us with that foreigner, then we stepped through that gate on your command, leading to my battle brothers dying by the scores. Now is perfect time to give up!"

Razarkha pointed her soulstealer at Adolita. *"Watch your tongue, Adolita. Even in Galdus, there must be sayings about the dangers of a person with nothing to lose."*

"Ah, 'even in Galdus', here we are, this is the true Praetor Erre, though praetor is too honourable a title and Erre too Galdusian a sound," Adolita ranted. *"You're a foreigner who wanted to ruin a nation that means nothing to you. All your talk of quashing the Sons of Sula and making Nortez better disappeared once you got your souls!"*

Razarkha scoffed. *"Are you accusing me of intentionally orchestrating this failure? Do you think I'd willingly subject myself to this humiliation?"*

"How can I be sure? Somehow that great Sulari ascendant knew to put off your death!"

"You're alive too, if you haven't noticed!"

Adolita blasted herself into the air, maintaining a fire-sustained hover. *"Perhaps your Ilazari pet wasn't briefed on your plans. You didn't brief your Arkheran necromancer to be valorous. I'm done listening to you—"*

Razarkha shot Adolita out of the air before she could attempt something similar, a lumomantic ray piercing the woman's chest. Her charred body plummeted, and her wounds were so cauterised that most of her organs remained within her as she hit the ground.

Weil, paralysed throughout, suddenly sprung into pointless Isleborn theatrics. *"What happened? Why did you do that?"*

"Don't you have eyes? She was preparing to bomb us!"

"Or fly away!"

"Would you have given her the chance to do either?"

274

Weil hesitated. *"I would have tried to talk her out of it!"*

Razarkha clenched her fists. *"Talking never fixes anything!"*

"Talking is what gained us our revolution!"

"And now it's gone, Weil, we're back at the beginning! Even you couldn't be talked into helping me. You would have abandoned me in Ilazar. Only your father's death got you to stay with me," Razarkha ranted as she involuntarily projected Tei and Rakh's faces onto the false ascendants. *"Fear, horror, and anger are the only things that grant me allies. I'm a monster, and monsters don't have real friends. Just people too afraid to oppose them."*

Weil took a sharp breath. *"I finished that book on the boat to Demidium, and—"*

"I just killed one half of my remaining allies and you're going to talk about some stupid bondage book? In case you haven't noticed, we're doomed! *I'm trying my hardest not to accidentally kill you,"* Razarkha babbled, her illusions becoming indistinguishable from the true ascendant effigies. *"If you have nothing worthwhile to say, if you're not going to support my decision to kill Rowyn, and Adolita, and every traitor there is, then hide in your stupid portals and leave me to my thoughts."*

"I'm sorry," Weil said. *"We should at least try to find somebody else. As you said, it's not over yet. Perhaps one of these two souls can help us find a reliable way back to Ilazar. I could rebuild my house and—"*

Razarkha shoved Weil to shut him up, then allowed her soulstealer's energies to flow through her. In fleeting pieces, the local arcana flickered red, and though the 'ascendants' lacked true conduits, they were propped up by tendrils of telekinetic magic that flowed towards the centre of the ruined citadel before them. Within were a pair of arcane sources, only one of which held these puppets' strings.

275

"We need to enter the citadel," Razarkha said. *"If we aren't doomed to eternally hop from portal to portal in search of food, our answers lie there."*

"Would you like a tentacle to fling us? Once we're in the air, you can use telekinesis to take us the rest of the way."

Razarkha held her last ally. *"You're loyal to a fault. Perhaps everybody betrayed me for a reason. You're the only person long-suffering enough to love me."*

"I don't know what to tell you, Razarkha," Weil said.

"That's all right. I don't know what to tell myself."

There was nothing left to say. With an open portal and a tentacular flex, the first and last of Razarkha's revolutionaries flew through the bright skies, heading towards calamity, hope, or something else entirely.

* * *

It had been centuries since an openly necromantic lord ruled within Arkhera, yet to Plutyn Khanas, it was like slipping on a surgical glove. He'd claimed a room that once belonged to one of the Fel'thuzes, and from its window, the snow-covered, peaceful city he'd produced lay before him like a scale model. The antlike citizens, twisting terraces, and gangrenous churches served as a reminder of the power his ancestors once held in the Flowerfields.

Quira Abraxas ruled her own mockery of a city pretending to be a spellbinder, but here Plutyn was, reminding Arkhera what true prosperity was without the masquerades. The Liquid Shade Cartel were afraid to eat lunch in this city, and thanks to Rowyn, the Malassaian Traffickers were a scum-laden memory. It was almost noon, and unfortunately Plutyn had more on his agenda than basking in success. He couldn't afford to be accused of flat-footing.

He walked to his dresser, picked up his pipe, and filled it from his sachet of bhang-weed. A match-strike later, and he was right again. He couldn't allow himself to grow comfortable. His father and poor, dear Mortyn fell into one or both of those traps, as did foolish, entitled Rowyn, albeit not to the grave.

Plutyn left his newly claimed room and moved through the silvery, chilled halls of Castle Selenia, then arrived at the wisdom's chambers, where Plutera was already sorting through the nobility's mail. She was so lost in the work that Plutyn entered the office without her notice. It was only after his pipe's smoke reached her nostrils that she turned around.

"Father! Heavens, you crept up on me like a spectre!"

"You cannot allow yourself to be so focused on a task that you're unaware of your surroundings," Plutyn stated. "What if I were an assassin?"

Plutera's face reddened. "I'm sorry, father. I know you're only saying this because you need me to be strong."

"Not necessarily strong, but alert. Be quick enough to see the strong coming, be clever enough to know what to do," Plutyn said as though a piece of gnomish clockwork. "I'm still proud of you, Plutera. I just want assurance that when I inevitably pass away—"

"I know. I'm not upset that you brought it up," Plutera said, her smile reminding Plutyn of the woman who died birthing her.

"What news from the surrounding cities?" Plutyn asked, taking a deep puff of his pipe.

"I'm just going through it. There's word from Wisdom Yugen of Parakos regarding the missing Amerei Gemcutter debacle," the girl said, scanning the topmost letter. "Would you believe it? A twelve-year-old bastard girl goes missing, and when the wisdom found her, not only was she in Yukishima, but she was *alive*. I'm glad for her safe return, but I must admit the circumstances are cosmically unlikely."

"A heroic tale we're the bystanders to," Plutyn remarked. "Perhaps one day we can have the wisdom over for some wine and bhang-weed. People of Madaki descent can appreciate a good smoke. The rest of the letters?"

"There's a few from Wisdom Khalver Veritas. Let's see…" Plutera mumbled, flitting through letters with dancing eyes. "…Erwyn starting his research with Melancholy, Lady Selenia proving irritating, Lady Selenia having gone—oh my."

"What is it?"

"Lady Selenia and Irikhos Foenaxas have gone missing, and Count Fel'thuz has started a search. She may already be found given the time it takes for letters to arrive here, but still, if the lady remains missing, what do we do?"

Plutyn's frown intensified, and smoking didn't alleviate it. "We keep this matter secret for now. If she remains missing, we could mobilise the Selenia troops to prove our loyalty, then 'lose' to thank the Foenaxases for letting such a tragedy befall our beloved overlady."

Plutera lowered her gaze. "Father, Lady Selenia's irritating, but she's soft-headed. She's no more to blame for her nature than a dog is."

"That's where you're wrong. A poorly trained dog's actions can be blamed on its owner's incompetence, but ultimately, the dog is the creature that bites, and when it mauls the wrong person, it is the dog that is put to the sword," Plutyn stated, then put a hand on his daughter's shoulder. "I envy your gentle heart. However, this world is as icy in temperament as this city is in weather. You must chill yourself to match it."

"Or I could warm the icy world up," Plutera offered.

"Even at your age, I couldn't possess such optimism. Perhaps I am wrong to teach you when you stand to teach me so much."

Plutera's green eyes flared up like the family skull, and with renewed vigour she continued to scan through the letters. She laughed and handed a few letters to Plutyn.

"Baron Oswyk's still sending us angry letters, isn't that amusing?"

"Quite," Plutyn said, almost cracking a smile.

"And then there's a few from— what's this sigil?" Plutera asked, tapping a sea-green smudge of wax imprinted with three 'claw marks'.

"I believe that belongs to the Saltclaws of Sandport," Plutyn said, taking the letter to confirm it. "Likely news regarding Amerei Gemcutter, if the girl was truly rescued from Yukishima."

Plutyn opened the letter and scanned its contents, mouthing along as he did.

"To Lady Kag'nemera Selenia of Moonstone and her court. This is a transcription of a telegram requested by Imperial Engineer Hildegard Swan. We write to inform you that, in his duties as a spy, Rowyn Khanas has died at sea by Razarkha Fel'thuz's hand. His remains will unfortunately will not be recovered—"

Plutyn couldn't finish it. He'd made jests of how, if the gods were just, Rowyn would die assassinating Razarkha, yet now that it happened, he couldn't help but curse the gods.

"What's wrong, father? I didn't quite hear you," Plutera said.

"It's about Rowyn," Plutyn answered. "He's dead, Plutera."

His daughter shook her head. "No. After he'd proven so heroic in Winter Harbour, after we'd said our goodbyes, he can't be gone forever, he— let me read it."

Heedless as ever, the girl snatched the letter from Plutyn and upon reading it herself, slammed it against the desk. "If Razarkha returns to Moonstone, I'll kill her myself."

"No," Plutyn commanded. "If she returns, we flee. We've lost Rowyn and I have no intention of losing you too. Mortyn, your mother, Rowyn, I've lost enough kin. You shall not throw your life away for a foolish notion like personal vengeance."

"You told me what you did when Mortyn died," Plutera said, rising to her feet. "You tore his killers apart, you massacred their families, all to avenge your brother. Why won't you let me do the same for Rowyn?"

Plutyn took his daughter into his arms. "I will not deny you your vengeance, my dear. But remember that I didn't personally plunge a single blade into my enemies. Come. Let us call in some favours. It appears Count Fel'thuz's concerns were vindicated."

Reforged

Chanting and a loud, droning speech in a language Rowyn barely recognised stirred him from unconsciousness. His eyelids shifted, allowing sunlight to flood in like water through a busted dam. Beneath him were soft, tropical sands, and once his vision cleared, he found himself in a small bay, nestled between a pair of lush, green cliffs.

The hubbub was coming from a set of Jaranese-looking, staff-wielding humans, clad in tasselled robes of blue and yellow, fervently addressing a crowd of singing, variably dressed humans. Behind the speakers were the ever-expressionless Ariel, her love, Ferrus, and Khun-Rax, the captain who'd made the best and worst decision of his life by harbouring Galdusians.

Once Rowyn stood and scanned the area, it became clear that most Galdusian refugees had already departed. If this was Jaranar's east coast, he could hardly blame them. Godswater of Arkhera was often considered the kingdom's 'Little Jaranar', and if their treatment of spellbinders was reflective of such a status, minimising time on the archipelago made sense.

It was probably the right decision for Rowyn too, but he needed to ensure Ariel was with him. He moved through the revelling Jaranese, a serpentine giant amidst the parting humans. When he reached the robed figures laying claim to Ariel, they stopped their speech and thrust their staffs forward, wielding accusatory tones in a language he didn't understand.

"Rowyn Khanas!" Ariel said in Old Galdusian. *"Please help me! I'm not sure what these humans are saying, but they are extremely agitated."*

In response to this, the priestly men lowered their staffs and began to conspire in Jaranese. Khun-Rax took one of them by the shoulder, speaking in a rougher rendition of the language, and following a small argument, the portly sailor hit his belly.

"Lucky that our new god-priest is your friend," Khun-Rax said in broken Common. "You can speak for her in the Common Tongue, then I tell the... what is your word for it, ah, yes, the Stormcallers what she says."

Rowyn took a moment to process the sailor's bizarre remark. "When you say god-priest, do you mean—"

"Yes, the blessed-by-the-Storm being of magic beside me. The saviour of my crew," Khun-Rax said, gesturing to Ariel and Rowyn while speaking Jaranese to the priests.

The men parted in response to the sailor's words and allowed Rowyn to get close enough to Ariel that he could whisper to her. *"Ariel, do you know what's happening? I don't think you're in danger."*

"I'm not? But why are they making all this noise?"

"They think you're blessed by one of the Jaranese gods. There are six: The Border, the Harvester, the Worm, the Storm, the Eagle and the Moon Man. If Khun-Rax's Common is accurate, they think you're associated with the Storm," Rowyn explained.

"Why do they have gods based on ordinary things? Do they not have ascendants? Do they not know of the conceptual apotheosis that pervades this cosmos?"

Rowyn's words tangled in his mouth. As with most people from the south of Arkhera, he was a Jaranese Pantheist himself, but the rituals and teachings were things he tolerated in exchange for harvest festivals rather than deeply held convictions. Translating these shaky beliefs into a second language compounded the issue.

"The Jaranese believe in embodiments of certain important aspects of life. For example, the Border is all about boundaries, laws, orderliness—"

"Like the Great Rakh'norv that generously enabled Galdurium and the future worthy to ascend?" Ariel asked.

282

"No, no, this isn't about order in the physical sense. It's more about right and wrong; morality. Anyway, the Storm's domain is the weather, unpredictability, and magic. Sailors pray for the Storm to be merciful when they set sail, even giving Stormcaller priests sacrifices for their blessing,"* Rowyn attempted to explain, only for Khun-Rax to butt in.

"You speak with the Storm's blessed for a long time. What does she say?"

"Will you—" Rowyn began in a sharp tone, before remembering his knighthood. "Firstly, her name is Ariel, and secondly, she doesn't understand the language. She's deeply confused and wants an explanation."

"Do you know and care about the holy significance of her rescue?"

Rowyn paused. "I've explained who the Storm is. I'm from Arkhera—"

"Oh, Arkhera, yes, very good, Petyr Godswater, only holy man in your kingdom!" Khun-Rax said with a laugh. "Tell me when Ariel dispenses her first wisdom. I can hardly believe a saviour sent by the Storm himself wouldn't know her own master."

Rowyn opted against trampling the captain's beliefs. Instead, he spoke to Ariel in Old Galdusian while the big man and the priests worked the Jaranese crowd.

"These people want to hear wisdom from you. I don't think there's a way to convince them not to worship you while I'm unable to speak Jaranese."

"Can't the nice Jaranese captain tell them?"

"If I tried to relay the notion to him, he wouldn't believe me," Rowyn explained. *"Your bravery has inspired him; think of how you saw Praetor Erre the day she liberated you."*

Ariel paused. *"They want to serve me unendingly? I never got to serve Praetor Erre. I betrayed her. Will they betray me?"*

"They're in a different situation to you. What matters is, they look up to you, they think you can help them, and..." Rowyn hesitated and shifted his gaze, "...well, they would probably be willing to guide us to a city, somewhere we can get food with ease."

"Oh! I forgot you need to eat! Ferrus, I'm so sorry, I never thought to ask you if you were hungry!"

Ferrus gave a slightly bestial, hunched shrug. "I'm more confused about you're talking to this Arkheran in the old tongue. Is it the only one he knows?"

"It is. I've decided what I'm going to say, Rowyn, but it's a lie. Lies are good if they help people, aren't they?"

Rowyn's rumbling stomach compelled him to nod. "They are."

"Then tell them that they are to provide food for all Galdusians that have not departed, along with my Arkheran friend, Rowyn. Then they shall take us to the nearest city, away from this disturbing green matter."

"Disturbing green matter?" Rowyn asked.

Ariel used her arm-shaped rocks to point at the beautiful vegetation atop the surrounding cliffs.

"Those are plants, Ariel," Rowyn said with a chuckle. "While Jaranar has cities, they're not like Galdusian ones. Just like in Arkhera, plants live alongside people. With time, I'll help you understand the world beyond Galdus. For now, I'll be your voice to the Jaranese," Rowyn promised. "Is food and passage to a city all you desire?"

"It would be wrong to ask for anything more," Ariel claimed.

With an incline of his head, Rowyn turned to Khun-Rax, who'd once again reduced his prominence for the loud-mouthed, elaborately dressed priests' sake.

"Ariel has made her first demand."

Khun-Rax's brown eyes grew eager. "Finally, a true messenger of the Gods! Her demands are surely those only the divine could understand!"

Rowyn scratched the back of his head. "Actually, she wants food for all Galdusians that are still here, along with passage to the nearest city."

Khun-Rax folded his arms. "Odd. I thought gods would want strange things, like the tale of the Moon Man's string spool."

"For now, she wants the people she brought with her to live. Where is the closest city?"

The fat sailor turned and pointed towards the plant-lined gorge between the two cliffs of the bay. "We walk through there, and if my map is right, we get on path to Ma-Hith, south-eastern port of all Jaranar, and most important, my home!"

"Tell your people what Ariel desires, then after that, we'll gladly accept your guidance," Rowyn said, taking in a lungful of sea air.

He couldn't go home. Even if Plutyn possessed the notion of forgiveness within his black heart, Overlord Verawor had a close working relationship with the Soltelles. The moment the Yookies found out he feigned his death, they would be furious, and if Verawyn had to choose between retaining a necromantic knight and a business relationship with the richest empire in the world, he would naturally pick the latter.

"Khun-Rax?" Rowyn asked.

"What is it, voice of Ariel the Storm's Blessed?"

"Can you teach me Jaranese? This is a personal request, not something Ariel asked for."

Khun-Rax laughed and hit his belly. "If I did not, how would you stay to bring the Storm's word to Ma-Hith?"

Rowyn uneasily returned the laughter. "I'm glad you understand."

* * *

Several awakenings later, and still, Farawan needed to be sedated. He lay unconscious, and though multiple patients had been given the cultivated disease Erwyn had dubbed 'wormblister', Farawan was the first infectee to be tested, and thus the man who'd prove his hypothesis correct or not. So far, the results weren't encouraging.

Worse still was Narina, his poor lover, sitting in the tent's corner with Rarakhi. While he was sure the boy was being tactful and kind, it couldn't have been enough to fill the void left by her beloved. As Erwyn stared at Farawan, Melancholy put a hand on his shoulder.

"Perhaps we should go back to the hypothesis stage," Melancholy said. "We have numerous experimental cases pending, there's no point staring at a loaf of bread as it bakes. If he's cured, he's cured. Until we see change, we're better off thinking of alternative measures."

"I'm in no condition to innovate," Erwyn muttered.

"Are you *still* worried about your little meal ticket? If Lady Selenia's dead, it's not a problem," Melancholy bluntly stated. "You were still born into privilege; you can just claim that estate in Moonrock your brother's taking care of—"

"Don't talk about Lady Selenia like that," Erwyn snapped. "I respect you as an academic and a healer, but you don't need to voice your displeasure with nobility at every waking moment."

"Until the deserving wield power, I won't stop."

Erwyn exhaled through his teeth. "It's a good thing you were my mentor, because I don't think I could befriend you naturally."

"I'm not anybody's friend," Melancholy said. "Such a notion is forced to somebody like me. I have something better than societal approval: Purpose."

"I'm happy for you. Please leave me to watch over Farawan. I'm sure you can formulate hypotheses without me."

"As you wish," Melancholy said, casually wiping blood onto her smock and preparing to leave, but as she did, Farawan started to move.

The patient's arms twitched against his restraints, and despite the relatively unfrenzied movement, he opened his eyes with unnerving speed. He opened his mouth, paused, then spoke coherently.

"What happened?"

Erwyn's enthusiasm rushed back into his body. "You're *speaking!*"

"Who are you? Why is it surprising that I can talk?"

Melancholy covered her mouth, then turned to hide her face. Erwyn, meanwhile, waved to Narina frenziedly.

"Farawan's awake and speaking! He's *cured!*"

The young woman quickly rushed to her betrothed's side, Rarakhi her lanky illusionist shadow. Her sapphire eyes were full of tears, but Farawan was still confused.

"Fara, Fara, you're back! You're truly back!"

Farawan tugged at his restraints. "What's going on? Why am I tied to this perverse old man's table? Why am I so hungry? Did I oversleep? I had the worst nightmare, Nar."

Narina's fair face whitened further. "It wasn't a nightmare."

Farawan's long face tightened. "You don't mean to tell me—"

"A horrible plague struck the city, Farawan," Narina recounted. "It turned men into animals. I was at home with mother, when you burst in and— you took us both. Mother went mad too, but somehow, I stayed sane. The wisdoms here were trying to figure out why I didn't become a monster while you did."

Farawan's voice shook. Before he could string together another sentence, Melancholy spoke over him.

"We finally have a cure. We don't know how pregnancy will be affected, but—"

"Let me out of this thing!" Farawan screamed, twitching and rattling against the table.

Melancholy sighed. "Typical, he's reverting."

Erwyn corrected her with a forcefulness even he didn't anticipate. "No, you imbecile, he's going to—"

There wasn't time. Erwyn tore off a piece of his sleeve, bunched it up, and gagged the patient before he could bite his own tongue. With the young man saved, he seamlessly resumed his rant.

"You're genuinely ill-equipped for matters of the heart, Melancholy. He's just awakened from a maddened state where he's hurt the ones he loves. Allow him a moment to be upset and consider that he'd likely want to die."

Melancholy's eyes narrowed. "I feared that the cure was too good to be true. Allow me, the woman who has spent decades failing to cure rapeworm non-destructively, a moment to be sceptical."

"Will you two scroll-heads shut up? This ain't about you two, Farawan's the guy who got cured," Rarakhi said.

Erwyn noticed Narina, silently resting her head on her weeping lover's chest. He adjusted his monocle, then addressed the young woman.

"If anyone can save this man's soul, now that his body's cured, it's you."

The high elven woman sniffled, and brought herself upright, looking over her silenced lover. "I'm not going to lie to you, Fara. I know that the monster who violated me wasn't you, but a beast with your body and voice. Still, my foolish side, the side that gives me nightmares, blames you. I know it isn't the truth, and I know you're not at fault."

Farawan grew limp, his eyes empty, defeated husks. Erwyn took a calculated risk and removed the gag, and though a suicide attempt wasn't the immediate result, it was a while before the young man replied.

"Even if you think the monster who... raped you wasn't me, I still need to know you forgive me," he said in an undertone.

Narina seized his tied-down hand. "Of course I forgive you! It's just— it's my animal self not separating your body from the man I fell in love with!"

"I still walked to your house. The monster shared my memories. I was looking forward to our marriage, and it must have used that against me. I don't know what I should do."

Narina's grip on his hand tightened. "We're going to get married! Mother will be cured just as you were, we'll explain everything, and we'll be together, forever. I'm stronger than what I've been through. I don't care about what that monster knew. The man I'm in love with is back, and even if the monster wore his face for a while, I'm not going to stop loving him!"

Farawan's tears rolled down his cheeks. "If your mother can forgive me, then we'll marry. Her blessing is the least I could ask for. I know it's wrong of me to make this demand after what I did to you, but when we marry, is it all right for us *not* to consummate?"

Narina enthusiastic agreement almost resembled frustration. "Why would I consider that wrong? I'm not ready for carnal... anything. I don't know when I will be. We'll just see how we feel when we're married. It's all we can do."

Erwyn was satisfied. He untied Farawan from his table, and before he could offer him a body covering, the young man hugged his lady love with a passion the wisdom knew he'd never fully experience himself. While he was overjoyed, he couldn't match the starry-eyed happiness Rarakhi had for the couple. Still, Erwyn at least outdid Melancholy, who expressionlessly brought the conversation back to work.

"I'll demand the appropriate culturing resources from Lady Foenaxas, then write a guide on how to cure patients for future healers. Be sure to check my notes when I'm done," she flatly stated. "Hopefully Wisdom Khalver will read the instructions carefully."

"Where will you go after that?" Erwyn asked.

"I'm not sure. Without rapeworm, I'm redundant," she admitted. "That's nothing you need to worry about."

Though he wanted to say something else, Erwyn knew that changing his mentor's mind was a futile endeavour. Somewhere in her task-focused soul, an ego remained, and it was likely too bruised to directly discuss its existence with a former student. Erwyn removed his smock, when the tent's entrance fluttered as somebody entered. Her hair was wetter than snows alone could have caused, and her clothing was mysteriously pristine, but it was Overlady Selenia.

"Wisdom Erwyn?"

Safety protocols didn't matter. Erwyn approached his lady and took her into his arms.

"You're safe, thank every god there is."

Lady Kag didn't hold him as strongly as he'd expected. "I won't be lady for much longer. I don't think I should be."

Erwyn's voice faltered. "What do you mean, my lady?"

Kagura released Erwyn. "Irikhos kidnapped me, and I let him know that Yar was going to be the lady. I'm sending him to Elarond, and if he brings Yar home, father's will needs to be found."

The news was hardly good, but the young woman was at least coming to terms with her limitations. "If that's what you wish, my lady. Would you like to stay in Castle Selenia?"

"No. Tor and Yar would hate me."

Erwyn nodded. "That's understandable. I'll find the richest artist in Arkhera for when the time comes."

* * *

Though Razarkha's arcane reserves were still plentiful, the flight above the sun-bleached city of Ante Tertia was tedious. There was no membrane to cross, no sirens or monotonous Watcher commentating over her revolutionaries' actions. She and Weil flew over statues of presumably great men, crumbled-down gates of norvite, and necromantic-styled mausoleums that wouldn't be out of place in the Plains of Death, yet not a word was exchanged. Weil was back to wearing his usual grim countenance, but it didn't give Razarkha the comforting familiarity she sought. Perhaps her crushing defeat had left her ego unsalvable, and the ever-nearing walls of the citadel were her only true escape from misery.

Survival instinct prevented her from slamming against the jagged, monstrous tower of deactivated magitech, but as she made to apply her own telekinetic 'brakes', an outside force did so ahead of time. Razarkha hastily attempted to regain control, but the same force yanked them upwards and through a likely millennia-old hole in the building's side.

"I don't mean to doubt your spellwork, but are you responsible for the current telekinesis?" Weil asked.

"Of course not, I'm trying to figure out what's going on!"

As they were pulled into the citadel, they beheld a large, blood-red crystalline pillar consuming much of the centre, spreading through the building like the lianas attempting to capture Ante Tertia's outer buildings. The telekinetic force dragged them downwards through the miserable hollow of smashed-through floors, the sunrays pushing through the citadel's many wounds illuminating nothing but more of this crystalline knotweed. At some point during the descent, the arcane stone began to glow and dim in time with an all-consuming echo of Old Galdusian so bizarre that at first, even Razarkha couldn't make sense of it.

"You thought you could cause chaos in my perfect empire, didn't you?" the very building appeared to say.

"Your empire? I don't even know who you are," Razarkha replied, almost glad for the enemy after slaughtering so many allies.

"Of course you Isleborn wouldn't consider yourself part of the empire, but remember this, you ingrates! I gifted you and your Plague Emperor freedom, yet here you come, with your monstrous chaos-speech and your blasphemous ascendant-killing devices, attacking an emperor who did nothing to deserve your hostility!" the pillar ranted. *"You tried to kill me once, but the Great Rakh'norv is brilliant and generous! My orderly form is immune to your false god's magical technology! You still cannot kill me, so go back to the Isle of the Tzar and* stop ruining our home!"

Weil shouted to Razarkha while her ears rang. *"What is this thing saying? Is he speaking a language at all or just making noise?"*

"It's mad," Razarkha concluded. *"It believes it's an emperor— I know who this is."*

"What do we do, then? Is it going to kill us?"

"I don't know. Let me speak to it," Razarkha answered, before switching to Old Galdusian. *"Are you the last Golden Emperor? Are those ascendants your people?"*

"Yes. They're perfect, they know the true meaning of obedience *and* civic duty! *Consigliere Luxifros abandoned me, but I'm still alive, despite the traitors and cowards who plagued me! Now the only enemies I face are you, Isleborn meddlers who don't know when a war is over, and that* beast *at the bottom of the citadel!"*

Razarkha paused, then spoke to the soulstealer. "That 'beast' is the other soul, isn't it?"

292

"I don't see what else it could be."

Razarkha and Weil's descent steadily brought them towards a plant-infested, hole-ridden section of the Ante Tertia citadel. After brief consideration, she addressed the seemingly infinite pillar of redstone once more.

"May we see this beast?"

"Of course! If you Isleborn have any sense of spellbinder pride, you shall eradicate it at once!"

Razarkha smirked. *"Why haven't you exterminated it already?"*

"It refuses to be affected by my arcana!"

"I see. Show me this beast, then."

With that, the pillar continued to safely lower the pair into the increasingly green citadel interior, before both the pillar's visible influence on the walls and its magic cut off, causing Razarkha and Weil to plummet. Though she begged the First Light for his telekinetic assistance, no spellwork appeared to be effective.

Just as the pair were about to become a red smear upon a verdant, surreal meadow, they stopped falling. They stayed suspended above a bed of milk-and-wine lilies for a breath's length of time before resuming their fall with non-fatal results. When Razarkha regained her wits, she took in her surroundings.

The sun patchily illuminated the meadow from numerous holes in the besieging walls, yet the entire floor was covered in life. Pomegranate trees greater than any Razarkha had seen stood proudly, ripe fruits waiting to drop from their branches. Occasionally, a stump would be seen, accompanied by a sign, and what the felled trees became was soon apparent; in the middle of the meadow was a wooden hut with a rocking chair beyond the porch.

Sitting upon it was what appeared to be a dark elf, though as Razarkha instinctively stumbled towards him, she realised his eyes were nothing like a true dark elf's, which were prone to browns, crimsons, and golds. Instead, they were a bright, beautiful salmon-pink, a colour only achieved by spellbinders and necromancers as far as she knew.

The grey-haired alleged elf stood and put his hand forward, causing Razarkha to stop as though she'd ran face-first into a wall, and when Weil inevitably caught up, the same happened to him. The 'dark elf' walked slowly and deliberately, tipping his gardening hat before properly acknowledging the pair.

"Welcome to my meadow. You can call me the Prospector, though given my current hobby, I suppose 'the Gardener' is better," he said in an accent of the Common Tongue Razarkha had no means of gauging.

"What is he saying?" Weil asked. *"Something about treasure and gardening?"*

Before Razarkha could answer, the elf spoke again, this time in near-perfect Isleborn. *"My deepest apologies, I didn't know I had a genuine Ilazari along with an Arkheran playing Ilazari. Would you two like to stay in my humble hut? I built it myself."*

"How did you do this?" Razarkha asked. *"This garden lies beneath that emperor, how in the world are you alive? Humans were mere tools to the Old Galdusians, and elves vermin."*

"I'm like a rat who moves traps so they're beneath a man's feet," the Prospector said.

"Razarkha, does that mean what I think it does?" Weil asked.

"He's an antimage," Razarkha confirmed. *"In Arkhera, elven antimages are semi-common, and strong enough to be directly below humans in that foolish magocracy called the Order of the Shade. Someone* this *powerful, however…"*

"I was born lucky," the Prospector said with a shrug. *"I never knew my father, but my mother was more than enough to nurture my skill and curiosity alike. Enough about me. Who are you two?"*

294

"I'm Razarkha Fel'thuz, and this is Weil of Zemelnya," Razarkha said before her Isleborn idiot could say something foolish.

"That's a name I didn't expect to hear," the Prospector remarked, moving close enough that if not for the barrier he'd created, Razarkha could have touched him. *"The same Razarkha Fel'thuz who begged Antique for one of the fruits of his bad habit?"*

"You know Antique? The orc that refused to— I offered him a perfectly good share of my fortune!" Razarkha ranted. *"It wasn't begging, I proposed a fair transaction, and he told me his soulstealers weren't for sale!"*

"And rightly so. As distasteful as his collection is, at least he knows not to allow such unholy technology to fall into the wrong hands," the Prospector said, turning his back to Razarkha and walking away.

"What's 'distasteful' about collecting soulstealers?"

The Prospector turned back around to behold Razarkha from a distance. *"You obviously acquired a soulstealer by your own means, and unlike Antique, you're using it regularly. How much have you grown since acquiring it, Razarkha Fel'thuz?"*

"I'm more powerful than I've ever been! I was once a pathetic hybrid with nothing but my family name! Now I'm a telekinete and lumomancer! I can detect arcane signatures and clear sectors of ascendants with ease!" Razarkha declared, allowing her heart to swell. *"I may have got an entire revolutionary army killed, but I'm beyond powerful!"*

The Prospector's salmon eyes glinted. *"To summarise, you haven't grown at all."*

Razarkha's anger burnt up as the deaths of Sorelli and Igneus inflamed her damaged self-worth. *"No, I— I just told you how I've grown!"*

"Looks to me like you're the same beggar who harangued my fellow explorer trying to get a quick ticket to

295

power. What can you learn from killing everyone who opposes you?"

"*This!*" she screamed, pointing her soulstealer at the arrogant elf and unleashing a blinding beam.

In moments, Razarkha's balance abandoned her, and nausea swiftly took its place. She collapsed onto her side and Weil rushed over, blocking her view of what she hoped was the charred remains of the Prospector.

"*Razarkha! What in the world were you thinking?*"

"*What do you mean? I'm fine, I'm…*" Razarkha rambled, before noticing her left leg.

It wasn't attached to her.

Alienated

Razarkha awakened from her nightmare, only to shift her tail and discover it hadn't ended. There was no left leg to brush against, and the bed she was lying in wasn't Galdusian in design. She was a cripple, just like Tei. She pawed about and noticed something worse than a missing leg; a missing soulstealer. The panic fully awakened her, and her breath became out of control. She stumbled from the bed and scanned the small, wood-cabin room she was in from the floor, crawling in futility.

"Help me, Weil! Weil, please! You're here, aren't you, Weil? Weil, Weil, *please Weil, help!*" she screamed in Common before rationality caught up with her fear.

She whimpered, then prepared to speak Isleborn Ilazari. Her mind was scattered, and different languages' sounds mixed in her head. Had the Prospector somehow broken her mind with her body? She pieced together the Isleborn she needed, but by the time she opened her mouth, her elven assaulter opened the bedroom door.

"Ah, you're awake," he said in a calm tone. "Unfortunately, Weil is busy training. Is there anything you need?"

"Training?" Razarkha spat from her undignified vantage point. "His mistress loses a leg and he's *training?* He should be grieving outside the room, concerned for my recovery!"

"One doesn't exactly recover from a missing leg. He seemed more disappointed than upset, being honest," the Prospector said. "Don't you remember what he said before you fell unconscious? If my Isleborn is correct, he asked you what you were thinking."

"Shut up! You've done something to him, haven't you?" Razarkha said between laboured breaths, crawling up to the elf and grabbing his legs. "You've destroyed my

297

soulstealer, you've killed Weil, and now you're going to kill me!"

The Prospector pierced her with his unnerving salmon eyes. "If I wanted to kill you, child, you'd already be fertilising my garden. Consider this: You've woken up in a soft bed, you're screaming in a tongue Weil has trouble understanding, and I've done nothing but deflect attacks you initiated. What's more likely? That I'm playing mind games and Weil's dead, or that you're growing overly paranoid?"

Razarkha became limp. "Where's my soulstealer? Did you destroy it?"

The Prospector shrugged. "It's not my business to meddle in the affairs of a vile god like the Sovereign. His philosophy is one-sided, same as my mother's is. Unity is admirable, but when forced, you get Galdus, a realm of faceless ascendants wasting their precious years avoiding death in unison. Individual greatness is also to be respected, but to pursue it while trampling thousands, friend and foe alike? Do you think that's admirable?"

"Better to change the world than waste your life!"

The elf folded his legs on the floor. "Some of the greatest people I've met have been ordinary folk. An old fisherman who lost his wife to illness in his youth found the strength to love again with a lonely old woman that he spotted on the beach. A librarian's assistant saved enough money to free herself from her abusive father and brothers, then bought a house on the other side of the city. These folks didn't change the world, but they moved me much more than people like you."

Razarkha's phantom leg failed to push her up. "Those people are worthless."

"To you, perhaps. Telling you the truth, that soulstealer is outside my house, free to retrieve at any time. Before you grab it, let an old man give you some advice. You aren't doing yourself any favours by indulging your addiction to power. Weil confided in me, and he doesn't like the person you've become."

Razarkha propped herself up with her arms. "You're lying! Weil would never say such things. He loves me. You come off as a man who's never experienced carnal pleasure, so you wouldn't understand, but he *adores* me, and some missing leg won't change that!"

The Prospector sighed. "I'd laugh if it wasn't so sad. I'm almost finished making your crutch, then you'll be able to walk again. With Weil's training, perhaps you'll be able to leave Galdus. Tragically, the boy doesn't believe you'd stop your crusade given the choice to."

"Of course not! That conglomerate ascendant, that— that *Darvith,* whatever it is, killed my entire revolution! He's probably the worst problem Galdus has, and he's a sinchild, if the energies I felt were any indication!" Razarkha ranted. "You hate the Sovereign, surely you'd agree that a sinchild getting killed by a soulstealer would be a fitting irony."

"Killing Darvith would only make another sinchild of pride appear somewhere else," the Prospector said. "I'm not some grand crusader against the Sovereign, nor do I take joy in the suffering of his representatives."

Razarkha scoffed. "You could have fooled me."

"How can you show such hostility to somebody who shows you hospitality? Weil mentioned that—"

"You took my leg!" Razarkha screamed. "Stop talking about Weil like you're his best friend! *I'm* the one who he loves, *I'm* the one he's bound to, *I'm* the one he'll follow to the grave!"

The Prospector stood, a morose expression on his dusky face. "If you wish to kill Darvith the Deceiver, I can't stop you. However, I refuse to let Weil die for your sake. When I finish your crutch, you'll retrieve your blasphemous device and listen closely. You'll need my antimagic to defeat him."

Razarkha's body was overcome with excitement and terror. "Please don't leave, just listen to me."

The Prospector opened the door. "I'm listening."

"I need to see Weil. I'm grateful for your hospitality, but I need to see him."

"As you wish," the Prospector said. "I'll send him in."

He left the room, and in the deafening silence, Razarkha dragged herself back to her bed. From there, she clambered onto the mattress and used her remaining leg to make the final push into her covers. The last thing she wanted was Weil to see the cauterised stump where her beautiful, long thigh once was. The horror of her injury finally took hold in her mind, and she squeezed her pillow with hatred. Every instance of her father mimicking what she did to Tei came back to her, only this time, the person towering over her was Tei herself.

"Two short legs are better than one, wouldn't you say, dear sister?" the false Tei said in a voice that resembled Razarkha's.

"You're not real, you ran away, you're probably dead. Rakh loved you best and that was your victory. You don't need to mock me too," Razarkha mumbled into the pillow.

"If I'm not real, who's truly mocking you?"

Razarkha dug her overgrown nails into the pillow, then screamed and threw it at the door.

"I'm a cripple!" she yelled. *"I'm naught but a freak, is that what you wanted to hear? I'm just like Tei, but no, that's not bad enough, because I'm also despised by everyone! Nobody loves me, and those who do die, die, they all die, they all die!"*

She pulled her duvet around her body and rocked until the imbalance of her missing leg forced her onto one side, which only prompted further incomprehensible gibbering. All she wanted was to be back in Moonstone, sniping at Rakh and thinking about pushing Lady Selenia down the stairs. The door opened, and this time, her brown-haired accomplice walked into the room, his expression a twist on the usual misery. Razarkha tried to cover her tear-filled eyes as Weil sat next to her.

"Are you all right, Razarkha?"

"I lost my leg, what do you think?" Razarkha snapped.

"Sorry, stupid question," Weil said flatly.

Razarkha's heart was tearing itself apart, wanting to kiss him as much as it wanted to strangle him. She couldn't be soft on him, not when he'd grown cocky enough to betray her.

"I hear you made a new friend," Razarkha finally said. *"I didn't realise you liked people who maim your allies."*

"You shot the ray," Weil stated without emotion. *"All he did was defend himself, then he did the Isleborn thing and showed me hospitality. He's not my enemy, even if he's yours."*

Razarkha's hands tensed up. *"You're leaving me too? You attached yourself to me because of my strength, and now that I'm a cripple, you're throwing me away?"*

"I'm not abandoning you," Weil said, though his tone was hardly comforting. *"You wish to kill Darvith, do you not?"*

"Of course," Razarkha said.

"Then we're still allies. We'll ensure that abomination is defeated once and for all."

Razarkha tried to meet his eyes, but he turned so his overgrown fringe covered them. Her next tactic was to put her hand on his thigh, but this led to him moving away.

"What's wrong, Weil? Why are you pulling away? What did I do? What did I say? You speak of me as an 'ally', as though we haven't been forged together through every fire there is!" Razarkha spluttered. *"You're not going to*

301

leave me once Darvith is killed, are you? Promise me you won't!"

Weil paused. *"You won't be alone after Darvith's death."*

"Because you'll be there? Don't word things cryptically, Weil. I'm not a native speaker but I know evasive wording when I hear it!" Razarkha said in frenzied Isleborn.

"I'll be with you when Darvith's dead," Weil promised. *"I have a plan to kill him, but you'll need to learn antimagic from that elf."*

Razarkha held the unresponsive young man. *"Thank you, Weil. I knew I could rely on you. I'm sorry for being a weakling."*

"You've lost a leg. It's my turn to be strong for you," he said, emotion finally returning to his voice.

Despite not having done so since that drunken night they'd spent dancing at War'mal's academy, Weil began to sing. It was a traditional Isleborn song about Rakh'dor ge Luzma, the Plague Emperor's daemonic lover. As Razarkha rested against Weil's shoulders, he serenaded her with words about loving a daemon despite her man-eating nature, and wondering if, when her big, striking eyes met his, he wished for her to devour him or pass him by.

* * *

At the southern gates of Ashglass, Kagura Selenia shivered next to her advisor-count, hugging her own body while children's wailing filled her ears. The four Foenaxas boys and single Foenaxas girl clung to their Uncle Irikhos with all their childish might, rooting him in place. Nearby, Lady Foenaxas looked ready to burst into tears at a snowflake's touch. Solyx Solerro was by his wife's side, stoic in the face of his brother-in-law's imminent departure, while their seerish wisdom milled about.

"I wish Erwyn was here," Kagura whispered to Rakh.

302

"You know he's busy," Rakh quietly told her. "After everything our visit to Ashglass has caused, don't you think it's fair to let him help with the curing effort?"

Kagura's heart wrenched. "If I didn't come with you, Irikhos wouldn't be leaving."

Rakh hesitated, then took her hand. "I wish I could tell you otherwise, but you're correct. We should have left you in Moonstone. The diplomatic gesture wasn't worth it."

"Thank you for being honest," Kag said, her words catching in her throat and pulling tears to her eyes on the way out. "Promise to be honest with me until I'm not a lady. I'm sorry everyone felt like they needed to lie to me."

The spellbinder looked down on her, yet his crimson eyes were somehow comforting. "I won't lie to spare your feelings anymore, I swear it."

She let go of Rakh's hand. "I hope Erwyn will do the same."

Lady Kagura edged towards Irikhos and his family as the children stopped swarming him. The eldest son, Morganix, stood in her way, his small orange cape billowing in the wind.

"You stay away from my uncle! You're the reason he's going away, so don't gloat!"

"I only wanted to speak," Kagura said, her poise ruined.

Solyx stepped in and put a hand on his son's shoulder. "Morganix, no. Remember that Uncle Irikhos did something extremely mean, even if you love him."

"I don't care! She's going to gloat, and I won't let her!"

Kagura hid her hands in her sleeves, then walked around the boy. He erupted into an impotent rage that his father contained, acting as background noise to the ensuing discussion.

"I'm sorry, Irikhos," Kagura said, lowering her head.

The knight looked as though he was prepared for a vacation rather than an exile, with numerous suitcases and personal effects around him. Even now, resentment simmered in his golden eyes.

"Stop apologising for an exile you ordered."

"Do you know what happened to that commoner, Almarax?"

Irikhos frowned. "Surprised you care. He's left with the money I gave him. Seems he got what he wanted."

"Hopefully you can get what you want too," Kagura said.

"I know that you're being nicer than I could hope for, but if Yar and Tor are dead, I'll hate you for the rest of my life," Irikhos stated, his voice as cold as his surroundings.

"I'll hate myself for the rest of my life too."

"I don't need your self-hatred!" Irikhos blurted. "If they're dead, I'm not seeing my family again. I know you hated your family so much you sent 'em away, but I love my nephews, I love Lexie, and I love Mor'kha. Fuck, I'm even gonna miss Solyx."

Mor'kha Foenaxas rushed between them. "My lady, please forgive Irikhos's outburst, I'm sure he— my lady?"

Kagura gazed at the snow-and-ash mixture upon the floor, tears slipping from her eyes. Rakh appeared from nowhere, having apparently played invisible bodyguard to her, and he helped her face upwards once more.

"Don't worry," he said. "He's being exiled. He has every right to say his peace before he leaves. You're free to do whatever you want with his words."

"He's right to feel how he does," Kagura said.

"I don't think feelings can be right or wrong. They just are," Rakh replied.

An uncomfortable silence of snowfall and staring caused Irikhos to address his sister. "Strakha, be sure to have Morganix keep up his swordplay. I know it's redundant in the age of guns, but he seems to enjoy it. Also, don't think about what mother would say."

Mor'kha smiled sadly. "Whenever I think of what mother would do, I do the opposite. Stay safe, Iri, and send letters back whenever you can."

"Of course," he said, then called over his wisdom. "Khalver, I take it you sent the letter confirming my exile?"

"Yes, to Overlady Selenia's exacting specifications," the seer said. "I'm sorry I had to write it, but I've seen visions of your adventures already."

This caught Kagura's attention, and she pushed herself into Irikhos's conversation. "You did? Did you see my sisters? Did Tor grow out of her fat?"

Khalver narrowed his red-green eyes at Kagura then continued. "I saw the Pantheist temples of Napolli, the Alaterran Mountains, and wyverns, wild and tame alike."

"Napolli? Why Napolli? Wouldn't Virella be better, given that's where King Morello is?" Irikhos said. "If I leverage Grandma Mina, I would have Elarondian royalty on my side!"

Khalver shook his head. "I saw a distinct path where you took a boat from Godswater to Napolli."

Irikhos folded his arms. "I was going to go from Crabber's Mouth, but if Godswater and Napolli are in your dreams, I s'pose it's fate."

"By all means, Sir Irikhos, go your own way, it's just— well, I was consulted as a seer, and that's what I saw."

Rakh offered his own insights. "Given he also thought Lady Selenia would turn back, be sure to take his words with a pinch of salt. I wish you no harm, Irikhos. Best of luck finding the Selenia sisters."

Irikhos barely acknowledged Rakh, as he was gazing at his sister. Behind him was the southern gate of Ashglass, and his only way out of the city given the trainlines were closed. Kag wanted to tell him it would be all right, but he would take it as an insult. She wondered what her sisters would do. She could see the ever-kind Tor stroking his hair and Yarawyn kissing him goodbye. They looked at men and raved about them in ways Kag didn't understand, so they would have both been good wives. Even if her brother came down from the Moon, her sisters would still be superior.

Irikhos left his luggage behind and rushed towards Mor'kha, hugging her with desperate, unprecedented force. Holding each other, the siblings truly looked like copies. They spoke to each other in words too quiet for Kagura to hear, and she froze in place, remembering when her sisters left. Tor told Kagura that she hoped this made her happy, while Yarawyn screamed incoherent threats of vengeance. Razarkha beheld this and told her that she'd never take Rakh's love for granted again, if this was how Selenias treated each other.

She couldn't take it anymore. She rushed from the scene, despite knowing she needed to officially witness Irikhos's departure. Nothing mattered more than escaping the reminders of her monstrosity.

Returned

Castle Selenia had never seemed less like Rakh's home. Its dark blue banners billowed in the wind behind numerous greenhouses, snow piling up by the gates they'd just entered. Lady Kagura was shoegazing, requiring Erwyn's occasional intervention to walk straight, while Rarakhi rushed ahead of the group.

"C'mon, we're walking too slow," the boy insisted. "You're not going to mope over everything, are you dad? Erwyn cured a fucking plague. Yeah, that dumb nobleman got sent away, but let's face it, if a commoner did what he did to Lady Kag, they'd be dead. Same with Aunt Razarkha. You know it, I know it. It's all a load of shit if you ask me."

The back of Rakh's head flared as he turned to his son. "If you like, we can return to Ashglass and you can say that to Lady Foenaxas's face."

"Fuck off," Rarakhi deflected. "You know I'm right, even if that god-kisser would burn me for speaking the truth."

The four had left Ashglass as quietly as possible due to the gaffe during Irikhos's departure, and while Mor'kha made a show of thankfulness to Erwyn, she couldn't meet Lady Kag's eyes. Rakh pondered over if bringing the lady to Ashglass had achieved anything positive. Aside from her reformation and possible abdication, nothing came to mind. It wasn't enough to justify the injury to Mor'kha Foenaxas, the lady who only wanted to save her people. All Rakh hoped for was that word regarding Razarkha had arrived, because as it stood, the Foenaxases' loyalty was more in question than ever.

When they entered the castle, he recognised the door guard as one of Plutyn's men, armed with an unusually long magitech rifle with coils around its barrel. As they moved through the foyer, more former Khanas Family members were seen milling about in Selenia colours, putting on a display of deference when Lady Kag passed them. Rarakhi's restraint vanished, and he rushed through the halls towards the castle's main lounge.

"Hey, Plutera! I'm back, Petal!"

Rakh caught up to Lady Kag and Erwyn, tapping the former's shoulder. "My lady, I advise caution."

"Why's that?" she asked.

"From the looks of it, Sir Plutyn's filled the staff with his own men. It might be he's preparing something unscrupulous."

Erwyn frowned. "I had a similar feeling. What can we do now that we're surrounded?"

"If the worst comes to the worst, I can help us escape," Rakh said.

Lady Selenia's expression barely shifted from her usual misery. When she finally mustered words, they were lifeless.

"Sir Plutyn hates me too. I don't have a friend in the world."

Erwyn put on a fatherly voice. "We're probably safe, but you should never view employees as friends. Perhaps when we find you an artist, you can make friends with them."

"You're not my friend either, then?" Kagura asked the wisdom.

"It's complicated. I've grown to love you, my lady, but I ultimately serve Moonstone first and you second."

Lady Kag didn't respond to this. Rakh offered his hand, but she pulled away from both of her advisors, marching into the lounge Rarakhi had already entered. The boy's lack of noise was somewhat disconcerting, so Rakh rushed after his lady, bursting into their destination around the same time as her.

The lounge was decorated in moon-themed trinkets, and a jaggedly-painted banner stretched atop the room, reading *'Welcome Home, Overlady Selenia!'*, with Plutera,

Rarakhi, and a group of thuggish-looking servants cheering as she came in. Behind them was a stone-faced Plutyn Khanas, who didn't even bother miming a cheer of his own.

"What is this? I don't understand," Kagura said as Plutyn moved through the crowd.

Rakh cast an illusion of himself while his true self vanished, but upon seeing Rarakhi and Plutera making moon eyes with each other, decided against retrieving a dagger from his inner pocket. The necromantic minister approached with his usual stormy disposition and stench of bhang-weed, then bowed deeply.

"We received Wisdom Veritas's letter, and prepared a celebration in honour of our brave lady's triumph over such vile treason," Khanas said, then turned to Erwyn as he arrived. "Ah, and here is the wisdom who cured a plague. A feast is being prepared in your honour."

The necromancer's straight face throughout this tall tale forced Rakh to twist his own. Even Lady Kag was compelled to speak up.

"Will I need a food taster for this feast?" Lady Kag asked.

"What are you implying?" Khanas said in a voice as convincingly confused as a clown's shoes were convincingly fitting. "I shall eat everything you intend to sample before you if it puts you at ease."

Rakh folded his arms. "No offense, Minister Khanas, but this is unusual behaviour for you. What exactly is your game?"

Khanas's voice became as grim as his expression, and he clicked his fingers. "Men, leave us. Enjoy the food, do as you wish. These three want business, so business it is."

As the former mobsters flooded out of the room, Khanas moved to a comfortable armchair and sat down, then filled his pipe with bhang-weed.

Plutera was still excited despite her father's crestfallen nature, and asked, "Can I take Rarakhi into my room?"

"You shall stay in the dining room and partake of the feast, and if any servants report you going somewhere secluded, I will cancel the betrothal," Plutyn promised.

"But father, you know I wouldn't do anything rash!"

Plutyn sighed. "If matters get out of hand, don't come crying to me."

"Thank you, father!" Plutera said, and with that, she kissed Rarakhi's cheek, then dragged the flustered young man out of the lounge by the hand.

"What is all this, then?" Rakh asked, taking a couch opposite Khanas.

Plutyn waited for Erwyn and Lady Kag to take seats of their own, then lit his pipe with a match. "My hope was to ingratiate myself with Lady Selenia. Is that such a sinister motive?"

"It is when you've never displayed such behaviour before," Erwyn pointed out.

The necromancer took a deep, smoky puff. "Notongue painted that banner himself. The idea was Plutera's, she's reminded me that we need every ally possible, and being candid, Lady Selenia usually responds to indulgence of her ego."

"Not anymore, it seems," Rakh said. "Her kidnapping has left a few scars."

"Is that so?" Plutyn said, shifting his ghastly verdant gaze to the overlady. "Speak, my lady. What troubles you so? Sir Irikhos has been exiled, has he not? If you fear a grand return such as Razarkha's, I wouldn't. He's an elf, not a spellbinder. Speaking of Razarkha, you no doubt want news of her exploits."

Lady Kagura slumped in her couch. "Don't worry about me. Rakh and Erwyn are the important ones, my concerns are stupid."

Plutyn Khanas hesitated, then abruptly continued. "Very well. Regarding Razarkha, there were numerous telegrams forwarded from the Sandport Radio Tower, and it appears Rowyn secured himself the backing of the Soltelle Empire. He reported on Razarkha absorbing the ascendants of Nortez, which initially didn't make sense aside from being an area with concentrated populations. It seems she's formed a revolution."

The necromancer took out a pair of letters and paused. "I'm sorry to say I didn't read most of the telegrams in a timely manner, but the latest two are particularly relevant. Following an attack on Demidium, Rowyn was killed at sea by Razarkha's hand. Another letter was sent from the Yukishimans, apparently to clarify matters."

He handed one of the letters to Erwyn, who unrolled it and read it out loud. "To Lady Kag'nemera Selenia of Moonstone. While it was once tactically viable to withhold this information, Razarkha Fel'thuz currently presents a danger to society at large. As the most likely target of her rampages and thus the first line of defence, I shall disclose an important tactical weakness of her soulstealer; its ability to steal souls is limited to—"

Erwyn cut himself off, and his eyes scanned over it once more. Rakh leaned forward.

"What does it say? How is her soulstealer limited?"

"Apparently it can only steal souls of ascendants or the recently-killed. The letter goes on to say that this power cannot be underestimated, she's consumed thousands of ascendants, but it isn't the all-killing weapon many perceive it to be. The writer, this Imperial Engineer, says that they're going to watch the situation as closely as they can without a spy on Razarkha's tail and may arrive to reinforce us."

Rakh emptied his lungs with relief. "Oh, thank the gods, the Yookies are on our side. Still, we can't rely on them."

311

Plutyn took another hit of his smoke. "Absolutely not. That's why I've called in numerous debts, and magitech arms previously in the hands of less-than-scrupulous entities have been confiscated. Plutera insisted that we form close bonds and prepare for Razarkha's return together. She may not appear angry, but she wants to watch Razarkha die following Rowyn's death. I fully intend to facilitate her vengeance."

"What about your vengeance?" Rakh asked. "He was your cousin, was he not?"

The necromancer's expression sharpened. "Regardless of whose vengeance it is, the time for dallying has come to an end. Are the Foenaxas armies secured?"

"I don't know," Lady Kag admitted. "We saved Ashglass but got Irikhos exiled."

"It depends on if Mor'kha values her people more than her family," Rakh admitted.

Khanas's eyes glimmered. "Foenaxases are likely not Fel'thuzes or Selenias. For now, I'll secure every magitech weapon I can, and as for the soulstealer's weakness, we should send word of it to every lord in the kingdom."

Erwyn frowned. "Sir Khanas, your tenure as acting lord ended the moment Lady Selenia returned to Moonstone. Your orders are reasonable, but bear in mind—"

"It's fine, Erwyn," Lady Kag said, standing up. "I won't be lady for much longer anyway. Thank you for preparing a feast, Sir Khanas, but I'm going to my room."

Overlady Selenia listlessly exited the lounge. Upon her exit, Rakh nodded to Erwyn, vanished, and rushed ahead of his lady, making sure to lock every window she came across.

* * *

In the Prospector's garden, Razarkha rested her weight upon her new wooden crutch, staring at Weil as he played with his chaotic portals. He would open a portal, jump into it, and rarely, come out of another portal on the other side of the garden, only closing both portals once he'd safely made the journey.

So far, the most common outcome was him exiting the same way he entered, which was useless beyond acting as a temporary refuge. Razarkha bitterly regarded her occupied hands, one acting as her new leg and the other holding the Soulstealer of Craving. Weil failed again and again, occasionally finding success, and a sharp sensation pervaded her chest.

"Well?" the Prospector asked, appearing from thin air. "For a woman so determined to gain power, you're taking a lot of breaks."

"I'm just keeping watch over Weil."

"His development is no longer in your hands. Your own, such as it is, remains in your control."

Razarkha instinctively folded her arms, only to unbalance herself, and after a scrambled job of correcting herself, she proceeded with her planned-to-be-snappy comeback.

"Such as it is?" she said, adjusting herself with a few hops. "Isn't he doing what you decried me for doing? He's just gaining new abilities, like I am. Where's all the growth that you like, all that nonsense about fishermen loving again?"

"Perhaps he's been growing beneath your very nose, as much as your kind have noses," the Prospector said with a chuckle. "I didn't need to do much aside from show him the way. You, however, are uninterested in balancing yourself. So I'll do the next best thing. Let us continue our lesson in antimagic."

Razarkha crutched herself away from the elf. "You borrowed my illusionism just then, didn't you? Yet you've only been willing to show me deflection and nullification antimagic. Why are you hiding the ability to hijack from me? Do you fear that I'll use your own tricks against you?"

"You're a fool if you think I fear you at all," the Prospector replied, taking his gardening hat off and fanning himself with it. "It's redundant in your circumstances, that's all."

"Is that so? Because it seems that the ability to take control of the vast reserves of arcana Darvith has in their possession is somewhat useful."

The Prospector put his hat back on and sat down in his flowers. "Look up at the citadel and the Ruined Emperor veining through it. If antimagic could hijack ascendants' arcana, do you think I'd allow this poor, deluded soul to continue denying itself the afterlife?"

Razarkha readjusted herself. "So hijacking antimagic only works on the fleshly?"

"Yes, and even then, in a limited way. Almost every elven mage worthy of consideration augments their skillset with spellwork, because natural antimagic alone is situational. For hijacking to work, the target must have an arcana node, and additionally the hijacking will only control their natural magic."

Razarkha's face untensed. "So, you're only able to steal my illusionism, and the rest of your powers are deflection, nullification, or spellwork?"

"You're quick to learn when you believe you'll earn power as a result," the Prospector remarked. "It's a shame you're so resistant to correction the rest of the time."

"Be quiet," Razarkha snapped. "If hijacking ascendants is futile, then let's stop wasting time. I want to know how to deflect magic, just as you did with my lumomancy."

The Prospector raised an eyebrow. "You want to know how to deflect magic into an incorporeal being that can't be harmed by it? Think about your priorities. I'll teach you how to nullify arcane activity first. This may be difficult for me to put into words, as it is as natural to me as illusionism is to you."

Razarkha withdrew from her soulstealer's arcane reserves and prepared a lumomantic beam. "Go ahead. Demonstrate nullification, instead of taking my other leg."

"Whenever you're ready."

She unleashed a deadly ray upon the Prospector, her inner animal wishing for the pointy-eared embodiment of smugness's death while her inner long-term planner wished for his survival. In the end, the light never reached him, vanishing as though blocked by a matte black wall she couldn't see.

"Impressive. What if I magically threw something at you?" Razarkha said, preparing a telekinetic spell before feeling a wave of impotence flow over her body.

"No," the Prospector commanded. "You will not tear up pieces of the garden. If you must throw anything, throw pieces from the citadel walls."

Razarkha trembled as arcana wriggled through her body and the Prospector's powers prevented it from spilling out. It was as though a thousand needles were pricking the inside of her skin.

"Stop it, I understand, I understand!"

The Prospector lifted his aura of antimagic. "It's irrelevant anyway. While antimagical nullification can stop magical energies in an area, if some telekinete flung a boulder from beyond that area of influence, antimagic wouldn't be able to nullify the inertia the rock has."

"What am I supposed to do in that situation?"

"Trust that Weil can protect you," the elf said with a laugh. "That shouldn't be too hard, seeing as the boy seems to consider it his full-time occupation."

"I hate how familiar you claim to be with him."

"Have you considered I do it specifically to annoy you?"

Razarkha's left side felt even heavier. It didn't matter what face he wore; Rakh Fel'thuzes existed in every race, creed, and culture. Powerful fools that contented themselves with mocking people for having ambition rather than doing anything worthwhile with their gifts were a plague, and one day, Razarkha would be the cure.

"For a man who prides himself on wisdom, you're petty," Razarkha remarked.

"I like to enjoy the simpler things," the Prospector said. "Now, petition the fractions of the Great Light, offer up your energies and ask them to prevent arcane interference with your surroundings. If your first attempts at spellwork are anything like mine, the Great Light will likely consider this request bizarre, but acceptable for the right—"

Suddenly, the Ruined Emperor's rocky body dimmed, and Weil's many practice portals shut. The Prospector's voice wavered before he could offer his snide commentary.

"How many souls did you consume to perform that? That was accidental, wasn't it?"

Razarkha grinned. "When *I* first learn a new kind of spellwork, I always start powerful, but imprecise. You may have arcane energies from, presumably, this little garden you love so much, but I have thousands of enemies reduced to fuel for my unstoppable rise."

"If you're so powerful, would you care to perform telekinesis on yourself?" the Prospector challenged.

The request was laughably simple, yet when Razarkha expected to levitate, she instead reduced her reliance on her crutch too early, falling onto a bed of cornflowers, whose pollen caused a sneezing fit. The Prospector knelt by the downed spellbinder, and she didn't need to see his face to know he was smirking.

"Shut up!" she screamed ahead of time. "Go ahead, laugh at me, tell me about how I've ruined my own powers by going too hard with the nullification antimagic! Go on!"

"I think you've told yourself everything I was going to, but I will laugh at you," he said, punctuating himself with a stilted guffaw.

Weil stopped trying to open another portal and rushed over to the pair. When he saw Razarkha, he helped her up and asked, *"What's going on? If you did whatever you did a moment later, I'd have lost a limb."*

"I just overdid the antimagic. I'll get it under control before we face Darvith."

The young man frowned. *"I hope you're right, because we both need to be precise for this plan to work."*

"Speaking of that, I want to know the specifics," Razarkha said. *"I know you're saving your juiciest secrets for your new best friend, but surely you can share your plan with me."*

Weil's orange eyes shifted about. *"I can tell you, but you'll need to undo this antimagic if you want a demonstration."*

Razarkha huffed, then shifted her tongue to Common. "All right, Prospector, Gardener, whatever you want to be called, put this farce to an end so Weil can explain his plan."

The Prospector shrugged. "Only you can do that. Learning how to is part of the experience. I won't be there to fix things when you're fighting Darvith, will I?"

Razarkha's fuchsia eyes narrowed into slits. No matter what they claimed, these two were acting as though they were her enemies.

* * *

Standing guard at the walls of Ma-Hith were six statues, depicting each of the Jaranese gods. The Border was a bird-winged humanoid of opal on one side and a bat-winged humanoid of jet on the other, the Harvester a cowled, dubiously-humanoid being of bones, the Worm a man-shaped tangle of their eponymous animals, the Storm a mage with a rocky 'cloak' carved to appear billowing, the Eagle a light-footed fellow with wings upon his shoes, shoulders, and hat, and the Moon Man, last of all, was a man wearing a crescent-moon mask over half his face, holding a rocky lantern in-laid with sapphires that represented the stars.

Rowyn Khanas took in their worn majesty as he and his crew of priests, sailors, and refugees passed them, then beheld the port city of Ma-Hith itself. Its buildings were nothing like the dull, square architecture of Sula; colour and irregularity sprung from constructs great and small. The tallest structures had many-tiered roofs and gilding along their edges.

Throughout the streets, deep blue flags dropped from sideways-stretching poles, with a red pair of Jaranese symbols that resembled looping snakes, albeit one appeared to have an accent above it. Rowyn's group weren't the only gathering in the city; plenty of brown-clothed, midriff-baring Jaranese were gathered outside a blue-and-gold monstrosity of a building.

"I don't like this place," Ariel said in an Old Galdusian breeze. *"Nothing's functional. It's too bright, and there's too many shapes that don't make sense."*

"It's what freedom allows for," Rowyn explained. *"If you wanted to express yourself in a manner other than speech, what would you do?"*

"I'm sorry, Rowyn Khanas, I don't understand the question. What means of expression are there but words? Actions, perhaps?"

"Yes, actions, but— you know how in Nortez, there were dance halls and music that Erre's insurrectionists enjoyed?" Rowyn asked. *"That music, bizarre and repetitive as it was, expressed somebody's creativity. They didn't make it with function in mind, just their thoughts and feelings."*

Ariel paused. *"But buildings aren't music. They serve a clear function."*

"That doesn't mean people can't attach ideas to them," Rowyn said. *"Once we've eaten, we can escape if you truly wish, but don't flee on account of confusing brickwork. Believe me, Galdusian architecture is just as unsettling to me as Jaranese architecture is to you."*

"I'll endure it for your sake. Sorry, Rowyn Khanas."

Rowyn considered telling her not to apologise, but before he could do so, Khun-Rax elbowed him and gestured towards the towering temple before them. There were six faces carved into its frontmost wall, rubies fixed into each one's eye sockets that only served to make their oppressive visages even more unnerving. Each domain had a pair of colours associated with them: Red and white for the Border, black and white for the Harvester, brown and green for the Worm, blue and yellow for the Storm, brown and gold for the Eagle, and blue and black for the Moon Man.

"Behold, Rowyn Speaker-to-Gods!" Khun-Rax said. "This is the greatest temple in Ma-Hith, the Temple of the Eastern Seas, last bastion of the Gods before the godless lands of Sula."

For all Khun-Rax talked it up, it had no grounds between the barely-paved streets and its entrance. While the Gods' faces were impeccably maintained, the stacked roofs that marked each of its floors grew sparser in tiling the higher Rowyn looked. Despite this, priests at the front of the group flooded into the building, one of them yelling Jaranese at Khun-Rax.

"Holy Adherent— er, how you say, *Ascetic* Pya-Thi says that the Storm's holy avatar must enter the temple."

"Will she be harmed?" Rowyn asked.

"Why would we harm the Storm's chosen? Her holy connections are undeniable!" Khun-Rax claimed, hitting his belly as though to add emphasis.

"If you insist, but I expect food for every Galdusian with us," Rowyn said.

"Oh, the priests always have food prepared for their pious visitors. It is their holy duty!"

Rowyn nodded, then turned to Ariel and the refugees. *"Come inside, everyone. They want to show Ariel to their holy men, and they apparently have food."*

"Will they eat us? The overseers told me that I was lucky to be born in the Demidium Breeding Facility, because wild humans are cannibals," Ferrus said.

"No, they won't eat us," Rowyn said in a short tone, then softened. *"Apologies. I know you've only just been freed."*

A Galdusian spellbinder cocked his head. *"Wait, so the Jaranese don't eat each other? Then what is the purpose of taking in Jaranese-blooded humans? I was told augmentation was a merciful fate compared to what undomesticated humans became."*

"They don't eat each other," Rowyn reiterated. *"They're showing us remarkable generosity, just go into this temple, nod along with whatever they say, and enjoy their food."*

The Galdusians, regardless of race, shrugged and complied. Rowyn rubbed his forehead and wondered how he'd become the effective leader of this group. Within the temple was an expanse of tiles, cushions, hookahs, statue-marked shrines, and the aromatic scent of Jaranese jasmine rice along with a meaty take on seafood wafting from a set of tables. His Galdusians didn't wait before taking advantage of the long-robed Jaranese men inside, with many sitting down with steaming bowls in their hands in the time it took for Rowyn to look around. Some winced at the flavours, but others were eagerly devouring the unusual cuisine.

Ariel floated beside a man in a six-coloured robe, her 'arms' dangling towards the floor as a flurry of Jaranese bounced off her rocky, uncomprehending head. While

Khun-Rax was nearby, he was apparently unwilling to translate. Though the intoxicating aroma of shellfish pulled him towards the tables, Rowyn had a duty to the woman he'd dragged away from home.

"Khun-Rax, with me, we need to translate for this man."

The fat man laughed. "You not eaten yet. I get you a bowl of white curry, then we talk. Gods and men alike cannot deny a starving man his food! That is why the capital city Meung-Chaydan is accursed in every realm!"

"I wish I knew what you were talking about. Still, if you're unwilling to translate before I eat, then there's no helping it," Rowyn said, calling to Ariel in Old Galdusian. *"That priest can wait, the captain insists that I eat!"*

Ariel, as bound to her submissiveness as ever, approached Rowyn. *"I'm sorry. I cannot understand their language."*

"We'll learn it together," Rowyn promised, taking a bowl Khun-Rax had retrieved. *"Once we're in a position to sail away, if you're still uncomfortable here, we'll think about where would be best to go."*

"Why can't we travel to your home?"

"Because if I return, the Soltelles will kill me."

Ariel paused. *"Is it because of me? If it is, I'll stop following you so you can go home."*

Rowyn squinted. *"Why would that ever be your fault?"*

"Consigliere Lesteris told me I wasn't allowed to be present for any meeting with the Yukishimans, because if they saw me, they would kill him, and I'd be all alone," she explained. *"There wasn't anyone Lesteris feared more than the Soltelles."*

This made Rowyn chew a little slower, and after swallowing, he said, *"For once I understand how that rat thinks. You're not the reason the Soltelles would kill me, but their threat is very real. If I can't return home, there's only one place I can think of that could become a second one. Perhaps I could even send letters from there."*

"Where is that?"

"Zemelnya," Rowyn answered, stuffing his face with a chunk of coconutty, zesty prawn as the scent of Jaranese white curry mingled with the ghosts of Vi'kara's fragrant oils.

Humbled

"*Demidium is finally stabilising, from what I can see,*" Siendros said from one of Darvith's many portals. "*Count Anvus Aurelion has promised to rebuild the Demidium Breeding Facility, barring some small niggles.*"

Axas, from his little room in Nova Tertia, spoke up. "*Small niggles? Considering what's happened, every setback should be treated as major!*"

"*An unascended cretin like yourself would treat such matters as great, but I assure you, they're small,*" the red-eyed ascendant claimed.

Darvith's soul danced with glee; another wedge to leverage conflict had presented itself. He moved a good portion of his eyes towards Siendros's portal and addressed the ascendant.

"*Axas is your superior, ascended or not. Your words are foolish, and you shall answer Axas's question. What 'small niggles' are there?*"

"*Galen Aurelium, one of Count Aurelion's stock, has convinced numerous members of the Demidium Citadel that breeding humans is more trouble than it's worth, and that their suicidal demonstration of individuality is proof of this,*" Siendros explained.

Axas snorted. "*That's of no concern to the Sons of Sula. All I desire is for Galdus to be united and restore order within its people. We have the right to take inferior races and augment them how we please, but given how troublesome they've proven themselves, perhaps foregoing the facility's reconstruction is wise.*"

"*Precisely why I considered the setback minor! It's some concubine's whelp making irrelevant rumblings. Demidium will move past this crisis,*" Siendros said.

"*Do people blame the Sons for the violence?*" Darvith asked, his stormy body rumbling with anticipation.

"Many do," Siendros admitted. *"Some soldiers have expressed mutinous thoughts regarding our expansion into Nortez. They say we've made enemies we can't afford to fight. Where are these fleshly scumbags' principles? If Galdus is truly great, no enemy will stand before us!"*

"Good point, Siendros," Axas said, his voice dripping with venom. *"Perhaps, if Praetor Erre resurfaces, you can lead ascended forces to stop her personally."*

"Are you saying you wish for my death?"

"You've undermined my authority multiple times; you should consider my tolerance of your existence a mercy!"

Darvith missed being able to smile. He watched the rebel leader and his coordinator bicker, then echoed over both. *"Neither of you are worthy of my glorious attention. Axas, tell Malderis to expect Praetor Erre in Moneri. Otherwise, be silent, knowing that none of you are capable of ushering Galdus to glory."*

The Sinchild of Pride shut the portals connected to Axas and Siendros, then opened a set associated with the citadel of Moneri, the first Galdusian city. He'd already concluded with his father's help that if Razarkha Fel'thuz resurfaced, she'd need a fresh batch of ascendants to feast upon. Nova Tertia was safe while Darvith persisted, Demidium was already ravaged, but Moneri was full of complacent ascendants, and had the second highest amount of enslaved augmentees within it, behind Demidium itself. It was a ripe pomegranate dangled before a breeder who'd known nothing but fungal food parcels.

Echoes of Luxifros, the boy Darvith once was, sent waves of melancholy through his myriad ascension stones, causing his smoke to shimmer. The Golden Emperor's men found him and took him in, their pride convincing them that they were using him. Everyone was the same: They could handle him differently, *they* were special. When Galdus woke up and realised their hubris he could finally rest.

A tugging sensation interrupted his reminiscence, and he shut his rifts to find a single chaotic portal at his side. He directed his eye-embers towards it, finding that the smoky arcane matter of his body was being sucked into the Soulstealer of Craving, thrust from the opening by the Praetor Erre's hand.

Oddly, the ascendants' bodies fizzled out a few feet away from the soulstealer, yet the device still glowed as though absorbing souls. When Darvith attempted to trace the portal's connected locations, the truth of the matter became clear; somehow, Razarkha was performing elven antimagic to protect their portal while it was in killing range. The ascendants died on contact with the area of nullification, then their disembodied souls were dragged through by the Sovereign's own godly phenomena.

"Very clever, Razarkha Fel'thuz," Darvith said as the portal continued to trim irrelevant souls from his side. *"I expected you'd gather your strength in Moneri, but instead fate had us reunite early. Your impatience will be your downfall."*

Directly influencing the soulstealer wasn't an option, but there were other ways to stop this. Darvith telekinetically tore pieces off the citadel beneath him, lifted them, then flung them towards the portal. Predictably, the hand retreated into the Chaotic Realm, its rift vanishing.

Darvith spoke in his internal voice. *"Really, father? Is this what your supposed champion devised? A fleeting attempt at murder that barely scratched me?"*

"What makes you think they're done?" the Sovereign asked.

"That chaos-speaker is unreliable. Last time they transported their allies, they moved to Ante Tertia. There's no way they can open such a lucky portal again—"

The tugging resumed, and once again, there was a portal with a soulstealer sticking out, shielded by antimagic. Darvith's eyes swivelled across his gaseous body, and before

325

he could say anything, the Sovereign burst into laughter within his soul.

"It appears the chaos-speaker got lucky again."

"Silence," Darvith snapped within himself, then projected his voice to the portal. *"Do you think you can keep this up? One of you will get tired and blunder. Perhaps you'll forget to maintain your antimagic, or not close the portal in time. What if I find out where you're operating from?"*

The rebels didn't respond, so Darvith flung more pieces of the citadel, perhaps occupied, perhaps not, towards the portal, prompting it to close and reopen again. He attempted to obfuscate the source of the projectiles, but eventually, the portal moved without a stimulus. The imitation of Andros had somehow gained control over the Rakh'vash, and every side of the Nova Tertia citadel was a possible drain on Darvith's carefully built collection of souls.

"How can you stand for this, father?" he internally asked.

"What do you mean?"

"Think of the souls I patiently took into my care, preparing the Underworld for a sinful immigration like no other," Darvith seethed. *"I know you produced the soulstealers with the intent of annihilating those who fled death, but these sinful, prideful people were ours to torment! I'm to be your warden, yet if you allow this to happen, you'll lose every subject you stood to gain!"*

"It's your fault for capturing them using a method I consider abominable," the Sovereign said. *"If some madwoman with a device of my own creation comes in and ruins it for you, that's nothing I can change. I'll just have to treat you like the warden who failed to harvest a single prideful soul."*

"But that's not true!" Darvith protested, his scream accidentally projecting into the city, his rage manifesting as

326

a thunderclap that shook the Nova Tertia Citadel to the point of shattering.

As the building he floated above collapsed beneath its proud weight, Darvith's form wavered. He attempted to telekinetically hold it together, and beyond the citadel walls, ascendants watched in horror. The Sinchild of Pride's many eyes betrayed him; he could see every ascendant growing fearful, losing their faith in the farce he'd tricked them into believing. He gave up on holding the citadel together, and black, stony shards the size of whales flew into its walls, causing a further destruction. Portals continued to dance about him, taking piece by increasingly significant piece.

"Time has taught me patience! You will slip up, and when you do, I, the infinite being impervious to your fleshly weakness, will wipe your smear of a legacy away!"

The portal didn't respond, but his godly father, ever talkative, did.

"Perhaps you have a point, Darvith. If you're the representative of modern Galdusian culture, it's a truly farcical society."

"I am not finished here!" Darvith screamed, unleashing a storm around him.

The collapsed citadel became a whipping tempest of rocky splinters, and yet the rebels still had an answer. Around the portal with the soulstealer, a pair of separate rifts opened, taking in any rocks that threatened to buffet the hand and soulstealer away. Finally, they'd made their mistake. From these extraneous portals, uncovered by antimagic, Darvith tracked their originating chaos-speaker's location. The answer utterly broke the ascendant's composure, and he unleashed a laugh loud enough for the entirety of Nova Tertia to hear.

"You must be joking. You're still in Ante Tertia? You're in luck, Razarkha Fel'thuz. You've forced I, the great conglomeration of minds, move from his millennia-long post. Consider yourself honoured."

Darvith dropped his storm of shards and opened an orderly portal beneath himself. He condensed his form into a brightly glowing set of gems and pressurised magical smoke, dropping into his path to the so-called revolutionaries that dared to humiliate him.

*   *   *

The southbound line from Moonrock reached its terminal station, and Irikhos Foenaxas dragged his luggage from the wheezing locomotive onto the colourful tiles of Godswater, the southernmost port city of Arkhera. Throughout its station, icons and statues related to the south's six gods could be seen, and even the ticket desk had a small figurine of a black-and-white winged man upon it, sitting in front of a chubby, olive-skinned human with folded eyes.

"All's in order. Have a wonderful time in Godswater, friend," the human said as he checked Irikhos's tickets, then gestured to the station's exit.

"Which harbour would have boats to Napolli, Elarond?" Irikhos asked.

"Not many boats visit Elarond from here, but those that do almost always go to Napolli," the ticket checker remarked as he tapped his upper lip. "If I were to think of elven converts, I would think of Eagle's Wing Dock, so try there. Buy a map if you can spare ten coppers. Surely a rich looking fellow like yourself can afford that!"

Iri pulled out his wallet and counted what may have been his penultimate transaction in Arkheran coinage. Landon's metal faces were handed over, the map was received, and he left the station unsure if he thanked the man for his help.

As he wandered out of the building, the city of Godswater appeared as a colourful blur. There were many facets the city had in common with the north; banners of the ruling family, a red shepherd upon white, hanging from every significant structure, winding residential terraces and sprawling plazas filled with stalls.

Despite this, the monotheism of Eternalists and Renewalists was foreign to the south. In residential and industrial areas alike, shrines to members of the six-god pantheon of Jaranar stood, adorned in colourful paint that clashed with their humble, dull surroundings. It was as though Godswater was constructed believing that while stereotypically Arkheran buildings got the job done, gods would only settle for gaudy, Jaranese-style architecture.

Irikhos's legs thoughtlessly moved while his mind drifted to the train he'd taken from Moonrock. The walk from Ashglass to the Sanguinas Territories was itself a quest that had taken him from merciless snows to mildly permeating frost, then the train revealed that as far as the south was concerned, winter was a mild chill at worst. The Great Vale's valleys and farms remained green despite their trees shedding their leaves, while the Forests of Summer's mangroves stayed leafy regardless of the season.

Nestled between swamps and the sea, Godswater was chillier than the preceding train journey, but only when a sharp breeze came Irikhos's way. The humans of the city dressed in clothing that was more focused on modesty than warmth, and despite the season he couldn't see a single coat. Arkhera was such a beautiful, varied kingdom, yet he'd spent his days limiting himself to three cities: Ashglass, his home, the Flowerfields, home of his cousins, and the Sunfort, home of his in-laws. He could have adventured into the Ashpeaks like his ancestors once did, or visited Parakos, Arkhera's first city.

Instead, he was exiled over a foolish woman who didn't deserve his attention. He'd always dreamt of hurting Kagura Selenia, and hearing her remorselessly talk about what she did was almost an invitation to the darkest corners of his mind. He should have remained rational, but what did the heart know of rationality?

The sound of screaming drew Irikhos from his musings, and though he had to leave Arkhera as quickly as possible, he approached the noise. He scrambled along a plaza, slipped down a nearby street, then sniffed a sharp scent that Ashglass knew all too well: Wood, flesh, and bone, aflame.

He reached the back of a great crowd, gathered before a manor-sized temple guarded by six graven images, wrought in colourful stones. Irikhos never cared to remember their names and domains; the concept of bickering, disunited gods that mortals were meant to equally revere was a queer notion to him. Still, the gods exuded a silent rebuke that the formless God of Renewal never could, pitilessly gazing at the blazing stake before their temple.

The burning woman had fallen silent by the time Irikhos saw them, having been rendered a crisp, featureless slab of overcooked meat. Mor'kha's passionate speeches came back to him all at once; every convicted explanation for why the horror the criminal and crowd had endured was somehow justified in God's eyes. Upon a nearby platform, a robed, short human with a shaved head and a black moustache that stretched like a pair of shoelaces raised his arms called to the people in a clear, confident tone.

"People of Godswater, rejoice! Know that the will of the Gods is always fulfilled! Those who slander their mouthpiece will be uncovered, then their folly will visit punishment upon them in this life and beyond. Though for most, this display should evoke exultation, it is also a warning for the heretics in our midst, hoping to sow discord amongst the faithful."

Next to the holy man was a girl, older than Morganix but, as far as he could tell regarding humans, not a woman grown. She shared his diminutive stature and wore a veil that concealed her hair. While the crowd erupted into applause even Irikhos was almost compelled to join, she cowered in fear whenever she wasn't focused on the charred human remains.

Irikhos's stomach wrenched within him. Mor'kha had burned criminals beyond count, yet when she did it, she didn't threaten the people afterwards. She would always say that her greatest hope was that the fires would purify the unrepentant sinners' souls, offering them a karmic clean slate and a chance to reincarnate into something with a chance to do good.

A glance at the blackened former human quashed Irikhos's familial pride. To the burnt, their burner's intent was irrelevant; all that mattered was that they were tied to a stake, dying in agony. If he ever returned to Arkhera as an overlord consort, would he finally have the willpower to make Mor'kha stop? The soldiers of Ashglass regularly became suicidal before the rapeworm epidemic, and the burnings of infected districts only exacerbated issues.

Overlady Kag'nemera was a contemptible fool, but her mercy was admirable. If it wasn't for her caveat, these Arkheran issues would be impossible for Irikhos to fix. As it stood, there was still a chance that he could improve his home; perhaps Godswater would remain a six-god torture pit, but at least he would be able to change the Forests of Winter.

He rushed away from the holy horror and hefted his luggage with vigour. There was no time for stalling; the quicker he found Yarawyn, the quicker he'd be reunited with his love, and more importantly, the quicker he'd return to Arkhera, more powerful than ever.

* * *

Razarkha pulled her hand from Weil's portal, and screamed in Isleborn.

"Why did you form those two portals without informing me first?"

"If I hesitated you wouldn't have a hand or *a soulstealer!"* Weil replied with equal volume.

"I suppose we're doomed now, because wherever we go, he'll follow!" Razarkha ranted, magical energies cracking her eggshell mind. *"I don't know why I trust you, every time it's your error that leads us further into danger!"*

"I'm always leading us out of the danger you *put us in!"*

Razarkha pointed her soulstealer at Weil's head, and just as the boy closed his eyes, she collapsed, screaming at the ground while tears poured from her eyes. They were on the roof of a long-abandoned inner-city library, so despite the numerous Rakhs, Teis, Terrezas and Ranis floating about her, she knew it was just the two of them.

"I wanted to be a hero, Weil! That's all I wanted!"

Weil's voice wavered. *"I know."*

"This can't be it. I refuse to die!" Razarkha insisted, telekinetically forcing herself up and burning some of the excess energy within her.

"If that's the case, you should probably— oh shit."

When Razarkha turned to see what cut him off, she was greeted by a hail of boulders. The oversized raindrops of bleached Galdusian stone flew towards them and the citadel while a throng of enraged Sulari voices rumbled through the ivory streets.

"You honestly thought that you, two upstarts, could end what Andros's entire empire failed to? Behold my magnificence before the end, disgusting, fleshly failures!"

Rising over the Ante Tertia skyline was Darvith's columnlike body, but more pressingly, the rock-shower he'd flung was close to impact. Weil portals wouldn't be able to defend them from the shrapnel that would travel through with them, and Razarkha was hardly in a state to telekinetically catch the barrage.

332

Razarkha seized Weil's hand. *"Is there anything you wanted to do before you died?"*

"I wanted to ask you if—"

"I was always open to having sex with you," Razarkha answered before he could finish. *"I don't like your tastes, the ropes and whatnot, but we could have been lovers if you asked."*

"No, that's not— wait, what's going on?"

Razarkha checked the sky to see that impending demolishment effort was floating in place. From the citadel, a shrill, echoing voice screamed into the abandoned inner city.

"Consigliere Luxifros! I'd recognise your arcane signature anywhere, and of course, you brought your army of cowards with you! It took you a while to attempt an assassination! Well, you're too late! I have my own army of ascendants, and the entire Golden Galdusian Empire shall avenge me!"

Razarkha and Weil froze. Even Darvith stopped drifting, though his gaseous form still wavered. A thousand eyes pooled together, pointing towards the citadel itself, before finally, he unleashed a laugh that shook all nearby foundations.

"Golden Emperor Aeternus! I always wondered what happened to you," the grand conglomerate said in mocking Old Galdusian. *"I fail to see this alleged army of ascendants."*

"Behold!" the Ruined Emperor declared from his citadel. *"My army!"*

Animated rags flew from throughout the inner city, occasionally releasing plumes of fire or rays of light. This only caused further world-shaking chuckles from Darvith, which brought Razarkha out of her silence.

"This is it, Weil! Our opportunity!"

Razarkha telekinetically tore their roof from its building and pointed to Darvith.

"I'll keep us moving, all you need to do is occasionally open a portal in front of us when we need to relocate," she commanded. *"The rest is up to the soulstealer."*

She pushed the roof forward, and Weil opened a portal ahead of it. They slipped into the Chaotic Realm, then out again, appearing behind Darvith as he 'absorbed' the Ruined Emperor's decoys.

"Watch, my Emperor! Watch as your subjects join me!"

"No, no, no!" the Ruined Emperor screamed. *"Your monstrous nature was plain from the moment I met you, yet I allowed myself to be deceived! Not anymore!"*

"Fool. You're deceiving yourself as we speak— oh, they're still alive," Darvith remarked as Razarkha resumed her consumption.

She was more precise with her antimagic this time, creating a field that surrounded her block of roofing while she retained her ability to perform telekinesis within it. She started to circle Darvith, moving her field with the slab, ensuring she never passed through it as it flew. Smoky arcane matter unravelled from the conglomerate ascendant, which only increased its rage. However, whenever Darvith attempted to raze the streets, the Ruined Emperor prevented him, announcing each foiled attempt with Old Galdusian babbling.

"Answer me, Razarkha Fel'thuz. How did you get Emperor Aeternus, the Plague Emperor's greatest enemy, to ally with you?" the steadily-shrinking Darvith demanded.

Razarkha smirked as Weil placed a portal in front of them. She dropped the antimagical field, they whizzed through, then came out in a different place, still sucking the life out of Darvith. She didn't want to give the sinchild the satisfaction of an answer, yet as more souls coursed through her body, the tingling excitement forced words from her.

"I didn't do that, you imbecile! He hates you all on his own. I figured that out with one conversation!"

"You're a fool to think you're safe! You'll misstep as you did before, and when fleshly people misstep, they die."

Razarkha grinned as Darvith's voice grew less thunderous. *"Do you want to know something beautiful about flesh? It's vulnerable. We can't afford to make mistakes. We can't stay still. Our lives are short and beautiful. You've grown complacent with your godhood, and now you can't handle a true threat."*

Darvith's steadily diminishing body rumbled, then unleashed a concussive screech which, predictably, didn't pass through Razarkha's antimagical field, even as surrounding buildings crumbled.

"Enough! A creature of your youth, of your faculties, will not kill me! Andros couldn't kill me with all seven soulstealers!"

Darvith's wispy form drooped towards the ground. Razarkha lowered her flying roof, held steady by Weil as the soulstealer continued to drain the conglomerate. It was as though he'd given up; he didn't cast magic, nor did he speak. He simply drifted towards Ante Tertia's outer city, apparently attempting to flee.

"Something's suspicious about this," Weil remarked. *"He used a portal to reach here, if he's fleeing, why would he—"*

"Shut up, Weil, this is our moment! Keep your eyes open and block anything my antimagic won't immediately nullify, while I keep up the chase!"

Weil was apparently proven wrong, as Darvith kept floating away, haemorrhaging ascension stones and arcane gas alike until he was a singular being, a small wisp with emerald-green embers for eyes. Suddenly, the soulstealer stopped consuming. The distraction made her pass through her own antimagical field, causing her low-flying slab of roofing to crunch against the ground as her telekinesis failed.

Weil grabbed Razarkha as they were flung by impact, but despite his efforts, she was still concussed when she hit the ground.

"What's happening? Why isn't the soulstealer working?" Razarkha spluttered to the Bold Individualist as her vision blurred.

Before the god answered, she felt her body get yanked towards the ascendant, who levitated her before his abstract form, his voice filling the air with pure hatred.

"Do you have any conception of the millennia *of work you've undone?"* Darvith asked, tearing the soulstealer from her hands and flinging it aside. *"I was already proving so-called civilisation's failures before a mindless sower of destruction like you came along and—"*

A portal opened in the middle of Darvith's body as he spoke. Razarkha was dropped, and the ascendant's smoky form slowly converted into an inky sludge. Despite this corruption, a glowing emerald from within the form made fuzzy, crackle-filled pleas.

"No! No! Father, this can't be the end! Reincarnate me, give me another chance, I won't ascend this time, I'll do things your way! Please, please!"

The speech stopped making sense and degraded into distorted screeching before cutting off entirely, and Darvith was rendered a pile of black, daemonic slime with a green ascension stone nestled within it. Razarkha instinctively tried to stand, then remembered the abundance of arcana within her. She telekinetically rose and drew her soulstealer towards her, taking a prolonged hit of magical energy before she turned to Weil. For some reason, he was wearing a strange, worried frown.

"Why aren't you smiling?" she asked in frenzied Isleborn. *"You just killed a sinchild! The man who got away from even the Plague Emperor! With these souls fuelling me and your newfound control over the Rakh'vash, we're*

unstoppable! We can conquer Galdus, even the world *if we desired!"*

Weil inhaled shakily. *"You're unafraid of anything now, aren't you?"*

"Of course! Do you know what all these souls feel like? The majority aren't even inside me, and even now I can feel the cosmos calling to me. The world feels so small, a tiny blotch of tissue within a great veined totality!"

Weil swallowed. *"Good. Then you'll answer me honestly."*

"Answer— what are you talking about? This is our great victory! The rest of Galdus is nothing compared to this! There are no questions, only conquest!"

"Allow me this one."

Razarkha scoffed. *"Fine. Your idiocy was always an endearing quality."*

Weil's expression hardened. *"Did you kill my father?"*

Arcane power spilled from her soulstealer while false images of Ivan fluttered into view. She almost stopped floating, and stabilised herself before she answered.

"I'll indulge you," she snapped. *"Yes, I killed him. What are you going to do about it? Kill me? He was dying anyway, he was suffering, he thanked me for killing him!"*

Weil clenched his fists and walked up to her. *"You let me believe Anya Kasparov killed him. You deceived me and let me think I'd avenged my father when really, I was helping his killer gain power! Did you ever care for me?"*

Razarkha pointed her soulstealer at Weil. *"Of course I did, but you* wouldn't listen! *The more time you wasted with that scammer, the more he suffered!"*

"You hid this from me all this time. I loved you, and you— you pretended to love me back! Pretended to be my friend!" Weil yelled. *"Was any of it real?"*

"Of course it was!" she said, her eyes filling up. *"You're the only person who's ever believed in—"*

Her speech was cut short by a fleshy blade piercing her lower back. She trembled, dropped her soulstealer, and looked at her stomach. The writhing end of a tentacle protruded from it. A wave of pain lashed through her as it slipped back through her abdomen, and she fell to the floor. The last thing she beheld was Weil, opening a portal and slipping away.

Unravelled

Between the darkness of death and the pale buildings of Ante Tertia, Razarkha lingered on. The old city tinged red and the streets blurred, filling with dissonantly clear images of Rakh, Tei, and the man Razander should have grown into. A great plume of smoke loomed over the nearest tower, then dived into the growing pool of blood before her. The liquid shifted into a humanoid she hadn't seen before; tall, clad in a black dinner suit and hat that topped an equally dark, obfuscated face. When he spoke, his tone was immediately recognisable.

"This is it, Razarkha. These are your final moments. What do you have to say for yourself?"

"Weil finally grew a spine. I don't know if I love him or despise him," Razarkha replied, though she didn't feel her mouth move nor did she hear her own voice.

"Despite all the murders you've committed, Ivan is the one that weighs the most on you. Why do you think that is? Is the aversion to murder itself, or something else?"

"Betrayal. That was my true sin. This world is a competition, and killing others to achieve my goals is natural," Razarkha said. "I should have accepted the consequences of my ruthlessness. I should have dominated Weil instead of cowering at his disapproval."

"His friendship was just as valuable to you as your goals," the Sovereign said. *"You were cowardly, but I cannot begrudge you on that count. You're one of my favourite people, Razarkha Fel'thuz. Amusingly delusional with an ideology so close to my own that I wish you could have been a sinchild."*

"It's too late now."

"Not necessarily."

Razarkha's soul coiled. "What do you mean?"

339

"I could lend you some extra time, but there won't be a moment you'll forget your days are numbered. If you thought Weil's debt was bad, you haven't seen anything."

It was tempting to leave this deal alone, but she knew that her soul would be stuck in an artefact in the middle of an abandoned megalopolis if she died here. Rakh would live on like she never existed, Weil would get away with his killing, and Darvith's arrogance would have been justified. She wasn't done with the mortal realm.

"I'm interested."

"I'm glad to hear it. As a consultancy fee of sorts, half the intact souls you never lived to use belong to me," the Sovereign explained. *"I will provide an apparatus to help you persist beyond death. Allow me to explain the conditions."*

The Sovereign projected an image of Razarkha with a crystalline chunk replacing her abdomen, along with a jointed set of crystals acting as her left hip and leg. Though spectating her body's demise from afar, she still had enough connection to her flesh to have concerns.

"Is there a stomach in there?"

"You could certainly eat for pleasure then spit your food out, but I wouldn't recommend swallowing anything that isn't water," the Sovereign replied. *"From now on, your sustenance is life itself, converted into arcana. I'll allow you to keep your share of the whole souls, along with the fragments of no value to me, but this still places your lifespan at around two years, assuming you don't use any spellwork along the way."*

"And how much time would be spent if, say, I unleashed a destructive ray?"

"That would cost you about a week, and telekinetic flight would burn through your borrowed lifespan. As for antimagic, I wouldn't attempt it. Arcane nullification, including your own, will lead to excruciating death. If I were you, I'd collect some more souls."

Razarkha pushed against her own body. "I'm fine with a short life, but from now on, no dilly-dallying with foolish Galdusians, no delusions of social reform. If I'm living on borrowed time, I'm going to punish everyone who's wronged me."

"So, you accept the deal? You wish to be modified in this manner?"

"I do."

"Good. Please stay in this Underworld waiting room while I fix your body," the Sovereign 'requested', forcing Razarkha's soul into a chamber with walls as black as a starless night.

Then she saw the courtyard of Castle Selenia thrust upwards to dash her head to pieces. Following that, she felt a knife stab her between the shoulder blades. Then she was helpless, burning all over, while some faceless wisp dumped fragrant oils upon her ravaged chest. After such agony, the feeling of a pillow against her mouth and nose was merciful.

* * *

Rakh sat alone on his own bed after what felt like a lifetime in Ashglass. Erwyn was a hero, Lady Kag was a victim, but all he'd done was fail to ease tensions with the Foenaxases. Perhaps he still had a purpose beyond worrying about Razarkha, but unfortunately, he didn't have a seerish friend ready to prognosticate at a moment's notice.

He'd sent a gallant knight to his doom. What would Verawyn Verawor say? Perhaps as a seer he expected it, but if that was the case, why send Rowyn at all? Despite the myriad magical varieties spellbinders could augment their natural abilities with, seerish prescience was impossible for them to learn. It was something to do with how their arcana node attached to their brains, but as Rakh was no necromancer, the bodily details evaded him.

341

Count Fel'thuz moved to the window and stared over Moonstone. Perhaps Overlord Verawor had seen the city in flames, or perhaps he'd seen something even worse. With Rowyn dead, it was all but confirmed that Razarkha would return, save any interruptions the knight's presence somehow facilitated. Rakh would have to write to Lord Verawor.

He watched a mother building a snowman with her son and scratched his wooden hand. He needed to make time to visit Tei with Rarakhi before the end. Perhaps he could even leave Rara with his mother and keep him out of danger. He'd need to inform Plutyn of the notion, as he would immediately demand Plutera be evacuated to the same area. Knocking came from the bedroom door, almost shocking Rakh out of the window.

"Come in."

Rarakhi opened the door, a few marks on his neck. "Hey dad, it's just me."

Rakh put on a non-illusory smile, though he was sure neither variant would have been convincing. "It's unlike you to voluntarily spend time with me. Are you in need of someone to brag to regarding your lady love? Because I know all about lady loves, and—"

"Look, I get excited about that stuff, but we didn't do anything," Rarakhi claimed. "After all the cut-up crotches I saw during Erwyn's experiments and Petal losing Rowyn, we're taking things slow."

"Ah, so she told you," Rakh said, moving back to his bed and sitting down. He patted a spot next to him. "Would you like to talk about it?"

Rarakhi paused, then sat by his father. "Only if you promise not to talk about any of your conquests. No offence, but nobody wants to know how many humans you've fucked or what illusions women requested."

Rakh chuckled. "There was one woman who asked me to become her—"

"I told you not to, fuck's sake," Rarakhi cut off. "Look, Petal's sad about all this, but you wanna know what's scary? She's *angry,* but in that quiet, simmering way. First time in my life I noticed how much the Boss has made her who she is, you know?"

"She must be her father's daughter to some extent. Did her mother survive her birth?"

"D'you think Plutyn would have given her the same name if she did?"

Rakh shrugged. "The late Lord Nemeron named his second daughter after his wife, and she went on to have a third. I was just wondering where she gets her kind side from. If she's only had Plutyn as an influence, she must have endeavoured to be gentler than her father. She's certainly admirable."

Rarakhi looked away from his father. "Yeah, yeah, that's enough of you mooning over your daughter-in-law. She wants revenge, dad. She wants to watch her cousin's murderer die, but she's a boss type, not a thug, you get me? I've taken on tougher people than my mad aunt. I wanna be her champion."

Rakh's hand tightened, and he could have sworn the phantom hand followed suit.

"Rara, I know you love Plutera, but you don't need to die for her. Dying for someone doesn't demonstrate dedication, it just gets you killed. Unless Plutera would die without your intervention, nothing is worth sacrificing yourself," Rakh said. "Am I understood?"

"The fuck would you know about love?" Rarakhi snapped, standing over his father. "Every woman you've been with was either out of duty or a one-night fling. Don't mention mum, 'cause from what I've heard, that was you taking advantage of a scared little sister."

Rakh met the boy's height. "It was nothing of the sort."

"Whatever you think, it wasn't love like me and Petal's," Rarakhi insisted. "I'm her muscle. One day, the Boss is gonna die and Petal will be my boss and wife all in one. I'll be her bodyguard, the one that makes people afraid to cross her!"

"You can't be her bodyguard if you're *dead!*"

"I'm not gonna die!"

"Razarkha tried to murder me when I was still on good enough terms with her to civilly agree to an honour duel," Rakh said. "She murdered Rowyn, who wasn't an enemy as far as she knew. You're a legitimised bastard son, the heir that she could never produce. If she learns of your existence, she will *kill you.* You've worked in the underground, Rara, I know you're not naive.

"Whatever powers she's got, think ten times worse and *hide.* I'm an adult, I've lived my life, and you're right; I have no long-term loves, and Erwyn's the only one who'll miss me. If anybody's going to die, let it be me. I won't let you play the self-sacrificing man because you think Plutera will thank you for dying. Do you think she'd be able to love your corpse?"

Rarakhi paused, his hateful expression shifting to amusement. Rakh's resolve faltered, and words slipped from his mouth.

"What's so funny?"

"Well, she is a necromancer," Rarakhi said with a laugh.

Rakh tutted. "I expect that sort of talk from Lady Kag, not you. Especially about your betrothed. Listen to me, Rarakhi. I know you want to prove your devotion and avenge Rowyn for your love, but if you want to marry her, you need to stay safe. It would be prudent for you and Plutera to stay in the south until Razarkha's death is confirmed."

Rarakhi's levity abruptly switched back to defensiveness. "You want me to spend time with *mum?* She hates me even more than you!"

"We don't *hate* you, we just—"

"Ignored me for the first twelve years of my life?"

Rakh's body moved on its own, taking the boy by one shoulder while his wooden hand clumsily smacked against the other. "Do you have any idea how terrified for your life we were? Why we were convinced Razarkha would murder you the moment she heard of you?"

"Just shut up, you're paranoid!"

"Rowyn is dead! Your aunt is a murderer!"

Rarakhi trembled in place. "I'm not gonna run away from her. Is there any way I can help? Plutera thinks there's gonna be a big battle from all the letters about Razarkha's power."

Rakh brought the boy into his arms. "I took you in hoping you'd never need to fight again. Because of Tei and I, you were killing from a young age. No age is good to start killing. We did wrong by you. Please let me do right by you this time."

"If I stay with mum and Plutera down in Deathsport, what's gonna happen to you?"

"That doesn't matter," Rakh said. "Promise me that you'll only come out of hiding once you *know* Razarkha's dead."

"I promise," Rarakhi said in a monotone.

"Like you mean it."

The boy shoved himself out of Rakh's grip. "I *promise,* all right, what's the point in making me say it if you're not gonna take me at my word?"

"My apologies, you're right," Rakh said, turning away from his son. "Go on, Rarakhi, leave me. You have better people to talk to, I'm sure."

Rarakhi paused. "Would you like me to get Erwyn, or maybe Lady Kag can act stupid and make you feel better about yourself?"

"No, I need some time alone," Rakh muttered.

"If you say so," Rarakhi concluded, and with that, the door was shut again.

Rakh moved back to the window, yet this time, Moonstone didn't lie beyond it. The back of his head burned as he saw a great, city-sized charnel pit filled with a million dead renditions of himself. Somebody had to be bait. If he couldn't unite the Foenaxases and Selenias, perhaps he could do this job right.

* * *

At the edge of Moneri, a geomantic augmentee named Brutus waited for a pyromantic co-worker to melt a set of freshly transported obsidian chunks within a fireproof pot the size of fifty men. Behind him lay the overly regular streets of the first Galdusian megalopolis, along with a gaggle of other augmentee workers and their keeper, a wyvern-armoured ascendant named Argentus. Rising from behind the urban skyline was the Moneri Citadel, a grotesquely large, uniform slab jutting into the sky as a storm swirled around it. Ahead, meanwhile, was an endless stretch of pale grasses and bulwarks of trees with glowing, deep red fungi clinging like tumours upon their trunks. Further still were gargantuan mushrooms whose stalks were too low to behold, but whose fruiting heads consumed the horizon.

Once the latest batch of obsidian was melted, Brutus got to work. He geomantically lifted a uniform ball of lava, flattened it, then pushed it onto the unruly grasses ahead of him, extending the city of Moneri by a single tile and removing one more sign of life from the Galdusian wilds. He thoughtlessly formed further shards of Galdusian lifelessness from the smelting pot's lava while his mind wandered to the days when he had a different name.

He was once Duncan Godswater. He had a brother he hated, a brother he pitied, and had grown too curious for his own good. He'd seen his apostolic brother's ability to

346

persuade people to believe anything he told him, yet Duncan, fool that he was, thought he was special. He may have resisted Petyr's words, but he couldn't resist fanatical ascetics' swords. To preserve his life, he'd accepted an exile to Jaranar. Then the Sulari ships came to Ma-Hith, and Duncan Godswater died. In his place, the wiser, quieter augmentee, Brutus, was born.

Duncan was once short, black-haired, olive-skinned, with facial hair too thin to grow a moustache like his eldest brother. Brutus was made of stronger stuff; when he lifted his hands, he saw rocky structures veined with heat, and when he touched his face, he felt nothing. Argentus 'took flight' as though he wasn't a ghostly being capable of wilful levitation, soaring around Brutus so he would be inescapably within his view.

"Brutus! Stop daydreaming! The whole point of an augmentee is that they're simple. They don't have a million great ideas distracting them all at once. Besides, whatever thoughts you have can't be worthwhile, given it's a human thinking them," the ascendant rambled in Sulari. *"Count Primero will be visiting this sector and checking us for city expansion progress any day now, and if he's displeased, he'll unleash his anger on* me, *not you!"*

"Yes, Argentus," Brutus droned in the ghost's foreign language. *"Sorry, Argentus."*

"You humans are incapable of remorse, so don't lie to me. Just complete your work. If Count Primero rewards me, you'll be rewarded. If he reprimands me, I assure you, displeasure will be conveyed the only way you augmentees understand: Disincorporation!"

"Of course, Argentus," Brutus said, instinctively laying another tile down.

Once the current row was completed, he and the pyromancer, Ignisi, fused its tiles, but more than ever, Brutus wanted to delay the extension of this great mockery of civilisation. Disincorporation had lost its threatening edge a

347

while ago; now it was closer to a brief respite from the pressure of controlling his body. Despite the fellow humans who'd be disincorporated with him for his inefficiency, Brutus slowed his work to a crawl right in front of Argentus.

"You say 'of course', but you seem worse than ever! I knew from the moment the farmers said that you were zeroth-generation stock that you would be a risk, but if you continue this behaviour, I shall treat it as deliberate sabotage!" the metal wyvern squawked.

"I see, Argentus," Brutus replied, keeping his voice flat and his eyes, such as they were, on the tiles before him.

"I don't think you do!" Argentus called, telekinetically pulling Brutus away from his work and tugging his hands off. *"Don't think there aren't punishments that would make you beg for an easy disincorporation."*

"What are they?" Brutus challenged. *"I cannot feel pain, so what could be worse than complete and utter helplessness?"*

"We still have necromancers amongst the ascendants of Sula. There are telepaths who can learn your every fear and leverage them."

"I see."

Argentus made an unusual noise that echoed within his armour. *"How very amusing. You must think your acting skills are extraordinary by human standards, but—"*

Suddenly, the beaked metallic monster stopped his crowing, and a great shuddering consumed the audial landscape. The augmentee turned to see the citadel of Moneri, once a proud, sky-consuming monument to Galdusian vanity, collapsing while its storm ceased to spin. Clouds of ascendants roiled through the sky, spiralling into a single aerial point.

"What is— Count Primero!" Argentus said, his echoing tones oddly panicked.

The wyvern aspirant reattached Brutus's hands and flung him to the floor. He opened a gold-and-white portal, only for Arkheran-accented Sulari to come from the other side.

"Oh, you're providing me an escape? You shouldn't have."

A spellbinder stepped out of the portal and extended her hand towards it. The resultant screech was deafening even by augmentee standards, ringing from beyond the portal while Argentus's gaseous entrails slipped towards her.

She was the most bizarre fleshly spellbinder Brutus had seen; she had a long tangle of black hair with grey streaks, a pair of fixated, pink-red eyes, and a tattered black-and-purple cape attached to a blood-soaked, torn dress. Her left leg and stomach resembled the rocky form of an augmentee. Practically welded to her hand was another gemlike construct of blue, red and pink, pulsing in response to the glow around the middle of her body.

She had an evident limp, as though her crystalline leg was only partially in her control. As she scanned the augmentee work crew, Brutus detected no fear, no disdain, almost nothing at all. Though she reminded him of Duncan's soulless brother, Petyr, the fact she'd killed Argentus was enough to restore a piece of his old self's foolish hope.

"Can you speak the Common Tongue? Are you Arkheran, by any chance?"

The woman stared at Brutus as though she'd found the Worm amidst a famine. "An Arkheran augmentee? Am I truly looking at an *Arkheran augmentee?*"

"Yes. I was once named Duncan Godswater, and I—
"

"You're a noble exile, too!" she squealed, rushing towards him while his fellow augmentees scattered towards the streets of Moneri.

"Don't touch me, I'll burn you," Duncan warned.

The woman halted just shy of him, then took a moment to wheeze. "My apologies. I never thought I'd see an Arkheran here. How did you get exiled?"

349

"I grew too suspicious of my brother, Petyr Godswater, then he set it up so a peasant woman, Nira, presented a bastard child as mine. If I recall, it had our family's look, so it must have been Petyr's. Regardless, he'd convinced Nira it was mine, and had ascetics beat me until I confessed."

The woman scoffed. "How could he convince the mother of such a falsehood? Surely she knew which brother she'd slept with."

"He's the Apostle of Godswater, and his words exert power beyond his holy station," Duncan said. "I don't claim to understand it fully, but I was unfairly exiled."

"I was unfairly exiled by my brother too— one moment."

The spellbinder leapt into the air with telekinetic assistance, then lifted her hand, consuming a set of ascendants that had gathered above them. Argentus and his ilk were naught but gaseous soup for this half-augmented abomination. Her body became luminous as she made the last of the ascendants flow through her, and slowly, she descended to the ground. For a moment, she stood, rasping as her hands twitched. Her tail whipped left and right, while her crystalline leg wobbled.

"My apologies. I'm Razarkha Fel'thuz. You may have also heard me referred to as Praetor Erre," she said with a grin so fragile it reminded Duncan how much he missed eggs. "I doubt Sulari citizens, let alone slaves, know this, but I killed Darvith, the Conglomeration of Minds, all by myself."

Duncan paused. "You're *the* Praetor Erre? My overseer said you were dead, your revolution scattered by Darvith!"

"Yet here I stand," Razarkha said, glancing at her crystalline leg.

"Are you going to continue your revolution? Are you going to end augmentee slavery once and for all?"

Razarkha shook her head. "No. Without Darvith, Sula can't recover from the damage I've already done. I'm here to harvest some souls, then return to Arkhera. Finding a kindred spirit was a lucky coincidence."

"May I accompany you? I've wanted freedom from this bondage for years, and if you're able to facilitate my return to Arkhera, I'll do whatever you ask of me."

Razarkha turned around, revealing that her spine was dotted with sharp, rocky spikes connected to the chunk of crystal at the small of her back. For a moment, she made noises Duncan could have sworn were sobs, before speaking in a disconcertingly flippant tone.

"Oh, if you insist. We can kill our treacherous brothers together."

Epilogue

Screaming above Lake Serenita, a great watery expanse nestled within the Alaterran Mountains, was a purple-and-red wyvern large enough to seat a light humanoid. Its wide, bat-like wings stretched as it soared over the waters, leaving ripples in its wake. With a deep warbling noise, it lowered its beak into the lake and pulled a fish from it, live and wriggling.

It flapped and ascended, then veered around, heading towards a pair of high elven women by the lake's northern bank. The creature landed by the shortest of humanoids, folding its wings upwards and fanning lengthy, man-like scutes around its neck. It dropped the fish and lowered its beak to the woman's level, who scratched along its dorsal side.

"Clever boy, good Moonrazer," Yarawyn Selenia said, patting the side of her wyvern's head. "Go on, cook your dinner."

Yar stepped towards the other woman, Torawyn, while Moonrazer opened his beak and unleashed a torrent of fire upon the unfortunate carp before him. The beast took the chargrilled remains into his beak and swallowed it whole, bobbing his head as he pushed it to his gizzard.

Tor had grown to be taller than Yarawyn, and since making it to Elarond, she'd consistently lost weight, to the point that was gaunt verging on frail. To her, not being the one Irikhos wanted was their undoing. When their father died, she was a woman grown but Yarawyn wasn't. Father would have left Moonstone to her and Irikhos without caveats, but instead Kag got to be acting lady for three years that became indefinite.

The saying that a right delayed was a right denied rang true to Yarawyn. The youngest Selenia's hatred crackled within her like a grassy bank surrounding

Moonrazer's dinner, and though she tried to keep herself measured, Tor always found a way through her mask.

"You're thinking about burning Moonstone again, aren't you?"

Yarawyn sighed. "Close. I just noticed how thin you've become. You know you couldn't have changed things, right? Iri and I got along well, and you were right to accept that. You're not at fault. Kag's the one who sent us away."

"I should have done *something*. I wonder if father would be happy with this situation."

"If Kag's had children, he probably wouldn't care," Yar muttered as Moonrazer took flight once more. "Kag, the perfect little model, posing for father. A far cry from the brat who killed his wife coming into this world."

"Father wasn't like that—"

"Yes he was, Tor!" Yarawyn snapped. "Everyone in Castle Selenia, Kag, father, Rakh and that Sanguinasi upstart, Erwyn, they're all stains upon Arkheran nobility."

"Don't start this again," Torawyn said. "Think about what we have here, Yar."

"You think being a healer in Alaterra, where nobody speaks the Common Tongue and looks at you funny for having the *slightest* of accents is a life?"

The thin woman's brow furrowed. "We've survived here for ten years. What about Naas'khar? Aren't you grateful for him?"

Yarawyn ignored her sister and watched Moonrazer return with another fish. He put it down and she welcomed him back to the ground, cuddling his head as he made contented rattling within his beak.

"Well?" Torawyn asked. "I have friends in Alaterra, and even if you're only willing to befriend cave-people, they're still precious to you, aren't they?"

Yar straightened her back, prompting Moonrazer to face Tor with dilated pupils. Her red eyes seared against Tor's blue until she huffed and turned from her.

"Naas'khar only lives in a cave because of this worthless nation's affiliation with the Soltelles. If he was in Arkhera, he'd be able to live in a city. Don't presume what he wants. I've promised that if I return to Arkhera, he's coming with me."

Torawyn withered under Moonrazer's predatory gaze and withdrew from her sister. "I'm sorry, I shouldn't have called him a cave-person. Still, what would you do if you returned? Hope Irikhos hasn't married someone like his cousin Elrax and take Moonstone as a couple? What if he's moved on, have you considered—"

"He can't have," Yarawyn insisted. "Wills and marriages won't matter anyway. Once I have the backing I require, I'm taking Moonstone by right of conquest, and King Silas or whoever has their arse on the throne by now is welcome to challenge my claim, provided he enjoys Moonrazer's flames. Go on, boy, cook your dinner."

The wyvern turned back to his catch and scorched the ground once more as Yarawyn hungrily eyed the flames. Tor was free to stay in Alaterra like the coward she was. Yar had a home to reclaim.

Appendices

Appendix I: Map of the World

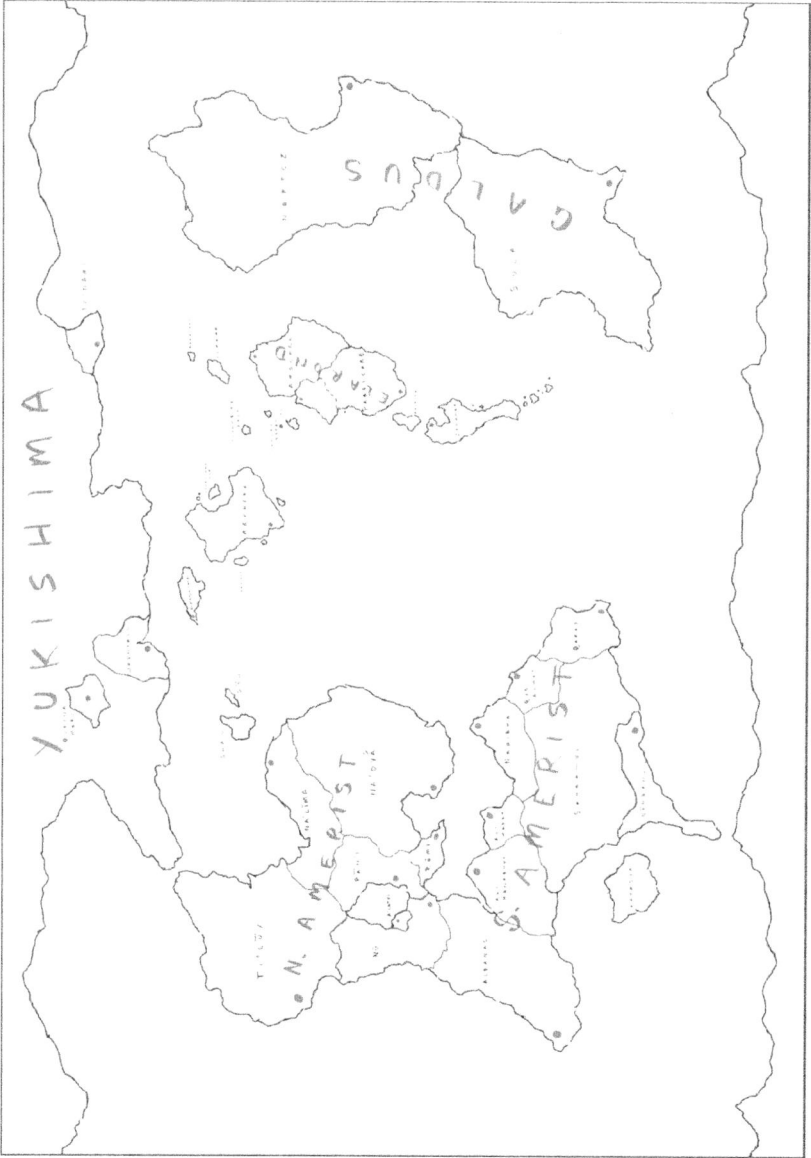

Appendix II: Races of the World

Humans: Humanoids much like the reader of this novel. Capable of magic in semi-rare cases, tend to be hairier than most other races save orcs. Populate most of the world and come in a variety of colours and cultures.

Elves: Beautiful, tall, dextrous humanoids who have long, pointed ears, youthful looks, and tend towards being non-magical. They have multiple subraces and cultures, such as pale-skinned high elves, charcoal-skinned dark elves, diminutive and red-haired forest elves, and the highly magical, mostly identical Kakajuan elves. Like humans, their presence is widespread.

Spellbinders: Willowy, pale, small-nosed humanoids who, while fragile, perform their natural magic with the same ease as breathing. They have long, rat-like tails and two primary cultures: The conservative, disciplined Galdusians and the bold, expressive Ilazari, both of which also populate Arkhera.

Necromancers: Cousins to the spellbinders, they are slightly shorter in both stature and tail length. Their magic, as their moniker implies, largely centres around control of the dead. An endangered race that is largely endemic to Galdus and Arkhera.

Orcs: Non-magical, apelike humanoids whose body hair makes them resemble sentient yetis. They are the dominant natives of Arkhera; the land is named for the Old Orcish for 'Orc Home'. Despite their lack of magic, they are tall, strong, and surprisingly quick.

Goblins: Green-skinned, scaly, and short beings who have more in common with monkeys than the apes most humanoids resemble. Bearing protractible claws, they are gifted climbers with large eyes they use to see distances other races cannot. Native to Malassai, though a healthy population exists in Arkhera.

Gnomes: Short humanoids with highly light-sensitive, myopic eyes and a sense of hearing that enables them to hear infrasound, gnomes are well-adapted to life underground. Modern gnomes that work in above-ground cities tend to wear goggles or sunglasses to avoid retinal damage.

Seers: Diminutive, waifish people native to Sanguinas Isle named for their race's limited prescience. Their abilities usually manifest as visions, but others experience their abilities the same way other humanoids anticipate events. Though they've spread to mainland Arkhera, they are relatively endangered after enduring multiple genocides.

Beastmasters: An endangered humanoid race endemic to the Arkheran Isles. They can bond with animals and share minds with them, enabling a unique, collaborative approach to animal husbandry other humanoids can't achieve. Most exist in the Iron Hills of Arkhera and as tribal communities on the Isle of Wor'ghan.

Printed in Great Britain
by Amazon